LP

EVERYTHING
WE
DIDN'T
SAY

Center Point
Large Print

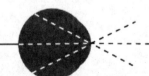

**This Large Print Book carries the
Seal of Approval of N.A.V.H.**

EVERYTHING WE DIDN'T SAY

NICOLE BAART

CENTER POINT LARGE PRINT
THORNDIKE, MAINE

For my Iowa Baarts

EVERYTHING WE DIDN'T SAY

CHAPTER 1

WINTER
TODAY

The murders took place on a hot summer night, but to Juniper it would always be winter in Jericho. Bitter and unforgiving as deep February, when frost edged the windows like salt on the rim of a glass.

It seemed fitting, then, that it was dark and profoundly cold when Juniper pulled into town. In the glow of her headlights she could see that the WELCOME TO JERICHO sign was riddled with bullet holes. Fifteen years ago there had been exactly three: puncture marks with saw-toothed edges that, if connected, would form a nearly perfect isosceles triangle over the yellow block letters of her hometown. They seemed intentional at the time. A warning, maybe, or a vulgar homage to three different bullets that had taken a much deadlier trajectory. But even barreling down Highway 20 at sixty miles an hour in the raw black of a February night, Juniper could see that the sign had become a target of sorts. At least a dozen holes had been punched through the metal, and the indentations of buckshot dimpled the gaping *O*.

A shot-up welcome sign was certainly an inauspicious reception—she could hardly believe that in all these years the city council had never bothered to replace it—but she harbored no illusions that her return to Jericho would be a happy homecoming. It was why she timed her arrival for the middle of the night and told Cora to slip the house key in the mailbox of the bungalow. Juniper had rented it, sight unseen, on a six-month lease. She doubted she'd make it that long.

Even over a dozen years later and in the dark, Juniper knew the layout of Jericho by heart. The population was just shy of four thousand and the streets were arranged on a grid, so Cora hadn't bothered to provide an address.

"It's the McAvoys' old place. One story, blue, tiny front porch. A block from the library. You know the one, right?"

She did.

Navigating the abandoned streets, she felt her skin prickle against the familiarity of a town she hadn't seen in years. Little had changed. Main Street was shuttered and quiet, gray snow piled against the sides of businesses that she had frequented as a kid. Juniper could almost feel the cracking sidewalks beneath her feet, the slant of concrete where the roots of gnarled trees had bubbled up. She used to burst into Cunningham's Cafe clutching a five-dollar bill. Cold Coke and hot, salty french fries, the backs of her bare legs glued to the green vinyl booth. The sticky-sweet memory felt like it was from someone else's childhood.

Beside the cafe was a secondhand store, then, in quick succession, a run-down Dollar General, a Kirby vacuum dealer, and a small-animal vet. Across the street there was the eye doctor, the bakery, a mom-and-pop hardware, and a shoe store that had been boarded up, windows plastered with faded FOR SALE signs. That was it: all of Jericho in the blink of an eye.

At one end, right before the corner where Highway 20 intersected Main, was the library. Just the sight of it made Juniper's heart unclench a bit, and she released the breath that she hadn't realized she was holding. Cora had offered her a reason wrapped up so neatly she had no choice but to accept. A perfectly packaged rationale to come *home*.

Because the town seemed abandoned, Juniper didn't bother to flick on her blinker when she turned at the end of the street. The small blue house was just where she knew it would be. It, too, hadn't changed much, and she could almost picture Harriet McAvoy rocking in her chair beside the front door. But the porch was empty, freshly shoveled, and someone had left the floodlight on.

For just a moment, the golden glow of it

mingled with the sudden flash of red and blue in her rearview mirror. But Juniper's foot was already on the brake, her subconscious aware of what was happening even before she turned her head and realized there was a police cruiser behind her. It was the first car that she had seen in nearly an hour. "Perfect," she groaned, easing to the side of the road instead of into the driveway of her new rental.

She threw the transmission into park and fumbled in the glove compartment for her papers, cursing under her breath. Of course her first few minutes back would end in a ticket. In a confrontation with the sort of small-town police officer who made her skin feel tight and itchy even all these years later.

Just as she located the little plastic folder with her papers, a shadow darkened the driver's-side window and gloved knuckles rapped against the glass. He was talking as the window rolled down, but Juniper knew the drill. "License and registration, please."

"Sorry, Officer," Juniper responded. "Was I speeding? I know I forgot my blinker back there, but no one was around . . ."

She handed everything over, hoping the fine tremor of dismay in her voice wouldn't come off as guilt. She couldn't see anything beyond the officer's waterproof black jacket and the dull glint of his badge. She tipped forward a bit to see if she could make out his features, maybe even recognize him from another time, another life. No such luck. Juniper didn't know if she should feel relieved or frustrated.

"I'm from out of town," she added unnecessarily. He had probably pulled her over precisely because of her Colorado plates. "Just got in."

"Juniper Baker?"

There was something in his voice that made her spine stiffen. "That's me." Instinct told her to fill the silence, play a little Jericho bingo to see if she could make a connection that would encourage him to let her off with a warning. But just as quickly as she fell into old habits, she remembered: Never answer more than asked. Never offer up unsolicited information. Never let down your guard. It was coming back to her.

"I'll be just a minute," the officer said. He disappeared with her papers and license, and in her rearview mirror Juniper could see him slide back into the cruiser. Tall, youngish, trim beneath his uniform. Unfamiliar. A far cry from Atkins, the round, elderly chief of police who had questioned her reluctantly all those years ago, as if he couldn't quite believe what had happened on his watch. The officer's skin had a blue tint from the dashboard light, and as she watched he punched something into the laptop computer she knew was attached to the console.

Juniper had nothing to fear, and yet her palms were suddenly damp in her lap. Knotting her fingers together, she pushed her laced hands out and away, tugging at the kinks in her shoulders and neck from the ten-hour drive. She was jittery, maybe a bit dehydrated, and unprepared for even this seemingly innocuous interaction. *What have I done?* she thought. Then: *Just give me a ticket. Write me up and* go away.

But when the officer came back, he only handed her a written warning. No ticket. "You were going a little fast back there, but I'm more concerned that your left taillight is out," he told her. "Dangerous. Especially in winter."

"Absolutely," Juniper agreed. "I'll call the shop tomorrow."

"Be sure you do. And welcome back, Ms. Baker."

Juniper's cheeks flamed, and she was grateful that the officer was already walking away. She watched the police cruiser drive off, pressing cool hands to her burning face and wishing that she was curled up on her worn corduroy couch in Denver. Or perched on a stool at her favorite bar. Or pulling a late night in the archives. Anywhere but here.

True to her word, Cora had locked the front door and left the key in the mailbox. It was likely an unnecessary precaution (no one in Jericho locked their doors) and futile anyway, because the mailbox was the most obvious place to look if someone *did* want to break in. Still, Juniper felt a modicum of control when she reached a hand into the letterbox and came up with an icy key. It slid effortlessly into the front door, and the lock clicked open.

The bungalow looked exactly how she imagined it would: shabby but comfortable. There was a tiny living room with a drab floral sofa and a boxy old television set that had a twist dial for channels and another for volume. The vintage piece paired perfectly with the charming avocado-colored appliances in the galley-style eat-in kitchen.

Juniper toed off her boots and lugged the carton she was holding to the off-white Formica table pushed up against the far kitchen wall. It was the only thing she had carried into the house. Her clothes and toiletries could wait—the contents of the cardboard box could not.

Dropping her cargo onto one of two padded kitchen chairs, Juniper yanked open the bent flaps. She lifted out nine slim Moleskine notebooks, each in a different color. They were labeled in her quick, willowy cursive with black, archival-quality ink. Flipping through them, Juniper confirmed nothing was missing.

Next were the binders crammed with clear sleeves protecting copies of every single blog post, newspaper or magazine article, op-ed, and mention of the murders she could find. Juniper had scoured the internet, unearthing microscopic scraps—from a comment about the Murphy murders on an unrelated case to the Facebook profile picture of the coroner who had performed the autopsies (she never did manage to get a hold of the actual reports). At the very bottom of the box were a few pieces of material evidence. A time-softened folder with a handful of glossy photographs that were just beginning to yellow. A label she had carefully peeled and pressed flat from a jar of the Murphys' famous raspberry jam. Her high school yearbook.

When everything was laid out on the table, Juniper felt the tension melt from her shoulders. It was all there.

She knew it was an impressive collection. If she had gone into law enforcement instead of library science, her box would have included forensic reports and interview transcripts, too, but this was enough. It would have to be.

The light was thin as spilled milk when Juniper woke. Without opening the curtains, she could tell that the day was dawning chilly and gray, the sun hidden behind long strips of clouds like cotton batting.

She had crashed on the couch, a musty afghan dragged over her shoulders and a binder open on the coffee table beside her. Thrusting back the blanket as if she had something to prove, Juniper hurried to her car and grabbed the suitcases she had left in the trunk overnight. *Early to bed, early to rise,* her stepfather had drilled into her, and even at thirty-three years old, seven a.m. felt downright luxurious. She could almost see Law scowl.

A quick shower and ten minutes in front of the mirror were more than enough. Sweeping on her signature dark red lipstick, Juniper tried to see herself as the rest of Jericho would. Like everything else around here, she hadn't changed much—at least on the outside—since she had last called Iowa home. Her skin was still warm as sunbaked sand, and she often wore her long tangle of hair in a thick braid that curled over her right shoulder. Freckles sprinkled her nose and cheeks, trailing stardust down her neck to where a Milky Way of constellations spread across her chest. A lover had once traced them all, drawing patterns with his fingertips.

It was just before eight when Juniper waffled at the front door. In theory, she knew exactly what she was getting herself into: she was here to help Cora, whose breast cancer had spread to her lymph nodes and lungs. The small college in a Denver suburb where Juniper worked as the Special Collections and College Archives Librarian had given her an open-ended leave of absence, a move so generous Juniper had teared up when the Director of Library Services had made the necessary arrangements. But standing with her hand on the door only a block away from the Jericho Public Library, nothing was theoretical anymore.

Cora was dying.

The reality was, Juniper's dear friend and only remaining confidante in her childhood hometown had decided not to undergo further cancer treatment, and Juniper had agreed to come back to keep the small country library afloat. Simple. But in the light of day, her reasons for coming were as labyrinthine as the contents of her box on the Murphy murders, which was now, she realized, strewn all over the kitchen table and on the floor beside the couch. She quickly gathered up the mess and restocked the cardboard box.

Then Juniper palmed her phone and tapped out a quick text message before she could change her mind.

I made it. See you tonight?

The text box turned blue when she hit send. Such a casual greeting when her fingers were tingling with proximity. Her child was in this place, only blocks away if she had already been dropped off at Jericho Elementary, the town's K–8 school. Lithe, lovely Willa Baker, all arms and legs and thirteen-year-old bravado and grace. Who loved winter and pink lemonade and ballet. Juniper had watched the videos over and over again, her girl in a black leotard flowing from position to position, each move so liquid, her chest ached with pride.

I can't wait to see you, she added, shocked by her own vulnerability and afraid of how Willa would receive it. Their relationship was light and happy, filled with funny gifs and a shared appreciation for cat videos. They didn't often tread into more serious waters. Too nervous to wait for a reply, Juniper slid her phone into her purse and stepped out into the frigid morning.

The Jericho Public Library was housed in the old mayor's mansion, a rectangular redbrick colonial with a wide front porch and two pillars that framed a double-wide black door. It was the most charming building in town, and the library board had fought hard to preserve it.

Inside, the floors were narrow plank and the color of clover honey, and the different book sections were collected in rooms on the main floor. Walls had been removed and columns erected to give the library better flow, but there was no way to completely erase the original layout of the home. There were two stone fireplaces and a profusion of floor-to-ceiling windows that filled the library with light, and scattered between the stacks were plush chairs in blue velvet paired with mismatched tables painted turquoise and canary yellow and apricot.

A little noise escaped her lips. Everything was so familiar it was like she had taken a step back in time. But then Cora came out of the small cluster of offices, and Juniper was jolted to the present reality.

"What on earth are you doing here?" Cora demanded, glancing at her watch with brows drawn together. In spite of her sixty-eight years and grim diagnosis, Cora's gaze was clear and blue. Still, she reached for a pair of reading glasses dangling from a beaded chain and perched them on the very end of her nose. She studied Juniper as if she were a puzzle to fix.

"Hello to you too." Juniper smiled around the sudden lump in her throat, taking in her friend's newly diminished form and the purple smudges beneath her eyes. They matched the lavender tips of her silver hair.

"You're supposed to be sleeping in," Cora chided. "I didn't expect you until ten, at least."

"I did sleep in. Come here." Juniper put out her arms and waved Cora into them. How long had it been since she had hugged someone like this? Someone who knew almost everything about her and chose to love her in spite of it all? She found herself blinking back tears, but didn't know who they were for.

It took her a moment to realize that something else was different.

"Double mastectomy," Cora said, as if she could read Juniper's mind. She pulled away and held Juniper at arm's length, giving her an unobstructed view of the flat plane of her chest. "Even if I was going to continue treatment I wouldn't bother with a reconstruction. And don't get me started on those padded bras. Are you crying, Juniper Baker?"

"No," she lied, and turned away to unzip her coat.

Cora led her behind the desk and leaned against it while she watched her old friend get settled. "I'm really glad you're here," she said, her tough-as-tacks facade wavering a bit.

"Stop it." Juniper couldn't handle gratitude. Not now. Not when her motives for coming back were so complicated she could hardly begin to unravel them all herself. She tossed her coat over the back of a folding chair and tucked her backpack in one of the square cubicles.

"You're a godsend. Truly."

"Enough. Or I'm leaving you with Barry."

"Oh, you're terrible." Cora coughed out a short laugh. "He has seniority, you know. He's the Assistant Library Director, you technically answer to him."

"He knows this is all temporary, right?"

"Of course. And since you're 'just the temp' "—

21

Cora curled her fingers into air quotes—"I've given you our Mom and Tot Hour. It's a barbaric group."

Juniper stifled a moan. "That's just plain mean. I'm home less than twelve hours and you've already saddled me with the worst event of the week."

Cora ignored her. "It'll be nice to have someone younger around. Barry's an old soul and I'm just plain old. Things have changed around here, June. The library isn't just books and a handful of DVDs anymore. I'm also fluent in *Minecraft*, *Fortnite*, and *Orange Is the New Black*. I'm trying to keep up."

Juniper was seized by a desire to plant a kiss on Cora's gaunt cheek, but that was out of character for them both. Instead, she turned away and lifted a stack of books that were ready to be reshelved.

Cora frowned, taking the books from Juniper and setting them back down. "There'll be time for all that. You just got here. I want to hear about everything. How was your trip?"

"Fine. Until I got pulled over in front of the rental. No ticket, but . . ." Juniper lifted one shoulder.

"You're kidding. Welcome to Jericho, right?"

"Something like that." Juniper reached for the books again, and this time managed to slip out from behind the counter with her cargo. She wasn't trying to avoid Cora, but she felt a frisson of disquiet. Maybe she had underestimated how difficult it would be to step back into her old life.

"What about the podcast?" Cora followed her a few steps, then stopped abruptly. She glanced around and lowered her voice, even though they were the only ones in the library. "Have you figured out who's doing it?"

"Not yet."

"Is it someone local?"

"I think so."

"Well, do you recognize the voice?"

Juniper felt a tingle of annoyance. "It's not even out yet. I don't know who's doing it, and I don't know how far along they are."

Cora nodded, but she looked a bit confused.

"I want to stop them *before* the podcast goes live."

"And Jonathan?" Cora changed tack. "Does he know you're here?"

It was an innocuous question, but it stung all the same. Juniper paused. There was no way for Cora to know the distance that stretched between her and her brother. The boy who had once been her best friend and was now a virtual stranger. "He knows I'm home," Juniper said finally, and hoped she could leave it at that.

"When are you going to see Willa?"

"What's with the twenty questions?" Juniper

sighed before answering. "Tonight." Then she disappeared between the floor-to-ceiling shelves of adult fiction. There would be time later for a heart-to-heart, to hear the scary details of Cora's illness and confide everything she dared to hope for Willa. Her plan to set things right. For now, there was work to do, and Juniper was grateful for it.

But after an hour or so, even the rustle of paper and the scent of old hardcovers wasn't enough to slow the scurry of Juniper's pulse. Her mind snagged at the thought of the podcast, and grateful for something concrete to focus on, she shifted the books to one arm and pulled her phone from her pocket.

Juniper had taken a couple of screenshots to save the thread from an obscure true crime message board. She always hid her identity online, which allowed her to gain access to information that might be concealed if her unwitting informants knew who she really was.

Posted by **u/cabgreckoning10** 11 hours ago
Working on a podcast about the Murphy murders. Already have a few production companies interested. Need advice re: editing. Any recs?

There were several comments. Links to editorial services and personal offers of help. A few users wondered about the Murphy murders, and then praised cabgreckoning10 for finding a compelling true crime story that hadn't yet been made into a podcast.

Of course, jumping into the conversation had been tricky, potentially even dangerous if she'd inadvertently revealed herself to have more than a passing interest. Still, she had longed to pepper cabgreckoning10 with questions: *Who are you? What do you know about the Murphy murders? Were you there?* She'd managed to restrain herself. Instead, she had thought long and hard about her comment, hands trembling as they hovered over the keyboard, and finally settled on:

BookishJ47 * Score hidden * 10 hours ago
  Got it solved?

cabgreckoning10 * 8.2K points * 10 hours ago
  Close enough. I'm going to prove that
  bastard Jonathan Baker did it.

It had flipped a switch inside her, and Juniper now lived with the constant tick of a countdown clock. Who was cabgreckoning10, and did he know the truth?

Rage and desperation made people do inexplicable things, and Juniper knew a thing or two about secrets. But "that bastard Jonathan Baker" implied that cabgreckoning10 was no stranger.

He—or she—was likely someone from Jericho. Maybe even someone Juniper knew.

And maybe it was all her fault that a killer in Jericho walked free.

CHAPTER 2

SUMMER
14 AND A HALF YEARS AGO

I wake to the sound of Cello Suite no. 1 in G Major, if my ear can be trusted. Mom is in a state, I can tell from the way she cuts through the prelude: a graceless thwack, a stutter of her bow when it should have slid like a knife through butter. Of course, it's still lovely, still enough to make me catch my breath and press my ear to the hardwood floor where I can't just hear the music but feel it reverberating like a whisper against my cheek.

The floor. Why am I on the floor? It takes me a moment to realize that I'm aching all over, my shoulder pinned beneath me, bare arm stitched with lines from the narrow planks where I rested. I press myself up, head hanging as I try to remember. Last night's cutoffs nip into my thighs and a spaghetti strap dangles around my elbow. I right it, recalling the night before in snapshots, Polaroid moments blurred around the edges.

There was a fire, a blaze we fed with old pallets and danced around like nymphs. An owl in the tree that spooked us all and made me scream. Ashley's arm thrown around my waist. Jonathan handing me a heavy, amber-colored bottle. I drank, obviously too much.

Mom is skipping through the courante now, her bow sure but somehow edged in anger. At me? Probably. I can't remember how we got home. Maybe Jonathan dragged me up the stairs and carried me into my bedroom.

I feel sick, my head thick, stomach churning and cavernous. This is why I don't drink. At least, not much. But the light slanting through my window is furiously bright, a reminder that it's officially summer. And I am a high school graduate.

The ceremony was in the gym of Jericho High, parents beaming up from folding chairs below the narrow stage where the graduates stood on bleachers. The entire place creaked and groaned in a chorus of metal on metal as we shifted our weight and shook out tired legs. But there were only forty-eight of us commencing, and the valedictorian was Lexi DeJong, who everyone knows would rather pluck her own eyebrows bald than speak in public, so we were in and out in just under an hour.

Afterward, there were sugar cookies and punch in the bright foyer of the newly remodeled high school. The punch dyed everyone's lips an unnatural shade of crimson so that we looked like a bunch of discreet cannibals, dabbing our mouths with embossed napkins. The good people of Jericho adhere to a family planning policy of "the more the merrier," so several of my classmates' much younger siblings were running around the room, making an unholy ruckus.

Shedding my robe when it was all over felt monumental somehow; this wasn't just my graduation, the end of my time at the mercy of the backwater Jericho school system. No, this is the beginning of everything, a rebirth of sorts. I'm gone, baby, gone. Or I will be in twelve weeks and three days, when I pack everything I own into my little black car, drive away to the University of Iowa, and never look back. Iowa City is merely a stepping-stone, a launch pad to bigger and better things. Maybe I'll do a semester in England, a leap year in Spain or Thailand. Maybe I'll nab a prestigious internship in our nation's capital, where I'll learn how to right the wrongs in the world from the inside. I could pursue a career in political science, art history, nursing, or architecture. I could wander the earth.

My mom never presses me about what exactly I plan to study in college, but Lawrence doesn't miss a chance to make me feel like a failure for not having it all mapped out. He believes it's his fatherly duty to be on my case. But to me he's less of a father figure and more of just . . . Law. "Lawrence" to Mom, "Dad" to Jonathan, and I avoid calling him much of anything at all. His well-rehearsed "A goal without a plan is a wish" speech falls on deaf ears.

Yet, if Lawrence saw me drunk last night, ponytail askew and reeking of booze, I'm a dead girl walking. No matter that I'm almost nineteen years old and weeks away from freedom. Never mind that I have never, not ever, done anything like this before.

I push myself off the floor and squint at the clock on my nightstand. 7:24. At least it's not noon. I wonder what time I got in, when the after-party dissolved and the eleven of us disbanded to sleep off unfamiliar hangovers. I hope my friends all made it home okay.

My bed is mussed up, sheets whipped into a twist that makes me believe I at least started out there. It looks so inviting, I crawl right back in, clothes and all, to try again. I can ignore the cello, my mother's passionate rendition of a new song I do not recognize. Sometimes she writes her own stuff, and this piece is building to an intense, bitter crescendo that will be hard to tune out. But before I can bury my face in the pillow, there is a furious rapping at my door.

"June? Hey, June, you up?"

"No," I call, my voice scratchy from bonfire smoke and laughter. I remember that now: laughing and laughing and laughing. I have no idea what we were laughing about.

"Are you decent?"

"No."

I hear the handle jiggle anyway. It is an antique glass knob that needs WD-40 and a few hard turns of a screwdriver. I know exactly how to fix it, but I don't because you can hear someone open my door from almost anywhere in the house. It's an alarm system of sorts. Not that anyone is in the habit of sneaking into my room. Who would? Lawrence avoids anything that bears even a hint of femininity, Mom is welcome with impunity, and Jonathan knows to knock. I bolt upright at the sound of him breaking this unwritten rule and am rewarded with what feels like a blow to the head. He finds me with the heels of both my hands pressed against my temples.

"That bad?" Jonathan says. I can hear the smirk in his voice.

"Worse. Was this your doing?"

"Pretty sure you swallowed all on your own."

I chance a peek and find my brother lounging against the doorframe, looking smug. He's obviously enjoying this.

"How did we get home?" I ask, closing my eyes again. The light glaring off my polished floorboards is too much.

"I drove."

"You were sober?"

"Of course." As if it's a given. Sobriety is never a given with Jonathan.

"How'd I get up here?"

"I dragged your ass. That's how."

I sigh. "Does Lawrence know?"

"No. He was out cold."

"Mom?"

When Jonathan doesn't answer, I look up to find him staring at me, one eyebrow cocked in that jaunty way that makes all the girls in Jericho and several neighboring towns catch their breath.

"Yeah," I say. "I know." It's impossible not to know. Mom's music is a far better indicator of her mood than the words she says or the look on her face. While you can still glimpse remnants of her storied hippie past—her penchant for bare feet, bangles, dresses that shift like shadows around her tall, slender frame—these days Rebecca Baker is buttoned up tight. It's hard to get a genuine emotion out of her, except for when she is playing her cello.

"We can deal with Mom later," Jonathan says, striding into my room. He opens my closet and yanks a shirt off a hanger, tosses it at me.

"What are you doing?"

"Get dressed." He glances over to where I'm still huddled on the bed. "I mean, in something other than last night's clothes."

"I'm sick, Jonathan."

"No, you're hungover. It's not the same thing."

"I need a shower."

"I know. It'll have to wait."

Even though Jonathan is younger than me by

less than a year, he has always felt like my older brother. When we were little, people assumed he was the oldest because he was bigger than me by the time we were toddlers, and now at eighteen he can easily pass for midtwenties.

"Wait for what?" I say, already bowing to his will, though crawling out of bed is the last thing on earth I want to do.

"Cal called."

"So?"

"Something came up. They need help."

I groan, but one leg is already curving off the side of the mattress, reaching for the floor. "What do they need me for?"

"I don't know, but Beth was crying. I think it's bad this time."

Grabbing the clean T-shirt Jonathan has thrown onto the bed, I wave him out. "Give me five minutes."

Cal and Beth Murphy live on the far side of the little lake that Jericho was named for. It's more of an oversized pond than a lake, a blue-gray smudge of spring water that bubbles up from the prairie and is ringed by gnarled oak trees and cattails that wave in the breeze. There are a few old docks scattered along the banks, and one gravel boat ramp that allows fishers to send out the odd aluminum skiff. Years ago, someone stocked the lake with bass, bluegill, and walleye, and optimistic fishermen still sometimes cast a line and hope for the best, but there isn't much to catch anymore.

From our farm you can drive to the Murphys' acreage in just a few minutes. At the end of our long dirt driveway, all you have to do is take a right on Delaware, then a left on County Road 21. Their place is on the corner, the pretty little homestead with classic red outbuildings and an ancient stone chicken coop that Cal has turned into a shop of sorts. On weekends, he swings open the wide windows along one whole side of the quaint hutch and sells uncertified organic fruits and vegetables that he and Beth have grown, as well as handmade goat milk soap and jams. When they are in season, Beth also cuts bouquets from her flower garden. Tulips and ripe purple hyacinths in the spring, peonies in early summer. My favorite arrangements are available in late July and August: bright dinnerplate dahlias with blooms as big as my open hand. I'll miss them this year because I'll be settling into my dorm room, not collecting flowers from the Murphys' stand.

I want to drive over, but Jonathan insists we walk. On foot, we take a different route entirely, cutting through the soybean field that stands beside our house until cultivated land gives way to the wild brush around Jericho Lake. We've worn a path between the trees and along the water, and we follow it in silence, Jonathan leading the way down a narrow trail of hard-packed earth until we come out on the edge of the Murphys' property.

"This was a stupid idea," I complain when I catch the hem of my shorts on the barbed wire fence. It's sagging between the posts of a single section, but I still have to stand on tiptoe to clear it. My balance is a bit off and a headache continues to thrum at the base of my skull and behind my eyes in spite of the ibuprofen I hastily swallowed. I'm not well equipped for an off-road adventure.

"Suck it up, buttercup," Jonathan quips. But when he sees me wrestling with the sharp end of a rusted barb, he comes back to hold my elbow.

I wince as the sharp metal finally pulls free of my denim shorts and bites into the soft skin of my thigh. It leaves a tiny dot of blood in its wake, and I lick my thumb and smear it away.

"I can't believe you dragged me out here," I mutter in Jonathan's general direction. But he has pulled away from me and is striding up the hill toward the Murphys' barn, trailing a quiet worry that belies his subtle jabs and carefree swagger. My brother is so much more than he seems.

And he loves Cal and Beth Murphy. We both do, though when I hit junior high I started spending less and less time with our older neighbors, and Jonathan started to spend more. The Murphys never had kids of their own, and I guess Cal needed Jonathan's young arms and strong back more than Beth needed my constant chatter while she rolled out pie crust or sheared the woody ends off cut roses. Jonathan still practically lives at the Murphys', while I've begun to feel slightly uncomfortable around them, guilty. Like an old friend who's lost touch and doesn't really have an excuse for it.

By the time I crest the hill at the highest point of the Murphys' property, Jonathan is jogging around the side of the barn. I curse him under my breath for dragging me out on a muggy June morning when it's obvious that I'm an afterthought, but just as I'm about to turn around and head for home, a thin wail pierces the morning calm.

It sounds like an animal in pain, or worse, dying. I hurry down the hill toward the barn, slipping and skidding in my rubber flip-flops as the cries intensify. The Murphys have a small hobby farm: a handful of goats that supply them with milk for their soaps, chickens that lay pretty speckled eggs, a pony named Penny, and a pair of horses they ride on Sunday afternoons. I don't like the thought of any of them suffering.

When I round the far corner of the large barn, I almost crash into Jonathan. He's crouching in the shade, arms wrapped around a hunched form. It takes me a moment to realize that he's holding

Beth, rubbing her back in slow circles like Mom used to do. Her dark head is bowed. She's sobbing.

"Thanks for coming, June." Cal's hand lands heavy on my shoulder and I jump. I hadn't realized he was standing with his back against the wide, shadowed side of the barn. "I was hoping you could take Beth inside and fix her a cup of coffee while Jonathan and I bury the body."

"What?" I jerk and feel Cal's hand fall away. It lands on a spade that's propped beside him. A nip of premonition lifts the fine hairs on my arm.

"Jonathan didn't tell you?"

"I didn't know," Jonathan says over his shoulder. "I couldn't make out what Beth was saying when she called."

As I stare at my brother, I realize that he and Beth are kneeling in front of something. It's a dark mass curled into a half moon and hidden in the gloom cast by the tall barn, but twin tufts of white help the picture slide into focus. There are markings on his paws and a milky plume on his muscular chest. Baxter. I'm looking at Baxter, one of the Murphys' beloved border collies. He's one of a pair—I never see Baxter without Betsy, his twin. But I don't have to ask where she is. In the beat of silence while I work out the scene before me, I can hear her whining and barking from inside the house.

"What happened?" I choke, stumbling backward a step. My head swims, and my stomach, too. I press a hand to my chest and gulp a ragged breath. It's obvious even at a glance that Baxter is dead. He's lying on his side, legs stiff in front of his body and stomach obscenely distended. The bloody froth around his mouth makes everything inside me twist and buck, and I have to look away.

"He was poisoned!" Beth pushes herself to her feet and spins to face me, eyes swollen and wild.

Cal shakes his head. "We don't know that."

Jonathan stands slowly, settling his hands on his hips. He catches my gaze. The message in his blue eyes is pointed, but for once I don't know what he's trying to tell me. Suddenly, I realize that I can smell Baxter. Rotten fish, a whiff of garlic. My heart quivers high and insistent beneath my collarbone and my lips tingle. The ground sways, but nobody else seems to notice.

"Come on, Beth. June is going to take you inside and make a pot of coffee," Cal says, wrapping one arm around his wife and brushing his lips against her forehead. "Take one of your heart pills, okay? And give Betsy a hug. She needs it."

Jonathan takes Beth by the elbow and motions to me. "Her heart pills are on the windowsill above the sink," he tells me as he leads us toward the house. It's postcard perfect: crisp, clean white with black shutters and a cheerful profusion of multicolored flowers spilling from window boxes. But behind the slanted roof I can see dark clouds rimmed in black. A storm is coming. The sky rumbles with thunder in the distance as Beth pulls away from us. When she's out of earshot, Jonathan says, "Cal and I will bury Baxter. All you have to do is make sure Beth is okay."

"But—"

"For once in your life, Juniper Grace, just do it."

I cross my arms over my chest and take a step away from Jonathan. Something has shifted in him between the moment he came into my bedroom less than an hour before and now. He knew something was wrong at the Murphys', but he hadn't been expecting *this*.

"What happened?" I say it quietly, but Jonathan's eyes dart to where Beth has just put her hand on the farmhouse door. She pauses with her palm against the lacquered wood, then sets her shoulders and slips inside. I can see Betsy framed in the narrow gap for just a second or two, her black-and-white body wriggling against Beth and trying to get past. To get to Baxter. The door snaps shut.

"Jonathan?" I spin back to him, but he's already heading toward the barn. Cal is nowhere in sight, but Baxter looks like a gaping hole in the shadows. It's a trick of the light that makes it appear as if Cal has already dug a grave. I hurry after my brother and catch his arm. "What the hell is going on?"

"I don't know," he says. He yanks away, and as he leaves I hear him say, "But this wasn't an accident."

CHAPTER 3

WINTER
TODAY

The lights were on inside the farmhouse, and framed in the picture window was a scene reminiscent of a Norman Rockwell print. They were setting the table, carrying stacks of plates and stemless wineglasses and a serving dish with potholders that Juniper knew her mother had knit. There was laughter—she couldn't hear it, but she could see it in the way that her sister-in-law, Mandy, tossed her head, lips pulled back in what could be considered a rictus. But no, they were happy, or at least pretending to be.

I could leave. The thought was tempting. She could whip the car around and speed away, past the little blue house and the library and the shot-up WELCOME TO JERICHO sign. This time, she would keep her promise to herself and never, *ever* come back.

But no. Juniper shoved the idea away. She had a plan. Besides, it was too late. As she watched, one of her nephews came running over to the window. Cameron? He pressed his nose against the glass, and his gap-toothed grin told her that he was indeed her four-year-old nephew. He

41

looked over his shoulder and shouted something so that everyone turned to stare.

The night was moonless and cold, so dark that Juniper could hardly see where she was going and had to pick her way carefully or risk breaking her neck on the icy walk. By the time she mounted the porch steps, Cameron had come outside and Hunter had joined his brother, one hand fisted around the collar of Jonathan's dog. Diesel was a Great Dane with classic fawn markings and the personality of a teddy bear. The little trio were the only family members willing to brave the night to say hello. Juniper didn't know if she should be disappointed or relieved.

"Did you bring us something?" Cameron asked in greeting. A towheaded carbon copy of Jonathan at four, he pressed himself against his older brother. Hunter favored his mother, but Cameron made Juniper feel strangely wistful.

"Of course." She smiled and held out a bag filled with lollipops from Hammonds. She didn't even tell them to save the sweets for later.

Hunter snatched it and murmured a thank-you. Then they both seemed to remember their manners and hugged her, quickly, before racing back into the house. Cameron left the door wide open for her grand entrance.

But Juniper's homecoming wasn't grand, and as she stood just outside the slash of light carved on the crooked porch of her childhood home, the full reality of it hit her like a blow. This was a moment so ripe with shame, she couldn't stop herself from recoiling a little. She was the runaway, the prodigal daughter who had split when the going got tough. And beneath the brittle layer of that ugly truth, Juniper harbored the fear that she hadn't left of her own free will— she'd been pushed out. Banished. Suddenly she knew that all the years between hadn't lessened the guilt and horror she felt. If anything, those feelings had intensified.

It was true that she made the pilgrimage home once a year—usually a quick weekend stay to celebrate Willa's birthday—but she avoided Jericho proper altogether. It was easy to bypass the entire town by taking gravel roads and then camping on the sagging couch in her parents' living room for a scant night or two. These whirlwind trips—though carefully structured and contained—were as sweet and fleeting as candy on her tongue. And while Juniper treasured the meager memories she made with Willa, she always drove back to Colorado with a bitter aftertaste.

In the early years, when Juniper came home, she would tiptoe upstairs in the middle of the night to hold Willa in the rocking chair. The child was so small and yet so heavy, a warm, sturdy weight in June's lap that threatened to anchor her to Jericho. And wouldn't she give up everything

43

for this? For the curl of her daughter's chubby hand around her finger? For the scent of her milk-warm breath in the air between them? For the chance to start again? But Reb had quickly put a stop to those nights. She'd snuck up the stairs herself and whisked the sleeping Willa up and away, chiding Juniper that the little girl needed her sleep. The message was clear: *Willa doesn't need you.* Juniper feared it was still true. She didn't belong here.

Crouching down, she buried both hands in Diesel's warm scruff. "What do you think, boy? Should we get out of here?" He licked her chin.

"June?" Her mother sounded hesitant when she stuck her head out the door, and in the dim glow of the porch light Juniper could see worry carve a deep line between the older woman's eyebrows. With one hand, Reb carefully smoothed her still-dark hair from her temple to the tight bun at the nape of her neck and attempted a smile. It wavered. Still, Juniper's chest flooded with something sticky and complicated at the familiar sight: wire-rimmed glasses, crooked half smile, knowing gaze.

"Hi, Mom." They met over the threshold and hugged awkwardly, like strangers. Reb smelled of wine with a faint undertone of sweat, an odor that reeked of anxiety. Juniper realized with a start that her mother had been drinking. It was in her shallow breath, the rheumy gaze of her

44

pink-rimmed eyes. Even more startling was the realization that her own mother was afraid of her—of those stolen nights with Willa in her arms and what they might look like now that Willa was old enough to make her own decisions. Now that Juniper was staying. Even if only for a while.

She had reason to be afraid.

"Welcome!" Mandy burst into the entryway, tipping the delicate balance toward pure mayhem. All at once, the private moment with her mother fell away and Juniper noticed that the boys were still screaming in the background, and the timer on the stove rang a shrill, insistent note. Before she could even return her sister-in-law's enthusiastic greeting, Mandy had stood on tiptoe to throw her arms around Juniper's neck. Into her hair she said: "Shut the door, you're letting all the cold air in," and then abruptly let go to call the dog inside. "Come on, Diesel."

Diesel loped past them, and Juniper pulled the door shut behind her before allowing Mandy to slide her coat off her shoulders. She had learned long ago that it was easier to just go along with Mandy's ministrations. Mandy had set up this dinner, probably planned the menu, and would no doubt orchestrate the conversation with a cache of benign questions that would steer them clear of politics and religion, Juniper's extended absence, and what had happened so long ago.

She sparked like a live flame, bright and warm and irresistible.

"Thank you," Juniper said quietly, surprising herself. But Mandy always made her feel vaguely grateful. *Thank you for the sincere welcome. For trying so hard. For saving my brother.*

"Everyone is so excited to see you, Junebug! We kind of can't believe you're here." Mandy looped her arm through Juniper's and sashayed them both into the dining room, presenting her to the group and declaring: *"Here she is!"* Juniper's cheeks bloomed crimson.

Law was closest, and he dutifully draped an arm across her shoulders. "Hey," he said, brushing the hard line of his jaw across her forehead. It was a wooden affection, but unexpected, and Juniper caught her breath. Then the brief moment of contact was over, and she was left staring at the only father she'd ever known.

Lawrence Baker hadn't altered his look in thirty years: buzz-cut gray hair, short clean fingernails, starched shirts. He even instructed Reb to iron a crease into his jeans and buff out marks on his shoes every night. Or, he used to. As far as Juniper could tell, he still did. He was scrubbed and neat as ever, even if his shoulders had rounded by degrees and his back was no longer ramrod straight. "Welcome home," he told her.

"Hi, Dad," she said, stumbling over the word

just a bit. She felt drunk. A little dizzy; a lot nauseated. The scent of her mother's pot roast and mashed potatoes was overwhelming, and the old-fashioned radiator that ran the length of the room was pumping out dry, hot air that made it hard to breathe.

"Boy, it's warm in here, isn't it?" Mandy slipped an arm around Juniper before she could swoon, and eased her into a chair. "Crack the window, would you, Lawrence? I think we all need a little fresh air."

Lawrence Baker wasn't the sort to be bossed around, but he left the room without a backward glance, and Juniper found herself alone with Mandy and, across the table, Jonathan. He was sitting on the long bench with his back against the wall and a glass of wine in his fist. It was mostly gone. He stared at her over the dregs, and for the life of her, Juniper couldn't make out his expression. Apathy? Disdain? Perhaps this was already his second glass and he was comfortably numb.

"Hey, J." It was all she could think to say.

He laughed. It was a wry chuckle, but in his blue eyes Juniper could see a flash of the boy she had known. Something inside her gave way, and when Jonathan pushed himself up from the table and leaned over to give her a brotherly kiss on the forehead, she had to squeeze her eyes closed.

"You came home," he said simply.

"I've been busy." Juniper's excuses were so tired, even she struggled to repeat them. "You're always welcome in Colorado. Best skiing in the States."

"We don't ski," Jonathan reminded her. "*You* don't ski."

"Hiking, then! Garden of the Gods or Estes Park or—"

"Enough. It was time. We're glad you're here."

Juniper wasn't convinced. She felt Mandy glance between them, but she couldn't begin to guess at what her sister-in-law was thinking. After a charged moment, Mandy clapped her hands. "Well, then. I'm going to go see if Rebecca needs any help finishing up."

"Tell the boys to take it down a notch or two," Jonathan said without removing his gaze from Juniper's flushed face.

"Boys will be boys," Mandy chimed.

Juniper caught Jonathan's eye roll, but Mandy was already gone. "I gave them candy," she confessed.

"It's official: you're out of the will." Jonathan downed the last of his wine in a gulp and grabbed for the bottle. He refilled his glass, then reached to pour for Juniper. She shook her head. "No?" He shrugged and put the bottle down between them. Lowering his voice, he said, "Look, June, we need to talk."

She felt herself go very still. "We are talking."

Ignoring her evasive response, Jonathan said: "I'll pick you up from the library on Wednesday. You get a lunch break, right?"

"Well, sure, but—"

"Mandy will be at work and the boys will be at school, so I'll grab something from Cunningham's and take you back to our place."

"We could go to the Admiral," Juniper offered, imagining crowded booths and lots of people. The thought of being alone with Jonathan made her a bit uneasy. They had very different ideas about how to deal with the past—it was one of the many things that made her brother feel like a stranger. Juniper had thick files and chat room aliases and a thirst for answers she couldn't slake. Jonathan vigilantly ignored the fact that their neighbors had been murdered in cold blood with no resolution, leaving him—in perpetuity—as the main suspect. Did he know about the podcast? Was she ready to tell him?

"I'll pick you up at noon." Clearly, Jonathan wasn't going to take no for an answer. He ran his hand through his dark hair and sat back against the wallpaper. It was faded and floral—from another era—and suddenly Juniper could see her brother as he had been: tall and lean, with a perpetual smirk that meant trouble. Back then, he could make her laugh with a goofy look. She missed that boy more than she dared to admit. His easy smile, happy-go-lucky way. They used to talk for hours about everything and nothing, and shared a bond that betrayed their connection as virtual twins. Now, at thirty-two, gray peppered his temples.

"Fine," Juniper relented. "I'll be ready."

"Ready for what?" Mandy swept into the dining room with the pot roast on a platter and set it on the table with a flourish. The boys were right behind her, and then Lawrence and Reb.

"Nothing," Juniper said absently as she half rose from her seat. Where was her daughter? She had been swept into the house and practically thrust into the chair where she was sitting, but she hadn't caught even a glimpse of Willa. Her heart vaulted at the mere thought, and she pushed back from the table to greet her. Would they hug? Juniper could almost feel the slip of a girl, shoulder blades against her arms like nascent angel wings. But when everyone found their seats and settled in, there was one empty place.

"Where's Willa?" Juniper finally whispered. She alone was standing, as if she had prepared a speech or was about to say grace.

Reb's forefinger caught the necklace at the nape of her neck and twined it round and round. Her eyes darted from mashed potatoes to Law to Jonathan and finally to Mandy. Juniper's pulse quickened as she turned her attention to her sister-in-law. Of course it would fall to her. This family of cowards would always defer to the woman who had stepped inside and set everything right. For one blinding moment, Juniper hated her.

"Willa's not coming down tonight," Mandy said matter-of-factly. "She's not feeling well."

It was as if Mandy had slapped her. Juniper felt all the air go out of her in a rush. "I could go to her," Juniper said, her voice splintering. She tried again. "I could bring her some food."

"Not tonight," Mandy said, gentler this time. "She's looking forward to seeing you, Juniper, really she is. She just needs a little time to adjust."

It was such a pathetic excuse. Generic and uninspired. Juniper had dared to let herself hope that maybe there was a chance for her and Willa. But thirteen years couldn't be erased with one overdue homecoming, no matter how noble her intentions. She hadn't *really* thought it would be easy, had she? That she could waltz in here and woo her daughter away from the only family she had ever known? Law and Reb might be her grandparents, but they were Grandpa and Grandma in name only. In reality? They were Mom and Dad. Juniper didn't know where she fit.

"You okay?" Mandy asked when the silence became uncomfortable. She reached out a tentative hand and gave Juniper's arm a fortifying rub.

Juniper looked around the table and realized that even the boys were struck dumb. They were staring at her, and Cameron was sucking on the tips of his middle two fingers—a nervous habit she thought he had left behind a long time ago. "Fine." She forced a smile and sat down, scooting her chair closer to the table. "I'm fine. I'll see Willa tomorrow."

"Of course." Mandy grinned and snapped her napkin, letting it settle over her lap as if Juniper's proclamation fixed everything. "Tomorrow."

Law cleared his throat then, and, recognizing the familiar prompt, everyone ducked their heads to pray. But instead of closing her eyes while her father pontificated, Juniper watched her family. Jonathan rubbed his forehead; the boys squeezed their eyes shut so tight they quivered. Mandy's lips held the memory of a smile, as if her face knew no other shape.

When Juniper looked at Reb, her mother was staring back at her. For a few seconds they studied each other, gazes thin and appraising. Then Reb softened a little, smiled. There was love in her look, but something else, too. Pity? Warning?

Juniper closed her eyes and knotted her hands in her lap. She hadn't come this far to roll over and play dead. She'd hoped it wouldn't come to this, but she was ready to fight for Willa. And it was obvious that Reb knew it.

Juniper returned to the bungalow early, allowed herself a single glass of the chardonnay that

Cora had left chilling in the refrigerator, and pored through an old phone book she'd found while rummaging for a corkscrew. She made a long list of people to call, dividing them into three columns: *Podcast* (for former friends and acquaintances she considered brave enough to attempt such an endeavor), *Interview* (for some long-awaited face-to-face conversations), and *Suspects* (because they were all, as far as she knew, still residents of Jericho). Whether their phone numbers were current—or even if they still had landlines—remained to be seen. But copying down the names and numbers felt like a step in the right direction. Juniper fell asleep on the couch again, with the dusty phone book splayed open on her chest.

When she woke, there was a stitch between her spine and shoulder blade. She rolled her shoulders to loosen up, and then stared at her phone, wondering if she should text Willa or leave her alone. Yesterday she had gotten three short letters: *cul*. See you later. Brief and painfully dismissive.

Being a mother was an art form. A complicated, intricate dance that Juniper had never learned the steps to. She swept in once a year and tried to match the rhythm of the life her parents had created for her daughter, but she always seemed to stumble. When Willa was five, she was enrolled in gymnastics, but by six she had left the gym behind for the dance studio. Somehow Juniper had missed the memo. The adjustable balance beam she had crammed into her trunk was almost immediately abandoned in the excitement surrounding Willa's first pair of ballet slippers. A gift from Law and Reb, of course.

There were other, less glaring missteps that left Juniper hovering at the edge of her daughter's world instead of leaping in. But this time would be different. The hole in her heart was exactly Willa-sized. And a couple of months ago Juniper's therapist had begun a line of questioning that ended with: "What role do you want to have in your daughter's life?" Didn't the question presuppose the answer? If Willa was her daughter, Juniper was her *mom*.

A poor excuse for a mother, to be sure, but Willa had grown in the space beneath her heart, had been ushered into this world by the soundtrack of her mother's body. That had to count for something.

Juniper dragged herself to the library just before eight, burdened by thoughts of her broken family and aching in the place where her back was beginning to knot. It was a dull but persistent reminder that nothing was okay.

"That bad?" Cora said in greeting when Juniper leaned against the doorframe to her cluttered office.

"That obvious?"

Cora gave her a wry smile in response. "Willa?"

"I didn't even get to see her. She wouldn't come down."

"Oh, honey. I'm so sorry." Cora was seated at her desk, face bluish in the cast of light from her computer monitor. She started to get up—ostensibly to offer a hug or some other form of tangible comfort—but Juniper shook her head, and Cora settled back with a heavy exhale.

"Stay put," Juniper insisted. "I'm fine. Or, I will be. I knew it wouldn't be easy—at least not at first. I haven't been a part of Willa's life for a very long time."

"She'll come around."

Juniper wasn't so sure about that. There was no reason for Willa to love her or trust her. "She hardly knows me. And let's face it, Cora, I'm not exactly mother material."

"So change that. Surprise her."

Juniper shrugged.

The sound of the double front door opening made them both glance toward the library floor. A cold gust of air followed the telltale squeak of rusty hinges, and Juniper called over her shoulder, "We open at nine!"

"Esther Harrison sometimes likes to stop in on her way to Cunningham's for coffee in the morning," Cora said.

"And you let her?"

It was Cora's turn to shrug.

"You're getting soft," Juniper teased. "I'll take care of her. What am I looking for?"

"Short stories, anything postwar. Think 1950s John Cheever, not Jack Kerouac."

"Got it." Juniper slipped out of the office, pulling the door closed behind her. *Cathedral*, she decided as she wove past the circulation desk and made her way toward the front door. If Mrs. Harrison was willing to branch out a bit, Raymond Carver might be a good fit. Subtle optimism, a sad flicker of hope. Maybe it would be just what she needed.

But it wasn't an elderly woman stomping snow off her boots just inside the door. "Mandy! What are you doing here?" Juniper couldn't hide her surprise.

"Hey, June." The younger woman forced a fleeting smile, and then surveyed the growing pool of dirty ice water beneath her feet with dismay. Her dark curls were crammed under a pink stocking cap with a jaunty pom—essential Mandy—but her eyes were downcast, her bottom lip snagged between her teeth. Gone was the happy girl from the night before.

When Mandy didn't say anything more, Juniper filled the awkward silence. "Are you looking for a book?"

"I'm looking for you."

"Okay . . ." Juniper felt something dark crawl between them, but she flicked it off.

"Look, I know Jonathan wants to talk to you," Mandy said quickly, "and I know that you're not just here for Cora."

Juniper glanced over her shoulder, but it wasn't as if this would be news to Cora. She knew Juniper's reasons were complicated. "It was time," she agreed, giving nothing else away. She had told Law and Reb that she wanted to be a more involved mother, but she hadn't admitted that she wanted Willa to move back to Colorado with her. No doubt they suspected as much.

"You want to be a bigger part of Willa's life, and we all get that, really we do." Mandy seemed to read her mind. "Even Reb."

"But?"

"But your timing is . . ." Mandy cast around as if she expected the right word to materialize out of the books around her. She settled on: "Uncanny. Things have been happening, June."

The library grew very small, the air delicate as spun glass. Juniper hardly dared to move, but she managed: "I'm not sure what you mean."

"Our car was keyed, for one. At first I thought it was just some punk teens with nothing better to do. But then our mailbox was destroyed a couple of weeks ago, and someone keeps calling the landline and then hanging up. The boys think it's funny, but . . ." Mandy shrugged unconvincingly.

Juniper was still struggling to breathe in the fragile, airless room. "What else?" she croaked.

"Footprints in the snow around our house. Headlights in our window late at night. Jonathan keeps telling me it's nothing, but I don't believe him."

"Do Law and Reb know?"

Mandy looked affronted. "We don't want to worry them."

Thinking about their family dinner the night before and the perfectly normal way Mandy had behaved, Juniper wasn't surprised that her brother and his wife managed to keep this from their parents. Clearly, she was an excellent actor.

A thought popped into Juniper's head. "Has anyone tried to interview you? Or Jonathan? About what happened back then?"

Mandy's nose wrinkled. "I don't know what you're talking about."

"Nothing," Juniper said quickly. Apparently, whoever was working on a podcast about the Murphy murders hadn't bothered to interview the prime suspect yet. Thank God. True crime podcasts peddled in the court of popular opinion—if damning recordings had already been made, there was little Juniper could do about them. "Look, I want to help, but I'm not sure what you want me to do."

"Isn't it obvious?" Mandy caught both of Juniper's arms and gave her a desperate look. "I want you to talk some sense into him."

"Me? We're not exactly close anymore."

"He'll listen to you about this. He doesn't talk about that summer, but I know you two were inseparable back then. Just persuade him that we need to get the cops involved."

Juniper didn't necessarily agree that calling the police was the best course of action. The people of Jericho had long memories, and though Jonathan had never been convicted of the murders, it was impossible to separate Cal and Beth from her brother. Guilty or not, he bore the stain of accusation—and had been treated accordingly for almost fifteen years. Plenty of people thought Jonathan Baker had gotten away with murder. Juniper knew her brother had had to start his own online web design business because no one in town would hire him. He had to marry a girl from out of town, stop going to church, keep to himself. There were unwritten rules that had shrunk Jonathan's world until it could be tucked away: out of sight, out of mind. Maybe it was best to stay there.

"My husband didn't kill those people," Mandy said as if she could read Juniper's mind.

Uncertainty coiled itself around Juniper's neck and she backed away, yanking out of her sister-in-law's insistent grip. Hurt registered so immediately on Mandy's face that Juniper quickly reversed course and folded her in a hug. "I know," she said, but the assurance rang hollow.

The distance between Mandy's confidence and

Juniper's own misgivings was razor thin. But it was there. When Cal and Beth Murphy were murdered nearly fifteen years ago, no one could have predicted it. And in some ways, everyone should have.

No one was entirely innocent. Not even Jonathan.

CHAPTER 4

SUMMER
14 AND A HALF YEARS AGO

My cell is a slim flip phone in sparkly pink. It was a birthday present to myself, a splurge that still gives me a little burst of pleasure when I slide it out of the back pocket of my shorts and thumb it open. I feel guilty for loving it, for having even a brief, happy thought when the sky is darkening to cinders above me and Baxter is buried beneath a couple feet of freshly turned earth in the grove.

I've missed several text messages, most of them from Ashley, who has undoubtedly been trying to get a hold of me all morning. But of course I didn't dare to answer my phone with Beth alternately sobbing into a crumpled-up tissue and muttering angrily under her breath.

"Where have you been?" Ashley demands when I call her.

"Long story."

"I have time."

I sigh, uncertain that she's ready to have this conversation. The low-grade drama that has surrounded Cal and Beth Murphy for as long as I can remember feels changed this morning. Darker, somehow dangerous. But if I'm honest with myself, the slow simmer has been

61

developing into a fast boil all along. First, there was the slur bleached onto their pristine front lawn. It took an entire summer for the four ugly letters to become indistinguishable from the rest of the carefully tended, bottle-green grass. *KOOK.* I wasn't even sure what it meant. What were they trying to *say,* those mudslinging, property-destroying tormentors? It seemed laughable at first. But the Murphys didn't find it funny. "It's not about property damage," Cal had said. "It's dehumanizing. They're trying to isolate us."

Then the Murphys' trees were toilet-papered, their roadside stand egged, and a single leaded window broken by a rock hurled through the vintage door. Later, Jonathan had told me about threatening phone calls and a truck that drove onto the Murphys' property one night and spun a few donuts in the gravel before honking madly and careening off into the darkness. Popular opinion pointed to teenage hoodlums as the culprits, but everyone knew there were other threats at play. Still are, apparently.

But I'm not interested in talking to Ashley about any of that right now. The strange angle of Baxter's neck is haunting me, making me feel jittery and scared. And Jonathan's proclamation: *This wasn't an accident.* I can't help but feel like whoever poisoned him is crouching in the ditch grass right now. Watching.

"Later," I tell Ashley as I hurry toward home.

I'm taking the road, too shaken to follow the footpath past the lake without Jonathan leading the way. Gravel crunches beneath my feet and sticks to the rubber soles of my flip-flops. I don't bother to stop and brush it off. "Anyway, I'm hungover. You too?"

Ashley hoots. "I *knew* it! You are the absolute worst. We have to build up your tolerance before you leave."

My best friend isn't going to college. She's taking a "gap year," if you can even call it that, because she doesn't plan to travel or even get a job. Ashley's mother had twins less than a year ago and, at late forty-something, is drowning beneath the responsibilities of being a round-two, brand-new mother. *I'll be like a nanny,* Ashley says, but I know what a sacrifice she's making for her mom.

"Not interested in being the college drunk," I say too brightly. My head still pounds and I feel like the scent of death lingers in my clothes, my hair. I'm desperate to scour myself. "I'm taking a quick shower and then let's go to Munroe."

"Today?"

"Yes, today."

"Mom wants me to watch the twins this afternoon—"

"It's the first day of summer break!" I interrupt. The thought of being stuck at home, of being trapped with Jonathan and my angry mother for the afternoon, makes me tense. "Camp starts next week, and you know I'll be busy every single day after that."

"Yeah, but—"

"Ashley!"

"Fine, okay." A big sigh whistles through the line. "I'll tell my mom I can't."

I sag a little in relief. "Half an hour. Can you drive?"

"Yeah, yeah." Ashley cuts the line.

When I slip in the side door of the farmhouse, a soft rain is just starting to fall. It splats on the black hood of Jonathan's truck and hisses at the sting of hot metal. The air is electric, charged with warm rain and summer ground, dusty and savage. It's a relief to shut the door and be enveloped by the smell of detergent, clean clothes. Mom's been doing laundry, and it's heaped on the counter beside the washing machine in neat piles. Whites and lights and darks. I can see the thin blue stripes of the master bedroom sheets spinning circles in the dryer. Clearly the ominous morning sky discouraged my mother from hanging the laundry on the clothesline outside. She's bound to be irritable knowing she won't fall asleep in sunbaked sheets tonight. I add it to the list of things that will weigh her down today, and I'm grateful that Ashley will soon whisk me away.

I can no longer hear Mom playing cello. Save the hum and bump of the washer and dryer, the house is eerily silent, holding its breath, and as my chest tightens, I realize that I'm not breathing, either. I'm rattled, even though I don't want to be. Even though I want to pretend that all of this is quite safe. Normal.

From the outside looking in, Jericho is as spit-polished and shiny as a pearl button. Friendly and close-knit, to be sure, but in the way that mob families are. If you fit the mold, honor the customs and routines that have been passed down for generations, you're gold. If not, well, don't let the door hit you where the good Lord split you, as Law likes to so eloquently say.

I have a feeling that's why the Murphys have targets on their backs. They're different. They dared to put up a political sign last year that didn't match every other one in town. Their vegetables are organic (or nearly so—Beth told me they're a year away from full certification), and their chickens free-range. Worst of all, they're smack dab in the middle of the biggest drama Jericho has ever seen. I think there are lawyers involved.

"Juniper?"

I slip into the upstairs bathroom quick as can be and ease the door shut. There's no use pretending I didn't hear her, but I can put off a face-to-face confrontation for a few minutes at least.

"In the bathroom!" I shout, yanking off my T-shirt and turning on the shower.

Even with the water running I can hear Mom

coming up the stairs. They creak, or at least some of them do, and Mom doesn't avoid the squeaky ones like Jonathan and I do. I kick off my shorts and hop in, even though the water is still cold. It spills over my warm skin and makes me gasp.

"We need to talk," Mom says, sticking her head in the bathroom. I forgot to lock the door, damnit. Thank goodness for plaid shower curtains.

"I'm showering here."

"When you're done."

"Ashley's coming. We're going to Munroe."

"It's raining."

"It'll stop." I duck my head under the lukewarm spray and silently curse myself. The beach is hardly appropriate for a stormy day. "We'll kill time at Starbucks, or Target."

I can't hear her sigh, but I know it's there. My mother's signature move, a low exhalation that's almost a groan—as if she's seventy instead of newly forty, and plagued by arthritic knees, failing vision, a lifetime of bittersweet memories. Mom is nothing like she sounds in those moments. First of all, she's gorgeous. The boys in my class have always made sure I understood that I've fallen short of the family standard. I'm cute, in a freckled, girl-next-door sort of way, but Rebecca Baker is capital-*S* stunning. A raven-haired, dark-eyed classic beauty. Of course, she doesn't realize it, and that just makes her all the more appealing.

Mom wears the same trend-blind clothes she wore when I was little, wide-legged pants when the fashion is skintight, and dresses that hide her slender figure instead of accentuating it. I'd kill to dress her just once. I'd put her in a pencil skirt that hugs her waist and some low heels. Her hair loose and just a little wavy. My mom wears her hair in a knot at the nape of her neck, bobby pins ensuring that no face-framing tendrils will ever escape. I'd have to hate her a little if I didn't love her so much. And when I look in the mirror, I can't help but wonder why Jonathan is all her, and I'm made up of the bits and pieces of a stranger.

Lawrence isn't my real dad. I don't know who is.

"Mom," I call, reaching for the shampoo. "Can I have some privacy?"

"I'll be in the kitchen," she says.

I don't answer.

When I come downstairs, freshly showered and feeling slightly more human, Mom isn't in the kitchen. She's in the laundry room folding towels—or at least I think she is. I tell myself she's busy, and instead of picking up the conversation like she so obviously wanted me to do, I pour myself a glass of orange juice and grab a blueberry muffin from the basket on the counter. I swallow the juice quickly and tuck the muffin in a paper towel, then go wait for Ashley from the protection of the covered porch. It's not long before she's pulling down the driveway.

"Ashley's here!" I shout through the screen door, grateful for my friend's punctuality. "We'll talk when I get back!"

There's a muffled reply from inside the house, but I'm already running down the steps into the pouring rain. For a moment I can't hear anything except the roar of water as it falls in sheets around me and explodes against the stone path. Then I'm wrenching the passenger-side door open and collapsing inside with a giggle.

"Some beach weather," Ashley says wryly. I can tell she's still irritated that I overruled her plans for the day. I'll make her change her mind. I'm good at that.

"Got a towel?" I grin at her, offering up my dripping arms as evidence of my need.

"You didn't take one?"

I shrug, but she reaches into the backseat and hands me a beach towel printed with multicolored popsicles.

"It'll pass." I squeeze the excess water out of my hair with Ashley's plush towel. It'll dry in a riot of dark blond curls, but I don't care. I rather like my lion's mane. It fits me.

"Are you even wearing your suit?"

I flash her, exposing my favorite green bikini top with the little white flowers.

My muffin is damp, but edible, and I tear off a corner with my teeth. A plump blueberry bursts against my tongue. "Thanks for getting me out of here," I say around a mouthful.

"What happened this morning?" Ashley's softening already, warming up to our comfortable chatter and the promise of a juicy story. "Did Law tear you a new one?"

"He's not even home."

"You dodged a bullet there."

"Look," I say, pointing in the rearview. "It's clearing already." There's a patch of sky behind us where the clouds have torn that looks exactly like the swirl in the blue peppermints my mom used to take to church. They cut my mouth, but I sucked them anyway, yearning for something sweet. I feel like that a bit right now, hungry in a way that's inexplicable and undefined.

"Spill," Ashley demands. "Where were you this morning?"

My story is thin, bare bones, though I'm not exactly sure why I'm hiding things from her. It just seems to me that there are too many loose ends, and I know exactly how my best friend feels about my prime suspect.

"Their dog was poisoned?" Ashley's nose wrinkles in revulsion.

"It was probably an accident." For some reason, I don't want to tell her what Jonathan said. Maybe I misheard him.

"Sure." Ashley laughs dryly. "Just like it was an accident when someone hit their car in the grocery store parking lot."

"Are you serious?"

"You didn't know?" Ashley shoots me a side-long glance as she slows for the corner that will take us to our favorite beach. "My dad had to file the incident report."

Ashley's dad is the manager of the Pantry and has a better grasp on local gossip than most. Maybe that's one of the reasons I'm hesitant to share just how upset Beth was. How Jonathan seemed oddly calm about the whole affair. No, not calm. *Accepting.* As if he suspected what had happened long before Calvin told him. There's simply no need to add fuel to this new development—and Ashley's family is a bit like gasoline. The Pattersons love to talk.

"Why would someone do that?" I'm talking more to myself than to her, but Ashley answers anyway.

"It's harmless." She shrugs one shoulder. "The Murphys make things hard for themselves, and then people like to tease."

"Tease?" I bristle, suddenly chilled in the blast of cold air pumping from the open vents. "Intentionally hitting their car in a parking lot is more like property damage."

"It was a scratch."

My anger is a sudden, solid thing, icy and

70

unyielding. But I don't want to fight with Ashley. Not now, not when I've orchestrated this outing, and the countdown to my departure has officially begun. I can feel the future tugging at me as I sit miserably in the front seat of her car. I don't want this—any of it. Not the bickering or the dead dog or the conspiracy theories that blow around Jericho like the tumbleweeds that occasionally waft through town on sweltering August days. So I swallow my snappy retort and focus instead on the fact that the blacktop beneath our tires is chalky gray and dry.

I could say, *I told you so*. Not only has the storm passed right over us, it looks as if it never even rained in Munroe. This happens sometimes in our corner of the Midwest. A tornado cuts through a cornfield tearing one stalk from the ground and leaving its neighbor tall and unscathed. It pours on the south side of town, but there's a mark on the pavement where the rain abruptly ends. Neatly drawn, impossible to miss. Life between normal and a life-changing tempest separated by a hair's breadth.

"Looks like we'll catch some sun after all," I say, bumping Ashley with my elbow as she pulls into the gravel parking lot on the north shore of Lake Munroe. There are other beaches, but this is where the boardwalk starts, where crowds of people stake rainbow-colored umbrellas into the sand and walk barefoot to buy hand-scooped ice cream cones and questionable corn dogs from Sweet Pete's. The north shore is also where GL Gas has pumps on the water. I can't help it—I love the way the boats coast toward the two long docks and guys come running out to catch the mooring lines. Sullivan is one of them, and he's the reason Ashley and I are both here.

He likes me. I've known that for a long time now, but Ashley's my best friend and I would *never*. Besides, it's impossible to know if Sullivan's thinly veiled attraction to me is sincere or if he's playing some sort of game. His friendship with Jonathan is strange, to say the least, and I've never quite been able to determine if I'm a conquest because he's genuinely interested or if it's all a ruse to get under my brother's skin. There are a dozen reasons why Sullivan isn't right for me, not the least of which is that I suspect he's a despicable human being.

Ashley, darling thing, is in lust. "He's here," she says, squinting toward the docks and shielding her eyes from the sudden blinding sparkle of sun on water. I follow her gaze and, sure enough, he's standing with one hand on a rusted off-white gas pump that's taller than he is. Sullivan is handsome, I'll give him that, in a brooding, slightly reckless way. He's older than us, two years free and clear of Jericho High, which makes him instantly more appealing than the toddlers we went to school with. Right now

I'm trying to dismiss the broad sweep of his bare back, the way his skin is already summer dark and polished. The knowledge that up close, he smells like coconut and lime.

Ashley flashes me a Cheshire grin, all hope and longing, and everything that came before is forgotten. It's a perfect June day and she's gorgeous in her cutoffs and gingham top knotted at the waist, poised for a summer fling that may blossom into more. I wish I could say something, that I could warn her away or somehow gently let her know that it's not going to happen. But Ashley is oblivious to the too-long stares, to the way Sullivan walks past me and brushes a fingertip along the underside of my bare arm. It rattles me every time, and he knows it.

But it's too late to second-guess anything now. Ashley is already out of the car and unloading the backseat.

"Take this," she says, thrusting a small cooler into my hands when I come around to help. I know it'll be filled with sparkling water and some of Ashley's favorite snacks: plain M&M'S and organic carrot sticks. As if they cancel each other out. "And this." She piles a faded quilt and a battery-operated radio on top of my outstretched arms. I feel only momentary guilt at the fact that I have contributed exactly nothing to this outing. Ashley's great at details. It's why she's so indispensable to her mom. To me.

It seems the entire county has come out to celebrate the first unofficial day of summer. The beach is dotted with blankets and towels, bucket sandcastles and questionably pink noses. I step around a mom who's chasing a boy with a floppy hat he clearly doesn't want to wear and drop to my knees in the sand. "The perfect spot," I declare, and Ashley must agree because she starts to set up camp.

"Thank you," Ashley says when we're finally settled side by side on the quilt. I don't know if she's grateful for my help unloading the car or the fact that I rescued her from an afternoon of baby wrangling. It doesn't matter. She exhales slowly, and out of the corner of my eye I can see her visibly relax, her chin going soft, her eyes drifting closed beneath her sunglasses. I'm hit with a wave of affection for her, a tenderness that chases memories all the way back to the swing set in fourth grade and the way we became inseparable over the course of a single morning recess. My best friend hasn't changed much over the years. She's still tall and skinny, though the lanky awkwardness of her middle school days has been replaced by a delicate grace. Ashley has rich auburn eyes and hair to match, cut so that it just grazes her shoulders and draws attention to the arching lines of her collarbones. I'm lucky to have her and I know it. I try not to think about how much I'm going to miss her.

"You're staring," Ashley says when I don't respond to her quiet thanks. "Weirdo."

"Your eyes are closed, how would you know?"

She smiles thinly, petal-pink lips pulled tight. "You didn't deny it."

"I'm going to miss you," I say, surprising myself. "When—"

"Stop." She bumps my hip with the back of her hand. "Seriously. This summer is going to last forever."

I smile, not wanting to spoil her fantasy.

"Besides," she adds. "You'll be back."

Again, I don't know about that, but I don't say anything.

Ashley finds our favorite station on the radio and we listen to Top 40 punctuated by the squeals of kids racing across the sand and the low rumble of boats on the water. The sun bakes our skin, flushing my freckles out of hiding, but I don't mind. The morning feels far away. I can almost forget about Baxter, my suspicions. Jonathan.

When a shadow crosses over my face, I'm half asleep on my back, fingers buried up to the knuckles where I was running them through coarse sand.

"Look who we have here." The voice is deep and vaguely familiar in my dozy state.

"Shall we write something on her stomach in sunscreen?" Ashley's giggle tells me all I need to know. Of course he found us.

I crack one eye beneath my sunglasses and find Sullivan crouching beside us, sandals abandoned in the sand and black board shorts riding up his thighs. Something darts through me quicksilver fast, but I can't quite catch it. It's impossible to pin down how Sullivan makes me feel. Other than mildly annoyed.

"I'm awake," I say before they can make good on their vague threats.

"Perfect. Move."

I comply, squeezing closer to Ashley to make room for Sullivan on the blanket. This wasn't how I planned it. We were going to join him on the docks later, when there were lots of people around and I didn't have to feel thrown by his subtle advances. Or heartsick about the way Ashley inhales high and shallow when he rubs the back of his fingers along his jaw in a move that feels calculated to me.

I sigh and sit up, pressed between my best friend and the boy she's wanted for years. We touch at unexpected places, ankle to ankle, knees bumping, my shoulder against the curve of his bicep until Ashley scoots over and we all have room to breathe.

"Break time?" I ask stupidly. My headache has dulled, but it still feels as if my skull is stuffed with cotton balls.

"You know, that's why I like you, Baker. Always on the ball."

Ashley laughs at Sullivan's non-joke as he mock-salutes me. I manage a dry chuckle.

"I was just on my way to grab a Red Bull." Sullivan leans back on his elbows and closes his eyes. "But Pete's is so far . . ."

"Suck it up," I say at the exact same moment that Ashley says: "I'll go!"

She reaches for her little teal purse, and I'm grateful when Sullivan digs in his pocket and hands her a five. Apparently, he'll use her to fetch him a drink but stops short of expecting her to pay for it. I roll my eyes behind my sunglasses.

"Thanks, Ash. You're a peach."

I watch Ashley walk away, but I can feel Sullivan watching me.

"A peach?" I say when she's out of earshot. "You're using her."

He lifts one shoulder casually. "I've never led her on."

It's true. Sullivan has been nice enough but clearly disinterested in Ashley's often conspicuous advances. If only she could see it.

I continue looking ahead and say without preamble: "So Baxter's dead." I didn't intend to be so blunt, but here we are.

"Yet another reason I like you, June. Your charming conversational skills."

"I'm being serious. I think somebody killed him." The heaviness of what I'm saying settles over us.

"When's the funeral?" Sullivan's nonplussed.

"Really?" I shoot him a disappointed glance. "That's your response?"

Sullivan pulls his aviators down with his index finger and regards me over the top of the gold wire frames. His hazel-green eyes are narrowed and his lashes unusually long. I can't read his expression, but for once he's not goading me.

I try to hold his gaze, but I can't. I feel a blush racing into my already warm cheeks. Suddenly I'm boiling, skin prickling all over and desperate for the siren call of the dark blue lake. I look out over the water, trace the peaks of whitecaps frothed up by boats crisscrossing the glassy surface. It's an unusually still afternoon for Iowa, calm in the wake of the storm that rolled through on its way to Wisconsin and beyond. But I'm disquieted.

"Come on, talk to me. Please," I force myself to say. "Tell me what you know."

After a beat he slides his sunglasses back up and moves to stand, raining fine grains of sand all over the blanket.

Almost against my will my hand shoots out and catches his wrist. It's thick in my grip, and when I realize what I've done, I start to let go. But it's Sullivan's turn. He twists his wrist and grabs my hand, tugs me so that I topple off-balance. Suddenly I'm pressed against his chest. I feel his breath on my skin, minty and warm.

"Tomorrow night," he says into my hair. "I'll tell you what I know." His lips just barely graze the curl of my ear before he stands, slipping on his sandals as I try to recover.

"What's tomorrow night?" My hands are braced beneath me, and Sullivan towers overhead, blocking the sun. His face is in shadow, and I can't tell if he's toying with me.

"I'll pick you up. Eight."

"But—"

"Just be ready," Sullivan says. He doesn't spare me a backward glance.

And he doesn't wait for his drink.

"Where is he?" Ashley asks when she gets back. The apples of her cheeks are rosy, her voice pitched higher than normal. She stands for a moment with her hand shading her eyes as she scans the beach. There's still the hint of a smile on her lips, and I'm grateful for that one small grace. Ashley didn't see Sullivan touch me.

"He had to go," I manage, pushing myself to my feet. "Here, toss it to me. I'll stick it in the cooler. I'm sure we'll find him later."

Ashley shakes her head. "It'll get warm. Is he on the docks? Was his break cut short?"

I don't know how to lie to her, so I try again to deflect by presenting my catch-ready hands.

Ashley's wistful gaze cuts to me, and all at once she's hardened. It's a tiny difference, a thin glaze of ice, but I know Ashley inside and out.

"I don't get it," she says, tossing me the black can. It's sweaty and nearly slips right out of my hands. "What did you say to him?"

I want to tell her that Sullivan's not worth her time, that he's a flirt and a liar and maybe worse. But if there was ever a good time to warn her off him, it passed ages ago, before her light feelings of attraction turned into full-fledged obsession. I can't dissuade her, and any attempt I make will only paint me into a corner that I can't get out of. I've seen the way Ashley looks at me when Sullivan is around. Skeptical, calculating, just a little hurt. It would be so easy for her to blame me. But this is our last summer together, and I can't lose my best friend.

"You know Sullivan makes me uncomfortable," I say honestly. "Maybe he picked up on that while you were gone."

I can see her thaw a little in relief. Better to think I scared him away than wonder if there's something else going on. I seize my chance and stick the energy drink in the cooler.

"Okay?" I ask my best friend. "Can we go swimming now?"

Ashley sighs and throws an arm lightly over my shoulders. She looks at me as though she's sizing me up. "You're a good friend," she says. "I think I'll keep you."

I just wonder how long.

CHAPTER 5

WINTER
TODAY

Jonathan was late.

Coming?

Juniper texted, hoping she sounded curious instead of passive-aggressive. The truth was, she was on edge. Her conversation with Mandy had kept her up all night. And though she had balked at the prospect of a private meeting only a couple of days ago, now she needed to see Jonathan face-to-face, to hear firsthand about all the supposedly unrelated attacks resurrecting a past he was trying so hard to dismiss. Between fretting over the details of her brother's harassment and all of her messages to Willa continuing to go unanswered, she was strung tight enough to snap.

Juniper stared at her phone, willing communication, but nothing appeared.

Ten minutes passed. Then fifteen.

"I thought Jonathan was picking you up today?" Cora called from the circ desk.

"He was." Juniper wandered over, still staring at the phone in her hands and beginning to sweat beneath her thick scarf and zippered-to-the-chin winter coat.

"Running late, I'm sure," Cora offered with a smile, but Juniper wasn't so sure.

She pulled up Mandy's number, but her call went almost instantly to voice mail, and when she tried a few seconds later, it happened again. Turning away from the trio of a young mother and her two littles who had approached the circulation desk, arms laden with bright books, Juniper tried to make her voice sound casual. "Hi, Mandy, it's Juniper. Jonathan was supposed to pick me up and he's late. No biggie, but I was wondering if he's with you . . ."

An incoming call interrupted her message, and Juniper drew the phone away from her ear to see who it was. She almost declined but accepted at the last moment, trying to muster patience. "Hi, Mom," she said, ready to tell Reb that it wasn't a good time, that they could connect later, when she realized there was a thin, desolate sound leaking through the microphone.

"June? Oh my God, June. He . . . there's . . . I . . ."

"Mom? Mom, what's going on?"

"He's . . . I—"

"Juniper?" Law's voice was suddenly on the line, solid and unyielding as a brick. "There's been an accident. Call Everett Stokes at the Jericho Police Station. He'll fill you in."

"The police?" she said, feeling her stomach

drop. "What happened?" She heard a honk in the background—were they on the road?—then what sounded like arguing, followed by a *click,* and they were gone.

Juniper felt her knees wobble, the room tilt precariously as the young mother and her kids brushed past, oblivious to the way her world had tipped sideways. What had just happened?

"Everything okay?" Cora came over. When she caught sight of Juniper's blanched cheeks and wild eyes, she took her by the arm. "Come on," she said, leading her to the nearest chair.

"Something's wrong," Juniper managed.

"Jonathan?"

"I don't know." But in a forgotten corner of her heart, his name echoed clear and resonant. Of course it was Jonathan.

Cora took charge. She put a call in to Officer Stokes, and a few minutes later, when Cora pressed a mug of steaming Earl Grey into her hands, Juniper realized time had become soft and pliable as clay. How long had she been sitting in the chair?

"I have to go," Juniper said, bolting upright and sloshing hot tea onto her fingers. She barely registered the burn.

"I don't think so," Cora countered. "The officer is on his way. Until then, there's nowhere for you to go. Come on, let's get you into my office so you can have some privacy."

Juniper didn't like being bossed, but she let Cora unzip her coat and slide it off her shoulders. She allowed herself to be led into the office, where she sat in the swivel chair, forced herself to sip the tea, and waited. Juniper was bracing herself to hear the news, however awful, but when the officer appeared at the doorway with a somber half smile, the first thing she thought was: *I know you.* Average height, average build. Brown hair with a glint of gold and eyes to match. The last time they crossed paths he was handing her a written warning for a broken taillight.

Neither of them mentioned it.

"Officer Stokes with the Jericho PD," he said, and then seemed unable to decide if he should shake her hand or hover in the doorway. He elected to hover.

"Look, I'm sorry to be the one to deliver the news . . . Your brother fell through the ice on Jericho Lake early this morning."

It was the last thing she expected him to say. She had steeled herself for the worst. Perhaps a hit-and-run, a split second of furious courage when Jonathan went after the car that kept driving by his house in the middle of the night. Or—God forbid—a baseball bat, a bit of poison, a bullet. Something fast and violent, an accident that wasn't truly an accident. Not this. This, Juniper didn't know how to process. Jericho Lake? Her brother wasn't a fisherman, and he wasn't an idiot. The lake was small and brackish; nothing worth catching lived there anyway.

"I don't understand." She was cold with shock—disconnected from her own body. She couldn't feel her hands on the mug anymore or even taste the bittersweet tea. "What the hell was he doing out there?"

"It's an ongoing investigation, ma'am. We're following every lead."

"What's that supposed to mean?"

"Exactly what it sounds like," Officer Stokes said. "Jonathan is very lucky that Mr. Linden was training his hunting dogs this morning out at the lake. We believe your brother was in the water for less than twenty minutes and unconscious for an even shorter time. He was airlifted to the nearest ECMO center in Des Moines for emergency treatment. His wife and your parents are en route."

"And what am I supposed to do?" Juniper snapped.

"That's between you and your family, ma'am."

She was irritated at this man and his dispassionate "ma'ams," but her anger quickly shifted at the mention of her family. The very same family that was at the moment hurtling toward Des Moines without her. Who had sent a stranger to tell her the news of Jonathan's condition. Juniper was an afterthought, as irrelevant to them as she was to her own daughter. She tried not to let the wave of nausea show on her face.

"Thanks for coming," Juniper said, because it was the only way she knew to dismiss him. But Officer Stokes didn't move from his post at the door.

"I'm afraid I need to ask you a few questions."

Could she say no? Juniper's memory was viscous and uncertain, but Officer Stokes was already sliding his hand into a hidden pocket at the breast of his parka. He pulled out a plastic bag. It looked just like the kitchen staple, but there was a slip of paper inside that clearly marked it as evidence. Officer Stokes shook the bag to settle whatever was inside, and then held it out toward Juniper.

Because it was obvious that she wasn't going to reach for it, Officer Stokes stepped closer. "It's a necklace," he said unnecessarily; she could see it now.

A silver chain, dulled to black in places. A delicately wrought branch with two tiny, dangling orbs that she knew to be berries because she had spent much of her young adulthood rubbing them between her forefinger and thumb. A good luck charm, a talisman. A hope for what might have been.

Juniper hadn't seen it since that night.

"I didn't know what it was," Officer Stokes said, seemingly oblivious to the change that had come over her: the sudden high flame at her core, heart racing, palms slick. "But one of the medics recognized it right away. Grew up in Nevada and said he knew it the second he saw it. Juniper berries, right?"

She didn't answer.

Officer Stokes shrugged. "We figured, well . . . Your name is a bit uncommon, so . . ."

The question hung in the air between them unvoiced. *Is it yours?*

Should she lie? Deflect? Pretend that she had never seen it before? But Officer Stokes wouldn't have to question many people in town to learn that it was, indeed, Juniper's. She had worn it every day from the moment she found it the summer she turned twelve until the night it was torn from her neck. "It was mine," she admitted. "I lost it a long time ago."

"Any idea why Jonathan might have had it in his pocket this morning?"

"No. I haven't seen it in years." That much was true.

"See, it's just that he wasn't carrying a wallet or cell phone, and he left his keys in the ignition of his truck. The only thing Jonathan had on him was this necklace."

Juniper took a tiny sip of air. "I don't know what to tell you."

"Listen," Officer Stokes said, settling both hands on his hips. "I'm guessing a lot of this will come out online tomorrow—we have a . . ." He paused, considering. "An *overactive* local journalist poking around, dredging up the past."

Journalist. Juniper's attention sparked at the word. *Who?* Maybe this journalist was the person she was looking for. All at once she wanted to flip the tables and interrogate Officer Stokes, but he was still talking.

"I wanted to give you a chance to hear it directly from me. We're taking another look at the Murphy case."

All the air went out of the room. "That was almost fifteen years ago," Juniper managed.

"I know this reopens a lot of old wounds in the community," he said, ignoring her, "but some new evidence has recently come to light."

She could hardly begin to imagine what that might be. Her necklace?

"And do you think what happened to Jonathan is somehow connected?"

"That's what I plan to figure out." Everett regarded her for a moment longer, his gaze direct and probing. But she didn't look away, didn't crack, and he finally sighed, then slipped the clear bag with her necklace back into his breast pocket. He reached across Cora's desk and laid a business card faceup on the surface. "If you think of anything, my contact information is all here. I really am sorry. We're all praying that he pulls through."

● ● ●

The halls of Jericho Elementary smelled exactly as they had when Juniper was a kid. Elmer's glue, hot lunch (chicken nuggets and tater tots, if she could trust her nose), and the slightly curdled, candy-sweet scent of small children. Juniper walked on the balls of her feet, trying to stop her snowy boots from squeaking on the varnished hardwood floor, and fought the urge to vomit.

Reb had texted Juniper minutes after Officer Stokes left, telling her to pick up Willa from school right away; Law would let them know she was coming. Their exchange had been quick and harried—Reb was clearly on the verge of a breakdown—and Juniper didn't ask many questions. Jonathan was in critical condition, and Law and Reb would arrive in Des Moines within minutes. That's all she really needed to know.

So Juniper had grabbed her purse, briefed Cora in the barest of terms, and driven over to Jericho Elementary with her coat flapping open and her gloves forgotten in a cubby at the library. She didn't even feel the cold.

Now she swung open the glass door to the office block as if she did this sort of thing every day, like a real mom would.

"They're waiting for you," the secretary told Juniper, and she wondered for a minute if the older woman could read tragedy in the slump of her shoulders. Of course, Jericho was a small town and outsiders rarely darkened the halls of the elementary school, but it still felt wrong somehow to not even flash an ID. It felt stranger still to walk around the curving desk and approach the principal's door as an adult (as a *mother*), but on the short drive over, Juniper had tried to prepare herself for anything. For tears and rejection, for Willa to refuse to go with her. She had rehearsed a short speech, but all her careful words disappeared the moment she lifted her hand to knock. Almost immediately the door swung open.

"Well hello there, June." Henry Crawford had been principal at Jericho Elementary when Juniper was a student, and he looked much like Juniper remembered him. Tall and lean with a navy suit too big for his frame, a tie that had been sloppily knotted, and a patch of fuzz on his chin that he must have missed when shaving. Somehow, it was endearing. Mr. Crawford was relentlessly kind and a lifelong bachelor—any shortcomings in the appearance department had been excused in perpetuity.

"Hi, Mr. Crawford."

"Please, call me Henry. It's good to see you, though I'm sorry it's under such unfortunate circumstances. Come on in." He stepped back and held the door for Juniper, ushering her into an office she had only glimpsed as a child. A few inspirational posters in cheap black frames, a tidy desk, and a circle of four small barrel chairs that looked brand-new. Seated in the farthest one was Willa.

Her knees were pulled up to her chest, the heels of her army boots hooked on the edge of the pretty, brushed upholstery and no doubt leaving a stain of muck and ice salt and cheap rubber. Mr. Crawford genuinely didn't seem to mind. Willa had wrapped her arms around her legs and was resting her cheek on her knees, face turned away from the door. The sweep of her long, dark hair hid her face, and for a moment Juniper was sure she was asleep. Her chest swelled with the desire to rush across the room and touch her daughter, even if it was just to lay her hand on Willa's back to feel the rise and fall of it as she breathed. She had grown up so much since the last time Juniper had seen her. Longer hair, longer limbs. More young woman, less little girl. Juniper felt the tug of her as surely as if they were tied together. Could Willa feel it too?

"Hey, Willa." Mr. Crawford naturally took the lead as he sank to the edge of the seat beside her. "Your mother is here."

Juniper felt the pinch of that word in her chest and wished she could ask Henry to take it back. But what was he supposed to call her? Willa called her both "Mom" and "June." One was natural, the other forced. Juniper had never been able to determine which was which—or how much Reb and Law had coached Willa one way or the other.

"I'm not going with her." Willa's voice was muffled, but there was no mistaking the words.

Juniper sank to the edge of the remaining chair and caught Henry's gaze. "Have you . . . ?" she began, unsure of how to finish.

"Willa knows about Jonathan's accident," Henry assured her, guessing the question so she didn't have to voice it. Juniper was grateful for both his competency and the way he said "accident" without hesitation or insinuation. "Our school counselor, Linda, has already been by to see her, but Willa says she doesn't want to talk about it just yet."

Juniper took a deep breath and leaned forward. "Willa, Grandma wants me to take you home. We all think it's best if you stay with me for a while—at least until Grandma and Grandpa come home from the hospital."

"No."

Henry gave Juniper a little nod of encouragement.

"It's just that there's nowhere else for you to go right now." She tried a different tack. "Grandma and Grandpa will be home soon, and then you can go back to the farmhouse, but for now they need to be with Jonathan. And I guess that leaves you with me."

"I'll stay with Zoe."

A friend? Juniper felt guilty that she didn't even know for sure. "We all think you should be with family right now."

This made Willa lift her head.

"And you're family?"

She fixed her mother with a withering look, and Juniper nearly melted beneath the icy heat of those hazel eyes. How could an eighth grader pull off a look of such contempt?

"Hey, now," Mr. Crawford cut in. "That's no way to speak to your mom."

Willa turned her laser gaze on him.

"I'm serious, young lady." He leaned in, ignoring her death look. "I know you're upset, but I expect better from you."

She put her head back down but didn't say anything more.

Juniper cleared her throat. "Why don't we go grab lunch somewhere? We could drive to Munroe or—"

"I'm fine," Willa cut in. "I'm staying here."

Losing her will, Juniper turned to Henry. "Is that okay?" she said. "I mean, do you think that's wise?"

He shrugged. "I suppose Willa can decide what she feels up for. Right, Willa? You can't sit in my office all day, but if you'd like to return to your class and be with your friends—and if your mother approves—I don't see why you shouldn't." He turned his attention to Juniper.

"You don't have plans to go to the hospital?"

"No. Not yet. Just waiting to hear more . . ." Juniper trailed off, uncertain what else to say. She was painfully aware that she had been left behind, barely even considered when her family rushed off to comfort and support one another.

However, if she was being honest with herself, Juniper was kind of glad to have been abandoned. Navigating the strained relationships within her family was difficult at the best of times. Surely the trauma of Jonathan's dire situation would only make matters worse. Juniper felt a stab of guilt at her own pragmatism, and the knife twisted deeper when she realized that time alone with Willa was exactly what she had hoped for all along. Too bad her daughter wasn't about to make it easy.

"Well, okay." Henry gave his knees an authoritative pat. "Willa, you're welcome to go back to class. I believe the eighth graders are in the art room for third period?"

Willa nodded.

"And your mother will be here after school to pick you up."

It wasn't a question, and though Willa rolled her eyes, she didn't argue. She slowly put her feet on the ground and reached beside her chair for the backpack she had dropped there. It was blue plaid and she had affixed a Breckenridge key chain to the zipper. Juniper instantly noticed the telltale green-and-white Colorado license plate design and felt a trill of hope. She had sent that key chain in a care package months ago. Maybe it was feeble to pin her faith on something so small, but Willa hadn't thrown her gift away. Instead she saw it—she used it—every day. Maybe, Juniper wished, it was a token of their connection, tenuous though it may be.

Mr. Crawford stood, too, effectively blocking Willa's path to the door until she looked him in the eye. "I want you to know that if you change your mind," he told her, "you can come back here anytime. You have a get-out-of-jail-free card today, courtesy of me. We can call your mom and she'll come right back for you."

Juniper stood and nodded. "I'll turn my ringer on high."

"Sometimes it takes a bit for our bodies to catch up with our minds, Willa," Mr. Crawford continued. "You know what happened this morning, but you haven't processed it yet. That's okay. Just be sure to let us know if you start feeling not like yourself."

Willa stared at her feet, thumbs hooked on the straps of her backpack and jaw tilted away from Juniper as if she couldn't bear to even acknowledge her presence. "Mmm-hmm," she muttered. "Can I go now?"

Mr. Crawford stepped back and swept his hand toward the door. Willa all but scurried away, not sparing Juniper a single glance on her way out.

When the door had snapped shut—just a degree shy of a slam—Juniper couldn't stop the heavy sigh that escaped her lips.

"She's thirteen," Henry reminded her.

"She hates me."

"No she doesn't. She just doesn't know how to be around you. You've been gone for a long time, June."

Why did everyone feel the need to remind her of her absence? It was as if the whole of Jericho was keeping tabs. "Thank you for your help," Juniper said, choosing to ignore Henry's comment. "Please call me if she changes her mind."

"Of course."

In the parking lot, Juniper banged her head softly against the steering wheel. Mr. Crawford was right—Willa's body hadn't caught up to what her mind had just been forced to acknowledge, and neither had Juniper's. But she was starting to feel it now. The high flutter in her chest, the prick of impending doom that twitched spider legs down her spine. Her therapist had taught her how to calm herself years ago, how to lean into the panic and count to ten. Inhale the future, exhale the past. But that was all a load of crap, wasn't it? Juniper couldn't exhale the past. It was catching up with her, circling her neck with strong fingers, choking her. Good thing she had become quite adept at living breathlessly.

Juniper's first meeting with Willa wasn't what she'd hoped it would be at all. She hadn't even gotten to touch her daughter, much less wrap her in the hug that Juniper's arms were aching to give.

Seeing her daughter in Mr. Crawford's office had been a sobering reality check. Still, like it or not, Willa was moving in with her, so Juniper did the only thing she knew to do and drove to her parents' farm. Of course, the least disruptive solution was for Juniper to just move into the farmhouse with Willa, but she couldn't bring herself to do it. In a way, she was getting exactly what she wanted—her daughter under the same roof—in the worst, most unimaginable way.

The door was unlocked, of course, and she helped herself to sheets from the linen closet, a faded quilt, and a lumpy feather pillow that had seen better days. The futon in the spare room of the bungalow would work in a pinch, and though Juniper wanted to set up Willa's room with things that would make her feel comfortable and at home, she didn't dare to enter the inner sanctum of her daughter's bedroom. Never mind that it was Juniper's old room and that her fingerprints surely crisscrossed every square inch. What she saw as unimpeachable, Willa would surely consider the gravest of sins.

But Juniper had already done her worst, even if she'd never been charged with any of it: perjury, obstruction of justice, trespass, abandonment. Was it treason to turn against your own flesh and blood? To wonder—even secretly, silently—if everything she believed to be true about her life was a lie? Juniper stood in her mother's kitchen with old bedding clutched to her chest and wished that she could click her heels together and go back to a time before everything fell apart. Before there was blood blooming from Cal's chest and spilled on the ground. Staining her fingers.

That kind of wistful magic didn't exist. But maybe the secrets she had buried in the Iowa soil were just now bearing bitter fruit. Maybe all she had to do was take a scythe and harvest the truth. Hold it, firm and heavy, irrefutable in the palm of her hand.

As Juniper slipped back into her car, outfitted with the barest essentials for turning the bungalow into a home for two, her phone buzzed in her pocket.

"Do you have Willa?" Cora asked, skipping the niceties.

"No. I—"

"Good." Cora cut her off. "I hate to be the one to tell you this, but someone poisoned Jonathan's dog."

"Diesel?" Juniper's mind stumbled, trying to keep up. That sweet dog had lain by her feet throughout the entire sickening supper at her parents' house only days before. Jonathan loved that dog.

Cora's heavy sigh was confirmation enough. "Apparently the cops found him floating where Jonathan was pulled out. Either Jonathan was trying to rescue him, or . . ."

"Or what?"

"Look, I'm just telling you what I heard, Juniper. I wanted you to hear it from me."

"So they think—what? It was a suicide pact? That if Jonathan was going to off himself, might as well take the dog, too?" Juniper pressed the side of her head to the cold window, trying to leech a little sanity from the cold pane. "Where did you hear this?"

"It's Jericho," Cora said. There was no need for more explanation.

"I have to go," Juniper said. "I'm driving."

But when she hung up, she sat in the icy car for so long that her fingers went numb.

CHAPTER 6

SUMMER
14 AND A HALF YEARS AGO

When Sullivan pulls down our driveway in his fancy new four-wheel-drive truck, Jonathan looks up from the mountain of pulled pork he's devouring and raises one dark brow. "What's he doing here?"

I know exactly how to needle him, so I lean with my elbow on my knee, chin in hand, and say all coy: "He's here for me."

We're sitting on the porch steps, me flush against the banister and Jonathan hunched over a plate heaped with food he has balanced on his knees. It's after eight o'clock, but he just got off work.

Normally when I sit with him at night, he teases me, tossing his filthy work gloves at me to get a rise, or regaling me with stories of his day. But he's quiet tonight, and when his eyes snap over to mine, Jonathan's not smiling. "You're hanging out with Sullivan now?"

I shrug. "He's my friend too." Which isn't strictly true. Sullivan is two years older than me—a senior when I was a sophomore—and our groups never overlapped. He ran with a wild crowd, a group of farmers' kids and cowboys who never cared much about their grades or fitting in, and who spent their weekends splitting cases of cheap beer and shooting at stop signs on gravel roads. Their futures were determined the moment they were born: they'd work with their daddy, then take over his farm, marry a local girl, have babies, and start the cycle all over again. Me, I've never considered myself a local girl and I certainly don't want to stay. Even after what feels like a lifetime here, I still don't feel comfortable with townies who think Jericho is the whole wide world. Sullivan tops that list.

"Yeah," Jonathan barks, wiping his mouth with the back of his hand. "You and Sullivan are besties, for sure." He's not happy.

"Lighten up," I tell him. But my heart is beating faster than normal, and my mouth is dry as dust.

Jonathan fixes me with one last unreadable stare, then sighs and puts his plate down on the step beside him. "Yo, Sully," he calls, pushing himself up as Sullivan hops out of his truck to meet us.

"Bro." They meet on the sidewalk and bump fists. It's strange and macho and not at all like my laid-back brother. But Sullivan has a way of making people meet him on his terms.

"Taking my sister out tonight?" Jonathan doesn't pull any punches.

That's my cue: I launch off the steps and slap on a smile. "Hey, Sullivan."

"Looking good, Baker," he tells me with a whistle. I'm wearing a pair of shorts and a vintage Tom Petty concert tee, my hair in a messy ponytail. My appearance is hardly worth a whistle. But I catch the wicked glint in Sullivan's eye and realize he's laying it on for Jonathan.

"This isn't a date," I tell them both.

"It's not?" Sullivan presses the heel of his hand to his chest as if mortally wounded.

"Definitely not," Jonathan agrees, then asks: "What is it, then?"

But Sullivan just laughs and turns toward his truck.

"I promise I'll bring her back in one piece," he calls over his shoulder.

"All good, my man." Jonathan says the words casually, but his mouth is a thin, serious line when he looks at me. I can tell that he doesn't dare to warn me with Sullivan close enough to overhear, but I can read his expression. *Be careful,* he's telling me. And, *I don't like this.*

Sometimes the connection between us is an almost tangible thing, a thread woven from shared experiences that tangles my brother to me. Our lives haven't been traumatic or marked by loss, and we aren't twins, but we're knit together in a way that's as inexplicable as it is comforting. Maybe it's because we shared a crib when Jonathan was born. I wasn't even a year old when he came howling into our tiny universe, and since

102

I was too small to be moved to a toddler bed, Mom tucked us toe to toe. Or maybe it's because we've always preferred each other's company, a trait that our mother was sure we'd eventually grow out of. We never have. Whatever it is, I can feel it fizzing between us now, a sparking, anxious sense of foreboding that only makes me more uncertain about my outing with Sullivan.

"You coming?" he calls.

What choice do I have? I lift my hand in a little wave at Jonathan and jog over to let myself in Sullivan's truck.

"Y'all are intense," he tells me as we leave the acreage behind.

"Who? Me and Jonathan?"

"Your whole family." Sullivan laughs. "Kinda oddballs, don't you think?"

I've never had anyone tell me that my family is odd—at least, not to my face. I suppose we are, in a way. Mom, the Jericho outsider who plays cello in the alfalfa field when it's a blooming sea of lavender, and who sometimes forgets to wear shoes when she goes into town. And Dad, almost twenty years her senior and already semi-retired. He looks old enough to be her father, and they get weird looks when they walk hand in hand. Even from people who know better. And then there's me and Jonathan. Polar opposites in almost every way, but attached at the hip. Still, I'm not about to try and explain myself to Sullivan Tate.

"You should talk," I say, rising to the challenge. "Wasn't your brother in jail?"

It's a low blow, and I know it. Another DUI, third offense. Dalton was driving with a suspended license, and there was no way the family could buy their way out of it. Two months, local jail, and a fine that was never accurately disclosed. I heard upward of twenty thousand dollars, but maybe that was exaggerated. Jericho's unwritten code would suggest I never, *ever* bring it up, but I'm not great at following the rules.

Sullivan doesn't respond to my jab, and I feel a tickle of remorse. Still, I can't bring myself to apologize to him, so I say: "Tell me about Baxter."

"Are you kidding?" He gives me a sidelong smirk, the put-down of his brother seemingly forgotten. "It's taken me years to get you in my truck. I'll tell you what you want to know, but I'm going to draw this out as long as I can."

I'm speechless, but Sullivan laughs. "Relax, Baker."

"But—"

"You might even have fun."

Is it my imagination, or did Sullivan's voice catch? I sneak a peek at his profile and realize his jaw is tight, a vein in his neck bright blue against his skin. Is he *nervous?* Sullivan Tate with his booming laugh and flirty wink and "I can have any girl I want" attitude? I'm unconvinced, but then his eyes dart to mine and I swear he flushes.

"Hot in here," he says, reaching to turn the air-conditioning up. I just nod.

I could put up a fuss, complain about the fact that he's basically kidnapped me, but I'm suddenly shy. Sullivan has a vulnerable side, and I don't know what to do with that.

He flicks on his blinker and I realize we're heading toward the river. North Fork River cuts through the county, narrow and deep, skirting Jericho on the west and sprouting tributaries that fan like veins through the rich farmland. One of the larger creeks borders the Murphys' property where it empties into Jericho Lake. The water is slow and muddy, a blur of dirty brown beneath the bridge that leads out of town.

"Where are we going?" I ask.

"You'll see."

The silence swells between us, making the cab of the truck seem humid and close even though the air is turned on high. We're awkward, both of us, glancing at each other and then away until Sullivan pulls down an overgrown lane and cuts the engine. I'm glad to finally be wherever it is we are. I'm not here to find common ground with him.

"Where are we?" We're hemmed in by trees and brush, branches scraping the windshield and poking bony knuckles at our doors.

"Access road," Sullivan declares, as if I'm supposed to find this information noteworthy.

"I can see that. But *why* are we here?"

Sullivan wrenches open his door. "Come on! You telling me you're Jericho-born and you've never been to Broken Bridge? How is that even possible?"

I've heard of it, of course, but no, I've never been. I don't feel like admitting this apparent blight on my character, so I climb out of the passenger side without answering. A branch scrapes me as I hop to the ground, and Sullivan hollers something about ticks from where he's half-buried in the bed of the truck.

Ticks? My eyes go wide, and I start frantically inspecting my skin: arms, legs, hands. Am I feeling itchy? Are ticks even itchy?

"Relax," Sullivan says, catching my hand and turning it over to inspect the pale skin of my wrist. "I could check you over if you'd like."

And just like that the old Sullivan is back. "No thanks." I pull out of his loose grip. "I'm all good."

"You're a little jumpy, aren't you, Juniper? Can I call you that? Juniper?"

"June," I say firmly. "About Baxter . . ."

"Yeah, yeah." But then he arches one eyebrow at me and takes off, heading away from the highway, deeper into the trees that flank the river.

I waver for a moment. I don't want to give in

to Sullivan, but if I don't follow, I'll be stuck out in the middle of nowhere alone. And I definitely don't want to call Jonathan to come and get me. I've come this far—what's a bit farther?

A few jogged paces and I fall into step behind him. The path is narrow but hard packed, and we walk together in silence. Somehow, out of the truck and beneath the trees it feels easy. I'm no arborist, but the cottonwoods are simple enough to pick out—they're tall and feathery, sprouting tufts of soft, fluffy seeds that drift like snow and alight on our heads. I pluck one off my shoulder and try to throw it at him, but it's lighter than air and floats away from my fingertips.

"Here." Sullivan tosses something over his shoulder, and I instinctively reach out to catch it. It's a canister of bug spray, and I give it a good shake, then liberally apply. The sharp, chemical smell makes me sneeze.

I toss him back the spray, and he tucks it in one of the cargo pockets of his camouflage shorts without using it himself, then pulls a beer from the plastic ring of the six-pack he's holding. He hands it to me and twists one out for himself. We pop the tops, bump cans, and then Sullivan shotguns the whole thing before I've even taken a sip. I worry momentarily about driving home with him but remember that Jonathan is on high alert. If he so much as sees an incoming call from me, he'll be on his way.

Sullivan is finishing up his second beer when we break through the trees at the edge of the North Fork River. There's a mossy, muddy smell of leaf rot and dead fish, and as I stand for just a moment I begin to sink in the soft bank.

"Rained yesterday," Sullivan reminds me. "Come on."

We follow the river around a bend until I can see the old train bridge peeking through the tops of the trees. Broken Bridge is the stuff of Jericho lore, a landmark that has stood for generations, though now it's little more than rusted struts and bracings, crumbling concrete. It's the perfect spot for parties because it's so hard to get to. The cops simply can't be bothered to chase teenagers into the brush. But tonight, we have it to ourselves.

Sullivan pulls himself up on the concrete piling and then reaches down to offer me his hand. I pause for just a moment before I take it, and then he hoists me into the air with more force than I thought possible. I'm yanked up beside him, half tipping off the edge, but he's got me. A laugh escapes before I can check myself, and Sullivan rewards me with a grin.

We scramble onto the bridge proper, all copper steel and sun-washed wood that's been baked to a flaking gray brown. I'm surprised to find that between every splintered tie is nothing but air. Sullivan doesn't seem to mind. He tightrope walks a rail to the center of the bridge, and then settles down on a thick stretch of rough wood with his legs dangling toward the water.

"Get over here," he says, patting the space across from him.

I'm less sure on my feet, and not a fan of heights, so it takes me a bit longer to get to where he's casually watching the slow current swirl beneath him. I feel woozy and disoriented when I finally reach Sullivan, and I can't decide if it's because of where I am or who I'm with. Maybe it's the beer. It was cold and I was thirsty. I finished it before we summited the bridge.

"Who says Iowa isn't beautiful?" Sullivan asks as I lower myself to a thick railroad tie. We're sitting knee to knee.

I'm surprised that there's a note of wistfulness in his voice, but I understand. It's lovely up here. The sky is darkening to velvet before us, and back the way we came is a watercolor smudge of citrus. Tangerine and grapefruit and blood orange spilled across the horizon. If I turn the other way there's a break in the trees where the train tracks once ran, and framed in leafy greens beyond the grove on the far bank is a farmer's pastoral field. It swells and dips like waves on the sea, and perfect lines of newly planted corn march into the distance. Every couple of seconds a firefly glints in the dusk, lending an almost magical quality to the deep quiet of this place. I realize I can hear myself breathe. And Sullivan, too.

"It's pretty," I admit, just to break the silence.

Sullivan nods. He catches my eye, and for just a moment I study him. Sandy-blond hair, unusual green eyes. They crinkle at the corners when he smiles, and almost disappear completely, but it's charming somehow. He's not handsome in the traditional sense of the word, and yet it's hard to look away from him. A single crooked tooth, a thin, pale scar above the curve of his eyebrow, the slightest cleft in his chin. I know he's trouble, but here on the bridge he seems like any other guy.

When his lips pull into a lopsided smile, I remind myself that he was suspended from school for starting a trash can fire in the men's locker room. That he has his own DUI on record, as well as a couple of minor in possessions. Because he's Jericho royalty—his family owns over half the farmland in the county—the general consensus regarding Sullivan is that "boys will be boys" and he'll eventually grow out of his mischievous streak. He's twenty-one now, and working for his dad full-time, even though he maintains summer hours at GL Gas. This he does, I'm sure, for the abundance of girls in bikinis lounging on the boats he fills up.

The thought yanks me back to reality. Sullivan is here for one thing only, but I have very different motives.

"Okay, spill. You promised you'd tell me

110

what you know about the Murphys' dog," I say.

"Why do you think I took you here?" Sullivan leans back with his elbows on the railroad tie behind him. The pose strikes me as risky. We're maybe twenty feet above the water, and one look at the river strewn with branches, sandbars, and who knows what else assures me I wouldn't want to fall.

I glare at him, losing all patience. I've played his game long enough. "They believe Baxter was poisoned. On purpose." I pause to let it sink in. "I'm pretty clueless when it comes to local gossip," I continue, "but even I know that the Murphys are feuding with the Tates."

"You make it sound all War of the Roses."

"Isn't it?" I'm mildly impressed at his historical reference. Obviously my standards for Sullivan have been set pretty low.

"Don't believe everything you hear," he says, and gives my foot a little tap with his so that it swings over the abyss. "You want to know the truth? It's pretty boring, June."

I don't say anything.

After a moment he sighs and pushes himself up. "Turn around," he tells me.

I swivel my head to look toward the field framed in the distance. The sun has slipped beneath the horizon and the rows are now nothing but dark shadows on black soil.

"That's our land. Or, at least, some of it." He

points southeast. "And beyond those hills, past what we can see, is the Murphys' acreage."

I nod.

"There's a creek that cuts through the land there, and"—he angles his finger further south—"a couple of sinkholes."

"You lost me."

Sullivan smiles a little. "Then I'll skip the whole aquifer water contamination bit and get straight to the goods: the Murphys say fertilizer and pesticide runoff from our farm is polluting their well and poisoning their little hobby farm. And the river, too."

I look down at the water churning beneath us. "Is it true?"

Sullivan shrugs. "We're farmers, June. And it's not illegal to spray our fields."

"But isn't there a way to stop the runoff?"

"Not our problem."

I think it is, but I don't tell him that. "What does this have to do with Baxter?"

"Those dogs trespass on our property every single day."

And there's my answer. Whether it was intentional or not, the Tates set traps and poisoned the Murphys' dog.

"So did you . . ." I don't have to finish before Sullivan shakes his head.

"It wasn't me. I couldn't . . ." He trails off, and for just a second his lips tug into a frown. But then he shrugs, grins. It seems forced. "We like to give them a hard time. Builds character."

"It's property damage," I say, quoting Cal. "And harassment and trespassing."

"Nah, it's all in good fun."

The night is warm, but all at once I'm chilled. I knew Sullivan Tate was cut from a different cloth, but his flippant disregard for the Murphys strikes me as cruel. How can he be so cavalier about the torment he and his family have inflicted on those two lovely people?

"Have I offended your innocence, Miss Juniper?" Sullivan reaches down to grasp my ankle. I pull away when he tries to lay my foot in his lap. "Maybe you should have a chat with your brother. He's not nearly as virtuous as you are."

I don't want to take his bait, but I can't stop myself. "What are you talking about?"

Sullivan winks. "You'll have to ask him yourself."

All at once I long to be anywhere but here. It's clear that Sullivan thought he was absolving himself, explaining exactly why it was within the Tates' rights to poison Baxter—or at least allow it to happen. But it's not so black and white to me. I can still see Beth sitting at her kitchen table with Betsy's mottled head in her lap. Her grief was real. And completely unnecessary.

"Take me home," I say, standing up. The bridge

pitches—or maybe I do—and Sullivan hops to his feet to slip an arm around my waist.

"I've got you," he says, and helps me go back the way we came, stepping carefully from railroad tie to railroad tie until all I have to do is jump off the abutment. The ground feels soothingly solid beneath my feet and I stand still for a moment to catch my breath.

Sullivan waits for me, and when I turn toward the path, we walk back to his truck wordlessly. But just before we reach the narrow clearing, he stops abruptly. I'm following so closely I bump into him, hands up to cushion the impact, and then I'm trapped against his chest when he spins to face me.

I don't have time to turn away when Sullivan bends toward me and brushes my cheek with a kiss so sudden and chaste it makes me blush.

"I like you, Baker," he says. It's completely unexpected and yet entirely predictable. Almost painful in its simplicity. For just a second I can see the Sullivan from earlier, hesitant and unsure. Hopeful. Looking at me like I'm Christmas morning instead of a gawky teenager in a faded T-shirt.

There's a hint of a smile on his lips, and for a moment all I can feel is the warmth of his chest beneath my fingers, the spark of possibility between us. But then I stumble backward, thinking about Ashley and dying a little inside.

"I'm sorry," I say, trying to hide the fact that he's left me winded. "I don't think I'm your type."

"And what exactly is my type?" Sullivan drags the back of his fingers along his jaw while he watches me.

"The staying kind." I step past him carefully, my hands curled into fists.

CHAPTER 7

WINTER
TODAY

Juniper watched as Willa slunk down the steps of Jericho Elementary at the end of the day, her backpack yanked tight across both shoulders. She pushed her long hair behind one ear and scanned the cars in the pickup lane, presumably looking for her ride. But when she caught sight of her mother leaning against a dull gray hatchback, she went rigid. Juniper knew that look: it was the raw panic of a feral cat in the split second before it bolted.

Juniper braved a smile and raised her hand in greeting, but that only appeared to make Willa even more upset. She teetered on the lip of the bottom step, considering, then seemed to realize that her fate was sealed. Willa ducked her chin into the loose collar of her coat and hurried over.

"You can't get out of the car," Willa muttered, brushing past Juniper to pull open the passenger-side door.

"What?"

"In the carpool lane! It's a rule!" Willa whisper-shouted, flinging herself into the vehicle and slamming the door.

Juniper squeezed her eyes shut and allowed herself a long, steadying breath before she stepped off the curb and came around the car. She tried to look on the bright side: Willa was going home with her. Her preteen daughter was moody and miserable, but at least she hadn't disappeared with Zoe (whoever she was) like she had threatened. It was a small victory.

"Sorry, Willa. I didn't know," Juniper said when she was settled in the driver's seat. "I'm new at this."

Willa had already buckled her seat belt and was staring out the window with her arms crossed over her chest. "Whatever."

Juniper put on her blinker and merged out of the parking lane, allowing herself to focus on what passed for rush hour in Jericho: a couple dozen minivans lined up in front of the school. As she waited for her turn at the stop sign, she contemplated driving to Cunningham's for a hot chocolate, or maybe to the grocery store so they could pick out a treat together. It seemed like a motherly thing to do. But it was obvious that although Willa was complying, it was under protest. Juniper didn't want to stir the pot. So she drove to the farm and waited in the car while Willa gathered up a few overnight things, then took her back to the bungalow.

Juniper had made up the futon in the spare room with the bedding from the farmhouse, but the room still looked like something from a seventies horror flick. Shag carpet, wood paneling, the faint odor of mothballs and damp drywall. It was a dismal offering.

"This is just temporary," Juniper reminded Willa, but she was really talking to herself. She hoped—prayed—the anger and distrust that frothed off Willa would recede.

When Willa didn't say anything, Juniper tried again. "Are you hungry? Thirsty? I always came home from school absolutely starv—"

"I'm fine," Willa cut her off.

"Okay. How about—"

"I have a lot of homework," Willa said pointedly.

So Juniper backed out of the small room, nearly losing a finger when Willa threw the door shut behind her. For the rest of the afternoon she found herself staring at the handle, willing it to turn, until she couldn't take it anymore and finally called Willa into the kitchen for supper. They ate beef stew that Cora had dropped off and crusty bread warmed up in the oven with cold butter, but Willa only picked at it, spearing the odd carrot or hunk of potato and then sliding it off the tines of her fork against the edge of her bowl.

They only attempted conversation once, when Willa sucked in a shaky breath and dared to ask: "Is Uncle Jonathan going to be okay?"

Juniper couldn't lie to her. "I don't know. Reb—Grandma—called a while ago to tell me that he's stable." How much to tell her? How much to hold back? Willa was a teenager, but could she handle the news that her beloved uncle, the man who stepped in as a father figure when she was still an infant, was in a medically induced coma and fighting for his life? It felt like too much. Juniper settled on: "They're doing everything they can."

Willa absorbed this without so much as a blink, and retreated to her bedroom as soon as Juniper gave her a nod. When Reb phoned later that evening with an update on Jonathan (no change), Juniper didn't even bother to tell Willa. The light in her room had already been shut off.

By the time Juniper dropped Willa off at school the following morning, she was eager to be rid of her and sick with guilt that she felt so exasperated by her own flesh and blood. Juniper could hardly wait to talk to Cora—to confide her fears and failings and get some much-needed motherly encouragement and advice. But even though the library door was unlocked and the lights were on, Cora wasn't in her office when Juniper arrived.

"You must be the new girl," someone said as she peered into the small staff room for a clue to Cora's whereabouts.

Juniper startled at the unfamiliar voice and spun around to find a stocky man with horn-rimmed glasses and a Mr. Rogers–style cardigan holding out his hand.

"Barry," she said, shaking his warm fingers and trying to hide her disappointment. "I'm Juniper." She had never met Barry in person, though they were Facebook friends and she had heard plenty of stories about him from Cora over the years. He was unctuous and a bit self-important, prone to writing rambling updates about his political views and posting almost daily links to his book review blog, which seemed to have a single reader: his mother. Cora kept him around because he was reliable and loved the library, his two best characteristics.

"It's nice to finally meet you in person," Barry said.

"You too." Juniper managed a shadow of a smile before asking, "Where's Cora?"

"She's not feeling well this morning," he said. "Texted to ask if I could open up for her."

Juniper felt a prick of disappointment that Cora had chosen to reach out to Barry instead of her, but she reminded herself that she couldn't have come earlier anyway. Juniper had Willa to take care of now.

"We have a busy day today," Barry said, turning toward the library floor and talking over his shoulder as if he expected Juniper to follow. She did. "Mom and Tot Hour is at ten. I've taken the liberty of picking a book out for you since you won't know what Cora's been doing the last several weeks."

"Sounds like you have it all figured out," Juniper tried. "Maybe you should do it just this once, and I'll watch."

Barry gave her a flat look over the rim of his glasses and thrust a binder at her. There was a glossy children's book on top. "I don't think so. This afternoon we have the Heritage Society meeting, and it will take me all morning to get everything ready."

Juniper took the binder and the book, dismayed by the fact that she would be reading and singing and leading chants with toddlers in just a couple of hours. Still, winging it would be worse, so she flipped through the binder and picked out a few activities so that she was ready to go when the clock hit 9:45 and the moms started rolling in.

The children's area was set up with a low stool for Juniper, a stack of carpet squares for the kids and their moms, and a plastic tote with hand puppets that had seen better days. As she tented the book on top of the stool she would soon occupy, Juniper found herself surreptitiously studying the women who had started to crowd the small library. The quiet space was bustling with activity. Apparently, the unwritten dress code was athleisure and high ponytails, and the women were all sleek curves and plummy lip gloss. They were also all near Juniper's age, which was what she had been worried about all along. Surely there were women she knew in this group. Women she had gone to high school with and who would recognize her and ask seemingly innocuous questions that would make her wither with shame. *What have you been up to since graduation? Are you married? Kids? Oh, Willa, of course . . .*

Juniper was nearly stiff with dread when the ladies had finished hanging up their coats and chatting and began to make their way to the children's section. They came with kids on their hips and travel mugs in hand, and broke into surprised grins when they caught sight of Juniper. It was clear that Cora had kept her promise and hadn't disclosed their agreement; Juniper hadn't wanted to make a big deal of her imminent arrival in Jericho, and begged Cora not to broadcast it.

"June Baker, is that you? Oh my goodness!" One of the women broke away from the group and stepped over the semicircles of carpet squares to give Juniper a one-armed hug.

Pressed between someone whose name she couldn't recall and a chubby two-year-old with strawberry blond curls, Juniper scraped the bottom of her resolve. She came up with a thin, determined smile on her face. "It's nice to see you," she said.

"India Abbot," the woman offered, readjusting her baby and studying Juniper with bald curiosity.

"You probably don't remember me. I was a bit behind you in school. What are you doing here?"

"Mom and Tot Hour," Juniper said, but she was being obtuse and immediately regretted it.

India's eyes went wide. "But, I mean, your brother . . ."

Of course. The news of Jonathan's accident had spread like a virus. Juniper was far outside the loop but could imagine the rumors that were pulsing around the community. No doubt they would reach a fever pitch now that she had been spotted in town. What was she doing here? Why wasn't she in Des Moines with the rest of the family? And what dirty secrets could they infer from this strange circumstance?

In her head, Juniper quickly tested and discarded a handful of answers. She landed on: "I'm helping out Cora for a while."

"Oh, of course, you're so sweet," India fawned, squeezing Juniper's wrist just a bit too tightly. "Poor, poor Cora."

Juniper knew that it would make Cora's skin crawl to hear that anyone pitied her, but she stitched her lips together and nodded sagely.

"And what a blessing that you can be here during this difficult time for your family. It's just so, so sad."

Clearly India felt things very, very deeply. Since Juniper didn't want to get drawn into a lengthy discussion about Jonathan's condition—

or Cora or herself, for that matter—she smiled politely, then indicated the book on the stool behind her. "Maybe we should get started."

"Of course. Welcome home." India pressed her nose into her daughter's plump cheek as if to self-soothe after talking about the tragedy that was Juniper's life, and then backtracked to the only carpet square left in the farthest corner of the bookshelf-lined area.

Juniper gave herself just a moment with her back turned to collect the book and flip through the binder of songs and activities that Cora had gathered. She was sure India wasn't the only person she knew in the crowd, but she was grateful that no one else had come forward. At least, not yet. After the finger-puppet play and the rhymes, and the lap bounce Juniper had picked out about bunnies, others would want to say hello. To poke around for some gossip to go with their lunch dates that would surely take place post–Mom & Tot Hour.

You can do this, Juniper told herself.

But when she turned around, a smile affixed to her face like an accessory and a benign introduction on her tongue, she knew she had been wrong.

Ashley sat front and center.

It had been almost fifteen years since Juniper had seen her former best friend, but Ashley was still immediately recognizable as the girl Juniper had known. Her hair was streaked platinum and longer than she had worn it in high school, and she was soft in all the places a mother should be. But she was Ashley through and through, from the fine line of her graceful jaw to the way she tilted her head just a degree to the right. Ashley had a little dark-haired girl balanced on her crossed legs, and her eyes were glittering with cold fury. The fact that Ashley had remained at the library when she realized Juniper was hosting story hour, and that she had taken the closest seat so she could stare Juniper down, spoke volumes to the scope and intensity of her ire. Clearly it hadn't abated in the years that Juniper had been in exile.

Juniper was horrified to feel her cheeks begin to redden, her eyes grow hot and damp. The children's section was small, and there were easily a dozen women with their kids seated on the floor in front of her, so she looked away from Ashley and made an offhand excuse about an overactive boiler. There were some polite chuckles and one of the little boys sneezed, setting off a flurry of "God bless yous" that gave Juniper the few seconds she needed to gather herself. She wrestled her emotions into submission, then proceeded to fill an entire hour with expressive book-reading and the kinds of nurturing, sensory-rich activities that she had rarely had the chance to do with Willa.

"That was amazing!" India told her when it was all over and the mothers were helping to put hand puppets and carpet squares back in their designated places. "One of the best classes we've ever had. You're a natural, June. I hope you plan on staying!"

Juniper was shaky and weak, as drained as if she had just finished running a marathon instead of reading books with babies. She could feel a sheen of sweat cooling along her hairline, and she was sure she looked like an absolute wreck. But she mustered a flimsy smile for India and a few of the other women who lingered. Ashley was not among them.

As if she could read Juniper's mind, India said, "And how great that Ashley Patterson came today! You two were BFFs in high school, right? I bet you have a lot of catching up to do!"

A noise from the entryway made everyone look toward where Ashley was struggling to pop her daughter's arm through the puffy sleeve of a quilted coat. She scoffed one more time, just to make her derision crystal clear. "June and I were never friends," she called over the space between them. "And it's Ashley *Tate,* India. I haven't been a Patterson in over twelve years."

How could anyone forget it? Ashley had married Sullivan Tate in a ceremony that had made a mini-splash in the tristate wedding community when it was touted as *The Perfect*

Prairie Wedding and picked up by a handful of bridal sites. Juniper hadn't been invited, of course, but that didn't stop her from furtively searching the internet for evidence of their nuptials. It had been gorgeous. Ashley in a dress the color of fresh cream, Sullivan in a gray tux that he somehow managed to render both casual and sharp. They posed in front of a wind-washed red barn and at the apex of an unmaintained gravel road with nothing but the sunset blazing like a wildfire behind them. It was exquisite, all of it. The stuff dreams were made of. In the end, Ashley's dream came true.

Juniper felt flayed open, her heart shuddering with each vulnerable, exposed thump. Ashley had known the real Juniper, the girl on the cusp of womanhood who had been simply, earnestly June. And Ashley loathed her. She dissected Juniper with a look, glared at her across the polished floors and the stacks of books and the shocked gathering of young moms. Then she swung her daughter into her arms, spun on the heel of her lambskin boot, and stalked out of the library. The door slammed behind her.

"She took a picture of you, you know."

"What?" Juniper looked up from paging absently through the Mom & Tot binder to find Barry standing right in front of her. He was so silent she hadn't even heard his approach—

127

or maybe she was too distracted to notice. But then his words clicked, and her eyes widened. "Ashley? She took a picture of me?"

"Not her. India. The one with the short hair and the purple eye makeup?"

Juniper didn't specifically remember purple makeup, but India had been carefully put together. A pretty, early thirty-something with a cute bob and a hundred-watt smile. It was no wonder that Barry had cataloged the details. "Why would India take a picture of me?"

"She has a blog. *Jericho Unscripted*. It's kind of a mix between a local gossip mag and a family photo album. She mostly posts stuff about her kids. But sometimes there's . . ." He paused, searching. "Other stuff. Let's just say it can be enlightening. If you believe what she writes, of course."

"*Jericho Unscripted?*" Juniper was still catching up. "You've got to be kidding me."

"I think it's supposed to be tongue in cheek. You'll probably be on it tonight. Just thought you'd like to know." Barry started to walk away, his arms full of old ledgers for the Heritage Society meeting. The library was dead after the excitement and drama of the Mom & Tot Hour, and Juniper was grateful for the chance to lick her wounds in peace. But she wasn't about to let Barry off the hook so easily.

"Wait a sec." Juniper came around the high

counter and grabbed a box that Barry had taken out of the storage area in the attic. She fell into step beside him. "Can she do that? Just post a picture of me without my permission?"

Barry shrugged, leading Juniper into the records room. It was a long, narrow room that was a leftover space after the interior transformation of the library. There was a rectangular table in the middle, an old microfiche at the farthest end, and the walls were lined with town histories, every Jericho High yearbook dating back to 1917, and thick dowels hung with newspapers like faded sheets on a clothesline. Barry set his stack of green ledgers in the middle of the table and then took the box from Juniper's arms.

"I guess so," he said. "She posts all sorts of stuff about life in Jericho, and I doubt she secures permission from everyone who pops up in her photos. You'll get lots of attention, I'm sure. *Jericho Unscripted* enjoys a broader audience than the *Chronicle*."

Juniper groaned. Clearly, she had discovered who Everett's "overactive" local journalist was. Though it sounded like calling India's blog posts "journalism" was more than generous.

"She'll probably write something like 'New Instructor for Mom and Tot Hour' or 'Welcome Home, Juniper.' "

"She wouldn't," Juniper whispered, her mouth suddenly dry as toast.

"Oh, she would. She will. That's why I told you. I thought you'd want to know."

"Thank you," Juniper choked, and Barry gave her a sympathetic look.

"Want to help me with these records?" he asked, but it was obvious that he didn't need her help. He was just trying to be nice.

"Looks like you've got everything under control. I should make a game plan for next week." Juniper was about to excuse herself when she caught sight of a row of Bankers Boxes lined up neatly on the floor beneath the shelves. "What's in those?"

Barry followed the line of her finger. "Old newspapers. They're on microfiche, of course, but Cora is having a hard time letting go of the originals."

"May I?" Juniper doubted Barry would oblige, but he nodded and swept his arm toward them magnanimously.

"Be my guest. We don't need them today."

Juniper crouched down and ran her fingertips over the striped boxes. They had been arranged chronologically, and she had to crawl on the floor to find the year she was looking for. Sliding the box out, she carried it to the circulation desk and lifted off the top.

There wasn't much inside. The newspapers were filed in order and separated by tabs that marked each month. Four, sometimes five weekly newspapers per section, plus the Shopper, a small insert that featured local ads and coupons. More than half the box was empty, a sad testament to the anemic existence of Jericho, Iowa. Or maybe it was a good thing. No news was good news, right?

Juniper flipped to the month of June and lifted out the flat stack of newsprint. As she knew it would, her graduating class grinned beneath the simple headline:

CONGRATULATIONS, GRADUATES!

Of course graduation would be the biggest news of the week. What else happened in Jericho?

In spite of the drama post–Mom & Tot Hour, Juniper couldn't tear herself away from the photo. She and Ashley were side by side, arms thrown around each other and mortarboards askew. They were flashing peace signs for no apparent reason, and Juniper found she could remember the way her hair clung to her neck in the heat, the way Ashley smelled of bubble gum and that dime-store body spray she loved. It felt like yesterday and like someone else's story at the same time. She didn't know what that kind of happiness felt like anymore. But even then, hadn't it been a ruse? A paper-thin likeness of joy that crumbled to dust at the first hint of adversity.

Every face in the photo was familiar, even

though Juniper couldn't name them all if she tried. Her time at Jericho High was a forgotten history, as meaningless and inconsequential as what she had for breakfast yesterday. But that wasn't entirely true. Some of it mattered. And try as she might to forget, little things came rushing back. Inside jokes, teachers she had loved—and hated. Her first kiss with Edward Cohen behind the bleachers at a varsity football game. He tasted of cinnamon breath mints and, underneath that, hot buttered popcorn.

Juniper traced her fingers around the frame of the photograph. Those kids had no idea what was coming. She felt sorry for them.

A quick flip through the rest of the newspaper confirmed what she already knew to be true: there was no mention at all of the storm that was brewing in Jericho.

The *Jericho Chronicle* came out every Wednesday, and there were only four editions between the graduation cover story and a headline that looked entirely different. Juniper already knew what she would find. Years ago she had scoured the photograph for evidence, pressing her nose to the paper so that she could get a closer look and coming away with black smudges against her skin. She never found what she was looking for. And although she doubted she would now, she pulled out the Fourth of July special extended edition and made herself look again.

JERICHO ROCKED BY DOUBLE HOMICIDE

"Rocked" didn't seem like quite the right word. Stunned, devastated, leveled. In many ways, destroyed. Jericho was never the same after the Murphys were murdered. It brought something dark and wicked home to roost: the gruesome, oily threat of menace; that unspeakable things could happen here, too—even in quaint little Jericho.

Though the heading was shocking, the photograph beneath was rather harmless. It was a shot of the Murphys' acreage the morning after, yellow police tape strung across the gravel drive and a scattering of official vehicles parked haphazardly in the grass. Cal would have hated that. Tires raking up his lawn, gouging long, ugly hash marks across the careful expanse of green. Afterward, the place sat empty for years, and with no one to tend the grass, those heavy trucks left bare patches like scars.

The article itself was pallid, devoid of any real information except for the line that made Juniper's lungs feel crushed every time she read it: *Suspect in custody*. They should have just written the truth: *Jonathan Baker in custody*. Everyone knew it.

Juniper glanced at her watch. Nearly three o'clock. The members of the Heritage Society would be filtering through the front doors soon, and she would have to go pick up Willa from school. This was neither the time nor the place for a more careful inspection, so after glancing toward the records room to make sure that Barry was still occupied, Juniper took the entire stack of magazines from June, July, and August and rolled them up. They made a fat cylinder that slid perfectly beside the laptop in her backpack. Everything about her petty theft was wrong, from the fact that she was essentially stealing from her dear friend to the atrocious way she had handled old documents, but Juniper didn't care. The newspaper was an incomplete history anyway. Riddled with holes and white lies. She knew the true biography of Jericho. At least, some of it.

Juniper helped a few patrons find the books they were looking for and sent Cora a "thinking about you" text while Barry welcomed the Heritage Society. They were a boisterous group of gray-haired men and women who shook Juniper's hand warmly and held her gaze as if to say, *We know who you are and none of that matters to us.* Juniper's pulse quickened when one of the older gentlemen pulled her into a hug and whispered, "Glad you're home, Ms. Baker. You belong here."

Although she didn't necessarily agree— not only did Juniper *feel* like an outsider, she wanted to be one—his words struck a raw nerve. The desire to belong was a weed that grew no matter how hard she tried to dig it up. Just when she thought she had it rooted out completely, a resolute sprout unfurled.

"Thank you," she told him, gripping his wrinkled hands in both her own. What she didn't say was that she suspected he was one of the only people in all of Jericho who was glad she was here.

When they were all settled in the records room and the library was quiet once again, Juniper unwittingly proved her point by looking up India's blog on one of the library's desktop computers.

Jericho Unscripted was sleeker and far more professional-looking than Juniper had expected it to be. She'd had visions of a pastel color palette and amateurish clip art, but India had obviously had help. The site was all silver and black, with a gorgeous photo of five women linking arms on the home page. Their backs were turned to the camera and the image was a little smoky, as if India had wanted to give the impression of inclusivity. These women could be anyone, but certainly not everyone, because they were all slim and perfectly coiffed and lovely.

"Good grief, they take themselves seriously," Juniper muttered. She wished she could share her derision with someone, perhaps Cora or Jonathan, but it helped to say the words out loud. She knew she was being petty, maybe even jealous, but she was too unnerved to care.

Juniper planned to scroll through old blog posts to get a bit of a feeling for the types of things that India liked to write about, but she didn't make it past the most recent entry. The title alone made her heart somersault.

LOCAL MURDER SUSPECT IN CRITICAL CONDITION

Good God, who did India think she was?

Juniper scanned the article quickly, her gaze alighting on phrases that made her simmer.

Jonathan Baker, a suspect in a nearly fifteen-year-old double murder . . .

No one was ever charged . . .

Murderer remains at large . . .

Jonathan's "accident" dredges up a lot of unanswered questions . . .

India had actually put quotation marks around "accident," but it was unclear what she was trying to imply. Was there any way she could know about how history was repeating itself? About the little "mishaps" and thinly veiled threats that Mandy had whispered about only days ago? Even if she did, India's insinuations read like a bad tabloid. She was clueless. Ignorant. She didn't know *anything*. India's faux friendliness—the way she had sidled up to Juniper at Mom & Tot Hour like an old friend—was galling.

Still. Juniper scrolled quickly through the

site, looking for anything and everything even remotely related to Jonathan or the murders. Could India be behind the podcast? And if so, was she capable of persecuting Jonathan— and Mandy and the boys—in such a sinister, traumatizing way? It didn't seem likely. India had come across as a little vacuous but friendly enough, and certainly not malevolent. Whoever was working on a podcast about the Murphy murders had a vicious vendetta against her brother. *That bastard.* It felt personal. And yet, India Abbot was definitely someone Juniper needed to watch.

She closed the browser and then tried to erase the search history before remembering that the function had been disabled—not that it mattered. If Barry was right, India's little online rag got lots of attention. Surely it had popped up on the library's computers many times before and no one who noticed it would think twice. Still, if Juniper had anything to do about it, India's days as an amateur investigative journalist were numbered.

Before she had time to change her mind, Juniper plucked the business card from where she had tucked it in her phone case and punched in the number. "Officer Stokes?" she said when he picked up. "I think we need to talk."

CHAPTER 8

SUMMER
14 AND A HALF YEARS AGO

Sullivan's kiss lingers like an illness. It clings to my skin and makes me feel dirty, even after I've showered and crawled into bed feigning an unspecified sickness. Jonathan leaves me alone at the insinuation of "girl problems," but I won't be able to avoid him forever. He'll insist on a play-by-play of my conversation with Sullivan, and I've never been able to lie to my brother. Not that I don't try—he can just read me like an open book.

Curled on my side in bed, I squint at the stars outside my window and try to get my story straight. Sullivan talked about water. About sinkholes and pollution and not much else. It scares me a bit to remember how cavalier he was about Baxter, as if taking a life—even the life of an animal—was really nothing at all. And I have much more to learn about the ongoing feud between the Murphys and the Tates. I wonder what Jonathan knows.

Layered in with all that worry is the knowledge that Ashley will never forgive me if she finds out what I let happen. It wasn't that big of a deal, of course. I know that. The logical side of me accepts that Sullivan kissed me and I backed away. But

Ashley will never see it that way because she's so head over heels for him. I'm pretty sure she'd forfeit our friendship over a misunderstanding. And isn't the growing distance between us all my fault? I've made no secret about the fact that I hate it here. My automatic dislike of anything and everything related to this town rubs Ashley the wrong way, and now that I'm half-gone, I can see our relationship is hanging by a thread. I wanted more for us than this.

Law and Jonathan are long gone by the time I drag myself out of bed and stumble down the stairs in the morning, but there's no way I can avoid Mom. No doubt, she'll be waiting in the kitchen for me, and I get ready as slowly as I can without making myself late. I pull my hair into a high knot and throw on clothes that are already paint-splattered and worn. By the end of the day I'll be a disaster, covered in smears of oil pastels and glitter glue if I'm not careful. I have the best summer job in all of Jericho—assistant to the Arts and Crafts Director at the community center—but it's definitely not clean.

I skip down the steps two at a time, planning to eat on the run. But Mom is leaning against the kitchen sink, waiting for me, it seems. She's not going to let me slip away so easily this time.

"Hey," she says, peering at me over a mug of tea.

"Hey." I can't exactly back out of the room now, even though I'm still not ready to face her. "About the other day . . ."

Mom sighs. "Juniper Grace, you're an adult. I'm not going to yell at you about grad night."

"You're not?"

"I don't want you to make bad decisions, but you're a good girl, June. Everyone is allowed a mistake from time to time."

I'm all set to argue with her—to remind her that I'm responsible and a straight-A student and not the kind of girl who makes a habit of getting drunk—but then she smiles at me over the rim of her mug and I realize she's already forgiven me.

"I thought you were mad. I've been avoiding you." I pull out a stool at the island and Mom comes over to lift a loaf of bread out of the basket on the counter. When Jonathan and I were little, she used to make something different and wonderful for breakfast every morning. Pancakes and waffles, omelets with fresh eggs we gathered from the small coop out back, lots of thick, crispy bacon. I didn't really appreciate it when I was a kid, the way Mom served us. I thought it was our right as her children, but I can see it now as something much different. An offering, maybe. A kind of tangible provision. Love.

"You don't have to make me breakfast," I say, but she's already slathering salted butter on a thick hunk of bread and reaching for the raspberry jam. In a few more seconds she slides the plate to me, open-faced sandwich cut in two triangles just the way I like it. "Thank you."

"You're welcome. There's a bag in the fridge with your lunch."

"You didn't have to do that," I say around a mouthful, but she waves me off.

"It's just leftovers. Don't get too excited."

I eat in silence for a few moments, and Mom just watches me. I can feel her gaze, but it's a soft touch, a caress. It hits me that I'll miss these moments with her when I'm gone.

"You wanted to talk to me about something?" I ask when I'm down to my last few bites. Mom needs to be prompted sometimes, to be encouraged to articulate the thoughts that whir so quickly, so quietly behind her dark eyes. And a hasty glance at the clock on the wall behind her tells me I don't have much time.

"I did?"

"You came into the bathroom the other day when I was showering," I remind her. "I thought you were going to yell at me about grad night."

"Oh." She waves her hand. "I don't remember. It must not have been a big deal."

I get up from the counter and rinse my plate at the sink before sticking it in the dishwasher. The air in our home hasn't been clear for days (weeks?), and I feel like Mom knows it. I just can't understand why she won't talk to me about it.

"You okay?" I give her my full attention for a moment, admiring the single white streak that sweeps from her temple and weaves its way through her braid. She doesn't bother to hide it, and there's a certain confidence, even rebelliousness in that. I heard Law tell her once to color it, and she laughed. "I earned it," she said. The thought makes me smile now.

"Fine, fine." Mom's lips curl to match mine, but her eyes are sad.

"You don't seem fine." I wrap my arms around her neck and hang on tight for a moment. She smells of oatmeal soap and fresh mint from the sprig she puts in her morning tea. There's a ceramic pot of peppermint in the window above the sink, and she clips and crushes a few leaves in her steaming mug every morning. The aroma of it brewing is the smell of my childhood. I breathe her in, let go. "Are you sure?"

"Positive. I just haven't seen much of you these last few days. Gotta soak up the time we have before it's gone, right?"

She means before *I'm* gone, and I feel a stab of guilt. "I'm going to college," I remind her, "not dying."

"God forbid." She laughs.

It feels wrong to leave her in such a strange mood, but I don't really have a choice. I need to arrive at the community center by eight thirty to set up for the first class at nine, and I'm already running late. I leave with a promise to help her in the garden (my mother's love language) on Saturday and drive faster than strictly necessary on my way into town, shaking off my worries as I go.

I unlock the double doors of the community center and bypass the gym to climb the wide staircase at one end of the building. At the top is the banquet hall turned art studio, a monstrosity of a room that spans the entire footprint of the gym below. Brick columns hold up the high ceiling, and tall, narrow windows span the entire south side. It's amazing in the morning when the sunshine pours in and the dust mites dance in the golden glow. Shelves have been built against the north wall and they're sagging beneath the weight of jars of paint, boxes of fresh canvas, and plastic totes filled with everything from cracked crayons to old buttons.

My first task is to set out cups of water to clean the brushes, refill the palettes, and make sure everything is ready to go when Tanya, the Arts and Crafts Director, breezes in just a couple minutes after nine.

At the end of my last shift I had left a wide tray with plastic cups on the counter next to the sink, and I start there now, filling each container half-full of water. I've never really considered the state of Jericho's water, but after my conversation with Sullivan, I find myself watching the faucet with a critical eye. I can't help myself—I lift one of the cups to my nose and sniff. It smells like chlorine to me, and faintly medicinal, not at all like our well water, which is trace mineral and earth. We run it through a water purifier, but the smell lingers.

City water is different. It's pumped through the water treatment plant, of course, and we all trust it comes out the other side safe and drinkable. Last spring they flushed the water main and for an entire afternoon the water ran brown. It smelled sharp and dirty then, like rust and damp cellars. Unhealthy. And a couple of years ago there was a notice about nitrates in the water. Pregnant women, small children, and the elderly were advised to drink bottled water instead. I didn't give it much thought at the time, but Sullivan's story of poisoned wells fills me with a sense of helplessness.

"Hiya, June!"

I turn to see one of the campers skipping toward me, blond pigtails bouncing. She's often the first through the doors in the morning, and I give her a big smile, shaking off any lingering doubts about the quality of Jericho's water. "Good morning! Wanna help?"

The day passes in a blur of activity and the never-ending chatter of small children, bright dust, and spilled paint. After Tanya has left and I've locked

144

up, I sit on the steps outside the community center and let the late afternoon sun raise goose bumps across my skin. Heat can do that—can make you shiver—just as surely as cold. I rub my arms to get rid of the prickling sensation and study Jericho spread out before me.

Suddenly I'm on my feet, leaving the community center and my car behind. It's a Friday afternoon in early summer and you can tell because Jericho is a ghost town. People leave work early, head to the lake, have a beer in the sun. I wouldn't be surprised to see a tumbleweed cartwheel across the street, but for once I'm grateful for the stillness.

The library is lukewarm, the air close and thick. It's also jarringly quiet, a reminder that even when no one is around the world is filled with sounds. Birds and a light breeze shaking the leaves, and cars in the middle distance. But in the library, there is just the sound of my breath. For some reason it's faster than normal, my heart beating high and hard. I came here because I wanted privacy, and I'm not even sure why. Or who I'm hiding from. I just know that I don't want the history of our home computer to betray the things I'm searching for.

"Hey, June."

Cora startles me, emerging from between the stacks with a children's book in her hand and a wide smile on her face. I'm a lifelong regular of the Jericho library, but it's been a while since I've popped by. I'd volunteered for the summer reading program when I was in middle school, but high school made me too busy for books. Still, Cora is an old friend, and after I gasp at her sudden appearance, I wrap her in a tight hug. Her dress is shockingly bright and printed with red and yellow birds in flight. She smells of essential oils: geranium and eucalyptus, if my nose can be trusted. Cora feels like every good thing from my youth wrapped up in one sparkling woman.

"It's good to see you," she says. One raised eyebrow scolds me: *It's been a while.*

"You too." I give her a smile of my own. "I saw you at graduation. I'm sorry I didn't get a chance to say thanks in person."

"The handshake line was a mile long. It was too hot to wait in the sun."

"I would have left, too."

"What can I do for you?"

"I just want to use a computer," I say. No books today, and I can tell she's a little disappointed.

Cora puts the book on the circulation counter before turning to face me, hands on hips. "We close at six on Fridays and I have plans, so make it zippy. Then promise me that you'll be back sometime when we can catch up."

"Cross my heart."

"Got your library card?"

I shake my head and Cora reaches behind the

counter. Grabbing a lanyard with a laminated card clipped to the end, she thrusts it at me. "Use this. Guest username and password are on the card. Search history is saved, so you'd better not be looking up porn or how to dispose of a body."

"You know me so well."

Cora laughs. "Don't worry, I don't have you pegged as the murdering type."

"There's a type?"

"Honey, I could pinpoint the ten people most likely to commit homicide in this town. And a dozen other things that would curl your toes."

I'm really not sure what to do with this information. Cora is a contradiction in terms, an ample fifty-something with the fashion sense of an eccentric yogi and a gaze so shrewd I feel like she can see right through me. When I was little and Beth Murphy used to take me and Jonathan to the library, Cora would sometimes pick out a book and read it just to me. It made me feel so special to be singled out that way. Like she saw something in me that I couldn't see in myself. Maybe it was the way that I could be both silly and serious, innocent and just a bit macabre. We share a weird sense of humor, and something makes me say: "Surely there are no homicidal maniacs in *Jericho*."

Cora takes the bait and belts out a laugh like a dog barking. But she doesn't say what I expect her to. "Oh, we're *all* capable of murder. Even—

maybe especially—the good people of Jericho."

"Not Jericho!" I fake-gasp, clutching my chest.

She gives me a stern look but softens it with a smile. "Don't be so sarcastic. It's true. People around here are a bit set in their ways, but that's true in most places. Communities coalesce around ideals."

"What are Jericho's ideals?"

She thinks for a moment. "Community. Family. Faith."

"Tradition. Uniformity. Compliance."

Cora laughs. "Tell me how you really feel!"

"It's true," I say, bristling a little.

"Maybe we're talking about two sides of the same coin," Cora concedes. "There's who we are at our worst, most base moments, and the shimmer of who we *could* be. Who we want to be. We're aspirational, I guess."

I've never thought of Jericho as the sort of community that aspires. We preserve. Circle the wagons. Protect our own no matter the cost, and sacrifice those on the fringes. It's not even close to being the same thing. "I guess we don't see it quite the same way," I tell her, and think for just a moment about sharing what Sullivan told me. About poison in the water and poison that put Baxter in the ground. This whole place feels poisonous to me.

"You don't have to agree for it to be true."

"Well, there's nothing that would drive me to

murder," I say confidently. There isn't. Of course not.

Cora shakes her head. "It's not about a *thing,* hon. The motivation to kill comes down to *who.*"

This conversation is suddenly making my stomach twist, my palms go clammy. I'm not sure how to get out of it, but Cora must read discomfort on my face, because she gives my arm a pat.

"Sorry. I'm not sure how we got here," I admit as I let her usher me in the direction of the small computer bank. There's a long table with four desktops, their monitors all dark.

"You know I don't do small talk," Cora says with a wink. "Can't tell if that's a good thing in a librarian or a liability. Anyway, when's the last time you've used one of our computers? We got new ones this spring. All you've got to do is give the mouse a little wiggle and follow the prompts. We default to Yahoo! but I'm sure you know how to get where you're going."

Cora disappears with one last comforting squeeze and I sink into a padded armchair. Keying in the guest username and password, I navigate to Explorer and type "water contamination" into the search bar. Over five hundred million hits unfurl before me, and I click through the first few, promptly realizing that I need to refine my results. I don't need to know that water pollution is usually the result of human activities or that runoff from fertilizers and pesticides is the biggest offender. I'm more interested in the effects, in understanding the reasons why the Murphys would fight so fiercely, so vocally about something that seems rather inconsequential to me. Drink bottled water. Buy a purifier. Find a way. Fertilizers and pesticides, chemicals themselves, are a fact of life.

After more than ten minutes of clicking and reading, refining my search and trying again, I'm surprised to discover that the science isn't nearly as exact as I thought it would be. In low concentrations, contamination from chemicals can cause anything from mild irritation to acute stomach distress. Higher concentrations of toxic chemicals are obviously much worse: burns, convulsions, miscarriage, birth defects, and certain types of cancer, including breast, ovarian, thyroid, non-Hodgkin's lymphoma, and leukemia. Scary stuff. But the Murphys don't have kids, and Beth is far past her childbearing years. They aren't convulsing on a regular basis—at least, not that I know of. As for cancer, doesn't it get us all eventually? Doesn't *everything* cause cancer?

It's hard for me to wrap my head around this kind of strife, the back-and-forth between people I don't know well, about an issue that doesn't seem all that significant to me. I'm missing something.

Cora is behind the circulation desk, gathering

things up and humming to herself. It's a subtle reminder that she has plans and I'm cramping her style as the only person in this utterly abandoned place. I don't blame her. It's a gorgeous summer day and I'm ready to be outside, too, but I key in one last search before I close the computer down. This time I'm a bit more specific. *Iowa water pollution cases*. The headlines scroll:

IOWA TOWNS FIGHT TO KEEP POLLUTION OUT OF TAP WATER

MORE THAN HALF OF IOWA WATER BODIES POLLUTED

IOWA CORN FARMS POISON DRINKING WATER

SMALL FARMERS BATTLE BIG AGRA

NASTY WATER WARS

Water wars indeed.

But this isn't my battle to fight. I turn off the computer and tuck my chair in under the table. Cora gives me a look as I approach her with the lanyard and guest card outstretched.

"Find what you needed?" she asks slyly.

"Poison," I tell her with a wink. "Quick, clean, undetectable."

Cora's laughter follows me all the way out the door.

It's hazy and humid when I jog down the steps, and I hurry to where my car is parked in the shadow of the community center. My hour at the library has unnerved me, and when I glance through the driver's-side window and see a yellow Post-it Note stuck to my steering wheel, a flutter of dread wings against my skin.

I don't lock my car doors—ever. Why would I? This is Jericho, where everyone knows my name and can recognize my car by the scattering of rust over the back wheel wells. Ashley has returned borrowed shirts by tossing them on the passenger seat, and my mom often slips treats in my cupholder just because. But this feels different.

I yank open the door and slide into the hot car, snatching up the little square of paper as if I expect it to be a death threat.

Hit play. —Sullivan

I'm confused for a moment, glancing around until my eyes fall on the cassette deck in my dash. I've never used it, not once, but now the little flap is pushed back and I can see there is a tape inside. My car is a hand-me-down, and it has both a CD player and a tape player that came with an impressive collection of my mom's old classic cassettes. She had once handed them to me in a cardboard box with a half smile and listening notes on her favorite composers and songs. I lugged the box around in my trunk for a while until Mom realized I was never going to develop an appreciation for her ten-tape ultimate classical collection. She reclaimed the box and stuck it in the attic.

A tape? I'm not even sure I know how to use one. And a pucker of concern makes me wonder if I want to follow Sullivan's instructions at all. What could it be? A confession? An in-depth explanation of water contamination? I turn the ignition and sit with my car running in park. Then, with some trepidation, I reach over. The play button sinks with a satisfying *click*.

It's a song I know, perfectly cued up to the first few lightly strummed guitar chords. I can't help the smile that tugs at my lips, nor can I stop myself from grabbing my phone and dialing his number.

"How did you know?" I demand, skipping the "hellos" and "how are yous" entirely. Tom Petty is singing "Wildflowers" in the background.

He laughs. "Your T-shirt. It was an authentic Tom Petty and the Heartbreakers concert tee from the 1989 Strange Behavior Tour."

I'm speechless. Almost. I can't believe he remembered the T-shirt I was wearing. That he recognized the three wolves howling at the moon. "My mom saw him play in Ohio that summer," I say. "We listened to him nonstop when I was a kid."

"Well, he didn't write 'Wildflowers' until the early nineties, but I took a chance."

"I . . ." I trail off, not really sure what to say next.

But Sullivan saves me. "Just a little nod from one Tom Petty fan to another. See you around, Baker."

He hangs up, cutting the connection before it has a chance to get weird. I'm not sure what to think, how to react. And in the quiet cab of my car, Tom Petty begins to sing "Free Fallin'."

CHAPTER 9

WINTER
TODAY

It took a couple of days for Willa to relax into life at the bungalow, and when she did, she carried with her a whiff of imminent flight. The air seemed laced with angst and expectation, the stubborn hope that her sojourn with Juniper would be brief. But when two nights turned into three, and Reb told them over video chat that she and Law had moved into a room at the Rainbow House, Willa seemed resigned to her fate.

"What's the Rainbow House? Can I stay there with you?"

"Oh, hon," Reb said. "You wouldn't want that. It's like a hotel for family members of long-term patients. We're in a room with a single queen bed."

"Long-term?" Willa's voice squeaked.

"Jonathan is doing better every day. 'Long' is relative, Willa."

Reb was quick to reassure, but Willa's narrow shoulders collapsed all the same. When they hung up, Juniper chanced a touch, and the girl withered into her arms. It was bittersweet—her daughter was finally clinging to her, but for all the wrong reasons—and brief. When Willa realized what she was doing, who she was embracing, she pulled back and crossed her arms over her chest. A signature Willa move. Juniper was getting used to it. And to the way her daughter thrust her hair behind her ears, crinkled up her nose when she was thinking, and hummed unconsciously while she ate. Juniper felt like an anthropologist, a veritable Jane Goodall noting and silently recording the behaviors and mannerisms, likes and dislikes, motivations and ambitions of her young subject. But it wasn't nearly that clinical. Juniper wanted to smooth the pale freckles across her daughter's cheeks with a thumb, plant a kiss on her forehead, watch her sleep.

"He's going to be okay," Juniper said belatedly, realizing that Willa was about to bolt back to her depressing room. The sentiment rang hollow even in her own ears. There were simply no guarantees. Still, the thrill of Willa momentarily softening in her embrace made her promise: "I'll make sure of it."

"How?" Willa sniffed, eyes narrowed. Running the back of her hand beneath her nose, she gave Juniper a doleful look that made her seem much younger than her almost fourteen years. It was unnerving how she could do that: flip-flop between poised young woman and guileless little girl. It was a marked change from last year and the gangly preteen Willa had been.

That visit, Juniper had woken her at midnight on her birthday and they drank hot chocolate in the kitchen and giggled like kids. For once, Reb hadn't caught them and broken it up. Where was the happy girl Willa had been?

"Well," Juniper said, studying her daughter, "Jonathan and I are virtual twins, you know. When we were kids we used to finish each other's sentences. We told each other all our secrets and were the very best of friends. I *know* him."

"That was a long time ago."

Willa was right, of course. It was disingenuous for Juniper to lean on a narrative so old and tired. And yet she and Jonathan were connected in so many ways. They still knew things about each other that no one else in the world did. And wasn't that exactly the problem? If Juniper wanted to resurrect Jonathan, she had to find a way to dig up the past.

"You're right," Juniper agreed, "that was a long time ago. But your uncle Jonathan is still my baby brother. I'm going to go see him tomorrow. I'll tell him it's time to wake up. That we all need him." She slipped the tidbit about her trip to Des Moines into the conversation as if it weren't a bombshell. Reb had warned her that Willa would want to go, that she would complain and fight and make Juniper's life miserable, but that Juniper was not under any circumstances to give in. Everyone agreed that it was not in Willa's best interests to see Jonathan clinging to life in the ICU.

But Willa didn't complain. Instead she seemed to do a bit of mental math. "It's Saturday. Where will I stay?"

"Well, I'll be back before it's late. Mandy has arranged for you to go to her sister's house after dance practice so that you can spend some time with the boys. Cameron and Hunter are anxious to see you."

A slight nod and it was settled. Willa went to her room for the rest of the evening and was moody when she woke up in the morning, but Juniper clung to those few moments of connection. Her therapist had admonished her to be calm, stable, and consistent. She'd told Juniper that earning her daughter's trust after all this time would be no small feat. Juniper was trying. True, she felt like she was attempting to catch a bird with a bit of seed in the palm of her hand, but she was willing to hold still for as long as it took.

She left Willa at the dance studio for an early morning class and took a shortcut through the outskirts of town on her way to the highway. Just before the neat, orderly lines of Jericho's only trailer park at the edge of town, she spotted a police cruiser pulling into a driveway. After guiltily checking her odometer (only two miles an hour over the speed limit), she realized that

Everett Stokes was climbing out the driver's side of the car. She recognized the distinct way he walked—shoulders thrown back, head tilted forward as he if couldn't wait to get wherever he was going. Besides, how many thirty-something police officers could Jericho employ? He was dressed in a navy uniform, billy club clipped to his belt and radio at his shoulder.

Before she could stop to consider what she was doing, Juniper pumped the brakes and pulled into the driveway beside his cruiser.

Officer Stokes turned, shading his eyes from the frosty glow of snow around him, and gave her a wary look. As he caught sight of Juniper, his features shifted just a bit, but she couldn't read his expression.

"Good morning," he called when Juniper stepped out of her car. To his credit, he didn't ask her what in the world she thought she was doing.

"Just driving past," Juniper explained anyway, already regretting her impulsivity. Too late to back out now. She crossed around her vehicle so they met in front of the garage doors. "This your place?"

He nodded. Now that Juniper had stopped and gotten out of her car, she was less convinced this bold move was the right one. When she had called yesterday, he had kind of blown her off. "My secretary would be happy to take your statement," he'd told her. But that wasn't what

Juniper wanted at all. She wanted this: a face-to-face with the man who told her they were taking another look at the Murphy murders. She decided to play nice Midwestern girl, remembering her roots: it was perfectly kosher, expected even, to stop and chat if you saw a friend. It was a huge stretch to call Officer Stokes a friend, but she braved a smile anyway.

"Night shift?" she tried awkwardly, and he nodded again. Because she couldn't think of anything else to say, Juniper ended up blurting out: "I spent some time reading *Jericho Unscripted* last night."

Something behind his eyes sparked. He gave a cynical laugh. "You discovered India's blog?"

"Not just her blog. We met at the library."

Officer Stokes sized her up for a moment, then said: "You're cold. And I need a cup of coffee. Come on."

Juniper hadn't expected to be invited into his house, but he was right—she was freezing. Her fingers were numb and her eyes were watering. She longed to put her hands around a mug of something hot, or at the very least get out of the icy wind for a moment. Mandy was expecting her at the hospital by lunchtime, but a quick stopover wouldn't throw anything off. Besides, now that she was here, Juniper couldn't shake the feeling that befriending Everett Stokes was the smartest thing she could possibly do. She had snuck a peek at his ring finger and noted it was bare. Not that she was even remotely interested in him romantically, but it certainly simplified things that she wouldn't have to deal with a jealous wife.

He led her to the side door, through the garage like they were old friends instead of relative strangers. "I haven't shoveled the sidewalk in a while," he said by way of explanation. What he didn't need to say was that he either didn't receive many visitors, or those who came by weren't the front door type.

Officer Stokes's house was tidy inside, so carefully kept that Juniper was instantly convinced he hired a cleaning service. She had never met a man so fastidious. The tile in the entryway-and-laundry-room combo looked like it had been scrubbed with a toothbrush. Even the grout was white and clean. And the whole place smelled of fresh citrus, lemony with just a note of cut grass.

"You don't have to do that." He seemed embarrassed that she was unlacing her shoes, but Juniper wouldn't dream of soiling his floor.

"It's fine, Officer Stokes," she said. "I'm a good Dutch girl. I don't wear shoes in houses."

"At least call me Everett," he said, flipping the coffee maker on and turning to lean against the counter. "How's your brother doing?"

"Okay. Stable. I'm actually on my way to Des Moines. I was just driving past . . ."

They were silent for a moment, studying each other across the tiny kitchen table. Then the radio at Everett's shoulder crackled, fragmenting the silence. He reached for it and turned it down, appearing almost surprised to find that he was still in full uniform.

"Give me a sec, will you?" Everett asked, patting his holstered gun.

"Of course." Juniper waved him away. "Where are your mugs?"

"In the cupboard above the sink. There's creamer in the fridge if you'd like some. I'll be right back."

Everett disappeared down a hallway. Juniper lifted two mugs from the cupboard he had indicated and positioned the creamer between them. In the quiet kitchen she could hear the tick of the clock above the stove and the low hum of the radiator. She wished she had her phone—it was in the cupholder in her car—but just as she was about to distract herself with the newspaper on the table, she became aware of the sound of running water. No, not running. Burbling like a brook; a happy, bubbly sound. Curious, Juniper peeked around the archway at the far side of the kitchen and into a small, bright living room.

There was a giant fish tank against the far wall, a monstrosity with what looked like an elaborate coral reef climbing up one side. Mesmerized, Juniper tiptoed into the living room for a closer look. The fish were far too vivid to be freshwater, and the gently waving anemones looked too real to be plastic. It was an exotic salt water tank.

For a few minutes, all Juniper could do was admire. Then she realized that she was essentially snooping in a stranger's house uninvited and turned to hurry back to the kitchen. But something caught her eye as she left. A door with opaque glass panels beside the fish tank had been left ajar. Behind it was a study: a scratched, obviously secondhand desk; an ergonomic chair; a stout, practical filing cabinet. But none of those things had grabbed her attention. It was the wall behind the desk that pierced Juniper like a hook.

The wall was filled with photos and clipped newspaper articles, Post-it Notes scrawled with words she couldn't read at a distance, and a handful of bold headings printed on stark white paper: *Tate Brothers, Franklin Tate, Carver Groen, Transient, Murder/Suicide, Jonathan Baker*. For a moment Juniper felt like she was falling, and she put a hand on the doorframe to stop herself from tipping into the sharp edge of the fish tank. A hinge groaned, but she hardly noticed. Everett had turned the wall of his office into a crime board: a scrapbook of clues and motives, suspects and alibis that rivaled her own. He wasn't kidding when he said he was taking another look at the Murphy murders.

Did he know about what was happening now? The calls and drive-bys, the insidious harassment of the most likely suspect? More important, what did Everett know that she *didn't?*

The room spun when Juniper turned from the door, but she was already calculating how quickly she could race back to her car to grab her phone. Would she have time to get it and snap a few pictures before Everett was done changing out of his uniform?

She was nearly in the kitchen when Everett emerged from a room down the hall. He was wearing a pair of jeans and a plain navy sweatshirt. His hair was mussed from when he pulled the crewneck over his head. Everett's thin smile made Juniper painfully aware of the wild knock of her heart, but she forced a grin and said, "You have a fish tank! Is it salt water?" She hoped she didn't sound breathless.

"You're welcome to take a closer look," Everett said. His voice was light, but he stared at her for a moment as if searching for something in her gaze. Did he know? Could he tell that she had looked inside his study? Clearly his interest in the Murphy murders bordered on obsession.

"I've lost track of time," Juniper said. "I'm so sorry, but Mandy's expecting me, and I don't want to keep her waiting. I really just stopped to see if you could squeeze me into your schedule sometime soon."

"Call the police department," he told her. "Susan will be able to take care of you."

He was blowing her off again. Juniper forced one last smile and chatted about the weather while she pulled on her shoes and zipped up her coat. Everett's goodbye was friendly enough, but as she pulled out of the driveway, Juniper could see him in the window, watching her.

It was almost noon when Juniper arrived at the hospital. Worry prowled in her gut as she steeled herself for what she would face inside. Reb had told her in unnecessarily great detail what Jonathan looked like, what machines he was hooked up to, and how the ICU was laid out. ECMO, or extracorporeal membrane oxygenation, was a form of cardiac and pulmonary life support that cycled Jonathan's blood through his body because his heart and lungs weren't capable of performing the necessary functions on their own. It was a lifesaving measure that would afford him time to rest and recover, but it felt like a last-ditch effort. A Hail Mary. The thought was terrifying.

Juniper hurried through the cold parking garage, coat clutched tight against her throat, and waited in silence as the elevator carried her up to the third floor. When the doors slid open, she followed the signs down the hallway and lifted the red receiver outside the locked ICU.

She carefully stated her name and the patient she had come to see, and after a log was checked and double-checked, the metal lock clicked open and she finally stepped inside.

The ICU smelled of antiseptic and recycled air. Just like any other hospital. But unlike other hospital visits, a nurse was waiting on the other side of the locked door to escort her to a small family waiting room where Mandy was slumped in a chair, head tipped back against the wall and eyes closed.

"Hi, Mandy," Juniper said softly.

Her sister-in-law opened her eyes and managed to pull her mouth into a semblance of a smile. She didn't move to get up, so Juniper went to her and bent down to wrap Mandy in a hug. "It's good to see you," she said. But the truth was, it was hard to see her. Mandy was a shell of the woman she had been only days ago. Her eyes were dark and sunken, her skin gray. It was obvious that she hadn't washed her hair in a while, because it hung lank and dull against her ashen cheeks.

"Here." Juniper took Mandy by the shoulders and turned her so that she could reach the back of her head. She deftly finger-combed her sister-in-law's loose waves, then pulled them into a French braid. Juniper was wearing a hair elastic like a bracelet and slipped it off her wrist to wrap it around the end of the improvised hairdo. When she was done, she gave Mandy's upper arms a squeeze.

"Thank you." Mandy's eyes welled with tears.

"Don't. It's just a braid."

"June . . ." A tear spilled down Mandy's cheek and she whispered: "I'm scared."

Juniper hugged her. "I know," she said. But she didn't want Mandy to fall down that dark hole, and quickly steered the conversation in a different direction. "Where are Law and Reb?"

"They went downstairs to grab some coffee." Mandy pulled back with a heavy sigh. "They're here all the time, June. All. The. Time. It's . . ."

"Exhausting?" Juniper offered. "Difficult, frustrating, annoying?"

That elicited a laugh from Mandy. It was short-lived as a hiccup. "Yes. All of those things. I love them, I do, but—"

"No need to explain. Why do you think I live in Colorado?"

"Smart girl." Mandy sounded wistful. "I wish I could fly away from all of this." Immediately, her gaze snapped to Juniper's and her eyes brimmed with remorse. "I don't mean that. I love Jonathan. I—"

Juniper shushed her. "This is hell, Mandy. I want to fly away too. You don't have to apologize for how you feel. Go get a cup of coffee. A bottle of wine. Do they sell wine in the cafeteria?"

"No." Mandy's lips held a fragile smile. "They

should. But there's a Starbucks around the corner. Maybe . . . ?"

"Go. I gotta talk to Jonathan about a few things anyway. I'll keep him company while you drink a large latte or two and do the crossword."

"I'm more of a *Better Homes and Gardens* kind of girl."

"Perfect. Grab yourself a magazine to go with your frothy coffee. Take your time."

"Thanks, Junebug."

Mandy hoisted herself to her feet and shambled down the hallway like an old woman. It hurt Juniper to watch her go, but she swallowed a shaky breath and steeled her resolve. After taking a moment to collect herself, Juniper approached the triage desk in the hallway. The ICU rooms fanned behind the low work counter, glass windows ensuring the patients were visible at all times. They were indistinguishable from here, bodies in beds attached to a network of machines that put Juniper in mind of the worst sort of science fiction. She felt like she should know which one was Jonathan, as if they were truly twins and shared a connection that went molecule-deep. But she didn't, and it wasn't until she had scrubbed in and donned shoe coverings, gloves, a gown, and a mask that she was finally taken to where he lay.

"He's in isolation because of the risk of infection," a nurse explained. She had frosted hair and matching silver wire-framed glasses that sparkled in the fluorescent lights. She looked like someone's fun grandmother. "Pneumonia is common in cases like his, but we don't want to tempt fate unnecessarily. Please don't remove any of your protective gear while you're inside the room."

"Okay."

The nurse smiled gently. "And you can't touch him. He gets agitated when we touch him, so we're keeping contact to a minimum. But you can talk to him all you'd like. In fact, please do. Tell him who you are. Talk about pleasant things, fond memories and the like."

It was a lot to take in. Juniper wanted to ask the nurse if it was a good sign that Jonathan became agitated when touched, but she was too busy worrying about what to say to him. Their past was littered with snares that she was sure would sabotage any progress he was making, but the present was filled with uncertainty, too. Juniper realized that there was much she didn't know about her brother. Although they remained close on the surface, it had been a long time since they had confided in each other like the best friends they had been. In many ways, Juniper was walking into the room of a stranger. The room of a man that she wasn't entirely sure she could trust.

The nurse opened the door for her and moved

over to the bed, where she examined complicated machines and checked levels that Juniper couldn't begin to understand. She must have found everything to be satisfactory, because in less than a minute she was patting Juniper on the arm and leaving them alone. The door closed with a soft thud behind her.

Jonathan was beset by an invasion of tubes. In both arms, his neck, his mouth, and snaking out from under a thin blanket. Still more were attached to his chest, his fingers, and coiled beside his swollen cheek. Reb had tried to prepare her, but everything was alien and terrifying, whooshing and pumping, filling the room with the soft hiss and whir of artificial life. Jonathan was in there somewhere, buried beneath the weight of all they had done to stop him from slipping out of his body and away. Juniper balked especially at the thick red pipe that so clearly cycled oxygenated blood into the vulnerable stretch of his pale throat, but she forced herself to take a few steps forward. To find his face beneath the towers of machines that surrounded him.

Jonathan. He was as still as a wax doll and puffy from all the extra fluid he had needed in those first awful days, but recognizable. His hair was charcoal against the white pillow and just a little too long, and even now Juniper envied his lashes. She smiled in spite of herself, and felt something inside of her crack.

"What have you done?" she whispered. And then, more loudly. "Hi, Jonathan. It's me, June."

There was a flurry of activity on one of the machines. She moved closer.

"I sent Mandy out for a coffee. I bet you'd like a dark roast right about now, wouldn't you?" She felt kind of stupid babbling at him, but there was a surge of energy in the room that made her step closer still. Maybe it was adrenaline. Maybe it was raw hope that he could hear her and was even now swimming back from the deep.

"You have to come back to us," Juniper said. "Mandy needs you. The boys need you. I need you."

Was she doing it right? Juniper had no idea, but suddenly there were a thousand things she wanted to tell her brother. Important things she should have said, and frivolous nothings that didn't matter at all. She wanted to ask him if he had any idea who was harassing him, and what had happened all those years ago. She wanted to apologize.

"Juniper and Jonathan." She smiled faintly. "When we were little it sounded like one word: *juniperandjonathan*. As if one couldn't exist without the other."

Something shifted. It was a quickening, a blip on the monitors that cataloged everything from Jonathan's kidney output to his brain activity. But before she could truly start to worry about it, the nurse with the silver glasses was back, her face a professional mask, her pace disclosing concern.

"Someone likes you," she said, catching Juniper's eye as she leaned over Jonathan. Then she turned her full attention to her patient. "Good morning, Mr. Baker. Are you thinking you might join us today?"

Juniper's heart stopped and then started back up painfully. She reached for her brother's hand, but caught herself at the last moment.

"Jonathan," the nurse called again, a bit more forcefully this time. "Are you with us?"

His eyelids twitched; Juniper saw it happen. But it was over in less than a second and she was left wondering if she had dreamed it or if Jonathan had flickered to the surface, if only for a single heartbeat. The nurse called his name a few more times, adjusted a dial that meant nothing to Juniper, and then straightened up with a small sigh.

"Keep talking," the nurse said. "Pull up a chair and tell him a story. Maybe today will be the day."

Her smile was reassuring, the hope she dished up carefully measured. Juniper accepted it gratefully, but somehow she knew that Jonathan wasn't going to wake up today.

After seeing what she saw in Everett's make-shift incident room, she was afraid that Jonathan didn't want to wake up at all.

CHAPTER 10

SUMMER
14 AND A HALF YEARS AGO

My mother's garden is an institution—and a ridiculous amount of work. Law tills the ground in the spring, then covers it in manure. Jonathan and I are set the very unsexy task of turning the soil by hand, layering in the natural fertilizer with metal rakes and sharp-cornered hoes. By the time the job is complete, we reek of dirt and sweet manure, and our fingernails are rimmed black.

After planting, the long, narrow rows seem to pop up overnight. Sugar snap peas climb bamboo teepees, and radishes sprout white stems with pretty, round leaves. When I was a little girl, I used to hide beneath the arching vines, popping cherry tomatoes like they were candy. I liked the purple ones the best. Still do.

But I don't like the hot hours it requires to weed and thin. It's humid where the earth exhales, and I'm sweating even though the sun is still low in the east. It doesn't help that Mom recruited Jonathan, too, and he's complaining down the row beside me.

"I should be at work," he mutters, adjusting the old towel he's kneeling on. The bark mulch Mom

173

spreads between the rows is chopped from our own felled trees and promises splinters. Jonathan and I are both in impractical shorts and making use of Mom's extensive stash of gardening supplies with little success. I peel off the pink nitrile-coated gloves I'm wearing and throw one at him.

"Why aren't you?" I ask as it bounces off his shoulder.

"We're between jobs. Nothing to do today." He tosses the glove back at me, but I don't want it. My hands are slick, and the rubber is stinky and damp. I'll take the dirty fingernails, the invisible cuts that won't hurt until I wash my hands later.

When I offered to help Mom with the garden, I thought we'd have some time alone together. My mother is a woman of few words, but they seem to flow a bit more freely when she gardens. With her hands in the ground she thinks less about the careful formation of each sentence, the way that others might perceive her opinions. I'm not sure what makes my mom so timid to express her own thoughts and ideas, so I love the times she lets loose even a little. But instead of joining me this morning, she conscripted Jonathan and then left with Law for town. I was not planning on a morning alone with my brother. I've avoided him for over an hour, working a row over and intentionally going in the opposite direction, but he's on to me.

After we finish up with the feathery carrots, Jonathan circles back around the garden to take a swig from the jug of ice water I'm currently drinking from. I hand it over when I'm done and wipe my mouth with the back of my hand. He drinks, says, "Let's stick together. I'll follow you."

Small talk. It's my only defense, and I prattle on about work and Ashley's mom's unreasonable expectations, and the fact that I think Reb is writing new music. Our mother doesn't compose often, but when she does start scribbling notes on staff paper, it usually means something. I secretly believe she's writing now because she doesn't quite know what to do with the fact that I'm leaving home. I wonder if she'll play it for me. Maybe it's a gift.

"Mom hasn't played the Braga in months," Jonathan says. He's huffy, but I don't know why. "If you'd listen, you'd know, too."

"I do listen," I tell him. I'm not sure what I've done to upset him, but of course I know that Mom only composes on one cello. The Braga is special. It was a gift from her grandfather when Mom turned eighteen and still dreamed of playing in a famous symphony orchestra. According to family lore, he sold an antique car to purchase it, and Mom's dad (an intractable man who died before I was born and whose name makes Reb's jaw tighten to this day) told him it was a waste of money. But Great-Grandpa Jordan believed that Mom had what it took, maybe even for a solo career and a single spotlight. The honey-colored sheen of the full-sized instrument would glow golden beneath the stage lights. Too bad it never did.

Years later, the cello still sounds like velvet and fine red wine, and even I can tell the difference in the quality of sound when she takes it out of the felt-lined case. Mom's "everyday cello," as she likes to call it, is perfectly functional and much less expensive. She uses it for teaching lessons and trying new music.

"You're so clueless," Jonathan says coldly.

"What do you mean?" I sit back on my haunches to watch my brother wrestle with himself. This is unfamiliar territory for us—Jonathan and I are never at a loss for words, and rarely fight. Suddenly the distance between us feels like a chasm.

"Forget it."

"Hey," I plead. "What's going on?"

Jonathan rubs his hands over his face, leaving behind a streak of mud that cuts from cheekbone to jaw. He looks exhausted and sad, and I want to step over the plants between us and wrap him in a hug. I don't dare.

"I'm stressed," he says finally. "Tired. We've put in fourteen-hour days this week."

It's a perfectly reasonable explanation for

his current mood. But I don't buy it. Jonathan is annoyingly easygoing, optimistic to a fault. Seeing him like this—as if the weight of the world is on his shoulders—isn't just unusual, it's unnerving. "Does this have something to do with the Murphys?" I ask.

"Does what have something to do with the Murphys?"

I jump at the unexpected sound of a voice from someone just behind me. Whipping around on my knees, I find Cal Murphy standing in the row a couple of feet away, hands in his pockets and a sheepish look on his face.

"Sorry," he says. "Didn't mean to startle you."

"It's fine," Jonathan answers for me. He's already on his feet, brushing dirt off his palms. "We were just about to take a break."

I giggle, hand pressed to my heart. "You scared me!" I accuse. The conversation has unraveled, and I'm grateful that Cal doesn't press me to explain why we were talking about him. Jonathan reaches over the row and pulls me to my feet, and I wobble a little unsteadily on the mulch, heart still racing.

"Sorry," Cal says again. "I should've called. Beth is working on some paperwork and I thought I'd walk over to see if I could catch Rebecca. Is she around?"

I slide my gaze to Jonathan and realize that he doesn't seem surprised by Cal's request as much as he seems angry. His mouth is a thin white line. "My parents are in town," he says.

"Do you know when they'll be back?"

I'm about to tell him that they just ran to the hardware store—with maybe a quick stop for a few groceries or a coffee at Cunningham's—but one look at Jonathan stops me short.

"We're pretty busy today." He puts his hands on his hips.

"Well," Cal says, "maybe tomorrow, then."

I can tell Cal is as confused as I am by Jonathan's behavior, but he smiles and appears to shake it off. "The garden sure looks good." He crouches down and brushes the tops of a row of bean sprouts with his fingers. "Heirlooms?"

"I think so," I say, when it becomes obvious that Jonathan isn't going to field this one.

Many of the seed husks are still attached to the new sprouts, and Cal carefully lifts one off a green bud. "Those labels might have gotten mixed up," he tells me, holding out the shell in the palm of his hand. It's light brown and speckled like a cardinal's egg.

I shrug. "I'll let her know."

"Does Rebecca use chemicals?" Cal asks. He pushes himself up, brushing his hands on his jeans and leaving behind dark smears.

I'm not sure how to answer this question to his satisfaction, but I don't have to consider my options for long. As I watch, a fast line of red snakes out of Cal's left nostril and begins to slip off his upper lip. The first drop lands in a splotch on his T-shirt, a crimson oval that looks almost exactly like a bullet wound. I can't quite register what I'm seeing, but Jonathan leaps forward.

"Cal! You're bleeding!" Jonathan reaches him in a second, but there's nothing he can do. He fumbles in his pockets for a tissue, for something, anything, but comes up empty-handed except for a bit of loose change and a crumpled gum wrapper.

By now, Cal's nose is bleeding freely, his T-shirt a ruin of red and his mouth slick and gory. I've had bloody noses before, but this is shocking. The thought flashes through my mind that he's dying before our eyes, of an aneurism or some horrific and unnamed disease. But Cal is unfazed.

"It's nothing," he says, tilting back his head and trying to stop the flow by pinching the bridge of his nose. I can tell that this won't help at all.

"Here." I grab the towel I was kneeling on and thrust it at him. It's ragged at the edges and peppered with dust and splinters, but Cal grabs it and presses it blindly to his face.

"Thank you," he mumbles from behind the dirty cloth. And then, again, "Sorry."

"Stop apologizing." I can't tell if he's embarrassed about the nosebleed or if there's something about the Baker farm and his business here that's bothering him. Either way, I can't take another apology.

"What can I do to help?" Jonathan has moved to stand beside Cal, one hand hovering behind his back. His eyebrows are knit together, his shoulders bent and miserable.

"Nothing, nothing," comes the muffled reply. "I'll be just fine."

But the dark stain on the towel seems to grow by the second, the fabric turning soggy and heavy with Cal's blood.

"I think we need to go to the ER," Jonathan says. He curls one arm around Cal and starts leading him in the direction of the driveway and his truck. Jonathan is just a little taller than Cal, and more than a little broader, and the older man allows himself to be led away. Cal is all leathery skin and tight, ropy muscle, but he looks like a child in Jonathan's half embrace, the salt-and-pepper tuft of his hair bobbing as they make uneven progress across the grass.

I jog to catch up. "I'm coming," I say without thinking, because what can I possibly do?

"No," Jonathan says at the same moment that Cal murmurs something from behind the towel. It's muffled, but the message is clear: I'm not welcome. "Call Beth."

And then Cal is buckled in the passenger side of Jonathan's beat-up old truck, his head thrown back against the headrest and hands pressed to the towel against his face, sticky with drying blood. Jonathan slams the door and hurries around the front of the truck. I catch him before he can swing open the driver's-side door.

"What's going on?"

"Cal has a bloody nose."

"Save it," I hiss. "There's more to it than that and you know it."

"Not now, June." Jonathan shrugs off my hand and yanks open the door, forcing me to hop back or risk breaking my nose on rusted steel.

The truck roars to life and Jonathan throws it in reverse, spitting gravel and making me spin away from the dusty cloud. When they're gone, I'm left coughing into the crook of my elbow. There's a narrow scrape of blood along my forearm and I have no idea how it got there.

Jonathan texts me Beth's number and one word: *clinic*. So he's taken Cal to the small Jericho medical clinic and emergency room instead of to the nearest hospital in Munroe. I don't blame him—it's a forty-five-minute drive to the hospital, and it certainly seemed like it was just a bloody nose. An aggressive, almost *violent* bloody nose, but a minor medical event all the same. Still, when I call Beth to tell her what happened, she hangs up after only a few moments without saying goodbye.

I'm left feeling jittery and shaken, but I know that if I go inside for a glass of lemonade or a cool break in the air-conditioning, I won't have it in me to come back out. Law doesn't like unfinished tasks, and I'm not about to explain to him what happened this morning, so I head back to the garden to finish up.

The mulch where Cal was standing is splattered with blood. I know that it will be black soon, an earthy, unrecognizable stain in the garden, but I kick the wood chips over it all the same. Then I scratch the blood from my arm with a fingernail, wondering for half a second if I should worry about getting sick from whatever made Cal bleed. But it's such a tiny amount, and I'm healthy as a horse. I push all thoughts of illness from my mind and try to focus on the task at hand.

By the time Law and Reb pull down the long driveway, I've wrapped up the last bit. I can feel that my cheeks are flushed, and my forearms are sprinkled with dirt that stands out against my pale freckles. I hope I look normal. Tired and dirty and normal. Not like my mind is racing and my heart pinched by the fact that I haven't heard a single word from Jonathan, good or bad.

"Nice job!" Mom calls, shielding her eyes with her hand as she steps out of the car. She can't possibly see what I've done from where she's standing, but it doesn't matter.

I wave back. "Thanks!"

"Where's Jonathan?" Law squints at me.

"He left a little bit ago." I jog across the lawn to take the brown paper bag my mom offers, and shift it to one arm so I have room for another. She loads me up again and we fall in step on our way to the house. Law's hands are free, so he lengthens his stride and swings open the door for us.

"What do you mean, he left?"

"It's no big deal. We were almost done anyway." The air-conditioning hits me like a splash of cool water. I set my bags on the kitchen table and lean against the counter to drink it in.

"But where did he go?"

I've turned this conversation over and over in my mind. I knew Law would ask and I knew I would have to come up with an acceptable answer. But lying is tricky, so I decide to keep it simple and true. "Cal and Beth needed help with something."

He's obviously frustrated, but to his credit, Law doesn't say anything. In fact, he reaches into one of the bags and starts unloading groceries.

I have never had to wonder if Lawrence loves my mother. They don't hug or kiss in front of Jonathan and me—for which I am eternally grateful—but he's gentle with her. He makes her tea when she's busy with her strings lessons, carefully setting the cup on the closed top of the baby grand piano in the sunroom turned music hall. Law even knows not to set the hot mug on the pretty walnut stain of the piano, and always makes sure to use a folder or some sheet music as a coaster. And he rubs her shoulders when she's tense, his huge hands dwarfing her tiny frame but somehow managing to be gentle enough that she closes her eyes and sighs.

I know that Law is a good husband. He's just not much of a father. Sometimes I get the feeling he wishes it was just *Lawrence & Rebecca* instead of *The Baker Family*. I get it: I'm not his real daughter. And we don't have much in common. I'm chatty and quick to laugh, determined and independent. Law's quiet and reserved, and he relies on Mom for everything from his fried eggs before work in the morning (three, over easy, with edges crisped brown in butter) to laundry and directions. When we drive somewhere together, he waits for her to say: "Turn right, Lawrence. And then the next left." They hardly go anywhere without each other. Law is huge, I'm small. He's rough around the edges and clumsy and provincial. I long for the twinkle of city lights.

My expectations are low when it comes to my stepdad. But it always surprises me when Law fumbles his relationship with Jonathan.

"When will he be back?" Law asks as he rearranges things in the refrigerator.

"Didn't say."

"Text him and find out."

I'd like to point out that I'm not my brother's keeper, but I'd earn myself a nugget of Law's ever-ready wisdom and I'm not in the mood. I pull my phone out of my back pocket and tap:

Home soon? Everything okay?

The reply comes quicker than I expected.

Heading to the Murphys. Home later.

How's Cal?

But Jonathan never responds.

"Home soon," I tell Law, slipping my phone back into my pocket.

He's done in the refrigerator and closes it with a thud. "I need him to help me reset the fence."

"So go get him," Mom says. She puts down the towel that she was using to wipe the counter. "I'll go with you."

"Forget it."

"I wouldn't mind picking up a jar of their blueberry-rhubarb jam—"

"I said no. I'll do it myself." Law walks away, and in a moment I hear the side door open, and then the accompanying slam.

"What was that all about?"

But Mom just stands there, worrying the edge

of the dishtowel with her fingers. Her hands are the hands of a seventy-year-old, and the only part of her body that matches her husband. "Dirt and water and babies," she told me once. "My hands were ruined by the three elements." She doesn't say anything now.

"You okay?" I ask for what seems like the hundredth time today. Jonathan is not okay, and Cal is not okay. Clearly Law is in a huff, and Mom looks like she might burst into tears. I feel like I am on the outside looking in, trapped behind glass as the world explodes before me. I have absolutely no idea what's going on. Or why.

When she doesn't answer, I finally say: "Want me to pick up a jar of that jam?" I have no idea if the Murphys' stand is open—I'd doubt it, considering they were just at the clinic—but I can pull strings. Jonathan once showed me where Cal kept the little brass key to the stone building (behind a loose rock just beneath the farthest windowsill), and I have no problem letting myself in and leaving behind some money for a jar of the blueberry-rhubarb my mother loves. Suddenly I want to do this for her so badly I can hardly stand it. She looks wistful, and I want to fill whatever hole is making her heart ache. I wonder if this is what Law feels when he crushes mint for her tea.

But Mom shakes her head. "No thanks. We

have plenty of strawberry jam here. I don't know what I was thinking."

"You were thinking you'd like something different."

She smiles at me, her brown eyes softening. "Don't we all think that, all the time?"

I'm not sure what to say to that, and after a moment Mom pats my arm. "Ignore me. Guess I'm feeling out of sorts."

Me too.

And I *do* decide to ignore her, to get the jam anyway, but as I jog down the porch steps, Sullivan's truck turns down our long drive. His window is wide open, and he smiles and waves me over.

"What are you doing here?" I ask him, trying not to sound as wary as I feel. I hang back, hoping he hasn't come for me.

"I have to make a delivery in Munroe and thought you might like to ride along." He grins and leans over to lift something from the passenger seat. It's a puppy. A wriggling, caramel-colored bundle of Golden Retriever perfection, and I melt like ice cream on a hot July day. "Are you a dog person?"

I don't answer, but Sullivan is holding the puppy out to me, and against my better judgment I take a few steps forward and fold it into my arms. I'm only human. The puppy smells of sawdust and sweet milk, and even though I should hand him back to Sullivan and walk away, I nuzzle his downy neck and feel the rest of my resolve crumble.

"This is the last of our Molly's pups. We sold him to a family in Munroe, and I could really use someone to keep him occupied while I drive."

Damn, he's smooth. Sullivan is playing me like my mother's cello, but even though I can spot his tactics from a mile away, I can't resist the squeaky whine of the ball of fur in my arms. I should lecture him about Baxter, tell him I'm not interested, and send him on his way. Instead, I lift the puppy to my face. "Hey, sweet thing. You want me to come?" I whisper. I'm rewarded with a lick.

"I think that's a yes," Sullivan says.

"You're a terrible person," I tell him. "Sneaky and manipulative and—"

"Yeah, yeah."

"If I go with you, it has everything to do with the puppy and nothing to—"

"Just get in the truck."

And I do. Heaven help me, I do.

CHAPTER 11

WINTER
TODAY

Juniper didn't stay at the hospital long. When she left Jonathan's bedside, she found her parents standing in the hallway, watching the door to their son's ICU room with expressions that seemed more guarded than hopeful. It was clear by the loose cuffs of Reb's sweater that she had been stretching the fabric in her balled fists, and Law's shoulders were so tight and close to his ears that Juniper knew it would take weeks to work out the knots in his tense muscles. A burst of pity bloomed in her chest. It was unnerving to see her parents so reduced. They had powered through her entire childhood and beyond with hard work and Midwestern pragmatism, but it was obvious that Jonathan's accident had shaken loose the bedrock. Law and Reb seemed to have aged years in a matter of days.

"Hey," Juniper said, pulling her mother into an embrace. Reb responded with a few limp pats on her back. "How are you two holding up?"

"Fine," Law responded. But his jaw stiffened as if he was holding back tears.

"Are you sleeping okay? Eating? You feel skinny, Mom."

"I'm fine." Reb pulled away and tugged the sleeves of her sweater over her hands, making fists with the droopy fabric. "Never liked hospitals much."

"Amen to that." Juniper began to strip off the protective gear that she had worn into Jonathan's room. It was light as air and obviously disposable. Within seconds it was all packed down into a ball that she tucked under one arm because there was no garbage can immediately visible. As the silence pooled between them, Juniper wondered if she should invite her parents out for lunch or offer to grab them something from the cafeteria. Maybe they needed a few basic necessities, toiletries or a bottle of ibuprofen, but before she could offer anything, Law narrowed his eyes at her.

"The nurses tell us that Jonathan responded to you."

"I don't know about that." Juniper shrugged. "It certainly didn't seem significant to me."

"What happened?" Reb asked, her voice tremulous and bright.

"Not much. I was talking to him and a few machines started to beep. The nurse came to check on him, but it was nothing. Jonathan's still . . . sleeping."

"What did you talk about?"

Juniper couldn't imagine what difference it made. "Nothing. Nothing important, anyway."

But in a flash of sudden, absurd disregard for an unspoken family rule, she added, "I wanted to talk to him about the Murphys."

The air around them seemed to freeze and shatter. At least, it felt that way to Juniper. Clearly Mandy was right: Law and Reb didn't know about how Jonathan was being tormented. Juniper hugged the wad of protective coverings to her chest and tried to suppress the current that pulsed through her limbs. She had done this. She had made her mother's face crumble like dry earth between her fingers. *I'm sorry.* The words rose to her lips, but she didn't speak them.

The Bakers didn't talk about what happened. Ever. It wasn't explicitly forbidden, but it was understood that to mention the murders of Cal and Beth Murphy was to call into question everything they feigned to be true. There were too many uncertainties, too many unanswered questions. So many things they couldn't say without inflicting irrevocable damage. But the alleged podcast, Jonathan's harassment, and Everett's makeshift incident room had convinced her the truth would come out. And they all had to be prepared for it.

Of course, her parents knew none of that. Lawrence was glaring at her, and Reb's eyes were swimming. "How could you?" Law said through gritted teeth.

Juniper took a tiny step back. "We have to

talk about this. What if Jonathan's accident has something to do with what happened?"

"That's ridiculous," Law hissed.

It wasn't, but she couldn't tell them about the private conversation she was supposed to have with Jonathan, her necklace that was found in his pocket, or the newspaper clippings and photographs that she had seen in Everett's house. She just wanted to tip off her parents so that when everything blew sky-high, they weren't incinerated by the blast.

"I think we need to be ready," Juniper said, lifting her chin so she could hold Law's gaze. "People are going to ask questions. They already are. We can't pretend they're not justified."

"And you can't pretend to know anything about us." Law's words were razor-sharp. "You've been gone a long time, Juniper Grace."

Know your place. Law didn't say it, but Juniper could read between the lines. It was the undercurrent of her life with her family, the careful boundaries that silenced her when the Murphys were killed, and then relegated her to little more than big sister status when Willa was born. Juniper couldn't deny that at nineteen years old she was terrifyingly young and unprepared to be a mother, and when Reb heroically stepped into the role, Juniper had been relieved. But that didn't make it right. Juniper understood now that she had probably been suffering from

PTSD and postpartum depression. She had needed professional help, not to be edged out of her daughter's life and sent off to college as if nothing had happened.

All of Juniper's questions about the night the Murphys were killed—and now, about Jonathan's fall through the ice—deserved to be heard. She wasn't going to be silenced this time.

"I'm sorry you feel that way," Juniper said. And then she walked away. She didn't feel bad about leaving her parents, but it hurt to go without getting the chance to say goodbye to Mandy. Instead, Juniper texted her:

Had to go. I'm so sorry. Back soon.

She hoped it was enough.

Juniper wasn't supposed to pick up Willa until after supper, but she found herself pulling into Jericho when the late afternoon light was just starting to bleed away on the horizon. It was snowing again, big, fat flakes that were postcard perfect but deceptively dangerous because they stuck to the road almost immediately. Her rental was the safest place for her, but Juniper didn't want to go there alone. She thought about popping in on Cora, or maybe seeing if Barry wanted to grab a bite to eat, but she dismissed both of those options without much thought. Juniper drove right through town and out the other side, not even sure where she was going until she found herself turning down County Road 21.

The old Murphy place was still picturesque in a run-down, forgotten way. A few renters had circled in and out of the farmhouse, but they never lasted long. Sober Midwesterners weren't prone to superstition, but there was something about the ramshackle acreage that conjured spirits. Juniper suspected she was one of the only people in Jericho who would call it what it really was: haunted.

Her tracks would show in the inch of snow on the curving driveway, but all at once Juniper didn't care. She needed to be here. Flicking on her blinker even though the road was abandoned, she crunched gravel and ice beneath her tires and pulled up beside the old coop where Beth had once sold dahlias the color of sunrise and pale, speckled eggs. Now the stones were sagging, the windows empty-eyed and jagged with smashed glass. The door that Cal had painted turquoise was gone completely.

She found she didn't dare to disturb the isolation of the farmstead further. She put her car in park beside the dilapidated roadside stand and crossed her arms over her chest, shivering in spite of the heat that blasted out of the vents. She studied the Murphys' buildings, the sloping property that had once been a jewel in the county.

Sadly, the rest of the buildings hadn't fared much better than the coop. The front porch of the farmhouse was slanting, and a few spindles had decayed and fallen loose. Sticks and bits of hay peeked out of birds' nests that had been built under the eaves, and she would have put money on the fact that other wildlife had taken up residence beneath the steps.

It took some effort for Juniper to drag her gaze to the barn, but when she managed it, she found that it wasn't nearly as horrifying as she feared it would be. It was just a barn, faded red and tilted slightly as if it couldn't help but hunch beneath the terrible weight of all it had seen. How sad it seemed. How quickly the world fell apart when there was no one around to shore it up.

She wasn't sure what she expected, but nothing happened as she sat in the driveway. She didn't cry or fall to pieces or remember everything in a flash of conviction. Instead, she thought of moments here. The day she rode her bike over to buy a jar of her mom's favorite jam. Cal had tucked the little mason jar in a brown paper bag and threw in a bar of soap, too.

"It's a new scent we're trying," he told her. "Blueberry-rhubarb, just like the jam."

Her mother had smelled tart and sweet for weeks. Juniper couldn't get enough of her and tucked herself beneath her mother's arm every chance she got.

Or the time she and Jonathan spent the night when their parents took a trip to Des Moines. If Juniper remembered correctly, there was a symphony orchestra traveling through and the tickets had been a Christmas present. But that was of little consequence, because Juniper and Jonathan were ten and nine, respectively, and sleepovers were few and far between. June had been pulled taut between excitement and dread in the week leading up to the big overnight, but when Reb dropped them off the morning they left, it became clear that there was absolutely nothing for her to be scared of.

"Cal's setting up the tent in the backyard!" Beth told them with a grin. "We'll make Dutch oven pizza over the fire for supper, and I bought everything for s'mores . . ." Her eyes twinkled as the possibilities unfurled like the whisper of pixie dust.

Their stay had been the stuff of children's books and folktales. They played hide-and-seek with Cal in the hayloft, found a nest of kittens, took turns riding the pony. When the cicadas began to sing, Beth lifted the lid off her black Dutch oven to reveal a brown, bubbling pizza wrapped in parchment paper like a present. It had seemed like bright magic to June, the sort of whimsy a good fairy might conjure. Later, fingers gooey with melted marshmallow, she fell asleep leaning back-to-back with Jonathan, and when she woke, she was tucked in a sleeping bag with the stars alight above her.

Had that happened? Juniper was sure that it had.

But it was hard to imagine that there had ever been happiness here. Laughter that echoed down to the shallow creek, and glossy bouquets held together with twine in the sparkling windows of the roadside stand.

Before she knew what she was doing, she wrenched open the car door and stepped out into the snow. It was falling hard and fast and was already accumulating in the grooves left by her tires, smoothing out the tracks. This was a totally unexpected storm that would likely end in the morning with water dripping like rain from tree branches and snowdrops blossoming through the white crust of ice. The kind of storm that could leave her stranded in this cursed place, calling for help because her wheels could no longer gain purchase on the slippery drive.

The inside of the stand was filled with paraphernalia. A long, narrow table missing a leg, a rail-back chair, some dusty crates with "Coca-Cola" painted on the side that would make an antiques dealer drool. It was dusty, but still, and Juniper stepped tentatively inside, avoiding the largest hunks of glass that littered the ground. Nothing changed. No flutter of wings or scuffle of clawed feet against the hard-packed dirt floor.

A few more steps and she was standing by the counter where Cal and Beth had proudly displayed their goods. The windows were French casement that could be swung wide so passersby were free to admire the buckets of flowers and soaps Beth had carefully arranged in glass jars, vintage crates, and on a chipped ceramic cake plate. The produce had beckoned from the window closest to the road, the siren call of gleaming bell peppers and bunches of slender green beans too tempting to ignore. It seemed like a dream to picture the coop the way it had been, though Juniper could close her eyes and smell the fresh tang of sun-ripened tomatoes.

Running her fingers lightly over the worn boards, Juniper scanned the small building for a remnant of what had been. A crate was too big, the penny she saw glinting in the dirt too ordinary. She wanted something distinctly *Murphy*. A token, a talisman. Juniper found it hanging on a rusty nail beside the farthest window. *Tags,* she realized when she reached for the dull glint. Two of them on a wire loop; an orange one that said RABIES VACC with a five-digit number, and a second that read BAXTER. Juniper realized that Cal or Beth must have hung them here as a reminder after he died.

Pocketing the tags was a bittersweet feeling, but Juniper headed toward the door with a renewed sense of purpose.

She didn't make it far.

The clouds were low and hushed, blanketing the sky and making it seem as if Juniper could hear every snowflake as it struck the earth. So when a vehicle came down the road, it was a racket she couldn't ignore. Juniper froze, praying the truck would speed on by, but she could hear it slowing even as her heart began to race. Her breath exploded in quick white puffs that evaporated in the cold air. There was no reason to think that the truck would pull onto the Murphys' old property. It had been abandoned for years. And yet, her car was a beacon against all that fresh snow, an aberration that would be noticeable not just because of its presence, but because the engine was still running and it was emitting a steady plume of gray smoke.

The truck turned. Juniper's car was parked maybe twenty yards from the road, directly across from where she was hiding in the chicken coop turned roadside stand. It was foolish to try and hide—she was trapped now—but she took a step deeper into the shadows of the low building anyway. Through the bank of windows she watched a silver pickup pull up behind her car. A moment later the door opened.

"Hello?"

It was a man in a heavy work jacket and jeans, his features obscured by an arm that he threw up to shield his face from the onslaught of snow.

"Who's there?" he called, but Juniper couldn't tell if he was angry or merely curious.

What choice did she have? Juniper swallowed a deep breath and stepped into the rectangle of wan light spilling through the doorframe.

"Hi," she said, raising a hand sheepishly. "Sorry, I was just—"

"June."

When he lowered his arm, Juniper's breath caught in her throat.

Sullivan. She hadn't seen him since their last night together. Juniper had been a teenager; she had believed she was in love. The man she had fallen for all those years ago existed only in the ethereal fog of her memories. Seeing him now, *here* . . .

"What are you doing here?" Juniper reached for the counter beside her and held on.

"I could ask you the same thing."

Her mind whirled through a dozen different responses, but in the end Sullivan spoke first.

"I own this property."

"What?"

"Bought it on foreclosure last year."

Juniper wasn't sure what to make of this news. Sullivan was the last person she thought would ever buy the old Murphy place. She couldn't decide if his purchase made him seem guilty or if it cemented his innocence. Either way, it didn't matter. Knowing that the Tates had finally swallowed up the property—the Murphys' former pride and joy acquired by their sworn enemies—filled her with a sharp, buzzing energy.

"I guess the Tates own most of the county now," Juniper said, a drop of malice in her voice.

Something flashed in his eyes, but the look passed quickly. In many ways, Sullivan was the same young man she had known all those years ago. Same sandy hair, same bright green eyes flecked with gold. But middle age had broadened his shoulders, thickened his neck. His face bore fine lines that he wore like badges of honor. Sullivan was just as handsome and even more intimidating than he had been at twenty-one. Juniper gripped the counter harder and felt a splinter prick the pad of her thumb.

"What are you doing here?" Sullivan crossed over the threshold, causing Juniper to shuffle back. He leaned against the doorframe, blocking her exit. There was a snowflake glinting in his eyelash, and as she watched, it melted and disappeared.

"I'm helping Cora with the library. She's—"

"I heard. What are you doing *here*." He patted the counter beside her fingers and her breath caught at his proximity.

"Taking a trip down memory lane," Juniper managed.

"Strange place to reminisce. Strange time, too. You know we're in the middle of a blizzard, right?"

Juniper glanced over his shoulder. The snow was still coming down hard, but it wasn't a blizzard. Not by a long shot. At least, not yet. She ignored his question and asked, "Do you always drive around your land in the middle of a snowstorm?"

"I have two hundred head of cattle grazing the section just east of here. I'm checking fences before the snow gets too deep."

It was ridiculous, but a part of Juniper wondered if he knew the moment she stepped foot on the acreage. Were they tied together somehow? Intrinsically bound by all that had happened that summer? Absolutely not. Sullivan's explanation made perfect sense. Still, she knew that when she looked at him there were things she couldn't say written in her eyes.

"Juniper Baker," he said. And then smiled, shaking his head. He ran his knuckles against his jaw like he couldn't quite bring himself to believe it. "How have you been?"

As if they were old friends. As if they could just laugh and chat in this dusty, decrepit building like they were swapping stories over coffee and cherry pie at Cunningham's. Juniper could rattle off five reasons why they should both leave now and pretend this unexpected meeting had never happened at all. *Ashley* was at the very top of the list. Juniper thought of Ashley's glare, her ugly words at the library. Jericho would have another

202

murder to solve if Ashley could see her husband and former best friend right now. Juniper's stomach flipped and her mouth went dry.

"Fine. I've been fine."

"I heard about Jonathan," he said. Sullivan sounded genuinely upset, and that more than anything pierced her. Everything that she had been tamping down, pressing deep into a place where she promised to deal with it later, came bubbling up. Not just Jonathan's accident and the possibility that she might never speak to her brother again. Willa, and Juniper's fierce desire to have her daughter back. What happened to the Murphys, who were like family. The uncertainty and rejection Juniper felt, the loneliness of being so far away from all that she had once known and loved. And, of course, there was Sullivan. Fifteen years later, and she still wanted him. She wanted to press her face against his warm skin. To trace the well-known and totally unfamiliar angles of his body and recapture those long summer nights when everything seemed so uncomplicated and pure.

But that was an illusion shattered by the events of that summer. Nothing about that time had been uncomplicated. Nothing had been pure. It was messy and messed up, a summer that didn't change the rancid heart of a hard community; it merely exposed it for what it was. Even if Juniper didn't know exactly what happened, she could close her eyes and feel the sickening pitch of her stomach as she came face-to-face with each difficult truth. There was darkness in Jericho. And this moment was a lie. Sullivan and her. Talking as if they were friends. They were strangers, not lovers. They were nothing to each other.

"I need to go."

Sullivan didn't move. "Are you okay?"

"No, I'm not okay! Nothing about this"—she gave her arm a jerky wave, encompassing the farm and Jonathan and Jericho itself in the gesture—"is okay."

"Is he going to make it?"

She wrapped her arms around herself and studied Sullivan for a long while. He didn't flinch beneath her gaze. Yet Juniper couldn't find even a hint of the cocky swagger that had characterized him all those years ago. Gone was the sly smile, the twinkle in his eye that made her feel like he knew all her secrets. The boy that he had been would have been cracking jokes by now, pushing her up against the counter and kissing her slow. Inviting her to forget that anything at all existed outside of the circle of their embrace. This new Sullivan, this man she didn't know, looked sad, his eyes lined with worry.

"We're not sure," Juniper said finally. Simply. There was nothing else to say.

"I'm so sorry."

Juniper took him to mean he was sorry about Jonathan, but there were a dozen other things he could be apologizing for. Still, Juniper wasn't entirely guiltless herself. The last thing he said to her that summer was: "I would have married you." Maybe she should apologize, too.

Instead she said, "We're hoping for the best." It was such a clichéd thing to say, but all at once Juniper was tired all the way down to her bones. She could have curled up on the floor of the roadside stand and slept with her head on the hard ground. "I really should go."

"Me too." Sullivan nodded. And yet he still stood blocking the door. "It's good to see you."

Juniper had been so good. She had done all the things they wanted her to do. She didn't talk about that summer. She had the baby and handed Willa to her mother. She went to college and moved away and didn't come back—partly because she didn't want to and partly because she knew she wasn't welcome anymore. Juniper was too broken, too complicated for quiet, orderly Jericho. And all at once she wanted to be the troublemaker they all believed her to be.

She wasn't the same wilting wallflower she had been for the nine long months of her pregnancy and the weeks of parting that came after. Juniper met Sullivan's gaze. "It's good to see you too."

Her confession was permission-giving, Juniper knew that, and she didn't back away when he moved toward her. He touched her softly. Just his fingertips on her cheek, his eyes searching hers for something they had lost a long time ago. Sullivan let his forehead fall to hers, and when she didn't pull away, he drew her close.

They stood like that for a long time, just holding each other, her head tucked against his chest and his arms tight around her. Then he kissed the top of her head, and when Juniper looked up, Sullivan brushed his lips against the pale curve near the corner of her mouth.

The shock of it startled them both, and they pushed away from each other at exactly the same moment.

"God, June." Her name sounded like a curse on his tongue.

Then Sullivan turned away and marched out of the old chicken coop. She followed him to the door, leaning against the frame because she wasn't sure she could trust herself to stand upright without help. Juniper watched as he trudged through the snow and climbed into the cab of his truck. After he slammed the door, he gave her one last hard look through the windshield, then slung his arm over the back of the seat and reversed out of the driveway, tires squealing as he punished them on the ice. He was gone before Juniper could even raise her fingers in goodbye.

She didn't fault him. She wanted to do the same

thing. To drive hard and fast, to break something, to scream. She knew exactly how he felt. And when he had studied her through the windshield, he was wrecked with warring emotions that she understood all too well.

He still loved her. But he hated her, too.

CHAPTER 12

SUMMER
14 AND A HALF YEARS AGO

"Let's go."

I look up from where I'm tucked into the very corner of the couch and close the book over my finger to mark my place. Jonathan is leaning on the doorframe, truck keys in hand. "Go where?" I motion to the novel I'm reading. "Kinda busy here."

"Busy" is a relative term. I'm in a pair of faded boxers and a tank top with a built-in bra. Pajamas, essentially. It's been dark for an hour already, and I was just thinking about bed.

"Bonfire at Phil's. Come on." He takes the book out of my hand gingerly, as if he's afraid of how I'll react. I let him do it, but only because I've changed my mind. If I was avoiding time alone with him before because I was afraid he'd drill me about Sullivan, I'm craving a few uninterrupted minutes now. We have a lot to talk about.

"O-*kay*," I say, exaggerating my reluctance. Pushing myself off the couch, I tell him, "I just need to change."

"Make it quick."

"Meeting someone?" I wink.

"No, but I think you are." He skewers me with a look so laced with meaning I stop in my tracks.

"What's that supposed to mean?"

"We have to talk about Sullivan."

"Fine," I say, an edge in my voice. "We have to talk about Cal, too."

"Just get dressed."

I throw on a pair of cutoffs and a long-sleeved Henley. It's late, and nights still get cool in early June. Stopping in the bathroom, I swish some mouthwash while brushing on a bit of mascara. A quick finger tousle and I decide I'm good enough. I've taken more than five minutes, and Jonathan isn't patient.

The main floor is dark and empty when I creep down the stairs, and I can see the glow of Jonathan's headlights through the kitchen window. I loop my fingers through a pair of sandals near the door and run out barefoot, jogging lightly over the gravel as the stones prick at my feet.

"What's the story, morning glory?" I ask, trying to keep it light as I slide onto the bench of his truck and slam the door behind me.

"No story, June. It's just a party."

"Where have you been all day? The Murphys'?" Law never bothered to track Jonathan down, and fixed the fence himself, presumably. He popped the tab on a beer when he came in the house around suppertime, and drank steadily from that moment until he lumbered off to bed. He hardly said a word to either me or Mom.

I glance at Jonathan's profile, illuminated by the dim dashboard lights. His jaw is set, and he nods tersely.

"How's Cal?" I finish up with my sandals and sit back, pulling on my seat belt and giving my brother my full attention.

"He's okay. They transferred him to the hospital in Munroe."

"Because of a bloody nose?"

"He has leukemia, June."

I'm stunned. Cal has always been the picture of health. Tall and lean with a head full of thick hair that you can tell used to be as black as Jonathan's. There's something vigorous about him. Hale. It's hard to imagine that someone like Cal could succumb to anything. Finally I manage, "I don't know what to say. I'm sorry."

"Tell Cal and Beth that."

"I will, of course." My mind is racing. "How long have you known? What do they need? Can I help? Jonathan, I want to help."

He sighs. "Slow down. They just found out. Still trying to wrap their heads around it, I think. And then Baxter was killed, and now Cal's in the hospital . . ."

"They admitted him?"

"They're keeping him overnight just to run

a few tests and make sure his blood pressure is stabilized."

"Is Beth okay?"

"What do you think?" He shoots me a grim look.

I can't stop myself from peppering him. I have so many questions. "Will he do treatment?"

"I think that's the plan. It's really early, June. I don't have a lot of answers for you."

We're silent for a few minutes as Jonathan navigates the dark county roads. The stars are out in full force, a scatter of diamonds in a black, moonless sky. Usually I'd lean forward against my seat belt and marvel at the constellations through the windshield, but I'm rooted to the bench tonight.

I whip toward my brother as a thought occurs to me. "Wait. Is this . . ." I can't find the words, and even when I do, they seem illogical. Impossible. I say them anyway. "Does Cal's cancer have anything to do with their water? With the trouble with the Tates?"

"Cal and Beth think so."

It's a sobering thought. Suddenly the fields around us seem ominous, the tufts of newly sprouted corn menacing. I've been told my whole life that this is a place of abundance. A fruited plain. It feels corrupted now.

"That's insane," I whisper, more to myself than Jonathan.

He pounces anyway. "It's not. It's all connected, June."

It's obvious he's been spending a lot of time with the Murphys. They talk like this all the time. About how we're poisoning ourselves with chemicals, sacrificing our own lives on the altar of corporate greed. According to the Murphys, big agra isn't just the end of the small family farm, it's the destruction of our planet. It's why they bought the acreage in the first place, and why they work so hard to grow everything, according to Beth, "the way God intended it." They hand out homemade pamphlets at their roadside stand, cultivate bee-friendly plants, and eat clean. They aren't strict vegetarians, but I do know that the only meat they'll touch is whatever they've raised on their own little plot of land and butchered locally. Admirable, I suppose. But it doesn't seem as if any of it has made a difference.

"I know," I soothe Jonathan. "It's not fair. I didn't mean that I don't believe you. It's just a lot to take in. And you have to admit, people get sick all the time. Cancer doesn't discriminate."

"Thanks for that, oh wise one." The sarcasm in Jonathan's voice is so thick I can practically see it dripping in the air between us.

"You don't have to be mean."

Jonathan ignores me. "Remember Petunia?"

Of course I remember Petunia. The Murphys

bought an Angus calf a couple of years ago and raised her in the pasture behind the small stable. She really was a sweet thing. Big brown eyes and a gentle manner that made her seem more like a pony than a cow. But when she was eighteen months old, Petunia disappeared.

"We'll have lots of steaks and hamburger, of course," Beth told me when I asked where Petunia had gone. "But also bone broth and liver and tongue. Don't worry, June, we won't waste a bit of her."

The Bakers are carnivores through and through, and I eat my fair share of hamburgers hot off the grill and Iowa chops with meat so tender it falls off the bone. But I have never named an animal I later ate. It seemed a little barbaric to me that the Murphys would do exactly that.

"What about Petunia?" I ask with some trepidation.

"When they butchered her, she was so full of tumors they had to condemn the meat."

I'm instantly sickened. Slapping my hand over my mouth, I groan. "That's disgusting. Why did you tell me that?"

"Because it's true. Because Petunia drank the Murphys' well water her entire life and she was so sick Cal said he'd never seen anything like it. It's why they started testing the water in the first place."

"You don't know that they're connected."

"How could they not be? Petunia was just the first of many. And now Cal?"

"What are you saying, Jonathan? Do you think this was intentional? Are the Tates out to get the Murphys?"

I can feel Jonathan clam up. He goes really still, really quiet, just like he used to when we were kids and I pressed him past his breaking point. My brother is all ice when he's angry, and the air in the cab is suddenly so cold that I reach to close the vents nearest to me. Of course, it's just the air-conditioning turned up high, but Jonathan's mood feels like a tangible thing to me.

"Talk to me," I say.

"We're here," Jonathan responds.

Sure enough, we're on yet another gravel road, pulling onto yet another rural farm where we're greeted by a muddy black lab and a row of cars and trucks parked neatly in the grass. Suddenly I could scream. If all this is true, why doesn't anybody care? Why aren't we raising hell and making changes and transforming the world? I've been told all my life that we are the salt of the earth, the quiet, hardworking backbone of a culture that offers life, liberty, and the pursuit of happiness. This feels like death, bondage, despair. I don't understand. But when I turn to question Jonathan further, I find that he's already half-gone, one foot on the running board as he hops out of the truck.

"Wait!" I fumble with my seat belt and slide out of the truck myself, running to catch up with him as he heads toward the field where a pallet fire is burning bright enough to signal space. I grab his arm, spin him to face me. "You can't just tell me all this and walk off. What are you doing? What are we going to *do?*"

Jonathan shakes me off. "Don't worry about it, June. It's not your problem."

"If it's your problem, it's my problem," I tell him, linking my pinky with his in a gesture of solidarity. When we were in grade school and kids used to tease us because of our unusual connection, we discovered that we could pass each other in the halls and twine our littlest fingers together for less than a second and no one would be the wiser. It was comforting for both of us to know that no matter what happened, we had each other's backs. I want Jonathan to know that now—to know that I'm here for him. Always.

But he jerks away. "You're leaving, June. It's not your problem at all."

"You dragged me out here," I remind him, feeling a nasty little sparkle of anger. "I thought you wanted to talk."

"Yeah, well, I changed my mind. Just stay away from Sullivan." Then he takes off at a lope and the darkness swallows him up.

Stay away from Sullivan. Really? Surely Jonathan knows me better than that. His warning is a challenge, and I have a sudden, perverse desire to find Sullivan and throw myself at him right in front of my brother.

I'm fuming, burning with indignation as I wonder if I should try to snag a ride home or go grab one of the beers that I'm sure is turning lukewarm in a cooler near the fire. When I feel something brush against my hand I startle, but it's just the dog nudging me for a pat. I oblige and give her a little ear scratch, too, even though she's filthy and smells like she's been swimming in a ditch. I'm still petting her when a form takes shape in the shadows and someone calls my name.

"June? *June!*"

It's Ashley. She's stumbling a bit but laughing, and I smile in spite of myself. "I'm here," I say. "Straight ahead. Keep coming."

When she's about ten feet away she can finally make me out, and her face splits into a wide grin. I can see the white glow of her perfectly straight teeth. "There you are!" Ashley wraps me in a boozy hug and gives my cheek a sloppy kiss.

"Seems like you've been here a while."

"I tried to text you," she accuses, "but you didn't answer."

I shrug and allow her to lead me toward the bonfire. Or maybe I'm leading her. Ashley has her arm slung over my shoulder and is hanging on for dear life.

"Good party?" I ask, slipping my arm around

her waist when the earth dips below us and she pitches.

"The best."

I know exactly what that means. Sullivan is here. My heart gives an annoying little tingle.

"You know what you need?" I tell Ashley. "A *nice* guy."

"I don't want a nice guy."

It's hard not to be irritated at her pigheadedness, but then I'm wrung out at the memory of just how unexpectedly nice Sullivan is. He does possess a certain infectious charm. And even knowing what I now know about Cal Murphy and the Tates' potentially unethical farming practices, my pulse still sprints at the thought of seeing him tonight.

Of course, he's the first person I see when we enter the warm glow around the fire. Sullivan is facing us, watching us as if he's been waiting for this exact moment. Ashley notices, too, and I can feel every inch of her body tense.

"He's looking at me!" she whispers, but loudly and clumsily.

I bite my lip, considering. But then, before I can fully weigh the consequences, I squeeze my eyes shut and blurt: "What if he's not?"

It's a bold thing to say, one step shy of a confession, and when I dare to look at her again, Ashley is stone-faced. Then all at once a smile lights up her face and she laughs. "Come with me!" she begs, as if I haven't said anything at all. As if it's ridiculous to imagine that he would have eyes for anyone but her.

"You go," I sigh. "I'd just be a third wheel."

"But what will I *say?*"

"Be yourself," I tell her. "You're amazing, Ashley. He'd be crazy not to fall for you." It's what she wants to hear, and she giggles.

My stomach twists as I watch her walk away. Partly because she's my friend and I love her, and partly because I'm remembering how easy it was to talk to Sullivan all the way to Munroe and back. The puppy squirmed in my lap and licked every square inch of my hands and my arms, all the way up to the cuff of my T-shirt. And every once in a while, Sullivan reached over to tug on the puppy's velvety ears. It was subconscious, a gesture of affection, and when he lifted the puppy from my arms to deliver him to his new family, Sullivan buried his own face in all that golden fur and said goodbye.

Damn him for turning out to be a decent human being.

Intentionally positioning myself directly across from where Sullivan and Ashley are talking with their heads bent toward each other, I accept a can of beer and strike up conversations with whoever's nearby.

I don't know what time it is when Phil decides to throw a few more pallets on the fire, but it takes us all by surprise. The sparks detonate ashes and cinders on everyone standing nearby, and, shaking a burning ember off the sleeve of my shirt, I decide I've had more than enough.

I scan the crowd for Jonathan, hoping I can convince him to call it a night even though he was clearly eager to come. Not to mention furious with me. My happiness is going to be at the very bottom of his priority list. But it doesn't seem to matter anyway, because after circling the now raging fire twice, I can't find Jonathan anywhere. Sullivan and Ashley are also missing, and I have to stomp down a wave of self-pity. They've left me here.

Almost immediately, I shift from feeling jilted to annoyed. Jonathan has been changing in the last several months, and it's not fair for him to pin all his frustrations on me. He's keeping me in the dark, and then holding me accountable for things that I don't know. That I can't possibly know. It was low of him to take me here and then abandon me to my own devices as punishment. For what? By the time I decide to stalk back to where he parked the truck, I'm in a foul mood.

Heading away from the bonfire proves much more difficult than walking toward it. Beyond the light cast by the flames, the night is black as spilled ink. There's no moon, and though the Milky Way is a silver ribbon in the sky, it's not enough to illuminate my way. I squint in the darkness, willing my eyes to adjust as I stumble along in the tall grass. I wish I had a flashlight.

"June?"

For the second time tonight, I hear my name in the void. But this time, it's not Ashley.

"Jonathan?" I call back.

There's a shuffle in the shadows, a curse and the bark of a laugh, and then Sullivan materializes in front of me. His silhouette is shrouded in darkness, and I'm glad it's too black for him to see my expression. I feel quite sure it's a complicated mix of aversion and raw, unwelcome attraction.

"Have you seen my brother?" I ask abruptly, crossing my arms over my chest as if to ward him off.

"He left. Maybe twenty minutes ago? Took Ashley home."

"What a gentleman," I sigh. I want to ask Sullivan why *he* didn't take Ashley home, but I'm too irritated to care. "What am I supposed to do?"

"Ride home with Callum."

Callum is one of Jonathan's friends who lives just a couple of miles past our farm. I've known him since he was a curly-haired toddler. "Okay," I say. "Have you seen him?"

"Couple minutes ago. He left." Sullivan is enjoying this.

"Stop messing with me. I'm not in the mood."

"I can see that. Come on, let me take you home."

I wonder if he planned this, but that seems far-fetched. I'm sure Jonathan didn't need any convincing when it became clear that Ashley needed a ride home—he's always been chivalrous.

"Fine," I say, because I don't have any other choice. The butterfly feeling in my chest has dissipated, and I follow Sullivan without pause.

His truck still smells faintly of puppy. I'm about to comment on it when I realize that Sullivan hasn't turned over the engine. We're sitting in the unyielding darkness, alone, and when I turn to Sullivan, he's facing me.

"I need to get home," I say preemptively. "I have church in the morning."

"Me too."

This surprises me a little. I didn't realize the Tates were churchgoing. I wonder where they attend. I don't have a chance to ask him, though, because Sullivan slides his hand across the console and grazes the edge of my hand where it rests on the seat. I catch my breath, ready to pull away, but he hooks his pinky through mine and hangs on tight. I'm shocked. I wonder if Jonathan told him, if there's some way that he can know what this gesture means to me, how important it is.

"Sullivan—"

"Just listen," he says. "I know you don't trust me. I know Jonathan is warning you away."

"It's—"

He squeezes my pinky to stop me. "And I need you to know, June, it's never going to happen with Ashley. Like, not ever."

Still. "Sullivan, she's my best friend."

"That's why I let her down easy tonight."

"You did?" My heart breaks for Ashley a little bit, but I can't say that I'm surprised. What *does* surprise me is my own reaction, the lift of hope that makes it hard to breathe for just a moment. I try to think back to the bonfire, to Sullivan and Ashley talking across from me. Did she look devastated? Did she cry? My heart wrings at the thought, but I don't remember seeing her upset. And it's true that Ashley's obsessions come and go almost as frequently as she changes the color of her nail polish. How many boyfriends has she lazily flipped through while I helped her pick out cute outfits and dissected their fleeting, would-be relationships? Maybe, just this once, it's my turn.

But I'm being ridiculous. Irrational. I want nothing to do with Sullivan and never have. I'm leaving for college in a handful of weeks, and I have no intention of ever coming back. At least, not to stay. So what could possibly happen between us? Nothing. And then there's the drama with the Murphys and what happened with Baxter . . . I should tell him in no uncertain terms that he needs to take me home. *Now.*

Except Sullivan has turned over my hand and is tracing the lines in my palm as if by memory. I'm losing my resolve, I can feel it, and when he leans over the console and carefully brushes my hair off my shoulder, I let him.

His mouth is warm and oh so tender on my neck. I try to think logically about what's happening so that I can justify it in the morning, but it's harder and harder to concentrate. And by the time Sullivan finds my lips, I'm not thinking at all.

CHAPTER 13

WINTER
TODAY

It took Juniper several tries to back her car down the gravel drive of the old Murphy place. There was a sheen of ice over the loose stones, and a thick layer of snow on top of that, and in the end she was forced to clear a path by scuffing up the gravel behind the wheels with the heels of her canvas tennis shoes. She cursed herself for bypassing boots that morning and assuming the only off-roading she'd encounter would be the hospital parking garage. But, inappropriate footwear aside, her low-tread tires eventually caught, and Juniper slid the rest of the way home.

By the time she finally closed the door at the bungalow, she was shaking uncontrollably. It could have been because her sneakers were soaked through and her jeans were damp to the knees, but she knew it had much more to do with the hint of Sullivan still lingering on her lips.

She wanted to yell a string of obscenities, but her teeth were chattering so hard she couldn't have done it if she tried. Instead, Juniper kicked off her wet shoes, peeled off her socks, and tiptoed on frozen feet to the bathroom, where she sat on the edge of the tub and ran hot water over her lower legs. But she had forgotten that icy extremities required a slow warm-up, and she let herself sob when the water pierced like needles.

It had been a very long time since she had cried over Sullivan Tate.

A sliver of her soul wanted to show up at his door and beg him to change his mind. For just a moment or two she wished there was a way to undo the past, to erase his marriage to Ashley, to put herself in her former best friend's place. But even as she ran her thumb beneath her swollen eyes, she knew that she didn't want that. Not really. She didn't know the man that Sullivan had become, and her starry-eyed memories of those weeks they were in love were a fairy tale that even she didn't believe. It had been a summer romance, nothing more. Besides, there was no way to forget everything she knew, everything she had learned along the way. Juniper had a life now, a job she adored, an apartment on the fourth floor that boasted a glimpse of the Rockies over the low-lying buildings of her modest, academic neighborhood. She was strong and capable, independent.

Never mind that her brief relationship with Sullivan had changed her life forever.

As she was toweling her feet and then stripping off the rest of her cold, damp clothes, Juniper allowed herself to consider her former best

225

friend. It was like pressing a bruise, but welcome in a way because thinking about Ashley yanked her head out of the clouds. Sullivan and Ashley were married now. They had children and a life together that Juniper knew nothing about. They shared a history—and a future—that she was not a part of, and as much as she wished that things had turned out differently, here she was.

Juniper pulled on leggings and a chunky cable-knit sweater, and layered two pairs of socks over her numb feet. Then she went into the kitchen and quickly spread some peanut butter on a slice of bread. Folding it in half, she ate it while she grabbed her backpack from the hook by the door. Mandy's sister was expecting her to pick up Willa eventually, but in the meantime, she needed to start collecting her thoughts.

Juniper was an archival librarian by trade, but her small liberal arts college didn't boast an enormous collection of precious books and documents that required her to appraise, process, and catalog new finds regularly. Instead, she managed a small library dedicated to the obscure theologian the college was named for—and spent the majority of her time helping students and academics conduct research and find often-esoteric information within the hundreds of thousands of pages she had come to consider her own. In other words, she preserved, maintained, and disseminated a wealth of knowledge and information. Juniper was a researcher. It was a safe, orderly, predictable job that offered a comfortable distance from which to dissect events she longed to understand. And there was nothing she had researched quite so thoroughly as what had happened in Jericho that summer.

Everett's little incident room seemed paltry in comparison.

While her laptop powered up, Juniper pulled out her notebooks and pens. Her hair was a damp mess, so she stuck the pen she was holding in between her teeth and swept her curls into a tangled topknot. She spread her notebooks and papers out on the coffee table, and when she ran out of room, she used the couch cushions beside her hips.

It was hard to remember when exactly she started digging into the murders, because it seemed to her that for nearly fifteen years she had thought of little else. She gave birth to Willa and left for college and secured a job and went through the motions of a normal, productive life—dates with harmless, unremarkable men, girls' weekends to Aspen, contributions to a modest 401K—but beneath it all, forever and ever, amen, was the low vibration of what had happened that night. She couldn't escape it, so she embraced it.

Each notebook represented years of gathered

information in the form of everything from conversations that she tried to recall verbatim to notes that she took on the articles, TV news segments, and blog posts she found relating to the murders. There hadn't been a lot of media attention, and Juniper had to scrape mentions from far-flung corners of the internet. The FBI had never gotten involved—presumably because the case was not high-profile enough—and the media was quick to turn their attention to more salacious stories when nothing immediately shook loose on the case.

Still, she was persistent. She'd managed to track down a former criminal profiler via a Reddit chat room, and learned that most rural or small-town homicides were crimes of passion committed by someone the victim intimately knew. After exhausting Juniper's patchwork anthology about the murders, he reminded her that the most obvious suspect was usually the right one. He favored Jonathan and wondered why the sheriff's department hadn't been able to make a conviction stick. He blamed the ineptitude of local law enforcement and the thunderstorm that had rolled through Jericho only hours after the shots were fired. Evidence was washed away before more capable crime scene technicians had a chance to collect the marks and traces and bits of ephemera that could have led to an arrest.

Bad luck and botched job all around,

he wrote.

I'm sorry the bastard walked free.

Juniper never shared that she was the bastard's sister.

And she didn't bother to tell him that her gut pointed her in a very different direction: to the Tate family—the only people who she could discern had a compelling motive. She knew things that nobody else knew, had spent more sleepless nights than she could remember with the weight of those secrets slowly grinding away at her soul. Wrestling with the question she could never answer: Had her silence let a killer walk free?

Selecting Sullivan's notebook from the coffee table in front of her, Juniper turned to a fresh page and dated it. She entered the information that she had learned—that Sullivan had finally purchased the Murphys' land—and wrote a series of questions for herself to research later. It was a bit of a half-hearted endeavor. There were lots of empty pages in the notebook dedicated to Sullivan. Mostly because in the weeks leading up to the murders, he had a pretty convincing alibi: her.

But Sullivan couldn't be discounted entirely.

He was intimately tied to the turmoil with the Murphys, and he had gone AWOL for a couple of hours the night of the murders. And in the years between, Juniper had learned so much about the fragile imbalance between small homesteads and big agra that she knew the debate had spilled beyond her own farming community into global markets and discussions of the future of food production itself. It was economic and political, and Juniper had only scratched the surface of the conflict. Still, she had an entire binder dedicated to water contamination lawsuits in the Midwest. It included the documents that the Murphys had filed in court against the Tates, and she supposed she could nearly be considered an armchair expert in civil action environmental lawsuits. Juniper would have to find out what—if anything—had been done to mitigate the runoff that had caused the legal drama in the first place. And how Sullivan was involved.

What if Jonathan had been asking similar questions? Juniper's pen froze on the page, and a dot of black ink began to spread beneath the place where the point dug into the paper. What if that was exactly why "things were happening"?

She wanted to be dispassionate, an objective observer who could pick the facts out of the case without the handicap of pesky emotions, but everything inside Juniper told her that Jonathan's accident was linked to the Murphy murders.

What had changed? What had Jonathan learned?

Jericho Lake bordered the Murphys'—now Sullivan Tate's—property. Had Jonathan been caught poking his nose where it didn't belong? It certainly wasn't out of the realm of possibility. Juniper still had eight-by-ten glossy prints from the last time that Jonathan played detective. They were safely tucked away in one of her Murphy murder files.

When Juniper's phone rang, her hand jerked across the page, leaving a long hash line through her notes. It was a local number. She took a steadying breath and answered, half expecting to hear heavy breathing on the other end. Or maybe nothing at all.

"Hey, Juniper. Everett Stokes." He sounded off. "Sorry, thought I'd get your voice mail. I assumed you'd shut off your ringer at the hospital."

"I'm home," Juniper said, cringing at the thought of Jericho as home.

"How's Jonathan doing?"

Juniper didn't want to be suspicious, but she couldn't help but wonder what Everett's motives were for asking. Did he care? Or did he just want to know if Jonathan was ready to be questioned? "He's doing okay. Not much has changed, but we're hopeful."

"Fingers crossed," Everett reminded her yet again.

Not everyone is hoping for Jonathan's

recovery, Juniper thought. She wondered for a moment if she should tell Everett about what had been happening to Jonathan. But it wasn't her place. She reminded herself that for most of the inhabitants of Jericho, the Murphy murders were an unprecedented, vicious incident that had appeased whatever savage god required such a sacrifice. Jericho returned to sleepy-little-town status much the way new shoots grew in the shadows of a scorched forest and life started over, hiding the scars of all that had come before. Jonathan had elected to stay in Jericho. He must have felt some level of acceptance. "That's the beautiful thing about a small town," Reb had once told her. "When we fall, we pick each other back up. We begin again."

"Thanks," Juniper said when Everett cleared his throat. She had lost the thread of the conversation and wasn't sure what else to say. "But I don't think you called to ask me about Jonathan . . ."

"No. Not just that, anyway. I'm actually calling to apologize. I think I may have given you the wrong impression, and I was hoping you'd be willing to come down to the station on Monday. I told you that we're taking another look at the Murphy case, and I think you could provide some clarity on a few things."

Maybe Juniper was imagining it, but there seemed to be an edge in his voice. Did he know that she had seen his incident room? It had struck her as personal—and unprofessional—at the time. If "we" were taking another look at the Murphy case, why had Everett's home office been turned into the staging ground? Still, this particular invitation seemed official if she was expected at the tiny Jericho Police Station. She knew the place. It was the old post office, a square brick building on the opposite end of Main Street as the library. People would see her going in and coming out. But there was no way to refuse him without making him question why.

"Sure," Juniper said. "I took the day off to drive down to Des Moines today, so I definitely can't leave Cora high and dry on Monday. How about over lunch? Does noon work?"

"You bet. I'll plan on seeing you then. Thanks for helping us out, Juniper."

"I live to give," Juniper muttered after they had said their goodbyes and she'd clicked off the phone. She was decidedly unsure about what to think of Everett. Why did he care so much about their small-town tragedy? The rest of Jericho was perfectly content to leave the past behind.

Pulling her computer onto her lap, Juniper flipped it open and connected to the hotspot on her phone. She felt a jolt of anticipation when she typed "Everett Stokes" into a search engine and hit enter. There was something uniquely satisfying about starting a new hunt for information. Juniper was hardly a private detective, but over time she had learned how to follow the breadcrumbs of even the faintest trail. The internet was layered and complex, a hash-marked map to nowhere and everywhere that she could navigate with an agility that surprised her. If Everett was hiding something, she'd find it.

Juniper's first search didn't turn up much. A couple of Facebook profiles (none of which were linked to the Everett that Juniper knew), a few obituaries, and the web page for a pediatric dentist in New Orleans. It was time to refine. Flipping to a new page in her general-purpose Moleskine, Juniper began to outline her plan. She'd vary search engines, try different keywords, and focus in on specific regions. A detailed log would help her keep track of which combinations produced results and which ones proved to be dead ends.

She was just jotting down some targeted key-words (*police, officer, Jericho, Iowa*) when there was a scuffle and the sound of muted words outside her front door. Juniper barely had time to look up from her notebook before the handle turned and Willa surged into the bungalow, dusting snow across the faded hardwood floor and trailing a blond girl in Dutch braids that Juniper had never met.

"She's home!" Willa shouted over her shoulder.

Juniper froze for a moment, then realized that her unusual fixation was on full display for the girls, who were studying her from the doorway.

She snapped her laptop shut and lunged to gather up the journals. They made a fat stack that she tried to cram into her backpack with a casual air. It wasn't working.

"Willa!" Juniper smiled, standing. "I thought I was supposed to pick you up in"—she glanced at her watch—"fifteen minutes. And I thought you were with . . ."

"Katie," Willa offered with a look of mild disdain. "Mandy's older sister's name is Katie. I was there for supper, but Zoe and I are working on a science fair project together, so I went to her house after we ate. Katie was supposed to text you."

"Oh." Juniper hadn't picked up her phone since she'd tossed it on the far side of the couch after Everett's unsettling call. But she remembered those quick trades, the back-and-forth free flow of junior high and high school. Willa and Zoe were exchanging a knowing look, and that was familiar too. "Hi, Zoe." Juniper took a few steps and stuck out her hand, wondering too late if it was weird to shake hands with her teenager's best friend.

But Zoe grinned, a sweet, gap-toothed smile that told Juniper her parents weren't concerned about orthodontics, and curled her fingers around Juniper's. "It's really nice to finally meet you, Mrs. Baker."

There were so many things wrong with *Mrs.*

Baker that Juniper wasn't sure where to begin. Instead of bothering, she just said: "Call me Juniper."

Zoe shrugged, making one of her long braids slide over her shoulder. "Okay. My dad's in the car. I'd better go."

She was gone before Juniper could wonder if it was normal for a father to sit in the car instead of coming in to say hello to his daughter's best friend's mom. But she didn't have long to consider it.

"What's all that?" Willa dropped her backpack on the floor with a thud.

"All what?"

Willa spread her arms wide to encompass the living room and the little nest Juniper had made for herself on the couch. The notebooks were stuffed out of sight, but her computer remained on the coffee table, and there was a profusion of different-colored pens and highlighters, a pad of sticky notes, and the uncurling roll of old newspapers that Juniper had "borrowed" from the library. It looked like a harried grad student had recently vacated the premises.

"Just working on some stuff," Juniper said with what she hoped was nonchalance. "I wasn't expecting you to show up. I mean, I was going to pick you up in just a bit. Mandy sent me the address . . ."

"But I wasn't at Katie's anymore. Cameron and

236

Hunter had to go to bed, and Zoe and I needed to work on our science fair project." Willa let her coat slide off her shoulders and down her arms until it was dangling by her fingertips. Then, instead of turning to hang it up on the hook behind her, she let it drop to the floor. She rushed across the living room and plucked a single Moleskine notebook from where it was peeking out beneath a throw pillow. Tracing a fingertip over the name written across the top, she fanned the pages and started to read.

It was all over in the span of a few seconds. One moment Willa was standing in front of her, and the next she was flipping through Juniper's case notebook on Jonathan. Juniper knew it was Jonathan's notebook because they were all color-coded, and his was a rich burgundy. She must have missed it in her hasty attempt to hide the evidence of her unorthodox research.

"Put that down," Juniper said, numb with shock.

"I know all about this, you know." Willa turned a page. "About what happened before I was born. All those things everyone said about Uncle Jonathan."

"Willa—"

"Grandma and Grandpa think I don't know, but I do. How could I not? *Everyone* knows. Like I wouldn't hear. Like I wouldn't look it all up myself."

Juniper could see that Willa was shaking with emotion. The pages of the notebook were shushing softly in the tremulous grip of her hands. Stepping carefully around the couch, Juniper reached out to ease the Moleskine from her daughter's grasp. Willa jerked away.

"You're just like everyone else!" Willa took a few steps back, and drilled Juniper with a glare that was filled with all the fear and fury, all the frustration of being locked out for years. " 'You're too young to know. It's in the past. It doesn't matter. Someday you'll understand,' " she singsonged.

"Willa—"

"Do you know what they call me?"

"What?"

"My nickname. Grandma and Grandpa won't talk about it, and everyone else says they're just trying to protect me, but I knew in kindergarten that my uncle was a killer."

Juniper's fisted knuckles turned white. "Jonathan didn't kill anyone."

"Oh yeah? Then why do you have a notebook with evidence that says he *did?*"

"It's not like that—"

"BeeGee," Willa interrupted, her voice cracking. "They call me BeeGee. It's short for Butcher's Girl, because Jonathan butchered Calvin and Elizabeth Murphy."

"Oh, Willa." Juniper's heart felt like a stone

in her chest. She struggled to breathe around the weight. "I'm so sorry. I can't believe—"

"I wish everyone would stop babying me."

Willa was holding the notebook, but she wasn't reading it anymore, and Juniper carefully moved toward her daughter. When she reached for the Moleskine, Willa let it slide from her fingers. It was a sign of resignation, the resolute understanding that nothing would change. The girl sank to the edge of the couch and curled her arms tightly around herself. She wasn't crying, but in some ways her lack of tears was unnerving to Juniper. This pain had been inured inside of Willa, lacquered by years of disregard and silence. It had calcified harsh and bright, the sort of tumor that could rot a person from the inside out.

"I'm sorry." Juniper sank carefully to the couch beside her daughter and held the notebook closed between them. "You're right—I think everyone was just trying to protect you. But clearly we've done more harm than good."

Willa was shrinking before Juniper. Wrapping herself tight with the thin whips of her dancer's arms, ducking her head so that her hair hid her face, pulling everything close. Juniper knew exactly what she was doing. She had done it a thousand times herself. *Shrink. Be small. Make yourself tiny, invisible, insignificant. Maybe if you contract to the size of a pinprick, no one will notice that your heart has shattered and scattered in the wind. Maybe no one will realize that you have ceased to exist.*

Juniper wanted to say: "I see you. I understand." But she didn't. Instead, she reached into her backpack and took out the entire stack of notebooks. Balancing them on her lap, she asked, "What do you want to know?"

This was Willa's history, too, and she deserved to know. Juniper remembered all too well what it felt like to be carved out of her own story.

Willa's eyes widened. First in suspicion, and then in shrewd calculation. "Everything."

"I don't know everything," Juniper said honestly. "Sometimes I think I don't know much of anything."

"Well that's definitely not *nothing*." Willa dipped her chin at the stack of notebooks and cautiously slid from the arm of the couch to the cushion.

It felt a bit like taming a wild animal. Or at least trying. Every move mattered, every word required careful measure. Juniper was well aware that there were some things Willa should never know, but surely she deserved better than whatever scraps she could salvage from a furtive Google search on the school's firewalled computers. Accurate information was always preferable to the theories of armchair detectives and crackpot conspiracists. And it was sobering to think that no one had ever sat down with Willa and had this conversation. Difficult as it would doubtless prove to be.

"Okay." Juniper exhaled hard. "Calvin and Elizabeth Murphy were murdered on the Fourth of July the summer before you were born. Cal was shot twice at nearly point-blank range, and Beth was shot once in the back."

Willa didn't flinch.

"No one was ever charged with their murders, but there are more than enough suspects to keep me constantly guessing."

"No witnesses?"

Juniper's teeth grazed the inside of her bottom lip, but she managed a thin smile. "No."

"But Uncle Jonathan was found at the scene of the crime." Willa sounded so adult.

"He made the 911 call." Juniper nodded. "When the police came, he was holding Cal's gun."

"And standing over his body."

"It wasn't like that."

Willa's eyes narrowed almost imperceptibly.

"He loved them, Wills. Cal and Beth were like a second family to him. Jonathan was wrecked when they died. I didn't think we'd ever get him back." In many ways, they never did.

"But why was he there? How did he *know?*"

It was exactly what Juniper kept asking herself over and over again. That summer had unraveled so spectacularly and then spun into such a complicated knot of deception and scheming, it

241

was nearly impossible to tease out the truth from lies. "I'm not sure," Juniper finally said. "He says he heard the gunshots from our farm, and I have to believe my brother."

Willa glanced at Jonathan's notebook still on top of the stack, but she didn't press it. "What about everyone else?"

"It could have been a murder-suicide." Juniper tugged that notebook out of the stack—it was black and nearly empty—and held it up. "But not likely."

"Why not?" she pressed.

Juniper inhaled. Willa wasn't going to let her off easy. "Well, Cal's back was to Beth, so if he shot her first and then shot himself, he would have had to turn away from her to do it. Seems improbable."

"And two shots? How do you shoot yourself twice?"

"Exactly." Juniper tossed the notebook on the coffee table.

"But Cal's fingerprints were on the gun."

"It was his gun; of course his fingerprints were on it."

Willa's eyes were a little too wide, her breath high and quick in her throat.

"Is this too much?" Juniper chanced a touch and put her hand lightly on her daughter's knee. Willa didn't shake her off. Nor did she budge even an inch.

"I know a lot already," she said with a calm that belied her age and contradicted the slightly panicked glint in her eyes. "The gun was taken from the glove compartment in Mr. Murphy's truck. It was parked beside the shed and unlocked. There were only two sets of fingerprints on the gun: Mr. Murphy's and Jonathan's."

"That's right." Juniper nodded carefully. "But Jonathan said he picked up the gun from where it had fallen in the dirt. It makes sense. There was a lot of debris on the gun, too." And blood. "Jonathan had no reason to hurt the Murphys. No motive." Motive, means, and opportunity. The holy trifecta of making a murder conviction stick. Every time Juniper dug deeper, she feared she'd uncover a motive strong enough to cast her brother in a whole new light.

Willa dipped her head once, and though Juniper couldn't tell if it was in agreement or doubt, she added Jonathan's notebook to the black one on the coffee table.

"It could have been a stranger," Juniper went on, holding up a blue Moleskine. "Someone passing through. But nothing was taken from the farm, and random acts of violence are less common than the news would have you believe." Another notebook discarded on the pile. "Besides, how would a stranger know that Cal kept his gun in the glove box?"

"What about the Carver guy?"

Juniper found the green notebook. It pained her to even have it, and she tossed it on the coffee table without pausing. "That was a terrible mistake. Carver Groen didn't know what he was doing."

"I thought he confessed."

"He did. He also wore a different-colored superhero cape every single day of the week and carried a pocketful of dimes that he left on windowsills around town." Juniper felt a hot, creeping shame when she thought of the photograph the newspaper had run of Carver grinning from ear to ear as they led him out of the police station. "He didn't understand. He just wanted to help."

Juniper didn't want Willa to know how painful that had been, how hard for the entire community to watch Carver—a beloved fixture in Jericho—insist that he had killed the Murphys. Did he want closure? Was he trying to make the people around him happy? Carver was a five-year-old in the body of a twenty-seven-year-old, but he knew the well-worn path between his mother's house, the grocery store, and several other key spots around town. Everyone looked out for him, which was why it was initially concerning that there were forty-five minutes during the night of the Fourth of July that Carver was unaccounted for. Some had seen him in the park, others walking home after the fireworks. But the time in between was as dark as the night had been. Carver's mother—a single mom and night shift factory worker at the processing plant in Munroe—took to drinking after his rash confession, and a couple of months later sent Carver away to a group home. Fourteen years had passed, and Jericho still felt bereft of his presence. Lessened somehow without the bright flash of one of his capes as he half skipped down the street.

"But he *could* have done it," Willa said. "I mean, if he wasn't quite right . . ."

And that was exactly why Carver's confession had been so devastating. There was always a lingering sense of: *What if?*

"His fingerprints weren't on the gun," Juniper reminded Willa. And herself.

"He could have worn gloves."

A small smile came unbidden to Juniper's lips. "Sounds like you could be a detective someday, Willa Baker."

"No thanks," she said quickly, with an accompanying movement inward; hands fisted, arms crossed tight.

Juniper pivoted back to facts. "There are five notebooks left. The Tates."

But Willa was already uncurling, pushing herself up from the couch to dismiss Juniper's final suspects. "It wasn't anybody in the Tate family."

"How do you know?"

"Come on." Willa rolled her eyes. "The Tates have been here forever. They're nice people."

Juniper knew nice people were capable of terrible things. "You can't say that, Wills. You can't *know*."

"Why would they hurt the Murphys? It doesn't make sense." Willa rocked from her heels to the balls of her feet and back again. "You haven't told me anything I didn't already know."

"I'm sorry, but—"

"It all comes back to Jonathan, doesn't it?" Willa shook out her hands as if they'd fallen asleep and she had to help the blood flow back into her fingertips. But it was more than that. Juniper could see she was trying to throw off the taint, the stain of suspicion on her family, her name. *Butcher's Girl.* Because before Jonathan found Mandy, before Hunter or Cameron were ever born, there was Jonathan and Willa. Juniper abandoned her baby, and the rest of her family stepped in. Willa had moved into her mother's old bedroom, right across the hall from Jonathan. He became her protector and best friend, an uncle who was more father figure than anything. Willa had always been his girl.

"If not Uncle Jonathan, then *who?*" Willa asked, her voice reedy with fear.

"Willa, sit down. Let's talk about this. There are things that—"

"I know enough," she said, turning away. "I don't want to know any more."

When Willa slammed the door to her makeshift bedroom, the sound of it reverberated for a long time in Juniper's chest.

CHAPTER 14

SUMMER
14 AND A HALF YEARS AGO

Every summer, right in between Jonathan's birthday and mine, we go camping at Lake Munroe. This isn't a family thing, it's friends only, and it's this dreamy little weekend that celebrates the several weeks that my brother and I are the same age. Mostly it's an excuse to leave work early on a Friday afternoon and spend a couple of days on the lake with our favorite people.

I was born on the night of summer solstice, when the sun had just slipped beneath the horizon and fireflies were beginning to spark in the fields. Mom doesn't recall much about that night—she claims she was in too much pain to remember anything past the blinding agony of childbirth—but she does remember the shocking purple of the night sky and the twinkle of lights that shimmered over the field outside the second-story window of her hospital room. Every other detail is lost to a fast and unmedicated delivery. I've never asked Mom if her pain was physical or emotional. I don't dare. I'm afraid of her answer.

From what I do know of the story, Rebecca

Connor had arrived in Jericho, Iowa, just six months before, following the promise of a job at the door factory. She'd circled the ad in a newspaper in Rapid City and driven into Jericho the very next day with nothing but her car and the contents of the backseat: some clothes and a pair of hiking boots, a shoebox filled with photos, the Braga, and two sleeping bags that zipped together but were now bundled apart. She had just under three hundred dollars in cash, and nowhere else to go. Rebecca's family was from another small town in eastern Iowa, but after a whirlwind romance lured her west, she returned to the heartland penniless, alone, and thirteen weeks pregnant. She couldn't bring herself to go home. It's probably for the best—neither I nor Jonathan have ever met our maternal grandparents.

My mother met Lawrence Baker a week after she arrived in Jericho, at the counter in Cunningham's. She'd gotten the job on the production line at the door factory, and was renting a furnished one-bedroom apartment above the cafe. It was dark and smelled of grease, but Patricia—the owner of both the cafe and the apartment—kept her mug full of hot coffee in the mornings and refused to charge her for it. Law found Rebecca nursing a cup at the farthest end of the long cafe counter early one Saturday morning. He watched her from his booth for the better part of an hour, and when he worked up the courage to finally slip onto the sticky green stool beside her, she rewarded his moxie by letting him buy her a caramel pecan roll for breakfast.

To hear Mom tell it, their courtship was quick and practical, nothing like the passionate affair that caused her to abandon her life and drive across the country for love. Of course, that's my spin on it, not hers. But I have to be right. When I was twelve years old and desperate for every scrap of information I could glean about my father—my *real* father—I found a small, cream-colored envelope hidden inside an empty cello case in my mother's music room. In my desperation to leave no stone unturned, I tipped it forward and realized it was hollow. Or, almost. The envelope was inside, tucked into the very bottom.

When I lifted the flap, there wasn't much to see. A pressed flower that turned to dust in my fingers was lying on top of a small sheaf of letters. I unfolded the first one and was surprised to find it written in a dignified, upright cursive. I read the first few lines, but even as a preteen I knew I was trespassing in an unforgivable way. Still, I turned the sheet over to find a signature. A name. They were all signed the same: Love, me.

Me. I wanted to take my mother by the shoulders and shake her. Who was *me?* I was so desperate for answers, I felt like my heart had been scooped out of my chest. But as I was replacing the envelope, something slid and tapped against the side. When I looked again, I found a necklace coiled in the corner. It was a tangled mess, the chain knotted in so many places I wondered if it could ever be undone. But the charms hung free, and it only took me a second to realize what they were. Juniper berries.

I didn't think twice: I grabbed it. Obviously, it was mine.

The knots took me hours to unravel, and I had to work with straight pins that pricked my fingers and left tiny dots of blood on my skin. But the next morning I walked downstairs with the necklace hanging bold against my T-shirt. When my mother saw it, she looked as if she had been punched. Her eyes went huge and hurt, and then she blinked and the expression was gone as quickly as it had come. She gave me a soft smile and never said another word about the necklace. But the next day when I looked for the envelope of letters, it was gone.

That was passion. That was the kind of romance that stories were written about, that launched a thousand ships. I knew the look in my mother's eyes; even though I couldn't fully understand it and had never experienced it myself, it strummed something deep and essential inside me. Something uniquely and painfully human. It was longing, an ache that was so real I could feel it exhale in the room between us. And it was the heartbreaking certainty that the thing she wanted most she could never, ever have. I witnessed the moment that she remembered—and lost him all over again.

My mother has never looked at Lawrence Baker that way.

And yet, for the entire month after they first met, Law showed up at Cunningham's on Saturday morning and bought Rebecca a caramel pecan roll. On the fourth week, he dared to reach out his hand and tuck a strand of dark hair behind her ear. She let him. She also let him call her Reb, take her out on a few real dates, and a couple of months later propose with his grandmother's wedding ring, a simple gold band that had been etched by years of wear and hard work. She still wears that plain ring.

I guess it's a different kind of love.

Law knew Reb was pregnant with another man's baby. And to absolutely no one's great surprise, he took her anyway. Who else would marry Lawrence Baker? There's no male equivalent—"bachelor" didn't quite do justice to his situation—but he was clearly an old maid, gruff and past his prime and not husband material. Of course, Mom has never used those words with me. She paints the picture much differently, insisting that they needed each other, that they were an unexpectedly perfect fit. But it's not hard to read between the lines. They've always been a mismatch: Reb with her music and her artist's soul, her slender wrists and hair black as the river at night; Law with his shock of close-cropped, steel-wool curls, acne-scarred skin, hands as big as a bear's paws. They're night and day, dark and light, and though they seem to work in their own surprising way, it's always a bit disconcerting to see. They're a curious pair and always have been.

A couple months after I was born, my mom was pregnant again.

This time, a boy. Jonathan was born on May 8, exactly six weeks and two days before my first birthday. Law had made a few bad investments (Mom would never say what, just that things were tight), so after Jonathan moved out of the bassinet, he moved into my crib. And I guess the rest is history.

Why we go camping with our friends to commemorate the window of time that we're virtual twins is a bit more murky, but this is our third (and probably final) year, and I'm not about to question tradition. Still, something about this trip hums in warning, like the charge in the air around an electric fence. I can't shake the feeling I'm in for a shock.

"I have the tent, the air mattress, and the cooler," Ashley tells me over french fries from the drive-in on the edge of town. We're sitting cross-legged on the lawn in front of the community center because Ashley's walked over to keep me company during my lunch break. I suspect she needs a little adult interaction, and as payment for intelligent conversation, she's brought a large order of Davey's crinkle fries and a chocolate shake to share. She's also brought the twins, and they're side by side in a double stroller, babbling to each other and gumming french fries to mush. Bella's fry squishes through her overzealous chokehold and hits the ground in pieces. I hand her another before she starts to wail.

"Sounds good," I say, but I'm distracted, and Ashley knows it.

"What sounds good?"

"What you said."

"Mmhmm. And what are you bringing?"

I lift one shoulder, hoping she'll fill in the blanks like she always does.

But Ashley just gives me a disgusted look. "You're half gone, aren't you?"

I'm not sure if she's talking about college, or the fact that my lunch break is almost up. A couple of my arts and crafts campers have already filtered past where we're sitting in the shade of a giant cottonwood. I wave and smile as another one walks by, then force myself to give Ashley my full attention and say, "Just a little distracted, I guess."

"Well, that's nothing new."

It's not like Ashley to be so tart, and that more than anything convinces me of my tenuous grip on my best friend. I watch as she starts to gather up the remains of our lunch—a couple squeeze packets of ketchup and the huge cup with an inch or two of chocolate sludge in the bottom—and wonder why she hasn't brought up Sullivan. The memory of our kiss makes me skittish, but when I open my mouth to come clean to my friend, the words shrivel on my tongue.

It was sweet of Ashley to come, and I'm blowing it again. I make a split-second decision to offer her an olive branch in the form of juicy gossip.

"Did you know that Calvin Murphy has cancer?" The moment I've said it I regret it. I have no idea if Cal's leukemia is public knowledge, and in light of how the Murphys have always been treated as outsiders by the close-knit people of Jericho, I wouldn't be surprised if they were hoping to keep the news under wraps—at least for a while. But Ashley has already devoured this information. She spins toward me, used ketchup packets still pinched between two fingers.

"Seriously?" There's something a bit alarming in her look. Hungry, maybe. I've seen it often. It's the look of someone starved for a sense of importance and worth. Eager to live vicariously, even if—maybe especially if—the vicarious living is tragic. The look on Ashley's face is one of the biggest reasons I'm so eager to leave Jericho behind.

"Yes," I say, almost against my will. "But keep it under wraps, okay? I don't think they're telling people yet. You know how Cal and Beth like their privacy."

"I don't know how long you can keep something like *cancer* a secret, but I won't tell anyone." Ashley leans over and gives me a one-armed hug. "I'm sorry, June. I know they're friends of yours. And I can totally understand why you're out of sorts. I'm just glad to finally know what's gotten into you lately. I thought you were hiding something from me!"

I'm winded by guilt. "Cal and I aren't that close," I protest.

"You don't have to pretend with me." Ashley fixes me with an understanding gaze. "I know you're neighbors. I know Jonathan is over there all the time. This must be absolutely killing him."

"He's upset."

"No doubt. And with the court case and all . . . I wonder if they'll just settle."

"Court case?"

"You don't know?" Jack is starting to fuss, but instead of preparing to leave with him and Bella, Ashley rises to her haunches and unbuckles her baby brother from the stroller. She settles back down in the grass, long legs casually crossed, and perches him on her lap. He burbles at me and grins, reaching for the french fry I've forgotten I'm holding. I hand it over.

"No." It's a little white lie. I've heard rumors, but I want to know what she knows. "I don't know anything about a court case."

"The Murphys are suing the Tates. It's ridiculous, I mean, there's no way they'll win, but they're not backing down."

"How do you know this?"

Ashley arches one eyebrow as if to say, *Really?*

I reframe the question. "What else do you know?"

"Everything, I suppose. At least, everything there is to know. The Murphys are suing for five million dollars in damages due to unlawful drainage resulting in property damage and water contamination." Ashley gives me a satisfied little smile, as if this is something she has worked hard to memorize and she's proud that she can recall it verbatim. But I'm too stunned to give her the affirmation she craves. Her smile falters and fades.

"I don't know what to say."

Ashley shrugs. "Not much you can say. They won't win. Everyone knows it."

My legal expertise wouldn't fill a thimble, but even I know that five million dollars is a significant amount of money for a civil case. And television has taught me that lawyers' fees aren't cheap. I try to picture Franklin Tate, Sullivan's dad, and wonder how he handled the news of a lawsuit. He's not huge, but he carries himself like a tiger, all sinew and swagger and snarl. Mr. Tate's the kind of man who makes baldness look intimidating, and his four sons surround him like a dangerous entourage. Well, not Sullivan. He's the baby of the family and as such has always seemed a little removed from the Tates' infamous reputation. Still, I wouldn't want to cross them—in a dark alley *or* a courtroom.

"Maybe they'll just drop it now. The lawsuit, I mean." Ashley lifts Jack into the stroller and fusses with the straps. He shrieks at her and Bella decides to join in. "I'm sure they'll be really busy with cancer treatments and everything."

This strikes me as incredibly cold, even though Ashley was expressing her condolences only minutes before. I raise my voice over the complaining babies. "Maybe they *shouldn't* drop it. Maybe they're right."

"The Tates know what they're doing," Ashley insists. "They've been farming that land for generations."

It's all I can do not to roll my eyes. But I'm not spoiling for a fight with my best friend. I've been angling for reconciliation. So I keep my mouth shut and focus instead on distracting the twins while Ashley gathers up the toys they've tossed in the grass and shoulders the oversized diaper bag. She's such a natural it almost makes me feel uncomfortable. Ash could be a mother at nineteen.

"Thanks again for lunch," I say.

"Not sure fries and a shake count as lunch." Ashley smirks. "But you're welcome. I'll pick you up on Friday at five. And, for the record, you're in charge of sleeping bags, lawn chairs, and firewood. Don't forget to check the email with food assignments. I think you're on for breakfast on Saturday."

I nod like I'm taking careful mental notes, but I'm thinking about the Murphys. About the battles we choose—and the ones that pick us.

It's a bittersweet weekend, heavy with a sense of finality. The sky is so blue it hurts to look directly at it, and in the morning the horizon is studded with tufts of white clouds whipped stiff as heavy cream. It's hot in the sun but cool in the shade, and I live in my swimming suit with a long, loose-knit sweater thrown over top. By the time Saturday evening rolls around, my skin is the color of cream soda and my hair is frothy with sun-bleached streaks to match. I smooth Ashley's expensive body cream onto my shoulders and carry the scent of coconut and driftwood with me wherever I go.

I don't often think about missing this little corner of Iowa, but days like this make me feel nostalgic for something I haven't yet lost. Or maybe I never had it? I can't quite decide why I'm so conflicted about this community and my place in it, but it might have something to do with the fact that it's filled with so many contradictions.

Now, in the dusky haze of a couple of days spent in the sun and water, everyone is just a little short, nerves exposed. Who we are is less artfully hidden because the veneer has been buffed away by sand and a bit too much time together. Ashley's forlorn, Jonathan is distracted. I can guess what's troubling him, but it doesn't make me feel any better to know the source of his sadness. Callum's sunburnt, Phil's hungover, Lexi's sour all the time. There are just over twenty of us spread over six campsites in a collection of tents, tent trailers, and one Suburban where Jeff and Blake are sleeping on the benches. To a person, we're done.

"Let's go home," I tell Jonathan when I catch him heading off toward the bathhouse alone.

He doesn't even glance at me as I hurry to match his long strides. "This is our party, June."

"Not really. It's an excuse to get together and you know it. Has anyone said happy birthday to you?"

"My birthday is long past."

"It's not about that." I snag his arm, and he finally stops to face me. "Come on. It's been fun, but I want to go home. I think you do, too."

"You're welcome to go."

I study my brother for a long moment, taking in

the beachy sweep of his dark hair, the warm glow of his skin. His eyes are bright but hard somehow, and they don't crinkle at the corners like they usually do when he looks at me. It makes me sad.

"What's going on?" I ask him. "What happened to you this summer?"

Jonathan sighs. He passes his hand over his face, and when he's done it looks as if he's drawn his mouth down farther still. It's a trick that should end with a reversal, with his hand sweeping everything up into the grin I know so well, but he just stares at me like his heart is breaking. I rise onto my tiptoes and wrap my arms around his neck. When Jonathan hugs me back, he shudders. I'm afraid that he's crying, but after a few seconds he steps back and gives the end of my ponytail a tug. His eyes are dry.

"I'm okay, Junebug. I'll be just fine."

"Why won't you confide in me?" I can't keep the hurt out of my voice.

"I'm not trying to keep you out. It's just . . ." He puts his hands on his hips and looks over my shoulder to where the moon has drawn a wavy line across the water. "I need some time."

"Time to what?"

"Figure a few things out."

"Is this about Cal and Beth?"

He lifts one shoulder. "In a way. But there's more to it, June. I just can't share it with you right now."

"Will you ever?"

"Soon," he promises.

It's not nearly enough, but at least I got him to admit that there's something going on. I'll take it. "You won't go home with me?"

Jonathan shakes his head. "I need to stay."

I can't for the life of me imagine why he has to stay at what's supposed to be a fun campout with friends if he's clearly stopped having fun. But after we roast hot dogs and Phil takes out a guitar and serenades us with classic country in a more than passable voice, a pair of headlights illuminates our camp. It's after eleven. We all look up to see who's arrived, but when I glance at Jonathan in the firelight, the set of his jaw assures me that this—whoever it is—is what he's been waiting for.

Car doors open and slam, but the interior lights are too dim and too far away for me to make out who it is. Four figures approach us in the darkness, but it isn't until one of them calls out that I realize it's Sullivan.

"Hey!" he says, entering the circle of light around the fire. "Great night for a fire. Got a chair?"

A few people shift around, spreading out another blanket and moving a handful of roasting sticks that were leaning against a lawn chair. But Sullivan's not alone, and when the others join our ragtag crew, my mind goes dark as a light switched off. It's the rest of the Tate brothers. Dalton is just a couple years older than Sullivan but he looks much older than that. Hard living has left his face lined, his expression perpetually harsh. He chews tobacco, and it pulls his mouth to one side as if frozen in a constant sneer. And the other two Tate brothers are no softer. I don't even know their names, but they're grown men, clearly out of place among the kids who have gathered around hot dogs and country music. *Kids.* I haven't thought of myself as a child in a long time, but next to the Tate brothers I feel small. Naive.

They commandeer chairs and produce bottles that I hadn't previously seen. They swig and laugh while Phil (who's roughly their age but half their size and clearly not cut from the same cloth) quietly puts his guitar away and slips off toward the scattering of tents. I'd like to follow him, but Ashley throws an arm around my shoulders and whispers: "Sullivan came!"

"And his brothers," I mutter under my breath. "They're not exactly a great fit here."

"Of course they are! The Tates fit everywhere they go."

I couldn't disagree more, but I don't have a chance to say anything more because Sullivan catches sight of us and comes to sit on our blanket. Ashley scoots over to make room for him and within seconds is regaling him with stories of the weekend. I burn with shame on her other side, trying not to catch Sullivan's eye and wishing that he would just leave us alone.

It's my abject avoidance of Sullivan that allows me to see the exact moment that Dalton Tate walks past my brother. He lays one hand on Jonathan's shoulder, and without saying a single word the two of them move off into the darkness. The older brothers follow.

I'm stunned. The familiarity between Dalton and Jonathan is startling enough, but the fact that the four of them disappeared together makes my stomach flip. I want to chase after them, to figure out what in the world is going on, but when I glance over at Sullivan to see if he's about to take off too, I find he's already watching me.

He cuts his chin to the side so slightly I doubt that Ashley even notices. But his intention is clear: *no.* It's his eyes that I can't understand. Sullivan is not amused or flirtatious or cunning. His expression is raw and unmistakable. It's filled with regret, and something that makes my blood run cold: fear.

CHAPTER 15

WINTER
TODAY

Juniper had to drag Willa out of bed on Monday morning, and then practically light a fire underneath her to complete every step of her before-school routine. If Willa would have tolerated it, Juniper would've gone so far as to drag a brush through her daughter's long, dark hair, and spoon-feed her oatmeal while she half slept at the table. But the bathroom door was resolutely locked, and though Juniper wheedled and made vague promises that she hoped Willa found enticing, it was after eight o'clock when the moody thirteen-year-old finally emerged. Her face was scrubbed pink and her hair pulled back in a messy ponytail, but Juniper wondered if she had remembered to brush her teeth. No matter. Willa was dressed and presentable, so Juniper thrust a granola bar at her and ushered her out the door.

"We're going to be late," Juniper muttered as she shut and locked the front door behind them.

"Whatever."

"Okay, *I'm* going to be late."

"What's Cora going to do, fire you?"

Juniper rolled her eyes at Willa's back. "That's not the point." She rummaged in the front pocket of her backpack for her car keys and nearly mowed Willa down when the girl stopped suddenly in the middle of the sidewalk. They both stumbled, and Juniper dropped her keys in the snow. "What the—"

"Look," Willa said, her tone brittle as the February air.

"At what? Seriously, Willa, my keys are buried in eight inches of snow. A little help here?" Juniper crouched down and plunged her bare hand into the snowbank to retrieve them. When she turned her attention to her daughter, she saw what Willa was pointing at.

The tires of her car were flat. And not just flat; they had been slashed.

Juniper had never seen a slashed tire before, but the six-inch gashes in the otherwise smooth rubber of the two passenger-side tires were a dead giveaway. Pushing past Willa, Juniper hurried to the driver's side. Those tires had been slashed, too. Her first, visceral emotion was fury. Tires were expensive. She could count on two hundred dollars a piece, plus the cost of a tow . . . The numbers ticked higher in her head even as she began to realize that she was more scared than angry.

Someone slashed her tires. Juniper's vision spun for a horrifying moment and she put both hands on the hood of the car to steady herself. Violence was always shocking—a reminder that nothing was as it should be—and Juniper couldn't help but recoil at the thought of someone plunging a knife into the tires of her car and tearing. Methodically, viciously. One by one. And Juniper doubted that the job could have been accomplished by a run-of-the-mill kitchen knife. This was the work of a weapon. Something saw-toothed and evil.

Juniper had been asleep only a few feet away. *Willa* had been. The reminder that her daughter had been curled up and oblivious beyond a window that could easily be seen from the driveway made Juniper's stomach pitch. Needing to ground herself in reality instead of the wrenching worst-case scenarios that were playing like a string of horror movie scenes in her mind, she reached down to run her thumb over the jagged line of split rubber. Juniper didn't flinch when a tiny wire pierced her skin. The pain helped. She could feel her heartbeat in the place where a line of blood quickly bubbled to the surface, and without thinking, she stuck it in her mouth.

"Are you hurt?" her daughter asked, reaching for her.

Juniper hadn't realized that Willa had followed her around the vehicle.

"I'm fine," she said, balling her hand so Willa

couldn't see the cut on her thumb. Juniper tried a smile; it didn't work.

"Who did this?" Willa looked very young in the pale morning light. She had raked back her hair unevenly and her ponytail was lopsided; her bottom lip trembled just a little.

Juniper thought about saying that it was an accident. But that was ludicrous. "I have no idea," she said honestly.

"What if . . ."

"Don't." Juniper put her arm around Willa and turned her away from the car. "Let's not speculate. It was probably just some kids. We'll walk to the library and see if we can borrow Barry's car."

"We should check for footprints. Maybe they left something behind." Willa tried to spin out of her mother's grip but Juniper held on tighter.

"I'll call the cops when we get to the library. Everett will know what to do."

"Everett?"

But she was too distracted to worry that Willa now knew she was on a first-name basis with a town cop. "What time does first period start?"

"Eight-fifteen, but I'm not going to school."

"A couple of flat tires don't equal a free pass, Willa."

They argued back and forth all the way to the library—a welcome distraction that they both automatically indulged—but it wasn't a long walk, and when Barry entered the picture, the drama was sucked right out of the situation. Juniper snatched a few tissues from the box on the counter to wrap around her cut while Barry listened to a pared-down version of the predicament they found themselves in.

"You probably overfilled them," he told Juniper with just a hint of superiority. "Tires will deflate in cold air, but a warming trend changes everything."

Warming trend? The temperature was barely in the teens. But Juniper didn't bother to challenge him, and when Willa opened her mouth to object, Juniper took her by the wrist and led her away. "Thank you so much for letting us borrow your car," she said over her shoulder. "I'll drop my daughter off at school and be back in just a few minutes."

When they were settled in Barry's tiny two-door import, Willa shot Juniper a scathing look. " 'You probably overfilled them'? How stupid is he?"

Juniper barked a wry laugh. "Amen, sister."

"I mean, there's *no way.*"

"They were slashed," Juniper agreed, putting the unfamiliar car in drive. "But it was probably just a prank, Wills. A sort of hazing for the new kid in town. Or a bet. Some self-proclaimed badass is going to be in a lot of trouble."

Willa's eyes widened at Juniper's word choice,

but the ploy worked: she seemed to relax just a little.

"Besides, I don't have any enemies in Jericho," Juniper lied, "so the chances of this being a targeted attack are pretty slim. Unless, of course, there's something *you'd* like to tell me . . ."

"Oh, you know me: I'm a total badass."

Law would have told Willa to watch her language, but Juniper grinned. If an off-color word or two put them on common ground, so be it. "Just like your mama," she said without thinking. It was the wrong thing to say, and she regretted it the moment the words were out of her mouth. Did Willa want to be compared to her? Was it insulting? Premature? A reminder of what might have been? But when Juniper glanced over at Willa, the girl gave her a rare, hesitant smile.

By the time they pulled up in front of the school, Willa was convinced that the incident was haphazard, and she seemed eager to share the whole salacious story with her friends. Juniper sat in the car for a moment after she'd left and watched her daughter race up the wide front steps. Willa turned around at the door and gave Juniper an unexpected wave, and when Juniper raised her fingers in return, she did so with a mixture of gratitude and dread. Gratitude because the thought of her daughter living in fear made her sick—Willa wanted to believe that her mother's tires had been slashed for some arbitrary, almost casual reason. After worrying for a few grueling minutes, she happily accepted it was random and unspecified. But Juniper also felt dread because she knew the narrative she spoon-fed Willa was hollow. Her ruined tires were a gauntlet thrown. Someone was trying to send her a message.

Juniper wished, not for the first time, that she had been able to have that heart-to-heart with Jonathan. Her conversation with Mandy had given her a faint impression of what they were up against, and she didn't like the trajectory of those seemingly innocuous intimidations. She knew where they ended. Had whoever harassed Jonathan moved on to her? Juniper's stomach curdled at the thought.

Calling Everett was the logical next step, but instead of punching in his number, Juniper called Barry.

"Hey, do you mind if I stop by the garage to get a quote on a tow and four new tires? I kinda need a car."

"Not a problem. I'll cover for you. Cora said she hopes to be in around nine, so take all the time you need."

"Thanks, Barry."

Juniper clicked off the phone and threw it on the passenger seat, then sped right past Tucker's Garage on her way out of town. If it hadn't been for that shadow of a smile from Willa, for the tender way that a strand of her hair had missed the swoop of her ponytail entirely, Juniper would probably be parking in Barry's designated space in front of the library right now. She would have called Everett and let him investigate instead of racing off to do something that was poorly considered and most likely a terrible idea. Maybe even dangerous.

But something had risen up in Juniper that made her wild and reckless and brave all at once. Juniper had dealt with the fallout of everything that happened that summer for nearly fifteen years. She could handle the uncertainty, the painful memories, the knowledge that beneath the surface everything was rotten and black. Willa, on the other hand, was innocent. The fact that someone would commit a crime with her daughter in the picture solidified Juniper's fear into fury. God help whoever brought the fight to the doorstep of a thirteen-year-old. *Juniper's* thirteen-year-old.

She didn't have a plan, but she did have a destination. The Tate Family Farms was where Sullivan had grown up, and though Juniper didn't know who lived there now, she knew that he was poised to inherit. "Someday," he had told her once, "this will all be mine." They were sitting cross-legged on the nearly flat roof of one of the machine sheds, a riot of stars poking holes in the night sky above them. June wasn't really paying attention—Sullivan was tracing lines on her bare arm with a single fingertip, and she was aching for more—but he was obviously proud, so she tried to focus.

"You're the youngest," June said. "You're fourth in line for the birthright."

"I'm the only one who wants it. And the only one my dad trusts."

She felt a swell of something in her chest then, an acknowledgment, maybe, that Sullivan was different, singular. And hers. June lifted her cheek from where it rested on his shoulder and looked around the property. There was the sprawling house with its layered decks and custom-built hot tub. The carefully maintained barns and outbuildings. The bricked-in sign that designated the entire farm a national heritage site. One of the smaller barns had been built in 1876 and meticulously reconstructed a hundred years later. Sometimes people came to take pictures in front of the rough-hewn stone. June had never wanted something so domestic, so predictable, but all at once the realization washed over her: It could *all* be hers. If she wanted it.

She felt the draw of that belonging even now, even as she traced the path to the Tates' farm, every muscle in her body stiff with rage. Sullivan had offered her something back then that she didn't even have the understanding to know she would want or need: home. The sort of fellowship that attached her to something greater than herself and ensured that she would never, no matter what, be alone. More than anything else, she felt alone. So whatever negligible claim she had to Willa, she would protect it with a ferocity she hadn't even known she was capable of.

If Franklin and Annabelle Tate still lived on the property, Juniper wasn't sure what she would do. Of course, they knew exactly who she was, and she doubted they would react kindly to her sudden appearance on their doorstep. But if she was right, and Sullivan and Ashley were now the patriarch and matriarch of the Tate Family Farms, she knew the confrontation wouldn't go much better. She was on a fool's errand.

The long roundabout in front of the Tates' palatial, columned house had been paved since Juniper had seen it last. Back in the day it had been gravel, just like every other farm driveway for a hundred miles, and Sullivan had driven right off it to park on the patchy grass beside the two-stall garage. Now there were four stalls, with carriage house doors and dormer windows in what looked like a loft above the new construction. The double front door was a confection of wrought iron and glass, and there was even a fountain iced over in the very middle of a bricked walkway. A dozen other little changes made the transformation subtle but complete: the Tate Family Farms were no longer an impressive property in a conservative working-class community: they were a manor, a plantation that made no apologies for a level of status and wealth that far outweighed anything in the entire region. It was breathtaking, but indecent somehow.

Juniper wavered in the driveway for a moment, but when she thought of the tiny house where she was living and how it could easily fit in the garage of the Tates' gorgeous estate, a lick of fury rekindled. *They slashed her tires.* She had no doubt it was them, and in the face of their ridiculous affluence, that level of cruelty was just obscene.

The front door was fitted with a knocker (a knocker!) in the shape of a teardrop, but no doorbell. So, hand shaking and thumb still wrapped in a tissue now matted with dried blood, Juniper lifted the knocker and let it drop. Twice. A few seconds after the pair of thuds echoed through the house, Juniper could see Ashley descend the central staircase at a jog.

Was it relief that flooded through Juniper? Terror? She only had a moment to consider what she had done—the confrontation that she had so blithely initiated—before Ashley caught sight of her between the twining curls of iron and stopped in her tracks.

They stared at each other through the glass. Juniper bundled in a dusty winter coat and boots, and Ashley barefoot in a pair of high-waisted leggings and a sports bra to match. Winter and summer. Polar opposites. Strangers.

That could have been me, Juniper knew, and she couldn't tell if she was recoiling because she loathed the thought or because she secretly wished for it.

At first Juniper worried that Ashley wouldn't open the door at all, but then her shoulders squared and Ashley all but lunged across the space between them. Yanking one of the heavy doors wide, she growled, "What do you think you're doing here?"

"Hi, Ash." It popped out before Juniper could stop it. It was snide, but she felt her former best friend's nickname pierce a forgotten place in her heart.

"Don't you dare call me that. You have *no right* to call me that. I won't ask again: What are you doing here?"

Juniper thought of her crappy, rusty car and the knife that had surely made quick work of the threadbare tires. She could almost picture it: bone-handled, custom-made. Perhaps Ashley used it to segment pomegranates for her post-workout smoothie bowl. "Why did you do it?"

"Do what, June? Go to your stupid library class? For your information, I didn't even know you were back in town. And yeah, I probably should have left when I realized it was you, but you know what? I wanted to make you uncomfortable. I wanted you to squirm. I hope you hated every single minute of it, and you need to know I'll do it again. And every week until you leave Jericho."

A fleck of spittle hit Juniper on the cheek, but she didn't move to wipe it away. "Why'd you slash my tires, Ashley?"

Some inscrutable emotion washed across Ashley's features, but then she steeled her gaze and the moment was gone. "I have no idea what you're talking about."

"Really? Because I can't think of a single person in Jericho who would be so spiteful."

"Spiteful? Are you kidding me? You're a despicable human being, June."

That stung. "We were kids. Sullivan and I fell in love—"

"Your little affair was *not* love. Don't cheapen my marriage, my *life*"—Ashley tapped her chest with her knuckles, hard—"by pretending that a few weeks one summer when you were a teenager was anything close to love."

"It was an accident."

"Oh, that's rich. Do you mean that your secret relationship was an accident? Or that Willa was?"

Juniper recoiled as if she had been slapped.

"Thanks for that." Ashley crossed her arms and gave Juniper a cold, tight smile. "If I had any questions about Willa's parentage, I don't anymore. The look on your face is all the proof I need."

"Does Sullivan—"

"He's willfully ignorant. And it's for his own good. I can hardly stand to look at her. My children do *not* have a half sister." Ashley gave a little shiver of revulsion.

Poor Willa. Blameless, naive, lovely little Willa. The line where "father" should be on her birth certificate had been intentionally left blank—a bitter tradition for the Baker girls— because June had confessed that in the weeks after the murders she had gone completely off the rails. She didn't know who the father was. Didn't want to know. Didn't care. But that wasn't true. There had only ever been one possible father, but because Juniper wanted to protect her daughter—and Sullivan and Ashley and, well, *everyone*—she bore her parents' quiet shame. She would rather have them believe that she had slept with half the county than chain Sullivan to her when he had already let her go. The girl that June had been was hurt and reeling, and she had believed with the ingenuous certainty of a crushed nineteen-year-old that Willa would be better off without him. That they both would.

Of course, no one came forward. There wasn't even the faintest whisper of who the father might be, and eventually people stopped wondering. June and Sullivan had hidden their relationship meticulously, making sure the only people who ever saw them together were their siblings. And none of them would ever come forward. Willa was the opposite of a virgin birth—she was anybody's baby.

But Ashley's derision changed everything. Juniper was suddenly, unshakably sure that she had made a terrible mistake. The thought shot through her like a bolt of electricity: *Sullivan should know.*

"She has his eyes," Juniper said. She didn't even realize she had spoken out loud until Ashley hissed at her through her pursed lips.

"Shut up. *Shut up.* Don't you say that. Sullivan Tate has *three* children, and they all have *my* eyes."

At that moment a cry rang out behind Ashley. "Mama?"

There was a toddler sliding slowly down the steps on her bottom. She was facing them, her chubby arms outstretched toward Ashley as she pitched forward and came precariously close to tumbling headlong.

"Turn around, baby!" Ashley called, her voice, her entire bearing, instantly changed. She took a few hurried steps toward the staircase, twisting her arms in front of her as if to remind the little girl how it was done. "Just like Mommy taught you. On your tummy. That's a good girl."

Juniper's throat felt thick, and unwelcome tears

sprang to her eyes. She quickly swiped them away while Ashley's back was turned.

In spite of everything, it was clear that Ashley was a good mom. She had a beautiful life, beautiful children. What was Juniper doing? What did she hope to accomplish by coming out here and confronting her? Juniper was the outsider, the exile who had abandoned everyone and everything—including her own daughter. She had relegated Willa to a life as nobody's girl. Or, maybe—horrifyingly—the Butcher's Girl.

But this. *This* was her birthright. Willa was Sullivan Tate's firstborn.

As Juniper watched, the curly-haired toddler finally descended the stairs close enough for Ashley to reach. She swung the child up into her arms and nuzzled her neck while the little girl giggled. "Big girl, Hadley! Look what you did! Mama's so proud of you!"

Juniper wasn't sure what to do. She contemplated quietly pulling the door shut and just disappearing, but before she could reach for the handle, Ashley spun around. "Look, Hadley. It's the lady from the library. Remember her? Should we go to Mom and Tot Hour this week?"

"Ashley—"

"Yes, let's go. We'll sit right in the front again. That'll be fun." Ashley's tone was bright and cheerful, but she bored a hole through Juniper with her glare.

She knew that she was supposed to feel scared and ashamed. She knew Ashley expected her to duck her head and run, sufficiently cowed and put well in her place. But though her words were sharp as cut glass, and though her eyes were dark with hate, Juniper could see something else in Ashley.

Ashley Tate was ruthless, but she was also frightened. It might seem like she held all the cards—house, husband, heritage and all—but if they were playing a game, Juniper was the wild card and Willa trumped all. What would happen if she simply told the truth? If she confessed to Sullivan that he had another daughter? Maybe he already knew. Maybe he just didn't dare to reveal her secret. It was obvious that Ashley was terror-stricken by the very thought.

What else did Ashley suspect?

The memory of Sullivan's simple, damning kiss made Juniper gasp. Thankfully, at the sound, a satisfied smile crossed Ashley's lips and Juniper knew that she believed she had won whatever battle they were fighting. Best to let her think so.

"Goodbye, Ashley." Juniper held her gaze for a long moment, hoping that the Ashley she once knew was somewhere inside. *I'm not going to steal your husband,* she wanted to say. *I don't want to ruin your life. But things might get messy. And if you come after my daughter . . .* Well, it was obvious that Ashley knew all about being a mama bear.

Juniper didn't look back when she pulled away, but she could picture Ashley framed in the front door, Hadley in her arms. What a mess. Juniper couldn't be certain if Ashley had slashed her tires or not, but she was definitely capable of it. And if her former best friend was as angry and afraid as Juniper believed her to be, what else might she do? What might she have already done?

CHAPTER 16

SUMMER
14 AND A HALF YEARS AGO

Mom always makes crepes with Nutella and fresh strawberries on our birthdays, and when I wake on the morning of the twenty-first, I can already smell the fruity tang of the berries macerating. It's a Sunday, the perfect day for a birthday because Jonathan doesn't have to go to work and we can be lazy and together all day. But before I've even thrown back the sheets, I remember that Jonathan and I have barely spoken since the campout. In my mind's eye I can see him walking away from the fire the last night we were there, flanked by the Tate brothers. Dalton, Wyatt, and Sterling, I know now. Cowboys all. Or maybe vigilantes.

"They're just some guys I know," Jonathan tried to tell me when I cornered him later.

"You're kidding, right?" I was disgusted because everyone knows not to tangle with the Tates.

"Look, June, drop it. You don't know what you're talking about."

"So tell me!"

"I can't."

"What do you mean, you can't?"

"I don't want to, okay? You're leaving in a

couple of weeks anyway. Let it go," he insisted. And then added, "And stay away from Sullivan, like I told you."

"Make me." I was getting all up in his face, and for the first time since we were kids, Jonathan put his hands on me in anger. He didn't hit me or push me or anything, but he grabbed my upper arms and held me away. We stood there, arm's-length apart, and glared at each other. Then Jonathan let go, spun on his heel, and walked away. I could see red marks on my skin where he had pinched me, and though they faded quickly, I felt bruised by him for much longer.

I don't want to fight with Jonathan. Not on my nineteenth birthday, and certainly not in the last couple of months that I have with him. I'm headed to Iowa City in mid-July for a two-day freshman orientation program, and then it's only four short weeks until I move into my dorm room on campus. A part of me wishes that I could just stay when I visit in July—especially now that my brother and I are barely on speaking terms. But a bigger part of me wants to mend what has been broken. And that's why when I crawl out of bed and throw on my favorite sundress, I'm mentally rehearsing all the ways I can let him know I'm sorry without actually saying the words. *He's* the one who owes *me* an apology, but I want to make amends, even if he's not ready yet. The clock is ticking.

"Happy birthday!" Mom says when I walk into the kitchen. She doesn't even turn around—she can tell by the way I walk that it's me.

"Thanks," I say, and go to stand beside her at the stove. I lay my head on her shoulder for just a moment and get a whiff of mint and vanilla from the homemade crepes.

"I can't believe you're nineteen."

"Right?" I palm a peach from the basket on the counter and grab a paring knife to slice it up.

"Rinse that," Mom says, tilting the pan so that the batter from the first crepe covers the entire bottom of the large, round pan. She always throws the first one away. When Law isn't around, she calls it a sacrifice to the kitchen gods. When he is, she just smiles a secret smile at me and turns it into the garbage can.

I run the tap ice cold and give the peach a gentle wash beneath the spray. I halve it and cut off a sliver, then pop it in my mouth and let the sweetness burst on my tongue. It tastes like a birthday present.

"Where's Law?" I ask, glancing at the hallway that leads to their room.

"Chores."

It's almost eight o'clock. Usually he's done by now. "And Jonathan?"

"Still sleeping."

That explains it. Jonathan helps with chores

on Sunday mornings so that we can get to church on time. The fact that he's still sleeping, and that Law let him do it, is shocking to me. There isn't much to do on our little farm—not when the crops are safely planted and growing, and especially not since Law culled the herd—but the few cattle we do have need to be fed and watered. The chickens, too. And the eggs need to be collected, leftovers set out for the barn cats, and traps checked. Jonathan and I used to do an every-other-day rotation, but since Law works less these days, he likes to putter around the farm and he usually doesn't care how long it takes him. But church starts at nine thirty, and he should be in the shower by now.

"Want me to wake him?" I ask, worried that the morning will erupt in drama. I'm nineteen, past the point of believing my birthday grants me special princess status, but that doesn't mean I'm eager for a confrontation today—or any day, for that matter.

"Nah. He'll be up soon." Mom sounds deliberately mild, as if she's trying to be as nonchalant as possible.

Is everyone hiding something from me? "I'll be back," I tell her, abandoning my peach on the butcher block.

"Where are you going?"

I mumble something in reply. I just want to be alone.

• • •

It's a beautiful June morning, the air already warm and laced with the scent of the lindens that line our long drive. They're in full, heady bloom right now, and the ground is littered with clumps of tiny yellow flowers like fallen stars. I breathe in deeply, trying to memorize the way the sun shines through the heart-shaped leaves and casts dappled, golden light on the gravel lane. As ready as I am to go, there are things that I'll miss, and this view—the way the hills roll away from our farm and the sky spreads so wide and blue it seems endless—is one of them.

I don't see Law anywhere, so he must be in the coop or in the barn, and I lean against the trunk of Mom's car where it pokes out the back of the detached garage. There's a breezeway between the garage and the house so that Mom doesn't have to get wet when it's raining or snowing, but in the summertime, we tend to leave the garage doors wide open and forgo the breezeway in favor of the porch.

Mom is fastidious about her car and keeps exactly two things in her trunk: a faded patchwork quilt for impromptu picnics in the summer and potentially hazardous road conditions in the winter, and a spare tire that she knows how to change without help from AAA. It strikes me that today is the perfect day for a picnic, and I go around to the front of her car to pop the trunk. But when I reach for the quilt, I realize the blanket is unusually high, tucked around something that's peeking out from beneath a loose corner. I peel the fabric back and find mom's suitcase staring back at me. It's a gaudy, floral print that she's had for as long as I can remember, though it usually collects dust in the attic. I haven't seen it out in years. What's it doing in her trunk?

It's absolutely none of my business, but I'm so sick of people keeping things from me that I reach out and grab a corner of the suitcase. I assume it's empty, but I can hardly lift it. The big case is clearly packed full.

Glancing over my shoulder to make sure that Lawrence is nowhere to be seen, I pull the suitcase toward me and hurriedly unzip it. I have no idea what I'm going to find, but it's filled with the most obvious—and unexpected—things imaginable: Mom's clothes.

Her favorite dress is on top, a soft cotton shift with a flattering silhouette and big flowers the color of ripe nectarines. She doesn't wear it often, but she loves it and glows when she does. What in the world is it doing in here? I carefully lift the folded clothes and finger through a couple pairs of jeans, a bunch of shirts, and her well-worn cream-colored cardigan. The mesh pocket sewn into the top flap is stuffed with underwear and socks rolled neatly together, a bra in black and another in blush. Tucked in the side are a pair of canvas tennis shoes and brown leather sandals that I've never seen her wear before. There are enough clothes in here for a week away at least.

But Mom's not going on vacation.

I try to yank the zipper closed, but the clothes have shifted from my probing and it won't go. Cramming everything in, I press on the top of the suitcase to try to make the zippers line up. Something crinkles in the flat exterior pocket. I know I shouldn't—I'm already buzzing with the fear of being caught, of having unintentionally discovered something that's much bigger and scarier than I could have imagined—but I've already come this far. I unzip the outer pocket and stick my hand inside. It's an envelope. It's *the* envelope. The one with the letters from my birth dad.

All the air leaves me in a whoosh, and I'm left breathless and gasping with my head in the trunk. I try to blink the darkness away, but my vision swims anyway and I feel faint. I can't even begin to imagine what this is all about. Why my mother has a packed suitcase hidden in the trunk of her car—the car that Law never drives, never even touches. When they go places, they take his truck, and I can't recall a single time that I have ever seen him behind the wheel of her practical little sedan. It strikes me that if Reb was trying to hide something from him, this would be the perfect place to do it. And she's clearly hiding things. The envelope is undeniable proof.

My hands are shaking when I finally return the envelope to its original location and force the zipper closed. I pull the blanket back over the suitcase and tuck everything in tightly, doing a better job than Mom did, so that if someone does happen to open the trunk, they can easily dismiss the lump that is her faded car blanket. I'm not sure why I'm protecting her, but I feel strongly that she needs protection, and I'm desperate to offer it.

I shut the trunk quietly, afraid to slam it and draw attention to what I'm doing. I don't want to arouse Law's suspicions and I don't want Mom to know what I've seen. But I'm not quick or stealthy enough, because after I double-check that it's latched and turn around, I see Law walking toward me across the yard.

"What are you doing?" he calls. No "Good morning." No "Happy birthday."

I swallow hard and force a smile. "Thought I'd grab the picnic quilt, but I changed my mind." It's the honest-to-God truth, but my palms sweat as I say it.

Law grunts, then gives me a strained, crooked smile and takes a few awkward steps toward me. "Happy birthday, June," he says, and gives me a gruff hug.

He's not much of a hugger, and I'm so stunned by his embrace that my arms are pinned to my sides and I can't reciprocate. It doesn't much matter. The hug is over in an instant, and Law seems embarrassed that he attempted it at all. "Is your mother making breakfast?" he asks, breezing past the almost-paternal moment.

"Crepes," I tell him unnecessarily. "They should be ready by now."

I follow him into the house, heart heavy with knowledge that feels like an anchor. I know things that I shouldn't know and don't understand, and the pieces of this particular puzzle do not—*cannot*—form into a happy whole. At least, not one that I can imagine.

But it's my birthday, and I have no choice but to shove my suspicions aside and play the part of a happy, newly minted nineteen-year-old. Jonathan has emerged from his room, and when I walk into the kitchen he pecks me on the cheek and hands me a small, carefully wrapped package. "Later," he whispers, so I tuck it into the deep pocket of my dress.

"Everything's ready!" Mom says in a singsong voice. We find our spots at the table, and Mom sets my plate before me with a flourish, just like she's done since I was little. It used to thrill me, the three fat rolls of fresh crepes dotted with ruby-red strawberries from the Murphys' field and dusted with confectioners' sugar. As per tradition, she's put a single striped candle in the middle crepe on my plate. When she lights it with a match, the three of them sing "Happy Birthday" badly. Only Mom can manage to stay on key.

I don't make a wish when I blow out the candle. I have no idea what to wish for. I'm supposed to talk and laugh, to eat, but my stomach is churning and I have the beginning of a headache. Still, I cut a bite with my knife, spear a strawberry, and force myself to smile. The chocolate hazelnut cream sticks in my mouth and threatens to gag me, but I murmur my thanks and make eye contact with each person in my family. Everyone looks wary to me. Suspicious.

As if we're all choking back secrets.

Late in the afternoon, a storm rolls in. For hours before the bank of dark clouds becomes visible and the thunder starts to rumble on the horizon, I can feel the electricity snapping in the air. It pulls everything tight, winding the atmosphere until it seems as if we've all been drawn and are about to be quartered. When fat drops finally begin to fall and a gust of wind blows the scent of cool water and hot asphalt across the farm, it's such a relief that I head to the porch to watch the lightning crackle against the seething boil of charred sky.

I opened presents after church. A thick sweatshirt with the University of Iowa logo proudly embroidered across the chest from Mom, and an emergency car kit filled with disaster essentials from Law. Practical and thoughtful, exactly what I've come to expect from my parents. Jonathan doesn't say anything about the little package he gave me, so I slip it out of my pocket while I'm sitting alone on the porch and open it in the watery gray light of the storm.

It's a small, leather-bound journal with a thin braided tie. The pages are thick hand-cut paper, and the whole thing is not much bigger than a deck of oversized cards. It's the perfect size for slipping into pockets, purses, small spaces. I love it instantly, but I can't help wondering what prompted Jonathan to give it to me now. The journal seems like the perfect place to pen all the frustrations I have with him. All the questions. It's almost like an invitation.

I begin to crumple up the wrapping paper, but stuck amid the glossy wrap is a small square of lined notebook paper. I hadn't noticed it before. Picking it out, I squint at the single line written on it.

For all the things you can't say. Love, J

It's a form of apology. Jonathan knows he's killing me with his silences and secrecy. He knows that everything has changed between us this summer. But instead of reaching out to me and confiding in me, he's given me a pathetic substitute. As if writing down my feelings is going to make everything better.

A part of me would like to throw the book

out into the rain, where it'll be ruined by the thunderstorm. But even though I'm annoyed, I know it's too pretty for that, so I wad up the paper and slip the journal back into my pocket.

I can't help feeling melancholy. The storm certainly doesn't help, though the relentless sheets of water seem to have passed, and now the rain is falling soft and steady, the sound a music all its own.

When a car turns down our driveway, I look up in surprise. Sundays are quiet in Jericho. People don't mow their lawns or disc their fields or pop by unannounced. But it only takes me a second to realize that it's Sullivan's truck, and somehow, although he's the last person I expected to see, his presence makes perfect sense. My gratitude is swift, the desire to see him overwhelming any sense of misgiving or twinge of conscience. I'll be gone in just over six weeks. Ashley can have him then. And Jonathan has abandoned me—in more ways than one. He left hours ago. He can't expect me to spend the remainder of my birthday alone.

I stand up from the porch swing and go to lean against one of the pillars framing the wide steps. From here, I can feel a mist of rain and it raises goose bumps along my bare arms. Sullivan waves at me as he parks, and I wave back, then laugh as he leaps out of the truck and sprints through the rain. He takes the stairs in two huge bounds, and lands hard on the porch, shaking his head like a dog and scattering droplets all over me.

"Looks like you were expecting me," Sullivan says with a grin. His shirt is splattered and there are rivulets of water running down his cheeks. Without thinking, I reach and brush the rain away as if I'm wiping tears. It stuns us both, and I take a step back as Sullivan stares at me.

After a moment he seems to get his bearings back. "Happy birthday," he says.

"Thank you." I'm suddenly shy, ashamed of the way I touched him and my obvious pleasure at his unexpected arrival. "Are you looking for Jonathan?" I know he's not, but it gives me a burst of satisfaction when he shakes his head.

"I'm here for you, Baker. I was hoping I could talk you into going for a drive with me."

"A drive? Where to?"

"Munroe."

"Got another puppy to deliver?"

Sullivan's mouth quirks as if he's trying hard not to grin. "Are you going to make me say it?" He runs his hands through his damp hair and sighs. "I'd like to take you out."

"Like on a date?" I sound coy, but my heart is thudding so hard in my chest I'm afraid he can hear it even over the song of the rain.

"God, you're impossible," he groans. "Yes, June, on a date. I, Sullivan Tate, would like to take you, Juniper Baker, on a date."

I can't stop the curl of my lips. But just as quickly as I smile, I remember. I'm leaving. My best friend is probably in love with him. My brother keeps warning me away. But here, on my porch, on my birthday, stands the only person who's seeking me out. His attention is so unanticipated, and so welcome, I answer before I have a chance to think twice.

"I'd love to."

"Good." He looks for a second like he's going to lean in and kiss me, or hug me, or something, but he puts his hands on his hips instead. "Do you need anything? A coat? A purse?"

"Yeah, I'll be just a second." I hurry into the house without inviting him inside. I know that I should, that it's the polite thing to do, but I don't feel like fielding twenty questions from Mom and Law. Besides, I'm not sure that we want any witnesses. There are plenty of people who wouldn't be happy about me taking off with Sullivan, and while I don't much care, I also don't want to go looking for trouble.

"I'm going out!" I call in the direction of the living room.

"Okay," Mom calls back. "Have fun."

I'm back outside in a couple of minutes flat. I've grabbed a jean jacket to throw over my sundress and a clutch purse that holds my wallet and has just enough room left over for a tube of lip gloss. I even took a moment to finger-comb my hair and put on a bit of lipstick. When I step outside and close the door behind me, Sullivan gives me an unmistakable look that fills me with a familiar mix of dread and desire. I know I'm not supposed to like him, but there's something here I want.

"How did you know I was free tonight?" I ask when we're buckled in and heading down the highway. "It's my birthday. I could have been out partying."

"Nah." Sullivan smiles. "You're not the type. Besides, Jonathan let it slip that you were home. I took a chance."

My mood sours instantly. I already know the answer, but I can't help asking: "So he's at your house?"

"Mmhmm." Sullivan seems nonplussed by the question and has completely missed my tone.

"And what's he doing there?"

That earns me a sidelong glance. "Hanging out. Look, June, your brother and my brothers are good friends. He's at our house a lot. Do you have a problem with that?"

I contemplate that for a moment, and then decide to throw caution to the wind. "Jonathan is good friends with Calvin and Elizabeth Murphy. They're like family to him. And from what I understand, your family has made life a living hell for the Murphys. Sullivan, you *killed their dog*. I guess I don't understand the attraction."

His hands tighten on the steering wheel, knuckles turning white. For a minute, I think he's going to yell at me, but then he visibly relaxes and the Sullivan I thought I knew is back. He's cocky, self-important. He says insolently, "Dramatic much? The dog was a menace—he was getting into our henhouse on a nightly basis. And he killed himself. We didn't stuff poison down his throat. You don't know what you're talking about, June."

When I give an exasperated cry, it takes us both by surprise. But I don't care. I'm not about to back down. "I am sick to death of being told that I don't know what I'm talking about. If nobody will tell me what's going on, how am I supposed to know?" I'm shrieking, but it feels good. "And why did you pick me up tonight? Why are you with me? Is this all some act? Are you—"

Sullivan slams on the brakes and hydroplanes for a few seconds, forcing me to brace myself against the dashboard. By the time he's straightened out and slowed down, I'm breathing heavy and near tears. It's mortifying. I don't want to get upset in front of Sullivan Tate, and I certainly don't want to cry in front of him. But I feel used. So confused. My whole world seems upended and I can't put my finger on what exactly is different or why.

The rain is a gentle patter against the windshield now, and there's no reason for Sullivan to stop, but he pulls down a gravel road and parks in a field driveway anyway. I'm about to let him have it, to unleash all my frustrations on the nearest Tate brother, but when he turns to me, he's the Sullivan I've been getting to know. Softer, kind. His expression has changed completely from the hard irritation of only a moment before, and the first words out of his mouth are: "I'm sorry."

"For what?" He's been so hot and cold, back and forth, that I lean away from him with my back pressed into the passenger-side door. I can't get an accurate read on him.

"First of all," Sullivan says, "I don't know what's going on with your brother. I know he's been like a son to the Murphys, but in the last few months he started hanging around our farm. He met Dalton at a party and they started talking . . ."

It sounds far-fetched to me, but I can't deny the signs—or the rapport that Jonathan seems to have with the Tates.

Sullivan shrugs. "They're tight. I don't know what to tell you, June. I think Jonathan feels taken advantage of."

"What do you mean?"

He passes his hand over his face, and when he looks at me again, he seems reluctant to speak. Still, Sullivan asks: "Jonathan works a lot for the Murphys, right?"

I don't understand the question but I nod. "Sure."

"And have they ever paid him?"

"Jonathan would never accept payment from Cal or Beth," I say, maybe too quickly. Years ago, when Jonathan would simply mow their lawn or help feed the calves, I remember Cal paying Jonathan in trips out for ice cream or tickets to the movies. But as far as I know, Cal has never truly compensated Jonathan for the time he spends on their farm. And if I'm being honest, my brother has put in a lot of work there over the years. Hard labor that would have earned him very good money anywhere else. What would that add up to over the course of, well, a decade? Maybe more. I couldn't begin to guess. But, I remind myself, it doesn't really matter. Jonathan loves the Murphys. He would never hold something like a little—or even a lot of—money against them.

"I think you're wrong," I say, but I don't sound very convincing.

"I'm just telling you what I know."

"What else?"

"What do you mean, what else?"

"What are they up to? Why did you show up at the campout a couple weeks ago and why does my brother keep disappearing?" A thought hits me, and all at once I know that I'm right. I speak around a lump in my throat. "What are they planning?"

Sullivan doesn't deny anything. "You know the Murphys are suing us, right?"

I nod.

He heaves a sad, heavy sigh. "It's a really big deal, June. Like, we could lose the farm. My family could lose everything."

"And?"

"And we just want them to stop."

A sense of dread washes over me. "Sullivan—"

"It's not what you're thinking," he says quickly. "We would never hurt anyone. But if they're scared or distracted or feel like they can't win . . . Maybe they'll give up."

"So you—and my brother—are planning to 'scare or distract' the Murphys?"

Sullivan looks pained. "Not *we*. Not really. I mean, I want the lawsuit to go away just as much as everyone else, but I have no part in what they're planning. In *this*."

"But Jonathan does?"

I can tell it's hard for Sullivan to say it. He swallows visibly and then nods. "Yeah."

The betrayal I feel is a scalpel to the heart: sharp and clean. I can't even begin to imagine how Cal and Beth would feel if they knew. I've never sensed an ounce of bitterness in my brother toward the Murphys, but if I'm honest with myself, I have to admit that it stands to reason. All that time, all those years of free labor and last-minute phone calls for help for nothing but a warm handshake and paternal pat on the back when the work was done . . . It's not unrealistic to imagine that Jonathan has had enough. But I can think of at least a dozen ways forward that don't include intimidation and property damage. Or worse.

"How could he?" I whisper, and don't even realize I've said it out loud until Sullivan has reached for my hand. When I don't pull away, he laces his fingers through mine.

"People are complicated."

He's right, of course. I could have never predicted that I'd be holding Sullivan's hand, drawing more comfort from his touch than I ever thought possible.

I push aside my misgivings and hold on tight, drawing strength from Sullivan's warm grip to ask the question: "What are they going to do?"

"I don't know."

I study his face, but his gaze is unflinching. Honest. I believe he's telling the truth. "What *do* you know?"

Sullivan doesn't waver. "Whatever it is, they're planning on doing it on the Fourth of July."

Less than two weeks away. My mind is off, wheeling through plans and possibilities, wondering if I should confront Jonathan or warn Cal and Beth or involve my parents. Should I call the cops? It all feels a little surreal to me, as if I've somehow stumbled into the plot of one of the true crime shows Law likes to watch on TV. But I believe that Sullivan is serious. And the Murphys have already experienced some pretty awful harassment. Roundup on their lawn, trespassers at midnight, a keyed car. A dead dog. What's next?

Sullivan reads me like a book. "I don't like it either," he says, leaning toward me.

His shoulder is so inviting I let my forehead dip toward his collarbone and close my eyes. When his arms go around me, I bury myself against him. It's impulsive, but a perfect fit somehow. Sullivan smells of fresh-cut wood and the sharp zest of a cold lime. "What are we going to do?"

I'm not sure where it came from, this *we*. But Sullivan doesn't contest it. Instead, he brushes his lips against my forehead and murmurs, "I don't know, but we'll think of something."

And just like that, we're together. In this moment, there's no place I'd rather be.

CHAPTER 17

WINTER
TODAY

"**Y**ou look flushed," Cora said when Juniper burst into the library a few minutes before it was scheduled to open. "Are you feeling okay?"

Juniper was not, in fact, feeling okay. Her trip to the Tates' estate took less time than she thought it would, but it had been deeply unsettling. She felt pale and clammy. Sick. But she said, "I'm fine. And far more worried about you. How are *you?*"

"Never better. They adjusted my meds and I'm good as new." That obviously wasn't true. Cora's skin had a gray cast and she looked as if she had lost a few more pounds. Juniper wanted to fuss over her, but Cora was having none of it. "Enough about me," she ordered. "What's going on?"

"Did Barry tell you what happened this morning?"

Cora nodded, then waved Juniper into her office on the far side of the circulation desk. "Barry can take care of opening. He's salting the sidewalk."

Juniper had already seen him outside with the

bucket and ice-salt scoop, and had passed off his car keys with sincere gratitude.

"Come here," Cora said, just over the threshold of her small office. She held out her arms and Juniper returned the hug, but she was too keyed up to take any solace from Cora's warmth. Apparently, Cora could sense it, because she squeezed Juniper's hands and backed away to lean against her desk.

"I'm sorry I was late."

"Never mind." Cora flicked off the apology with a wag of her fingers. "Barry was here. I've been here for half an hour at least. Tell me: Who did it?"

"Slashed my tires?"

Cora's lips pulled tight. She didn't suffer fools.

"Yeah, sorry. There's a lot going on."

"Have you called the police?"

"Not yet."

Cora took this news with a slight nod. Juniper couldn't tell if she thought it was wise or foolish that the local police hadn't been contacted yet. She glanced toward the door to make sure that Barry hadn't crept into the library soundlessly. The floor was empty. Turning back to Cora she said, "I think it was Ashley."

"I don't know." Cora tapped the thin line of her mouth once. "She's all bark and no bite."

Juniper didn't agree, but she didn't argue. "One of the Tate brothers?" They hated her, and they had good reason to. Though she had been leveled by the murders and later by the knowledge that she was pregnant, in the months that June remained in Jericho, she hadn't missed an opportunity to accuse the Tates. Anything to take the focus off her brother. Anything to draw attention to what she knew to be true: the Tate brothers had been plotting to do something to warn off Cal and Beth Murphy. June spilled it all—or *almost* all—over and over again, to anyone who would listen. If there had been any chance that she and Sullivan could make it work, she had annihilated that possibility with the drumbeat of her allegations against his family.

"More likely. Sterling's wife left him last year. Took the kids. He hates everyone now. But I guess that's nothing new." Cora looked thoughtful for a moment. "Sullivan? If Ashley is upset that you're back, maybe he's defending her?"

Juniper went very still. Cora didn't know about her relationship with Sullivan, and she didn't want to let a single detail slip. As far as Cora was concerned, Ashley's animosity toward Juniper could be chalked up to June's relentless assertion of the Tates' culpability. It had nothing to do with Willa, or what Sullivan had once meant to her. "Maybe?" Juniper said, hoping her hesitancy was understandable, given the circumstances. "I don't think he'd jeopardize his family that way. They seem solid."

Cora lifted one shoulder. "Depends on your definition of solid. If you ask me, Ashley is a bit unbalanced. Besides, she has a lot on her plate. I believe their oldest is ten and the baby is still in diapers."

Sullivan's oldest isn't ten, she's almost fourteen. The thought came unbidden, and Juniper banished it immediately.

Cora snapped her fingers. "You know who you need to talk to?"

Juniper was numb and jarred by the sudden conversational pivot, but Cora didn't seem to notice. The older woman shuffled behind her desk and started tapping away at the computer. After a few seconds she turned the monitor toward Juniper.

"India Abbot," she said with something that sounded like pride.

"India?" Juniper was shocked out of her stupor by the glossy main page of *Jericho Unscripted.* "You've got to be kidding."

"Oh, no. She's something else. You'd love her."

"I met her," Juniper said. "At Mom and Tot Hour."

Cora wrinkled her nose as if she smelled something unpleasant. "She comes off a bit ditzy, but the girl graduated from UCLA and is working on her capstone project for a master's in psychology. She's great. Seriously."

"*Jericho Unscripted?* It's a little *Real Housewives*, if you ask me." Juniper held out both hands, palms up toward the computer screen as if it were all the evidence she needed.

"It's ironic. India's really bright. She went to a crime-solving convention last fall where the attendees dove deep into a cold case and tried to solve it over a weekend. India came home with an embroidered deerstalker hat because she did the most to advance the case." Cora paused, taking in Juniper's obvious skepticism. "You know, deerstalker because—"

"Sherlock, I get it." Juniper's mind was whirling. Crime-solving convention? Surely she'd found her podcaster. But she had a hard time reconciling the sparkly young woman at Mom & Tot Hour with: *I'm going to prove that bastard Jonathan Baker did it.* What did India have against Jonathan?

"Don't be judgmental," Cora chastised her, oblivious to what Juniper was really thinking. "Give her a chance. I think she could help you with your vandal and . . ."

"And what?"

"And Jericho's own cold case. You haven't let it go, June. Don't pretend that you have. I think you're right to believe that Jonathan's accident has something to do with what happened to the Murphys."

"I never told you that," Juniper said quietly.

"You didn't have to."

Juniper held Cora's steady gaze. Her mentor

308

and friend had never steered her wrong before, but Juniper was annoyed that her instinct had been so off about India. She was usually a very good judge of character. "Fine," Juniper said eventually. "Give me her contact info. I'll reach out tonight."

Cora's eyes glinted. "I think you'll hit it off."

"We'll see." Juniper tried to give Cora a stern look, but the woman was already scrawling on an index card. Apparently, Cora knew India's number by heart. Juniper couldn't help but feel a twinge of jealousy—and irritation. What secrets had Cora unknowingly shared with the woman who seemed hell-bent on ruining Jonathan?

"Here." Cora slid the card to her. "Be open-minded. India might be just what you've been waiting for."

Juniper sincerely doubted it, but she took the number and stuck it in the back pocket of her jeans.

Around lunchtime, Juniper realized that she hadn't eaten a single thing all day. Hustling Willa out the door and then dealing with the drama of her slashed tires had made food a moot point, but by noon her stomach felt hollow and the room swayed gently when she stood. She had promised to meet Everett at twelve but decided a few minutes wouldn't make a difference since she would be late anyway. Although Barry had offered to lend her his car again, she assured him she needed the fresh air and would enjoy the walk. She stumbled into Cunningham's half-frozen with cold, a stiff wind at her back, and her fingertips blue after only a few blocks.

Of course the place was packed. Too late, Juniper considered all the people she might bump into during lunch break in February. But before she could duck back out the door, an older couple pushed in behind her, crowding the small entryway, and any hope of an easy escape was extinguished.

Thankfully, a quick scan of the restaurant didn't immediately reveal any familiar faces, and she was able to order a tomato bisque and grilled cheese to go without any fanfare or fuss. While she waited, she slid her phone from her coat pocket and texted Everett.

> *Sorry, running late.*
> *Grabbing lunch from Cunningham's.*
> *Want anything?*

She watched for the three dots of an impending response, but they never came. Strange, since it was 12:10 and he was supposed to be meeting with her. But she didn't have long to wonder about his silence, because only a few minutes later she was walking out with a greasy paper bag and a hot to-go cup in her hands.

Juniper sipped from the cup as she hurried toward the Jericho Police Station. It did much to fortify her as she prepared to meet with Everett on more formal ground. She didn't know what to expect. Was this a routine Q&A? Or was Officer Stokes going to drop a bombshell? The thought of new evidence, of the Murphy case being cracked wide open and spilling secrets like a rotten egg, made Juniper's pulse quicken. She just couldn't decide if it was in anticipation or fear.

Juniper let herself in the front door of the police station and discovered a small, tiled entryway with a single, unassuming desk. No one was behind it. Against one wall was a line of four blue plastic chairs, and Juniper considered sitting there to wait, but the clock above the desk told her it was already twenty after twelve. She had to be back at the library at one so that Barry could take his lunch break, and she wasn't going to be a minute late. She would not be indebted to Barry any further than she already was.

Instead of sitting down, Juniper walked around the desk and peered into the hallway behind it. "Hello?" she called. "Everett? Is anyone here?"

No answer. No movement at all. There had been a police cruiser parked in front of the squat building, but Juniper had no idea how many cars and officers Jericho employed, and frost on the windshield made it seem as if the cruiser had been parked there for a while. Maybe overnight.

"Hello?" she said again, louder this time. When there was still no answer, she started down the hall, peeking in the rooms that faced each other across the narrow space. A dark kitchenette with a stained coffeepot and a box of bakery donuts on the table. A small, messy office with piles of paper stacked on every available surface. Juniper had been here before, had been questioned in a conference room that she could barely remember because she had surely been in shock at the time. What had she said? She couldn't even recall that. But no doubt Everett possessed a complete transcript and had pored over her every word. The thought made her angry.

"Officer Stokes?" Juniper called one last time, irritated that he had forgotten their appointment and that she would have to walk back in the cold without first having a chance to eat her grilled cheese and warm up a bit. But just as she spun on her heel to go, a door wrenched open at the very end of the hall.

"Juniper." Everett gave her a half smile and eased the door shut to the room he had just vacated. "Sorry to make you wait. I was working on something and got caught up, I guess."

"Jonathan's case?"

His smile faded. "You'd be surprised at how busy we are. Jericho isn't as innocent as it used to be."

"It wasn't innocent then."

"Fair enough. Let's meet in here. It'll be easier for you to eat at a table while we talk." Everett stepped across the hall and motioned that Juniper should follow him into the conference room. Juniper could picture it: Glass insert in the door. Two folding banquet tables pushed together, and cheap office chairs scattered around. It had smelled of Lysol and body odor the last time she had sat picking at a bit of snagged plastic on the arm of her swivel chair.

Juniper wanted to tell him no, but she walked dutifully over the threshold and plopped into the seat nearest the exit. She busied herself with taking the lid off her soup and unwrapping the grilled cheese from Cunningham's while Everett retrieved a thick blue folder and a ballpoint pen and chose a spot across from her.

"Thanks for coming today," he said by way of introduction. "Again, I'm sorry the front office wasn't staffed. I'm alone here over the lunch hour."

"No problem." Juniper took a bite of her sandwich and wiped her fingers on a napkin. She hoped she appeared casual, collected. In reality she was feeling anything but. Talking to Everett had seemed innocuous when she agreed to it only yesterday, but now that she was in the same conference room where she had been interrogated about Jonathan, his connection to the Murphys, and his whereabouts on the night of Fourth of

July, she had completely lost her appetite. Still, it would be telling if she left her food untouched. She took another bite.

"I just wanted to clarify a few details with you."

She nodded. Swallowed.

"Where were you on the night that Calvin and Elizabeth Murphy were killed?"

Juniper nearly choked on her sandwich. "Excuse me?" she said, between coughs into her napkin.

"I've upset you."

"No," Juniper argued, taking a swig of her soup. It was the only liquid she had. She longed for a bottle of water but wasn't about to ask. "You surprised me. I didn't realize I was a suspect in your new investigation."

"I never said you were a suspect."

Juniper had to admit, this guy was good. He was studying his notes, or pretending to, but when she least expected it, he snapped his eyes up and gave her the full brunt of his attention. It was a great way to catch her unguarded. She steeled her features.

"What are you saying, Officer Stokes?"

"Please, call me Everett. I'm saying that there's a discrepancy in your timeline that night. See, you were at the Pattersons' party"—he ran his finger across the page and tapped something that Juniper couldn't see—"from approximately nine until nearly ten. Several witnesses saw you there. With your brother."

Juniper nodded but didn't say anything.

"And then it says you drove home by yourself but met up with your brother and Sullivan Tate at your farm to watch the fireworks."

"Yes," Juniper said, but her mind was reeling. What had she said? What time did she arrive at home and who was supposed to be where, when? She folded her hands on her lap so that he wouldn't see them tremble.

"Can you see the fireworks from your farm?" He smiled at her suddenly. "I mean, you're a ways out of town. There have to be better places to watch."

"There are. But we can see well enough. We wanted to avoid the crowds."

"Sorry if I'm making you nervous, Juniper. I just want to clarify a few details." He turned another page and scanned it. "So you watched from the back of Jonathan's truck. Together. And then Sullivan left for home around ten thirty and you went inside."

"That's right."

"And your brother . . . ?"

"Heard the gunshots and went to the Murphys' farm."

"But you didn't hear them."

"I was in the shower at the time."

"So Jonathan placed the 911 call at . . ."

Juniper's palms began to sweat. She hadn't talked about any of this for almost fifteen years, and she couldn't remember how exactly she had accounted for each minute. What had Sullivan said? Jonathan? At the time they made sure their stories matched, but it was hard to separate fact from fiction with Everett staring at her. He didn't blink. Pure determination. He was trying to prove something, but she didn't know what.

"I don't remember," Juniper finally said.

"Ten forty-one," Everett said. "That leaves eleven minutes unaccounted for."

"I was showering," Juniper reminded him. "Sullivan was driving home. Jonathan was probably doing chores. And we weren't glued to our watches. I have no idea what time Sullivan actually left and I went upstairs. It could have been ten thirty-five or forty."

"Yeah, that's what the investigating officer said at the time. You were"—he put air quotes around the words—"'a bunch of kids who had been drinking and couldn't be specific.' But eleven minutes is a long time, Juniper."

She held his gaze and lifted her chin a fraction of an inch. "What are you saying?"

Everett ignored her question. "Sullivan was home by ten thirty-five. That has been corroborated by both of his parents. And the Tate Family Farms are in the opposite direction. His timeline fits."

"Mine doesn't?"

"You and Jonathan are each other's alibis for eleven minutes."

"You're assuming the timeline is accurate."

Everett closed the file with a snap and sat back with both hands laced behind his head. "A minute here, a minute there. I get it. I'm trying to make nearly fifteen-year-old evidence make sense, and no one was paying attention to the clock that night. Today, we'd subpoena cell phone records and know exactly where everyone was and when. The records we do have indicate that you all—Jonathan, Sullivan, and you—pinged off the cell tower south of town. I'm sure three-quarters of Jericho would've pinged off that tower. Three thousand potential suspects."

"But you're only worried about two," Juniper said coldly.

"Eleven minutes is a long time."

"It wasn't an issue then. And there was no gunshot residue on Jonathan's hands. There's no way he shot that gun."

Everett leaned forward with his arms on the table and gave Juniper a caustic look.

"You think . . . ?" But Juniper couldn't complete the thought. Did he think *she* had killed the Murphys, and Jonathan had covered it up?

"I'm just asking questions. Honestly, Juniper, I'm most interested in a witness. I can't shake the feeling that someone knows something they're not telling."

Juniper held his gaze even as her stomach filled with bile.

After a second he shrugged. Sat back. "Know what I did a couple weeks ago? It warmed up a bit, so I went for a jog. And going at a good clip it took me just under six minutes to run from your parents' farm to the old Murphy place." He counted off five more minutes on his fingers. The intent was clear: Jonathan (or she?) could have easily pulled off three shots in the five extra minutes. Or at least seen who did.

"I'm done here." Juniper was propelled to her feet by fury. Officer Stokes had acted so nice, so personable, but she should have known that he was only playing her. He was out for information, and she was afraid that she had already given him far too much. She had taken him at face value and arrived guileless and unafraid. Just the way he wanted her to. She should have brought a lawyer.

"Hey." Everett stood, too. "Thanks for coming. I didn't mean to upset you, Juniper. I'm just poking around. Comes with the badge. Let me walk you to the door."

"I know the way," she said, abandoning her cup of soup and nearly untouched sandwich on the table. He could clean it up.

"Juniper, wait."

She paused at the door for just a second, wary.

"Just answer me this: Why did Jonathan have your necklace? It seems strange to me that the only thing he would have on him the day he fell through the ice is his sister's necklace. That's weird, right? And to think, you had just arrived in town a couple nights before . . ."

But Juniper was already gone. She stalked down the hallway and wrenched open the front door, pausing for just a moment when Everett called her name.

"Wait," he said, stopping a few feet from where she stood letting cold air into the stuffy building. "Here. I thought you might like to have this back."

Everett tossed something into the air between them and Juniper automatically put out a hand to catch it. It was the evidence bag with her necklace inside. She stared at it for just a moment before cramming it in the pocket of her parka and storming out the front door, letting it slam behind her when the wind caught it. It wasn't until she was walking up the steps to the library that she realized she hadn't even had a chance to tell Officer Stokes that her tires had been slashed. Thing was, she no longer dared to.

He'd made her situation crystal clear: Juniper was on her own.

CHAPTER 18

SUMMER
14 AND A HALF YEARS AGO

Sullivan and I are a detective team—sort of. He keeps me apprised of what's going on in the Tate house and I share what I learn from Jonathan. It's not much, and we're not very good sleuths, because by the time the Fourth of July rolls around, we really haven't learned much.

We have, however, spent more time together than I ever imagined possible. Late nights melt into early mornings that find me sneaking in through the upstairs bathroom window. It's a narrow double-hung with a view of the towering maple in our side yard, and I can't believe it's never crossed my mind before to use it as a secret entrance. I suppose I've never really needed to. In many ways I'm grateful; my arms and legs are scored with fine cuts from climbing up and down the old tree, and a layer of guilt sticks to me like grime. I'm not a liar. One morning Mom runs her fingertips over my wrist when she sees one of the red welts, and though her eyes search mine for a long moment, she doesn't say anything. In some ways, her silent acceptance of the secrets between us is worse than an interrogation. *Ask me,* I want to whisper. But she walks away. And I text Sullivan.

It's a reckless, butterflies-in-my-stomach, heart-made-of-paper-and-kite-string feeling to be with Sullivan Tate. We riffle through the receipts in his dad's farm office, then lose track of what we're doing when Sullivan presses me against the filing cabinet and kisses me hard. We spy on Dalton and Jonathan, but they slip away when Sullivan asks me a question and then leans forward to listen to every single word of my answer. I learn to wait when he holds up one finger, a thought forming in the silence between us before he begins to speak, each word carefully chosen and full of weight. He discovers that a single kiss at the base of my spine will undo me completely.

We are our own worst enemies, but our digging is also compromised by the fact that Jonathan is still icing me out, and Sullivan doesn't have a very close relationship with his brothers. Only Dalton and Sullivan, the two youngest, still live at home. Sterling is married—no kids—to a girl who used to bully me in junior high. Her name is Kari and she's a good six years older than me, but that didn't stop her from calling me "Mop Head" when I was in sixth grade and she was a senior. Sure, my mom cut my wild hair in a ridiculous bob, and I did look exactly like a dirty mop with my frizzy, dishwater-blond hair, but Kari was a legal adult and felt the need to pick on a twelve-year-old. She made my life miserable, and I think that perfectly summarizes the sort of person Kari Tate is—and by association, her adoring Sterling.

Wyatt's not married but lives on his own in a farmhouse on a property the Tates own. It borders their land, and the Murphys' land, too, and everyone knows that Wyatt throws crazy parties there that sometimes have to get broken up by the cops.

When I bring up Wyatt's reputation—carefully, worried Sullivan might take offense—he laughs.

"Wyatt's a pup. He's wild, but he's not mean. My mother has the corner on that particular market."

"Did you just say your mom is mean?" I tug on the hem of his T-shirt and he laughs.

"As a snake."

"That's terrible."

"It's true. She pulled a gun on my dad once."

The look on my face must startle some sense into Sullivan, because he hurries to explain. "Oh, she'd never shoot him, she was just trying to get his attention."

I try to imagine it and can't: Reb pulling a gun on Law "just to get his attention." The scene doesn't translate.

Sullivan tells me other things. About the time a cop pulled his dad over and got the "Do you know who I am?" speech. He got off with a warning. Of course, Franklin Tate wasn't quite as lucky when he broke a guy's jaw in a bar fight and spent a couple nights in the county jail before Annabelle posted bail.

"Settled out of court," Sullivan says, a dark cloud passing over his features before I smooth it away with a kiss.

The Tates are certainly eccentric, prone to a bit of trouble, and not unlike many of the families in Jericho. If there is a clinging sense of peril to them, it's insubstantial as a whiff of smoke. A warning, maybe, but not enough to keep me away. They are churchgoing and gift-giving—the new atrium of Jericho High bears their name—and from the outside looking in, they are as inconsistent and complex as any family. A clash of reputation and reality.

Sullivan himself is probably the greatest contradiction, and as much as I wish I could push him away, as the days peel off the calendar, I find myself pulling him closer and closer still. His forehead wrinkles when he tells me about his family, and while it's clear to me that he loves them and understands them—that they are home—I can also tell that he's conflicted. He's not like them, not exactly, and that vein of something different that runs through his very core is the exact thing that keeps me up at night thinking about his touch. Sometimes, you want to run away from home.

It's dangerous, this feeling. I know that.

One night, tucked in the bed of his truck as we stare up at the glittering sweep of the Milky Way, I tell him, "Ashley will never, ever forgive me."

I'm laying with my head on Sullivan's chest. His arm is curled around me, fingertips just inside the fold of my shirt where he's stroking the warm curve of skin beneath the jut of my hipbone. I shiver, but he doesn't respond, so I push myself up to look at him.

"I mean it. I'm going to lose my best friend over you."

Sullivan has one arm propped beneath his head, and he lifts the other to cup my face. "I've told you a dozen times. I'm not interested in Ashley. Never have been, never will be."

"Don't you know anything about girls? It doesn't matter. She'd hate me if she knew."

"Then she's not a very good friend."

"We've been best friends since fourth grade. We can't throw it all away over a fling."

Sullivan sits up and leans so close our noses are almost touching. "This isn't a fling."

My heart stutters. We're not even a couple, not really, but I know exactly what he means. Still, I whisper, "What are you saying?"

"I hope you don't lose your friendship with Ashley over us. But June . . ." He traces my lips with his fingertip. "I think I'm falling for you."

It's a crazy thing to say. Way too early. He barely knows me. And yet, I know that he's telling the truth. I know it because I feel it too.

It defies explanation, but isn't that the point? Sullivan brings out things in me that I didn't know existed. Dreams about the future in which I'm not alone, adventures that include him. My world has expanded to embrace someone other than just myself, and it's more than lust, different from friendship. Even as I look at him in the pale moonlight, I know that I'll say goodbye to Ashley if I have to. My heart will break over it, but I don't want to give this up. I can't. I don't know where we're going, but I want to find out.

I put my head in my hands and whisper: "What have we done?"

"Nothing." Sullivan tucks a strand of hair behind my ear. "We haven't done anything wrong."

"I'm leaving for college in August," I protest, letting that reality sink in. "Then what?"

I half expect Sullivan to beg me to stay, to tell me that I can study online or delay my freshman year so that we have more time to figure out what exactly is happening between us. But he doesn't. He says, "I've always liked Iowa City."

I'm stunned. "You'd come?"

"Maybe."

"What's that supposed to mean?"

He considers. "People do long-distance relationships all the time. They work."

"What if I don't want to do a long-distance

relationship?" The thought of not being able to see him when I want, of forfeiting nights like this, is agonizing.

Sullivan shrugs. "If it doesn't work, we'll find another way."

"I don't want to stay in Jericho."

"Who said I did?"

I think of his family, the over two thousand acres of the Tate Family Farms consortium of land and cattle, development and real estate. Sullivan is not just the baby of the family, he's the favorite, and an heir to what feels like half the county. I have a hard time believing his parents would just let him leave. Never mind his brothers.

"Jericho is in your blood," I tell him.

"Then it's in yours, too."

"It's not the same and you know it." I twist away from him, ostensibly to stretch out a kink in my back, but when I'm done, the distance between us is greater than it was before. I sigh. "We're a regular Romeo and Juliet."

"Come on." I can hear the eye roll in his voice as I'm looking at the stars. He edges closer and wraps his legs around me so I have no choice but to lean into his chest. Sullivan ducks his head and begins trailing a line of kisses along my bare neck, but he's not trying to distract me—he's laying claim. "One day at a time, okay? But know this, Juniper Grace: you're mine."

Yes, I think. And it's the most absurd, unexpected, and frightening thing imaginable. I don't know how it happened, but it did. I'm in love.

The morning of the Fourth of July always begins with a pancake breakfast in the park. Hope Reformed rents giant electric griddles and greases the surfaces with bacon fat before spooning on homemade batter that bubbles up and makes the whole park smell like a bakery. If you're early, the first few pancakes are crisped at the edges with drippings from all the bacon, and you can forgo syrup entirely because they're so delicious plain.

I can hear Jonathan get up in the morning to help Law with chores, so I drag myself out of bed even though I could sleep in. I know they'll drive into town when they're done, and I want to join them. Not just because this is probably my last Fourth of July in Jericho, but also because I'm hoping Jonathan will let something slip.

He's been distracted lately, and careless. When he goes out with the Tate brothers, he doesn't bother to lie about it anymore, and he seems to have accepted that Sullivan and I are friends. Well, it's less *acceptance* than *resignation,* but he no longer lectures me to stay away from Sullivan. I'm grateful that he has no idea about the real nature of our relationship.

Since I'm up and dressed, I head out to the chicken coop to collect the eggs and feed and water the hens. It's hot, and they've been laying less than usual lately, which means I only find six eggs, even though we have ten layers. But there's enough for an omelet or to boil for the potato salad my mom will make for the picnic later today.

By the time I've set the eggs on the counter in the kitchen and washed my hands, Mom is up, too. It's not quite seven o'clock, but we head out to the porch to wait for Jonathan and Law anyway. We'll be just in time to be among the first people at the pancake breakfast, and somehow, that feels appropriate for my last Fourth of July at home.

As Mom and I sit in the early morning silence on the farm, I consider asking her about the suitcase I found in the trunk of her car. But even though I'm dying to know, I can't bring myself to form the words. Reb is sitting with her head tilted back against the chain of the porch swing, and she looks more relaxed than I've seen her in a long time. Lighter. If I didn't know better, I'd say that she seems like a woman unburdened of something that had been weighing her down. I wonder if she would confide in me, but I don't dare to ask. It feels like an invasion of her privacy—and I have secrets of my own.

It doesn't take long for Law and my brother to clean up after chores, and shortly after seven we're all buckled into Law's truck. This is usually only a Sunday morning occurrence, and though it feels a bit strange to be shoulder-to-shoulder with Jonathan in the backseat, the drive into Jericho around the Fourth is always a treat because this is one holiday we know how to celebrate.

Nearly every farm and every house as we enter the outskirts of town is decorated with stars and stripes. Flags hang from poles and porches, red gingham tablecloths cover picnic tables, and kids are dressed in red, white, and blue. It's a slice of Americana straight from a Hollywood movie, but there's an earnestness to our celebration that defies cliché. We aren't *trying* to be this way, we just *are*. I know that there will be American flag toothpicks on top of our pancake stacks, and someone will undoubtedly be serving in a sparkly headband that looks like a firework exploding. Later, the actual fireworks will be small but spectacular, and I already have plans to watch them with Sullivan. Just the thought makes me feel warm all over. And then ice cold. Even if Sullivan and I are fuzzy on what exactly they're doing, tonight's *the night*.

"You meeting up with the Tates later?" I ask Jonathan innocently as Law pulls into a parking space near the shelter house.

He shoots me a barbed look and yanks open the door. "Maybe," he says.

"Well, either you are or you aren't."

"Not now," Reb says, shutting her door just a smidge harder than necessary. "I can't take the two of you going after each other this morning."

Apparently, Jonathan and I haven't done a very good job of pretending lately.

The shelter house is open air, and I can see the long picnic tables decorated with paper sparklers and flag napkins. There's already a bit of a crowd gathered, but Ashley is the very first person I see. She's behind the serving table, helping people collect plates and plastic utensils before they walk through the line. In shorts and a bright white tank, she looks impossibly tall and thin. Gorgeous. My heart snags at the sight of her and her quick, easy grin when a little girl drops her plate and reaches for another. I've betrayed Ashley in the worst possible way. It would have been one thing if I was honest with her about my surprising feelings for Sullivan. But I'm falling for him a little more every day, and she has no idea.

I feel almost feverish as I join the line, but when I get close to Ashley, I smile and reach over the table to give her a hug. I'm wicked—a lying, backstabbing Jezebel—but, God help me, I love her. I wish it didn't have to be this way.

"You going to the barbecue later?" Ashley asks, a glint in her eye. She hangs on to my arms even when I back away, and I wonder what's gotten into her. But then her eyes flick off to the side and I follow her gaze. Sullivan. Actually, the whole Tate clan—minus Sterling and Kari—though I know that Ashley hardly notices the rest of them. My heart sinks.

"Yeah," I say, wondering how I can avoid the Tates. There are less than a hundred people here, and although hundreds more will come, the crowd isn't big enough to get lost in right now. I accept a plate, fork, and knife from Ashley and wrinkle my nose in apology. "Actually, I don't know. I've got some packing to do and . . ."

When I trail off, she stares as if I've lost my mind. "You're kidding, right? June, you don't leave for weeks. It's the *Fourth of July*. You have to come. I insist."

"She'll be there," Jonathan says from behind me.

A flash of anger almost makes me spin around to give my brother a piece of my mind, but now is not the time or place. I have enough balls to juggle without worrying about what will come crashing down if Jonathan and I get into it in public.

"I'll be there," I affirm, hoping my smile doesn't look as thin and insincere as it feels.

"Good." Ashley nods maternally as I continue to move down the line. "I've invited someone else to come, too."

When she winks, my heart sinks.

"You have to tell her," Jonathan whispers in my ear as someone slides a stack of pancakes onto my outstretched plate.

I don't acknowledge his comment, but I'm quietly horrified. Maybe Sullivan and I haven't been as stealthy as we think we've been. Or maybe Sullivan is kissing and telling. But the second that thought enters my mind, I dismiss it. He wouldn't.

I head to the drinks table for coffee in a Styrofoam cup and end up in a conversation with one of my former teachers about the merits of the University of Iowa and whether I think the Hawkeyes can go all the way this year. I'm not even sure if we're talking about basketball or football (maybe baseball?), so I smile and nod, and by the time I turn around, my family is nowhere to be seen. I scan the growing crowd, and to my utter panic watch as Law takes a seat next to Franklin Tate. Reb is reaching out her hand to Franklin's wife, Annabelle, clearly oblivious to how rigid Jonathan has gone beside her. From thirty feet away I can sense his discomfort like a crackle in the air.

What choice do I have? To sit apart from my family would draw unwanted attention, and I can't think of a single logical reason to do so. I walk slowly toward the table where the Tates and Bakers have cozied up, hoping that I'll catch sight of a former classmate or someone who might entice me to join them. There's no one. Even worse, by the time I arrive, there's only one spot available at the entire table, and it's next to Sullivan.

I take my spot gingerly, sliding onto the bench as if I'm mounting a green-broke horse instead of sitting down to a breakfast of pancakes and bacon. Surely Sullivan can feel my hesitation, but instead of scooting over, he remains exactly where he is, so I have no choice but to sit with my hip pressed against his. Even touching him in such a discreet way is comforting, and I let out a quiet, ragged breath. Maybe this won't be as bad as I'm expecting. I actually feel like I can draw strength from Sullivan's presence. I would lay my head on his shoulder if I could.

"I don't think we've officially met," Dalton Tate says, reaching across the table to shake my hand.

"We haven't. I'm June Baker." I put my hand in his and try not to wince when he squeezes it tight. He looks a lot like Sullivan, though his hair is much darker and shorter, and he weighs a good twenty pounds more. I'm probably reading into things, but he has a cruel look about him, or maybe he's just serious. He doesn't smile at me to soften his automatic greeting.

"Oh, I know who you are." Dalton lets go of my hand and returns to the pancakes he was shoveling in when I sat down. "Jonathan doesn't really talk about you, but I know who you are."

Jonathan is across the table, sandwiched in between Law and Wyatt, and I can't stop myself from glaring at him for just a second. I wish it didn't, but it hurts to know that he doesn't talk about me—even to the Tates. I catch myself almost immediately and focus instead on the strips of bacon that are crisscrossing my pancakes, but not soon enough.

Dalton hoots. "I like a good sibling rivalry. She could kill with that look, man."

"Stop it," Annabelle tells her son. "Leave her alone." To me, she says: "I'm Annabelle, you can call me Anna. I invited your family to join us because we have so enjoyed getting to know Jonathan."

Her comment stings, but she can't possibly know that, and we shake hands across Sullivan and Reb. Anna fixes me with a direct, appraising look, and I feel like I'm on trial. Her tone is cordial enough, but this is not a woman I would like to cross, and I let go of her rough hand as soon as I can without appearing rude.

Soon we settle into eating and chatting, almost as if we're good neighbors and friends casually enjoying a Fourth of July community breakfast together. But there's tension in the air, a sense that not everything is as it should be between the nine people crowded around the picnic table.

Anna Tate clearly knows my brother better

than I would like her to, and she leans across the pinwheel centerpiece a couple of times to say something to him that demonstrates their familiarity. Dalton acts like he and Jonathan are best friends, and Wyatt has a strange habit of slapping him on the back at regular intervals.

Jonathan's not the blushing sort, but I can tell that it makes him feel awkward to be included among the Tates as if he's practically a family member. It's making Law crazy, too. When we were young and still begged Law and Reb for a boat, a vacation to Disney World, a bigger house, he used to shut down our requests with the same tired line: "Do I look like Franklin Tate to you?" It was meant to remind us that our parents weren't made of money, but there was an edge to his reminder, too. We understood by that one line and the way he delivered it that Law didn't *want* to be Franklin Tate. And the reason behind that always seemed mysterious—and slightly ominous.

I've lost my appetite, but I force myself to take a bite every few minutes anyway, and while I listen in on the conversations around me, I study Franklin and his boys. He's a large man with a thick neck and a bald head that's been baked brown by the sun from years of working outside. Still, he's attractive, and I can tell that he used to be distractingly so. It's obvious where Sullivan got his looks, but I'm not sure what to do with that information. It's hard to gaze at Franklin—at the marble-hard glint of his eyes and the way he watches the room as if taking stock of everything and everyone—and see bits of Sullivan reflected in him.

For just a moment I imagine what it would be like to join the Tate clan, to be a daughter-in-law to a man who, according to the Murphys, willfully and intentionally poisoned their wells and scoffed at the consequences. Who swallows up small farms when people get behind on their mortgage. Who allegedly pays off the cops when his wife gets a speeding ticket and bails his son out of jail and turns a blind eye when another son throws parties on his land that include meth and strippers. (I asked around—turns out the nature of Wyatt's parties is hardly a secret.)

A tremor passes through me, and without thinking, Sullivan wraps an arm around my waist. We both stiffen immediately, and he makes a show of rubbing his hand on my back and then looking at the floor. "Spider," he says roughly. "I think I got it."

I'm not sure that anyone would have noticed the familiar way that he touched me, but Dalton barks a laugh and then gives Sullivan a knowing smirk.

"What?" Reb says, looking around the table and, frankly, sounding a bit batty. Her eyes are wide and confused, and I feel sorry for her because it must seem like there's some inside joke that she is simply not a part of.

"There was a spider on my back," I say, getting up. "It's gone now."

I'm the first to gather up my things, and once I've done so, everyone else moves to do the same. Our table disperses quickly, Franklin leaving without a backward glance, and Anna offering a cursory wave before heading off to say hello to a group of well-dressed, perfectly coiffed ladies who look like a much better fit for her than my sweet mother.

Jonathan grabs Mom's plate and says in one breath, "I'll take this for you; I'm going with Dalton," as if a trifling act of kindness will soften the unexpectedness of his departure.

Mom opens her mouth to say something, but Jonathan doesn't wait around for an answer. He's weaving through the growing crowd before she can even say goodbye. "I thought we were going to the Pattersons' together," she muses, sounding sad.

Ashley's family has been hosting a Fourth of July picnic and barbecue for as long as I can remember, and as of last night, Jonathan had been planning on going with us. But obviously he has more important things to do with Dalton and Wyatt, and I wish more than anything that I could follow. It's a futile hope, though, and I turn my attention to Reb. "I bet he'll come later," I say, hoping to console her, but I doubt he will. I wonder if we'll see him at all today, and what that means for the plan he's allegedly hatching for the Murphys.

"It was so nice to meet you, Mrs. Baker." Sullivan steps beside me and gives my mom a warm smile. I had almost forgotten that he was nearby, and I feel a rush of gratitude and something that's a lot like pride as I watch him study my mother. His expression is open and genuine, and she smiles right back.

"Nice to meet you, too, Sullivan. You're welcome at our home anytime. I'm sure Jonathan would love to have you swing by."

I have to look down because I'm afraid my eyes will betray me. Is it written across my face? Does she suspect I love him? It's so unlike me, so terrifyingly uncharacteristic, but I want to press myself against him and link his fingers in mine. It would feel so good to claim Sullivan right here and now, in front of my mom and Law, in front of everyone. But as much as I want that, I fear it, too. I'm scared of what's happening to me because of Sullivan Tate.

We say our goodbyes, and Mom follows Law in the direction of the car. But before I can take a single step, I feel something brush against my hand. Sullivan's knuckles barely graze mine, and I know at once that we're feeling exactly the same way. I glance up and find myself looking into his eyes for the first time all morning. There are a dozen things I want to say to him, a hundred, but now is not the time or place. Still, he must see desire written all over my face, because he nods almost imperceptibly as if to say, *Later*.

Now, I wish, but I content myself with linking my pinky with his for just a heartbeat or two. Then he walks away, and I'm left standing in the shelter house surrounded by acquaintances and friends, people I've known—and who have known me—since I was born. They feel like strangers to me. I'm pulled taut between wanting to run and wanting to stay, and I'm convinced I have never felt so torn and confused in my entire life.

Until I catch Ashley staring at me across the crowded space. Her look is like a slap to the face, and anyone watching her would know beyond a shadow of a doubt that hitting me is *exactly* what she wants to do. I'd love to pretend that I'm reading her wrong, but I can't deny it: Ashley knows.

CHAPTER 19

WINTER
TODAY

"Why aren't you answering your phone?" Cora demanded the second Juniper cracked the library door, a full twenty minutes before her lunch was up. She didn't have time to stomp the snow off her shoes or unzip her coat before the older woman had caught her in an uncomfortably tight grip. "Where have you been?"

"Lunch," Juniper said, confused. The door fell shut with a thud behind her. "It's not even quarter to. I'm not—"

"Jonathan's awake," Cora blurted.

"What?" The room went airless and still.

"Your mom called here when she couldn't get you to answer your cell phone."

Juniper sucked in a frantic breath. "I turned the ringer off," she said, shaking off Cora's hands and fumbling in her backpack for her phone. She hadn't wanted to be interrupted during her supposedly innocuous conversation with Everett. Sure enough, there were four missed calls, all from Reb's cell. And then a text:

Call me.

"I don't know any details, just that he's awake and he's asking for you."

"I have to go." Juniper felt molded from clay, her mind slow, her fingers fat and clumsy as she dug deeper in her bag for the familiar ring of car keys. As she snagged them with a finger, a thought tried to worm its way to the foreground, but it was sluggish and slow to form. She stared at the keys.

"Your tires were slashed," Cora reminded her. "You can take my car."

"No, take mine." Barry stepped from behind the circulation desk—Juniper hadn't even realized he was there—and held out his keys. "It's no big deal. I live a couple of blocks away."

"But—"

"I insist. Cora lives across town—it's too far to walk. And clearly you have to go. Take my car. You can return it tomorrow."

Juniper's eyes felt hot, but she didn't know if it was because of the kindness of a near stranger or the fact that Jonathan was awake. Maybe both. "Willa—"

"She can go home with a friend." Cora solved the problem with a wave of her hand. "Zoe?"

Yes. Zoe. Juniper could call the school, get the number. Make arrangements as she drove. Suddenly nothing was as important as getting to Des Moines. Juniper held out her hand and Barry dropped the keys into her palm. "Thank you," she said around a lump in her throat. Then Cora swept her into a gruff hug and shoved her out the door.

"If you leave now you'll be there shortly after three. Call me on your way home, okay? I want to know how he's doing."

Juniper nodded as she rushed down the steps, but she didn't look back.

Barry's car still smelled of strawberry lotion and spearmint gum—of Willa. Her daughter had left a pack of gum in one of the cupholders in the console, and Juniper reached for a stick. Her hands were quivering. She wasn't okay to drive, not quite yet, so she chewed the gum in the cold interior and tried to take a few deep breaths.

In all these years, Juniper and her brother had never spoken about that night. It was scorched earth, barren and ruined. But Jonathan had been there, he could testify to the way their bodies fell, and Juniper was keeping a secret so big it was destroying her from the inside. Everything came back to this. She had come home, and Jonathan had almost died. She had no doubt her brother had wanted to talk to her about the night of the Murphy murders, and now, finally, it was time.

She slipped a hand into her coat pocket for the car keys and came up with an evidence bag. Her necklace was pooled in the bottom, a tangle of tarnished chain and pendants she hadn't worn in years. She thought it had been lost that night.

How did he find it? And why did he keep it? As a memento? Leverage? Proof? Maybe he thought he was protecting her.

The clasp stuck a little, but even with cold, stiff fingers Juniper was able to fasten the chain around her neck. She inhaled sharply when the berries hit her chest just as they had done in another life. If she closed her eyes she was nineteen again, and her whole world was about to explode.

Again.

But she wasn't that girl anymore. She turned the keys in the ignition and stuck her phone in the car cradle so that she could make all the necessary calls and arrangements while she drove. It was impossible to guess what Jonathan would say, what ghosts he would resurrect, but their reckoning was so long overdue Juniper hardly cared anymore. Whatever came next had to be better than almost fifteen years of looking over her shoulder, of wondering and waiting, of exile.

She made the trip in record time and found a parking spot in the hospital ramp. She had only been here once before, but the steps were all the same: elevator to ICU, lift the receiver, wait for entry, follow a nurse down a chilly, wide hallway. But this time felt different. Jonathan was awake.

"Your father is waiting for you in the family room," the nurse said when they reached the doorway to the same room that Juniper had met Mandy in before. Surprise must have registered on her face, because the nurse continued, "I believe your mother stepped out for a little fresh air, and Mandy went back to the Rainbow House for a shower."

"Thanks," Juniper managed, but it didn't sound very sincere. She had spent the majority of the two-and-a-half-hour drive imagining what she would say to her brother. Law hadn't come into the picture at all.

The nurse continued toward the triage station and Juniper didn't have much of a choice. She turned the handle to the family room and let herself in.

Law was standing in the corner of the small room, a Styrofoam cup clutched in one large hand. When Juniper opened the door, he didn't even flinch.

"Hi," she said carefully, hesitant to break whatever spell had been cast over the room. "I came as soon as I heard the news. How is he?"

Law waved one hand as if shooing her away, and his forehead descended in a heap of wrinkles.

"What is it?"

"Yeah, he's awake," Law confirmed. "Kind of. But something's off. He's not . . . he's not *Jonathan.*"

Juniper had no idea what to do with this information, but she had to see her brother for herself.

She peeled off her winter coat and tossed it on a nearby chair, stowing her backpack underneath. No one would cross Law, but if he decided to riffle through it, he'd only find her wallet with exactly seven dollars in cash and a couple of tampons. She said, "I'm going in."

"I'm coming with you."

"No." Juniper shook her head, and then employed a word she rarely used with Lawrence. "Dad, please, I want a few minutes alone with him."

But Law already had the door open and was holding it for her. "He's my son. I'll see him when I like."

Juniper knew there would be no reasoning with him. It was clear that he was going whether she liked it or not. Maybe he'd tire of the ICU room quickly, or they'd only allow one visitor at a time. Juniper gritted her teeth and followed her father to the triage desk where they were cheerfully informed, "The more the merrier!"

Because Jonathan's risk for infection had decreased significantly, they were no longer required to suit up before entering his room. However, the nurse directed them to the hand-washing station, and Juniper and her stepfather scrubbed up before pushing open the glass door to Jonathan's room.

As far as Juniper could tell, not much had changed. The machines still whirred and beeped, and the room still smelled of antiseptic and something much more base and corporeal. Juniper didn't want to know. But someone had thrown open the window shades, and a flimsy late-February light bathed the entire room in a soft glow. And on the raised bed, buried beneath a mountain of blankets and attached to more tubes and wires than Juniper could possibly find uses for, was Jonathan. Awake.

A sob caught in her throat, but Juniper swallowed it down and gave her brother a watery smile. "Hey," she said, moving closer to the bed.

Jonathan was staring out the window and hadn't so much as flinched when Juniper and Law walked into the room. Nor did he register Juniper's soft greeting. He was probably used to a steady stream of doctors, nurses, and therapists cycling in and out of his room, and there was no reason for him to assume that Juniper was anyone other than another person sent to poke and prod, test and adjust.

She paused for a moment, uncertain of how to proceed. Did Jonathan know she was coming? Would he be excited to see her? Or upset?

Jonathan's mouth was obscured by a breathing tube that was fastened to his head by a plastic contraption that pinched his cheeks and caused the hollows beneath his eyes to look cavernous. One cheekbone was tinged yellow and green from the remnants of a bruise that must have formed when he fell through the ice. When he was rescued? It didn't matter. It looked painful. Worst of all was the way that Jonathan stared at the smudged gray sky, unblinking, unseeing, as if he wished his eyes weren't open at all. Juniper watched her brother and knew that this was not how he wanted to wake up. It gutted her.

"No need to hover!" A nurse came bustling past Juniper and went to stand beside the hospital bed. "You have visitors," he told Jonathan.

She felt almost shy as her brother's eyes swept from the window to Law and then, finally, to her. She lifted her hand in a little wave and took a single step closer to the bed, her heart beating madly in her chest. Jonathan stared at her, his blue eyes achingly familiar but clouded with medication and emotions she couldn't begin to guess. Pain? Regret? It was impossible to read his expression.

The nurse had lifted Jonathan's left arm from beneath the mass of blankets and was studying an IV in the crook of his elbow. "I'm going to have to move this soon," he said, giving her brother an almost paternal pat. Then he turned to smile at Juniper. "Your dad is a seasoned pro at this, but you should know that Jonathan tires really easily and might drift in and out. It's nothing to be concerned about. Also, he obviously can't talk around the breathing tube, but there's a marker board on his table if he wants to use it."

Juniper glanced at the small table on wheels beside Jonathan's bed. The bed was in the middle of the room, presumably so that doctors and machines were afforded full access for his care, and the table had drifted off to the side, far out of Jonathan's reach. It struck Juniper that without the marker board, he was rendered utterly speechless. She felt a wave of panic at the thought. But Jonathan didn't seem to care. He didn't reach for the board or acknowledge the nurse's departure or make any move to communicate with Juniper at all.

It's Law's fault, Juniper thought. *If he wasn't here . . .*

But Juniper didn't know if Jonathan would behave any differently if she was alone. She studied her brother on the bed and understood that Law was right: something had happened. Jonathan was changed. Maybe it was his fall through the ice, but Juniper felt like it had to be much more than just that, because there was one word that came to mind when she looked at her brother: *hollow.*

Juniper decided to ignore the fact that her stepfather was in the room. She went to stand over Jonathan's bed, where she could hear the whoosh of the air being pumped into his lungs and look straight into his sunken eyes. He watched her move closer and didn't look away when she leaned over the side of his bed to lay a sisterly kiss on his warm forehead. His skin felt feverish beneath her lips, just slightly, and dry as paper. Juniper feared if she blew, he would disintegrate in a cloud of dust before her eyes.

"Hey there," she whispered. "I'm so glad you're awake."

For the first time since she had arrived in his room, Juniper wasn't confused about how Jonathan was feeling. His eyes filled instantly, and tears slid down his temples. Her mother had warned her about this, about how ECMO patients were often intensely emotional when they woke: crying or feeling angry or hopeless. But it was hard to watch Jonathan cry all the same. It felt wrong to see her baby brother—who acted like her big brother—so reduced. He was strong and protective and always in control. Not like this. Juniper had seen him cry just a handful of times in her entire life, and it killed her to see his tears now.

"I have about a million questions," she said. "But I'll save them all until I can buy you a beer and some hot wings."

That earned Juniper a small smile that was nothing more than a crinkling around his eyes.

"My treat."

Another brightening of his eyes. It was painful to watch him try to smile around the breathing tube, but the starburst of laugh lines at his temples made her heart lift. Juniper wanted to keep that smile coming, to remind Jonathan that life was beautiful and he wanted to be a part of it. Even though she longed to ask him why he was on the lake that day, why he had her necklace in his pocket, and what exactly happened that summer, this urge took precedence, and Juniper tucked her hair behind her ears and leaned forward to keep finding ways to make him smile.

"You look like a million bucks, Jonathan. Seriously. Never better."

He laughed a little, and then convulsed. Jonathan was choking on the breathing tube, and as he gagged, he began coughing furiously. Juniper felt a flash of dread and cast around frantically for the emergency call button. Why weren't alarms going off?

"It happens all the time," Law said from his seat near the foot of the bed. "It'll pass."

"He's choking!"

"It's a reflex. He can't actually choke because there's a breathing tube down his throat."

Law sounded frustratingly dispassionate, but the experience was unnerving. The coughing fit left Jonathan exhausted, and in the wake of new visitors and choking on his own breathing tube, it was apparent to Juniper that he had already reached the end of what he could handle. As she watched, Jonathan blinked, and it was a long moment before he opened his eyes again.

"You need some rest," she said, trying to bite

back her disappointment. Her expectations had been unrealistic. There would be no heart-to-heart, no answers today. Jonathan was still hooked up to ECMO. He had a very long road ahead of him. Scariest of all, he was a shell of the man he had once been.

Juniper leaned over to say goodbye, to make eye contact one last time before she let him drift off and rest. "Get some sleep," she said, touching Jonathan's face with the very tips of her fingers. "We'll talk later. We've got lots of time."

He looked at her, and then his eyes widened in shock. Jonathan tried to lift his head from the pillow, but he couldn't.

"What?" she whispered, keenly aware that Law was just behind her. Something was really upsetting Jonathan, and she desperately wanted to know what. "What's wrong?"

Jonathan's eyes cut hard to her chest and back again. When he did it once more, Juniper looked down. Her necklace had fallen loose from her shirt and was dangling in the air between them.

"This?" She touched it briefly, and when he tugged his chin down in affirmation, she slipped it back into the loose collar of her sweater. "Officer Stokes found it. It was—"

Jonathan silenced her with a look.

"What do you want?" Juniper whispered.

He pointed to the marker board and she went behind his bed to grab it. There was a blue dry-erase marker stuck with Velcro to the top, and Juniper pulled it off and uncapped it, then handed it to Jonathan. When she held up the board for him, he wrote a single word in a shaky hand.

Dad.

Juniper felt herself deflate. "He's right here, Jonathan. He's been here the whole time." To Law she said, "He's asking for you."

Lawrence lifted himself with some difficulty. At seventy-five, he was aging quickly, rapidly pulling away from his much younger wife simply because his knees and shoulders, even his mind, were tired from wear and tear. Still, he pushed himself to his feet and shuffled over to stand on the opposite side of the bed from Juniper.

He hovered there awkwardly for a moment, but then Law reached out and rubbed Jonathan's arm with his own gnarled hand. It was just a few seconds of contact, but it affected Juniper in a way she hadn't thought possible. Those arthritic fingers touching Jonathan with such unexpected tenderness was almost her undoing. Juniper blinked back sudden tears. She didn't know Law had it in him.

"I'm here," Law said, his voice thick. "I'm right here."

As Juniper watched, Jonathan studied his father's hand on the blanket. But he didn't look at Lawrence's face. And instead of saying anything to him, instead of using the marker board to communicate what Juniper believed had to be an important message, Jonathan turned his face toward her, away from Lawrence, and very deliberately closed his eyes. Tears leaked from beneath his lashes and dampened the starched pillowcase.

After the ventilator had pushed a few breaths into Jonathan's lungs and he didn't stir, Juniper caught Law's gaze. "What was that all about?" she asked quietly.

There was something fragile in Lawrence's look, but she could tell he was hurt, too. He sniffed once, hard, and then walked away from the bed as quickly as he could manage and yanked open the door.

"I told you he wasn't himself," Law said over his shoulder. "That's not my Jonathan."

CHAPTER 20

THAT NIGHT

When we get home from the pancake breakfast, I head straight to my room and call Sullivan. He doesn't answer, nor does he respond to the multiple texts that I send him over the course of the next hour. I have no idea where he is or I'd hop in my car to go find him, and then the level of my hopelessness hits me and I feel sick. It strikes me that I hardly know Sullivan. And, up until very recently, I deeply distrusted and even disliked him. He was insolent and arrogant and downright creepy at times. Sullivan never tried to disguise his attraction to me, and haven't I given him exactly what he wanted?

I think of his fingers tracing the curve of my hip and feel cleaved down the middle by longing and fear. What if all of this has been a game to him? What if Sullivan has been playing me and I've pushed everyone away?

Jonathan and I are practically estranged, and by the look on Ashley's face at the pancake breakfast, our friendship is over. I haven't seen the Murphys in weeks, Mom's keeping secrets from me, and all my other friends have already begun the slow drift into their own futures. Some to college, others into full-time jobs that have changed the landscape of their lives entirely. Me? I'm stuck in Jericho making terrible decisions that have the potential to unravel my world.

I'm frantic with regret and terrified that it's too late to undo what has been done. I want to drive over to Ashley's house and try to make her understand, but I know she needs some time to cool off. And I'd love nothing more than to talk to Jonathan—to *really* talk to him—but he's been sidelining me all summer. I pace the floor of my bedroom, unsure of what to do next, when I realize that I've had enough. I'm done with being lied to.

Mom is downstairs making potato salad and Law's drinking a pre-party beer on the porch, but I still tiptoe out of my room as if I'm in imminent danger of being caught. The second story of our farmhouse is small but efficient, with four doors opening onto a landing that boasts a single bookshelf with Jonathan's and my childhood collection. The first room to the left of the stairs is mine, then there's a tiny closet-sized room that houses Mom's sewing machine. The bathroom is kitty-corner from where I'm standing, and across the hall is Jonathan's bedroom.

It's the last thing I want to do, because I love and respect my brother, but I don't see another way. I step around the creaky boards of the landing and put my palm on Jonathan's closed door. His handle is as squeaky as mine, but I know the trick from years of sneaking in to play practical jokes on him. We did it all the time when we were younger: frogs in each other's shoes or cornflakes in the sheets. Once, Jonathan went so far as to put a live snake in my sock drawer, and when I opened it in the morning, I screamed loud enough to wake the dead. It was just a garter snake, but I cried for an hour. Law put an end to our shenanigans after that and threatened the belt if we ever did it again. We knew better than to cross him, and our prank war ended, but I still know how to open Jonathan's door so that it barely whispers in my hand.

Jonathan's room is cooler than mine because his side of the house is shaded by one of the largest maple trees in Jericho. It's dim in here, and smells faintly of cologne, as if the last thing Jonathan did before he left this morning was spray the bottle. It makes me unaccountably sad, because I associate his scent with laughter and amusing conversations about everything from string theory to local gossip. A stab of conscience makes me pause just over the threshold, but then I catch sight of a photo of the two of us on his desk. We're little in it, maybe four and five, and we both have dark rings around our mouths from the chocolate ice cream cones we're clutching. Although I'm his big sister, I'm staring up at him as if he hung the moon.

This is why I'm here. Because our relationship is worth more than every single one of the Tates combined. Worth more than any alleged slight he feels over the Murphys' exploitation of his time and talents. More than Ashley, even. And I won't let him shut me out anymore. If what Sullivan said is true and my brother is planning to do something dangerous or illegal tonight, I'm going to figure out what it is. And I'm going to stop it. For his sake, and for mine.

I ease the door shut and latch it, then stand with my hands on my hips and scan the room. Jonathan keeps his things neat and tidy—much more so than I do—which makes any sort of snooping more difficult because he'll notice if a single thing is out of place. And I'm not really sure what I'm looking for. Of course, I don't think for a second that Jonathan wrote out a play-by-play of whatever it is they plan to do. Nor do I think I'll find a stash of brand-new cans of spray paint or a journal entry confessing all the angst my brother feels toward the Murphys. But surely there must be something that will help me understand what on earth has gotten into Jonathan in the last couple of months. A receipt, a letter, *anything*. At this point, I wouldn't be surprised to find a baggie of pot or a bottle of prescription meds.

I'm sorry, I mouth, hoping my apology will linger in the air even if Jonathan never knows what I've done.

The desk is the most logical place to start, and I methodically begin to open drawers and examine the contents. There's not much—a couple of geodes that he's had since we were kids, a pair of headphones, a worn copy of *A Wrinkle in Time*.

The closet, dresser, and bedside stand are equally innocuous. If you studied the contents of my brother's room alone, you'd think he was the most boring person on the planet. Everything is organized and purposeful, from the rolled pairs of socks in his underwear drawer to the careful line of cologne, body spray, and deodorant on his dresser. I roll my eyes, even though there's no one here to see it.

I'm leaving the room feeling dirty and defeated when I realize his backpack is hanging on a hook screwed into the back of the hardwood door. The zipper is gapped open, and inside I can just glimpse a manila envelope. Not an old notebook left over from the school year or a folder containing his term papers, an envelope that looks like nothing I've ever seen my brother with before. Jackpot. My head spins a little, like I've stepped to the edge of a cliff.

Easing open the zipper, I slip the envelope from the bag. The outside offers no clues: it's addressed to Law, and the return label is for our family accountant. Looks like Jonathan lifted it from the recycling bin. When I open the top flap and tip out the contents, I'm left holding a stack of eight-by-ten photographs. I fan them quickly to see if I recognize anything, but they're grainy and seem hastily snapped. Maybe that's why it takes me a few minutes to grasp what I'm seeing.

The top photo is of a heap of dead animals. I live in rural Iowa, I've seen dead animals before, but it's still jarring when my mind finally makes it out. There are at least five cows piled on top of one another and bloated from the sun and heat. Stiff legs jut into the sky, lending the grisly scene a darkly comical air. Even though the picture is a bit pixelated, I can see a black cloud of flies hovering over and on the tangle of bodies. I feel bile sting the back of my throat and swallow hard.

It's disgusting, and I have no desire to examine the photo further, but if Jonathan has this picture, it must be for a reason. I study it again, looking for evidence of where it might have been taken and why. But after combing every square inch, there are only two things I can say for sure: (1) The animals are not by the side of the road to be picked up by the rendering truck, and (2) They've been in the sun too long to be properly carted away anyway.

I've grown up on a farm; I know what happens when large animals die. They're dragged to the side of the road and a rendering company is called. A truck removes the carcasses, then processes the dead animals. For what? I don't want to know. It's a gruesome undertaking that I'd rather not think about, but the alternative is even worse: dead animals rotting all over the county and polluting the ground and air as they decompose. I think it might even be illegal.

Sliding the gory photograph to the bottom of the pile, I quickly flip through the others. There are several pictures of a tractor in a field. It's a shiny green John Deere pulling what looks like a disc, and behind that there's a white tank. I can't make out the lettering on the side of the tank, but the red and orange warning triangle is familiar enough. I've seen these tanks all over the Midwest, and I'd bet a hundred bucks it's filled with anhydrous ammonia.

I don't know much of anything about anhydrous ammonia, but I've read the warnings on the side of the tankers while waiting at stoplights or for the train to pass through town. I know that it's caustic and flammable and poisonous. The tanks are all plastered with the universal sign for danger: a skull and crossbones. I also know that anhydrous ammonia is used as a fertilizer. It's hard to understand how something so hazardous could be beneficial, but I've never claimed to understand farming.

The last picture is dark, obviously taken at twilight, and filled with blurry silhouettes. No flash was used. Still, I can see that it appears to be a group of people with shovels around a skid loader attached with a saw-toothed dirt bucket. I couldn't even begin to guess what they're doing, and I'm starting to feel like I don't want to know.

I stack the photos in the same order that I found them and carefully slot them back into the envelope. When I slide the package into Jonathan's backpack, my entire body prickles with goose bumps, even though the air is warm. There's something really wrong about those pictures. Something foul. It's not just the dead carcasses or the warning signs all over the tank. The perspective is off, and every shot has a rushed, furtive quality to it that makes the photos feel urgent somehow.

I'd love to run out of Jonathan's room and slam the door, but I can't shake the feeling that I saw something familiar in the pictures. Something that I missed the first time around. So I grab the envelope again and flip through them over and over until I spot it.

On the third tractor picture, the one with the tank, I can just make out a truck in the foreground. There's only a thin sliver of the vehicle visible, a portion of the black tailgate, but at the very edge is a stylized paint job. Or maybe it's a decal of some sort. It looks like the distinctive mark of a branding iron, all burnt and black at the edges, with intersecting perpendicular lines. Suddenly I know exactly what it is: the Tate Family Farms logo. The *T* almost looks like a cross with two interlocking *F*s on either side.

I replace everything again, then hurry out of Jonathan's room, neglecting to be as stealthy as I probably should. But what does it matter? If Mom hears me banging around upstairs, she'll just assume I'm getting ready for the party later, shuffling between the bathroom and my bedroom. Even if she caught me closing Jonathan's door, I wouldn't care. Not anymore.

My messy room feels like a sanctuary after snooping through Jonathan's deceptively perfect space. At least my dirty laundry is out in the open, scattered across the floor and balled up in a corner of my open closet. I sink onto the side of my bed and close my eyes, head aching and heart threatening to pound out of my chest. I can't make sense of what I've seen, but I know that it's the key to everything.

Why would Jonathan have photographs of the Tates' farm? I can only assume that they're of a set, because it's completely illogical to imagine that my brother has been traipsing around the county taking pictures of random fields. So, dead animals, anhydrous ammonia, digging in the dark. I'm no scientist, but it seems pretty clear to me that any one of those things could cause the sort of contamination that would compel the Murphys to sue.

So maybe Jonathan isn't angry with Cal and

Beth after all. Maybe he's collecting evidence to help them.

The thought sends me to my feet. If it was difficult for me to believe that Jonathan would be willing to hurt the Murphys in any way, it's even harder to swallow that he's a sort of double agent. Hardworking, earnest, what-you-see-is-what-you-get Jonathan Baker is neither conniving nor a great actor. Surely if he's trying to cozy up to the Tates to get dirt on their unethical farming practices they can see straight through him. Yes, Jonathan likes to party from time to time, and yes, he has a mischievous streak, but his character is solid and he's a terrible liar.

I just don't know what to make of any of this, but as the sun shifts to the west and Jonathan continues to ignore my texts, I decide that there's only one course of action for me to take: I'm going to the Pattersons' party. Of course Ashley will be there—it's her house, after all—and I'm certain I'm the last person she wants to see right now. But their annual barbecue is also the place that I have the greatest likelihood of seeing Jonathan. And Sullivan. This time, they won't shake me off.

The party is in full swing by the time I arrive. I've taken my own car instead of catching a ride with Law and Reb so that I can leave when I want to, but also because I can't stomach the thought of spending hours at the Pattersons' house when I know I'm not wanted. I pull up when the sun is low on the horizon, and I have to park nearly two blocks away. No worries. I'm in no hurry, and already battling a sense that I shouldn't have come at all.

Still, I step out of my car into the July heat and begin to make my way toward the house that feels like a second home to me. Ashley's rich—or, her parents are—but that never bothered me growing up. The Pattersons are generous with their time and resources, and I was always welcome at their pool, in their boat, or curled up on the trundle bed in Ashley's giant room. When I was little, her life felt like a bit of a fairy tale to me, but she was always willing to let me be a part of it. I've repaid her kindness with betrayal, and it guts me.

I've intentionally missed the potluck picnic and neighborhood barbecue that's become a Jericho tradition. And I've missed the pool games and cannonball contest, too (Jonathan won last year). I feel a pang of disappointment mixed with a premature sense of nostalgia. This was not how I pictured spending my last summer at home, and I'm queasy with a sense of loss.

As I near the Pattersons' house, I begin to encounter pockets of people who have spilled out of their large, fenced-in yard and onto the street. It's getting dark enough for fireworks, and several children are holding giant sparklers.

Others are shooting off small mortars on the road.

"Look out!" someone shouts, and at that very moment a Roman candle pops and emits a ball of fire only a few feet away from where I'm walking. I jump into the grass and back away, watching the firework until the final burst of light sputters out and the pipe on the cement is left smoking.

"Sorry about that!" A teenage boy laughs. He's young; I don't recognize him. "Enter at your own risk."

He has no idea.

The wooden gate that leads to the Pattersons' yard has been propped open, and I duck inside as another knot of laughing people slips out. I can smell the alcohol on them, a sour-sweet scent that reminds me of pickling spices and sweat. Ashley's dad always taps a couple of kegs for the Fourth of July party, and the polished cement bar on the far end of the patio houses a vast collection of liquor bottles so that guests can mix their own drinks if beer isn't their thing. In fact, admission to the party is a hot and cold dish to share, and a contribution to the outdoor wet bar. It's teeming with glass bottles of expensive whiskey and cheap rum, fine wine and Boone's Farm. Law isn't the party type, but my parents always come to the Pattersons' Independence Day soiree, and I'm convinced it's because of the bounty of alcohol.

Even though it's getting late and people will soon head to the fairgrounds to lay out their blankets for the city fireworks show, the yard is still crowded. A group of girls in bikinis lingers in the pool, laughing at some private joke and preening for any appreciative onlookers. And I can't even see the bar for the circle of people around it.

I don't know where to begin. The grassy expanse beyond the in-ground pool is filled with lawn chairs and crisscrossed with strings of festive lanterns and Christmas lights, but it's not bright enough for me to make out individual faces. I want to find Jonathan, but would rather not run into Ashley, and the thought of Sullivan leaves me conflicted. I stand frozen just inside the gate and wonder if I should leave. What do I think I'm doing here, anyway?

As I'm about to turn on my heel and go, I catch sight of something unexpected: my mom. Reb is leaning against one of the high tables that have been scattered around the pool deck. She's holding a drink with an umbrella in it, and she's smiling. Grinning, actually, and now laughing at something that Peter Knapper, the local dentist, is saying.

Mom looks relaxed, pretty. She's wearing a pair of dark jeans and a white T-shirt that sets off the sweep of her long, loose hair and accentuates her classic beauty. I can't look away from her.

I'm not sure I've ever seen her so luminous and happy. It's an innocent conversation—I know that. Dr. Knapper is a devoted husband and father, but his friendly attention makes people blossom somehow. And yet, I feel like I'm spying on my mother. Witnessing something I was never meant to see.

I can feel a full-body blush coming on, and I'm about to disappear out the gate when Law comes up behind Mom. As I watch, he puts one arm around her waist and roughly grabs her upper arm with his other hand, causing her to spill her drink. Dr. Knapper leans forward to help, but he stops short when he catches sight of the look on Law's face. Even from a distance I can feel the ire in that glare. It's a cold fury, the kind that burns. I just can't tell if it's directed at the dentist or my mother. Maybe both.

Without a single word, Law begins to steer Mom to the gate where I'm still trying to decide whether to stay or go. There are people in between us, but Law seems unsteady on his feet, and completely focused on Reb anyway. Still, I turn my back on them and hurry in the opposite direction, weaving through the crowd of people as I go. I don't want them to see me. I can't explain why, but the need to fade into the background is so strong I don't stop until I'm on the far side of the enormous yard.

There's a wrought-iron gazebo back here, but

it's too far from the pool and the bustle of the picnic tables and speakers blaring country music to draw much attention, and I have it to myself. I sink to a bench gratefully because my legs feel as if they won't support me much longer. What did I just see? I can't quite get my head around it. I've never caught Law looking at Reb like that before, and I'm not sure I fully understand the implications. He wasn't just angry, there was disappointment and betrayal and resignation in his face. He looked as if what Mom had done—talking to a neighbor—was unforgivable.

I want to go home. No, not home, because I'm sure Law and Reb are headed there. I want to be somewhere that I don't have to worry about the Murphys or Jonathan or Ashley or my parents. If I'm honest with myself, I want *Sullivan,* and the ache of it nearly brings me to tears. My phone is in my pocket with the ringer turned all the way up, so I know I haven't missed any calls or texts from him, and my heart deflates. I've been such an idiot.

Standing up, I resolve to find Ashley, apologize, and then go home with my tail between my legs for the rest of the summer. Jonathan's right: none of this is my business, and I should never have allowed myself to get dragged into things so far beyond my ken.

When an arm goes around my waist from behind, I gasp in shock, but the sound is almost immediately blocked by a rough hand against my mouth. I'm pressed head to toe against the body of a man not much taller than me, but significantly stronger. I struggle, but his fingers are cutting off my breath and stifling my cries. "Hi, June," he whispers in my ear. I don't recognize the voice.

Just when I begin to truly panic, blood zipping through my veins, another voice carves through the growing gloom. "Grow up, Dalton. Let her go."

As quickly as I was seized, I'm released. I whirl to see Dalton smirking and Jonathan cringing not far behind.

"Don't you ever touch me again," I spit. For a second I'm not sure if I'm talking to Dalton or to Jonathan. I can't believe my brother let that happen.

Dalton assumes my target and laughs. "She's a spunky one, eh?" To me he says, "You let Sully touch you, darlin'. This is practically the same thing."

I bite back a retort, because what do I know? Maybe Sullivan and Dalton are exactly the same. I haven't heard from Sullivan since we talked at the pancake breakfast.

"Where have you been all day?" I ask Jonathan. It sounds like an accusation because it is. I'm furious for a dozen different reasons, but right now my anger is wholly directed at my brother and the fact that he allowed Dalton to put his hands all over me.

Jonathan has the decency to look stricken by what just happened, but his repentance clearly doesn't change anything. He shrugs. "Nothing, really. Just hanging out."

I scowl at him for a moment, fighting back the urge to cry out all the things I think I know. I could tell Dalton about the pictures I found, about the fact that I believe my brother is lying. Just exactly who he's lying to is beyond me, but it would feel good to throw fuel on that fire all the same. Something volatile hovers in the air around us, and I feel a bit like a child who's walked in on her parents fighting. There are things going on that I just don't understand. So I turn and walk away without another word.

"Stop!" Jonathan jogs a few paces and falls into step beside me. Across the yard, someone cannonballs into the pool fully dressed and a howl of collective laughter drowns out his next words. It seems for a minute as if he will reach out to take me by the arm, but my expression must deter him. Instead, he leans in. "Don't go that way. Ashley's on the warpath."

When I waver for a second, he takes his chance. "Follow me. There's a back gate."

Of course I know the Pattersons have a back gate. I've used it a million times. Still, I don't want to give Jonathan the satisfaction of taking his advice. Nor do I want to run into Ashley. My earlier bravado is shaken, and I just don't know if I can handle a face-to-face confrontation right now. *No,* I decide, and wordlessly stalk off in the direction of a much smaller gate set into the far corner of the Pattersons' eight-foot perimeter fence.

Dalton and Jonathan follow. "Leaving so soon?" I ask, my voice dripping with snark. I'm furious; I can feel it sparking and white-hot in my chest.

"We've been here for hours," Dalton says, clearly unmoved by the way he affected me. "Had to take advantage of the Pattersons' booze."

Naturally. Dalton does, indeed, seem drunk. But when I glance at Jonathan, his gaze is steady and his stride sure. He's stone-cold sober, I can tell.

What Dalton sees in my brother is beyond me. Jonathan is just eighteen, still in high school, and so different from Dalton and the rest of the Tates; it's almost jarring to see them together.

Halting, I cross my arms over my chest. "I want to talk to my brother," I say. "Alone."

Dalton laughs, but Jonathan fixes me with a stare that says: *Don't do this.*

Whatever. I'm past playing nice.

"No problem," Dalton says, seemingly oblivious to the nonverbal exchange between me and my brother. He waves at Jonathan as if to shoo him in my direction. "I'll just be waiting at the car, drinking a beer, keeping myself company . . ." he trails off as he walks away, his path wavering.

Jonathan hangs back reluctantly, but the moment Dalton is out of earshot I take my chance. I punch my brother in the shoulder. Hard.

"What the hell?" I cry, pulling back to hit him again.

He sidesteps my fist and lifts his palms in surrender. "I'm sorry, June. Really I am. I didn't know Dalton was going to grab you like that. I would have stopped him if I did."

"That's it? That's all you have to say to me?" I'm panting, my heart pounding. "That's just the tip of the iceberg, and you know it."

For just a moment the facade crumbles, and the Jonathan I know and love peeks through. His mouth twists down like he's about to cry— something I haven't seen him do in years—and in a split second everything changes and I want to take him in my arms like the big sister I am. But then he clears his throat and squares his shoulders, and the mask is back in place as if it never slipped at all.

"Just go home, June. Take a long bath, read a book. I don't care what you do, just *go home.*"

He wheels away from me and is swallowed up by the darkness. Almost as soon as I can't see him anymore, the first big firework explodes above me. It's brilliant, enormous, a crimson bloom that fizzles to gold as it streaks across the sky. When I was little, fireworks always made me cry. They were loud and terrifying. Clearly dangerous. I couldn't understand why everyone smiled and laughed while the world was ending around us.

They keep coming, an onslaught of light and sound accompanied by the suggestion of gun smoke and sulfur. Of course, I can't smell the fireworks from where I'm standing, but over the years I've held the punk and lit enough cherry bombs, bottle rockets, and fountains to know exactly how they sting at the back of your throat. Fireworks engage every sense, and for a few minutes at least, it seems the whole earth is entranced, faces turned heavenward.

Suddenly, I know what I have to do.

But as I hurry off toward my car, someone calls my name. I spin without thinking, and her blow catches me completely off guard. Before I realize what's happening, I'm on my hands and knees in the grass, left cheek flaming and eyes watering so hard tears drip onto my knuckles. I've never been slapped before.

"You bitch," she spits. I can hardly recognize Ashley's voice, but her sandals are familiar and so is her sparkly purple toenail polish. I bought it for her. "How could you?"

I could tell her that Sullivan had explained over and over again that it would never work between them. I could confess that it was an accident, that I never meant to fall for him. I could throw myself on her good graces, whisper that I had fallen in love. That this thing between Sullivan and me is *real*. But I know her well enough to know that her fury is all-consuming as a house fire. There is nothing for me to do but watch it burn.

Ashley stands over me for a few ragged breaths, and I worry the whole time that she will kick me while I'm down. But she doesn't.

So I sit back on my haunches and scrub at the tears with the heels of my hands. I dare to say, "I'm sorry," and she laughs.

"You're dead to me," Ashley says, which seems both ridiculously melodramatic and perfectly apt, and suddenly I'm just as angry as I am sad. I push myself up to face her, but Ashley is already walking away, leaving me behind as if we were never anything at all.

"He didn't want you," I call after her, my voice fracturing over the words. "He never did."

Ashley pauses just a moment, a stutter in her step, as a firework rips apart the black sky. It's red and fierce, the mouth of a dragon, and I'm reminded that there is much more at play tonight than the annihilation of our friendship. Because it *is* over. I've cemented it. She'll hate me forever, but I'm crushed, too, winded by not just her palm against my cheek, but the fact that she can simply walk away. If she ever loved me at all . . .

But I don't have time to cry over Ashley Patterson tonight.

I turn my tearstained face away from the place where she's fading into the shadows and take off in the other direction at a sprint. Maybe I'm not too late.

CHAPTER 21

WINTER
TODAY

"Barry's car again?" Willa asked, hopping into the passenger seat. She waved goodbye to Zoe through the windshield as she clicked on her seat belt. The girl was almost chipper, clearly invigorated by the excitement of the day and Jonathan's unexpected awakening. In some ways it was as if he'd come back to life.

"Yup," Juniper said automatically. She was really in no condition to deal with a hyper teen.

"How's Uncle Jonathan?"

"Awake."

"I mean, did he ask about me? Can I go see him? When can I see him?"

Juniper paused in the blue light of the dashboard and regarded Willa. She looked much younger than her thirteen years in the pale glow, her lips parted in expectation and the forward slant of her shoulders pitched with hope. She was so pretty Juniper couldn't speak for a moment.

"Soon," she forced herself to say. "You'll get to see Jonathan very soon. He misses you." Whether it was true or not didn't matter right now.

As Juniper navigated the dark streets toward

the bungalow, she felt drunk with the bitter elixir of all she had missed. She wanted to stop in the driveway and tell Willa everything there was to know. About who her father was and how they had once been so in love. About what had happened the night that everything changed, and the role that her mother had played in it.

But the game wasn't over yet, and as much as she wanted to leave the past behind and move on, seeing Jonathan with his eyes vacant and his body dependent on machines only underlined the fact that nothing had changed. Not yet. Jonathan was still the most likely suspect; Willa, the Butcher's Girl. Juniper bore the weight of her flight and her exile, the abandonment of her daughter, who was nobody's baby—not really—because teenage June didn't have the courage to tell the truth back then. Did she now? Juniper snuck a sideways glance at Willa as she drove down the dark streets toward home. The girl was nibbling on the tip of one fingernail, brow furrowed as she studied the windshield. She looked small and uncertain and lonely.

I do, Juniper thought. *I'm brave enough.*

"Willa, I'm so sorry, but there's someone I need to talk to."

"Is it about Jonathan?"

"Yes." Juniper pulled into the driveway of the bungalow and called Cora. Willa tried to insist that she'd be okay alone for a while, that this was *Jericho* after all, but that was exactly what Juniper was afraid of.

A few minutes later, Cora pulled up in front of the house and met Willa in the driveway. They hugged like old friends, and Cora waved over Willa's shoulder and gave Juniper a knowing wink.

Juniper watched until Cora and Willa disappeared inside the house and had enough time to turn on the lights and lock the doors. Willa swept the curtains shut and then she was finally blocked from view.

There was so much Sullivan in the girl. Juniper could see it now. The lightheartedness, the innate desire to laugh and have fun. Willa was fearless and bold, with just a hint of her mother's learned watchfulness. She was no dummy, that was for sure. And though there were things about her daughter that were wholly unknown and even a little scary, Juniper felt feverish with the desire to know her. To make up for all the lost years between them.

But first: this.

The number Cora had given her was now saved in her phone. She thumbed through her contacts until India Abbot was highlighted, then punched the call icon.

"Hello?"

"Hi," she said, hoping she didn't sound as flustered as she felt. "It's Juniper Baker. From the library?" It wasn't a question, but she couldn't stop her voice from tipping up at the end.

"Juniper! Hey! Cora said you might call. What's up?"

What's up? Juniper didn't know if she was more irritated by the fact that Cora had warned India about her or that India made it sound like a social call. They weren't buddies. Still, Juniper decided to push on. "I was hoping I could talk to you about the Murphy murders. Cora says you're kind of a true crime buff and that you might have some insight into the case." What she didn't say was: I want to know what you know. I want to know if it's *you* who's hell-bent on proving that Jonathan did it.

"Oh my gosh. This is like a dream come true. I mean, I've wanted to talk to you about Calvin and Elizabeth Murphy for years. *Years*. I never imagined I'd get the chance. Can you come over? Like, now? My husband is at a Beer and Hymns night at the Admiral and my kids are all in bed. I've just popped the cork on a bottle of pinot and it's not going to drink itself!"

"Sure," Juniper said, putting Barry's car in reverse. "Now works great."

India lived in a freshly constructed house at the end of an unpaved road that was part of a new subdivision in Jericho. Juniper hadn't realized that new developments were going up, or that there was a market for the type of upscale two-story Craftsman that India called home. The lot beside her modern-farmhouse-styled mini-mansion was under construction, and across the street were two more lots with SOLD signs staked in the dirt. As Juniper turned off gravel onto the paved driveway, India came to stand on her bright, homey porch.

"Sorry about the mess!" India called over the distance between them.

Juniper clicked the locks on Barry's car and jogged down the curved sidewalk toward the place where India waited, rubbing her arms against the cold. She was wearing a plush oversized sweater that fell off one shoulder and a pair of gray camo leggings. Clutching a delicate wineglass and sporting a perky grin, she made Juniper feel instantly frumpy and older than she was.

"It's fine," Juniper said, conscious of the snow and dirt that had accumulated in the tread of her hiking shoes. She couldn't possibly wear them inside India's new house.

But India already had an arm around her and was ushering her through the door.

"I can't believe you're here," India said, pulling Juniper's coat off her shoulders and hanging it with a flourish on a fleur de lis hook. "I mean, I've imagined it a dozen times. The chance to interview you, to hear what you have to say about what happened that night . . . The insight no one but you could provide into the case that was never solved."

"Wait." Juniper froze in the entryway, unwilling to take another step until she knew the truth. "I'm not here for an interview. And before we go any further I need to know: Are you working on a podcast about the Murphy murders?"

The question was abrupt, but it achieved the desired result: India's reaction seemed genuine. "What?" she asked, eyebrows arching. "Someone's doing a podcast about the Murphy murders?" Envy flashed across her features, and then she sighed. "I don't know what to tell you. It's not me. But it's a *great* idea—kinda wish I would have thought of it."

The look in India's eyes was too raw to be faked; Juniper believed her. She toed off her shoes and forced herself to smile. "How about that wine?"

India laughed. "I'll make it a very generous pour. I'm a lot to take."

The house was quiet and softly lit, and when Juniper followed India through to the kitchen and a cozy hearth room just beyond, she saw that a large-screen TV was on. But instead of HGTV or a charming Hallmark Channel romance, there was footage of a scruffy-looking man with dark hair and a quirky half smile staring straight into the camera.

"Is that Ted Bundy?" Juniper couldn't stop herself.

"Oh my gosh. Yes! I'm watching *Conversations with a Killer*. The man was a total psychopath, but there was so much more to it, you know? No doubt that he was a narcissist, but I'd bet the farm we're also dealing with some borderline personality disorder, possibly some schizoaffective disorder or bipolar. Where did that come from? I mean, what happened in his past to fracture his psyche to the point where he could hardly even be considered human?" Catching sight of Juniper's expression, India trailed off, then grabbed the remote control from the arm of an artfully distressed leather sectional and clicked off the TV. "Sorry. Weird stuff. I know."

"It's why I'm here," Juniper admitted. "Cora says you're finishing up your master's in psychology."

"Abnormal psychology with an emphasis on behavioral neuroscience," India said, pouring Juniper a glass of wine. "I'd love to be a psychological profiler for the FBI, but . . ." She shrugged, gesturing to the trappings of her domestic, small-town life and the wicker basket of toys in one corner of the hearth room.

"Life gets in the way?" Juniper suggested, taking the glass India offered and swallowing a mouthful of what tasted like cherries and cloves.

"Exactly. I'm not complaining. And we'll see what the future holds. Besides, I have to finish my coursework first."

Juniper felt quite sure that the capstone project wouldn't be a problem for India. There was clearly much more to India Abbot than her pixie cut and casual demeanor suggested. Her chic nail polish and the impressive collection of braided bracelets on her left wrist almost seemed like decoys.

"Thanks for meeting with me," Juniper said. "Cora speaks so highly of you."

"And you. She adores you, you know that, right? You're like a daughter to her."

Juniper wasn't sure what to say to that, so she took another sip of her wine and followed India to the couch. They sat on opposite ends, and India pulled her legs up beneath her.

"So . . ." she said, drawing out the word. "What exactly can I do for you?"

"I need help." It practically burst out of Juniper. "I'm sorry, India, but I read your blog—"

India laughed.

"—and I know that there are many people around here who still think that my brother killed Cal and Beth Murphy."

"You don't?"

Juniper was stunned silent. "He's my brother."

"Ted Bundy was someone's brother, too. That didn't stop him."

Juniper opened her mouth to speak, but nothing came out.

"Look." India set her wineglass down on a natural-edge coffee table and leaned forward with her elbows on her crisscrossed knees. "I don't think Jonathan killed them either."

"You don't?"

"He doesn't fit the profile, and his actions after the murders would either classify him as a sociopath—which neither of us believes is true—or point to the fact that he didn't do it. That he *couldn't* do it. I don't think for a second that he would kill Calvin and Elizabeth in cold blood over some free labor. Did they fight about it? Was it something he complained about often? Did he stop going over and running errands and doing odd jobs for them because he felt taken advantage of?"

Juniper realized that India was waiting for an answer. She shook her head.

"No," India confirmed. "And what did he do the second he realized they had been shot? He called 911. Who does that? You'd be hard-pressed to find a case study where the killer called in his own crime and then stuck around to be arrested for it."

"So, who?" Juniper could hardly choke the words out, her throat was so tight.

"That's the million-dollar question, isn't it? Of course, we have all the usual suspects."

"The Tates," Juniper supplied, and India tipped her head in acknowledgment. "Weighted equally?"

"No." India grabbed a tablet off the end table behind her and flipped through a couple of screens until she found what she was looking for. "I wrote up psych profiles on the entire Tate family. Of course, this is all speculation, considering I've never interviewed them about it and all I have to go on is hearsay and reputation, but it's better than nothing."

Juniper put her wine down on the coffee table.

"The way the murders happened would indicate a crime of passion," India said. "There was no forethought in this—at least, I don't believe it was premeditated."

"What makes you say that?"

"It's far too sloppy to be planned out. First of all, it happened outside, well after dark, on a holiday. Whoever killed the Murphys couldn't have known that they would be awake or even home on the night of the Fourth. If the murders had been orchestrated by some criminal mastermind—or even a newbie hack—he would have chosen a different date and time. Why not wait until the following night when he knew they would be in bed together? Why not learn their patterns and schedules and make a safer choice?"

Juniper's Reddit profiler had said something similar, but it was fascinating to hear how much thought India had put into everything. She knew Jericho. She knew the people who lived here. Juniper felt adrenaline spike in her chest.

"No," India continued, "whoever shot the Murphys did it spur of the moment. Something set him off. Something compelled him to make a terrible choice."

"Him?"

"Statistically speaking," India said matter-of-factly. "Is it possible that it may, indeed, be a woman? Sure, but I doubt it. So let's talk about bullet trajectories. The first bullet hit Calvin in the shoulder." She reached out to put a single finger to the place on Juniper's shoulder. It was just below the bone in the soft meat at the far edge of her collar. Juniper stifled a shiver. "Could have been a lethal shot, but it missed the axillary artery by a couple millimeters and exited out his back at a downward angle. What does that tell us?"

"The killer was taller than Cal?" Juniper guessed.

"Good girl. And not an excellent shot. Although, let's give him the benefit of the doubt and assume that it was dark. Now, when Cal didn't instantly go down, our killer realized his mistake and shot again, this time puncturing the chest and obliterating his left ventricle. Ninety-four percent of patients with penetrating thoracic injuries die before they reach the hospital, but I doubt Cal even made it another minute."

Juniper's head was swimming, and her vision felt a little clouded around the edges.

India noticed. "I'm going too deep," she said, setting the tablet aside and taking Juniper briefly by the hand. "I'll dial it back, okay? I know you knew these people. I know you loved them."

"I did," Juniper managed.

"Then I'll keep it simple. I think that whoever killed Cal was someone he knew. Someone who could walk onto his property undisturbed—who could come within a few feet of him without causing alarm. Someone who knew that Cal kept his gun in the glove compartment of his truck and felt no compunction grabbing it and killing Cal with it. Someone who was taller than Cal, and who was probably shooting out of anger or desperation, not premeditation."

"Besides Jonathan's and Cal's, there were no fingerprints on the gun," Juniper reminded India, but India was already shaking her head.

"That's easy. It's much easier to dispose of gloves than a gun. Or a cloth, handkerchief, you name it."

"And Beth?"

"Collateral damage. She must have come outside when she heard the shots, and the killer had no choice but to finish her, too. I think she recognized him."

"So you don't buy the stranger theory."

India sat back. "You mean that someone

passing through randomly knocked them off? Absolutely not. It's ridiculous, but I understand that it's easier to imagine evil existing outside Jericho than in."

"We're back to the Tates."

"Annabelle is too short," India said, ticking off the Tates on her fingers. "So is Wyatt. That leaves Franklin, Sterling, Dalton, and Sullivan."

"Your best guess?"

India sighed. "Beats me. The papers were already filed in court, the Tates—and the entire county—knew that the Murphys were suing them. And like it or not, the Tates were going to win. They had more money, better lawyers behind them. So a crime of sudden passion doesn't quite fit. And they all used each other as alibis. Except Sullivan."

India didn't need to say it, so she tapped one manicured finger against her pursed lips and waited for a response. Juniper held her tongue.

Juniper was Sullivan's alibi, and he was hers. That had caused some confusion, a few raised eyebrows, but it was easily explained away because Jonathan was the linchpin that linked them together. They held fast, a cord with three strands that had remained unbroken for all these years. Even though that night drove them so far apart they were now virtual strangers.

Juniper felt the fire seep out of her veins. She was left empty, a little chilled. She was back at square one.

"What we need is a witness."

"What?" Juniper crossed her arms over her chest, trying to ward off the familiar dark spread of despair.

"Somebody who saw something," India said, her eyes suddenly flinty. "Heard something. County Road 21 isn't busy, but on a night like the Fourth of July there would be people traveling home from town. Nearby farmers still up. Neighbors enjoying the fireflies and a warm summer night. Your farm was just around the corner from the Murphys', wasn't it? I think your parents still live there."

Juniper didn't like what India was insinuating. The would-be criminal profiler was a couple seconds away from asking: "Where were you at ten thirty on the night that Cal and Beth Murphy were killed?"

"You know," India mused, "I think a witness would crack this whole thing wide open. I just don't understand why no one is talking."

Eager to divert India's attention away from herself, Juniper quickly asked: "What about Carver Groen?"

India held Juniper's gaze for a long moment before responding. "You're kidding, right?"

"Officer Stokes still considers him a suspect."

"Everett?" India laughed. "He absolutely does not. You know who he is, don't you?"

Juniper felt her stomach clench as she watched

a smile play at the corners of India's lips. "No," she admitted.

"Everett Stokes is Carver Groen's cousin. Things were bad for Everett at home, so his Aunt Roxy—Carver's mom—took him in, and he lived with them for as long as I can remember. When Carver admitted to the murders, all hell broke loose. Roxy said she couldn't handle it all, so Everett was forced to move back in with his own mom and stepdad."

"I had no idea."

"It's not a happy story," India said, bringing one knee up and wrapping her arms around it. "The state removed him from their care after just a couple of months. He left Jericho his sophomore year of high school—we were in the same class—and bounced around foster homes, from what I understand. Nobody could believe it when he came back here wearing blue and a badge."

Juniper's mouth had turned into a desert. She lurched for her wine and took a big swig. It didn't help.

"He didn't tell you about his connection to the murders?" India said.

Juniper shook her head.

"Have you spoken to him?"

"Yes."

India sucked her teeth for a second. "You need to know he's on a witch hunt. Whoever killed Cal and Beth Murphy also ruined his life. He wants to pin this on somebody once and for all."

"Jonathan?"

India lifted one slender shoulder. "Would be a whole lot easier than convincing all of Jericho that someone in the Tate family was behind it. Do you know how many people they employ? How many donations they've made to keep this town afloat? Without irrefutable proof, the Tates are untouchable."

So all Juniper had to do was rewind the clock and prove beyond a shadow of a doubt that someone in her former lover's family was a cold-blooded killer.

"I can't shake the feeling that we're missing something. Like there's a giant piece of the puzzle we've overlooked. What else happened that summer, Juniper?"

Something nibbled at the back of Juniper's mind, but she pushed a strand of hair behind her ears and ignored it. "Thank you so much for your hospitality," Juniper said, standing. "I really appreciate it."

"I hope I haven't chased you out." India rose too, her pretty brow wrinkled in concern. "There's so much more I'd like to talk about . . ."

"Another time," Juniper assured her. "I have something I need to take care of."

"Sounds ominous." India followed her to the entryway and leaned against the wall while she watched Juniper slip on her shoes and grab her coat. "But then again, I see the world through a bit of a bleak lens."

Juniper coughed out a stale laugh. "You certainly do," she said. "Somehow, it suits you."

India waited until Juniper had slid behind the steering wheel in Barry's car, then clicked off the porch light and disappeared. Juniper couldn't help but think that in another life she'd love India—her quirky interests, the mismatch of her charming exterior and dark inner life.

She turned the ignition in her borrowed car, then took out her phone and tapped a message.

We need to talk.

The three dots of an incoming message appeared and disappeared. After a full minute, Everett finally responded:

About what?

Juniper ignored the question.

I'm coming over.

CHAPTER 22

THAT NIGHT

I might be too late already, but that's a chance I'm willing to take. Jericho's shoestring police force and volunteer fire department are busy at the fairgrounds setting off the fireworks, so I careen through town with no regard for posted speed limits. Everyone knows that the annual fireworks show is the darling pet project of Jericho's finest, and that for half an hour every Fourth of July the town is essentially defenseless. Not that we really need protecting. I think the worst crime that's happened here in the last twenty years was when Wyatt Tate lifted a couple of stereos from people's unlocked cars and sold them on eBay. Now it's a story that's relayed with a chuckle and a shrug, as if to say, *Boys will be boys.*

I'd love to believe that we're still as innocent, but I don't buy it for a second. My heart knocks painfully in my chest as I reach nearly seventy on the country roads, but I know that Dalton and Jonathan got a head start, and God only knows where Wyatt and Sullivan are. But I can't go there, I just can't. I push all thoughts of Sullivan out of my mind as I make the final turn down County Road 21 and accelerate toward the Murphys' acreage.

I have no idea what I'm getting into, but as helter-skelter as this plan is, I do have the common sense to realize that I'd better take it slow. So instead of turning onto Cal and Beth's property, I drive right past and pull into the lane that leads to Jericho Lake. It's deserted, of course, because I'd dare to bet that the entire population of our small town is at the fireworks show—or at least somewhere they can watch it.

With a spray of gravel and a squeal of tires, I whip into a makeshift parking spot near the lake. It isn't until the car is off and I'm hurrying along the path that Jonathan and I have worn down over the years that I realize just how dark it is. And how scared I am.

There's no moon tonight, or maybe there is, but it's hidden behind a wall of high, dark clouds. Although I can't see the fireworks out here, every once in a while there's a glow on the horizon, and for just a heartbeat the long, dark tendrils of withering fire etch themselves onto the face of the sky. It's apocalyptic. It looks as if bombs are being dropped on my hometown, and I'm the lone survivor running through the wilderness.

Stop it. I'm freaking myself out, making matters way worse than they need to be. This is not a zombie movie and aliens are not invading Jericho. I'm on my way to do a little reconnaissance, to make sure that my friends and neighbors are safe, and that nothing gets out of hand. That's all.

The raspberry canes are over my head, and when I jog down one of the rows, my skin crawls from the scrape of serrated leaves. Or mosquitos. Maybe both. By the time I finally crest the small hill at the top of the Murphys' farm, I'm itching all over, hyperventilating a little, and convinced that I'm about to stop something truly terrible from happening.

But the farm is quiet. I falter in the darkness, squinting at the curved drive. As far as I can tell, there's nothing there. No mysterious trucks. No one slinking through the shadows. If Betsy is outside, she's found no need to bark, and the rest of the pastoral acreage is equally hushed. Every couple of seconds I can hear the faint retort of the fireworks, but when I check my watch and realize it's almost ten thirty, I know that they're nearly done. I was sure that if the Tates were going to do something, now would be the time. With everyone's attention fixed elsewhere, it would be the perfect moment to strike. But I was wrong.

Except, it's unusually dark. It takes me a moment to realize that the light pole near the old chicken coop is conspicuously dim. It should be lighting up the whole yard, but the bulb isn't just faded, it's out. I wonder briefly if it fizzled out on its own or if it was helped along by a rock or a pellet gun. But now that I'm here, my suspicions seem almost silly and I dismiss them out of hand.

For a minute or two I stand just outside the raspberry field and try to catch my breath. The high cloud ceiling is changing the weather, and I can feel the humidity rising. I'm unbearably hot from the run and the sudden shift in pressure, and for a moment I consider walking down the hill to the farmhouse to ask for a drink. There are lights on inside—I can see silhouettes moving behind the windows—but I'd probably scare Cal and Beth half to death.

I'm about to turn and go when a breeze lifts the hair off my shoulders and blows the barn door open. It slams against the side of the large building, making me jump, and causing Penny to snort and neigh in alarm.

Before I can consider what I'm doing, I lope down the hill in the direction of the barn. It's so dark out that I don't worry about anyone seeing me trespassing on the Murphys' property. The only light comes from the glow of the farmhouse windows, and everything else is layer upon layer of shadow and black. But I can make out the bulk of the barn, and even if I couldn't, I know the way.

At the door of the barn, I pause. What if someone is in there? What if it's Jonathan? Or

Sullivan? I gasp a few shallow breaths and force myself to take the last several steps. I'm pressed tight against the side of the building, head cocked and ears craning for the slightest movement, the slightest sound.

I hear the shuffle of Penny's feet in the hay. The creak of old wood in a rising wind. A hoot owl in a nearby tree.

Nothing more.

My breath leaves me in a hard exhale, and I lean against the open door, spent. This has been a waste of time, and I will clearly be the butt of every joke forever. I can almost picture the Tate boys and my beloved brother holed up somewhere and laughing at my expense. At the way that they have all strung me along and made me see a specter in every trick of light. I swallowed it all, hook, line and sinker, and greedily gulped down the lie that Sullivan could want me. Could maybe even *love* me.

Tears sting my eyes, but I won't let them fall. Not for Sullivan and not for the Tates. Not even for Jonathan, because my almost-twin has proven himself to be no brother of mine.

I'm about to retrace my steps when the sound of a door opening draws my attention to the house. For just a moment I can see Cal framed in the warm rectangle of light, then he pushes Betsy back inside by her nose and shuts the door with a bang. He must have heard the barn door too.

Or he remembered that he left it open or he has other work to do. Whatever the reason, I'm stuck standing against the rough wood with nowhere to go. If I run for it, there's a chance that he'll see the movement and panic. I'm obviously much bigger than a raccoon or a possum, and for all I know, he's carrying protection because of the harassment he's experienced.

The thought sends a chill right through me. Farmers have guns. Period. Rifles for hunting and handguns for fun or for nuisances around the farm. Law has dispatched many a skunk with a little silver pistol that he keeps in his bedside drawer, and he even let me shoot it when I turned twelve and he wondered, briefly, if I might show some interest. I didn't. But if I were Calvin Murphy, and people had been driving onto my property at night, spraying my grass, keying my car, poisoning my dog, and otherwise making my life a living hell, you'd better believe I'd tuck a little something in my waistband.

He's getting closer—I can hear the melody of his whistle, but I can't make out the tune—so I make a split-second decision. I duck into the barn and press myself against the wall behind the open door. There are two doors, of course, double wide so they can be swung open to admit equipment and animals, and I pick the side that's open so that I can wedge myself in the sliver of space between door and wall. A smaller back door will be my escape when the time comes, but if he steps inside and turns on the lights, I don't want Cal to catch me racing through the barn as if I have something to hide. A couple of minutes. All I have to do is keep still for a couple of minutes.

My whole body is pressed tight against the wall, and I can feel the prickle of the splintered boards against my bare legs and arms. I squeeze my eyes shut and try to regulate my breathing, hoping that the wild beat of my heart and the ragged gulp of each inhale isn't a dead giveaway that I've taken sanctuary in the Murphys' barn.

But after a few minutes I realize that the footsteps I expected have faded away instead of come closer. I hold still and struggle to hear, but I can't make out a single noise above the songs of crickets and the complaints of the old barn. Turning, I press my face against one of a thousand gaps in the boards and squint into the inky night.

It appears as if Cal has angled away from the barn and is standing near where the driveway curves toward the roadside stand. I can barely make him out, but he's a moving smudge in the darkness, and as I strain my sight toward where I think he is, I realize that he's not alone.

Not alone. A thrill of vindication washes over me, but it's short-lived. If there's someone out there in the night with Cal, it means that whatever the Tates have been planning is going down. I wasn't supposed to be hiding in the barn, frozen.

I was supposed to be the voice of reason, the one person who could talk sense into them and fix it all. Or, if I couldn't make everything better, at the very least I could document it. Take pictures, call 911, do something. But I'm not out there. I'm hiding in the barn.

I push myself away from where I'm cowering behind the door and race out into the open. It's impossible for me to tell who is who—the two figures on the gravel drive are little more than stains on the velvet night—but I assume that the figure closest to the farmhouse is Cal. Either way, neither Cal nor the stranger make any indication that they know I'm there. They're talking, loudly, animatedly, but I'm too far away and can't make out the words. Against the backdrop of their argument, the soft scuff of my feet is mere background noise. But just as I'm about to call out to them, one of the figures raises his arm.

There's a flash, and a crack splits the night. Cal stumbles back. Another flash, another pop, and Cal makes a guttural, bubbling sound halfway between a shout and a cry.

My mind is far behind the animal reaction of my body. Before I can rationalize what I'm doing, I've stopped mid-stride and am scrambling backward, retracing the few steps I've taken from the sanctuary of the barn. Nature overrules any uncertainty I may be feeling, and pulsing in every pore of my body is a single message: *run*.

There's nowhere to go that isn't out in the open, and I'm hysterical with the thought that I may have already given myself away. But the barn is only a few steps off, and I've closed the distance before his body has hit the ground. I know because I hear the heavy thump of his weight against the earth. The groan of his breath as it's ripped from his lungs.

Oh my God. There are no words for this, no way to make sense of what I've just witnessed. I slam against the inside wall of the barn and collapse on the ground with jagged boards at my back. My shoulders sting, and my hip where I've landed too hard, but the sensations are meaningless. In the absence of rational thought there is nothing but noise. The white noise of my pulse as it floods through my veins, of the excruciatingly loud scuff of my scrabbling feet on the dirt floor. Of a whimper that must be coming from me and must be *silenced.*

Shut up. *Shut up.* Be quiet as whisper. Be soft as sleep.

But Beth is not quiet. I hear her burst from the farmhouse, shouting, but I can't make out the words. Behind the closed door, the dog is barking madly, the muffled yelp the warning of a siren and just as steady. It's a cacophony, a riot, a signal fire that lights up the night until another explosion rips through the air.

Then there is nothing but silence. One bullet,

and the woman has been hushed. The dog is quiet, too. Maybe Betsy knows. Maybe now she's whining.

My mind spins away from what this must mean, and finds a frantic, anguished home in nothingness. I hear nothing. I feel nothing. From far away, I discern a nudge of conscience, a murmur that compels me to look, to listen. But I'm on the ground somewhere, and it is not safe, but it is away.

I claw my fingers at the hard-packed earth, and it comes apart as dust beneath my nails. There is pain, and I realize that I must have torn them, that the wetness against my skin is blood. But when I think of blood, my soul begins to howl. It's a clamor that I cannot contain, that threatens to rip out my throat if I dare to open my mouth. I do not.

It's impossible to hear the footsteps, but I feel them. A reverberation in the ground that echoes through my very bones. He's so close I can feel him over my shoulder, sharing the air that I can barely breathe for shock and horror. If I were a different person—braver—I would surprise him in the darkness. Throw myself against him. Look him in the eye.

But I cower. Press my cheek against the hard boards until splinters bite my skin.

"Who's there?" he whispers. Two hissed syllables, a voice I almost recognize.

And then he's upon me. So close I could reach out and touch him through the narrow gap behind the door, but instead I tuck my face into my knees. It is dark as pitch all around us, dark as the grave. I hold so still, I am stone. I am nothing. I do not even exist.

The world is blackness and wailing somewhere deep inside my chest. I am unseeing, unfeeling. Undone. The earth has come apart around me and there is no way that I can go on after this. That *life* can go on after this. It's over.

But behind my raw fear and the way my heart and mind skitter away from reality, I realize I can smell him. It's uncanny, this odor he carries with him. It pricks my nose and invades my mouth. It makes me gag, and I do so silently, noiselessly, wishing him away, wishing everything away. But I'm hemmed in by shadows and he's trapping me there.

He smells of death.

CHAPTER 23

WINTER
TODAY

I am the witness.

The thought tattooed itself on Juniper's skin, driven deeper and deeper by her every frantic heartbeat. *Wit-ness. Wit-ness. Wit-ness.*

She had been there, on the Murphys' farm, from the moment that Cal stepped out of the house until everything had been reduced to the freckle of starlight between heavy clouds and blood seeping into the dirt. When she pulled it apart, dissected that night, Juniper could see everything reduced to fragments of a whole. Puzzle pieces that fit somehow, but she couldn't seem to put them together.

Or maybe she didn't want to.

I think a witness would crack this whole thing wide open.

Juniper's skin tingled at the memory of India's direct gaze, of the fine line of her delicate jaw as it hardened in anticipation of what Juniper would—or wouldn't—say. India was savvy. She'd solve the mystery sooner or later. Realize the same thing that Everett already had: there was time unaccounted for. Long minutes nobody could explain.

When Officer Stokes looked back at police reports, what would he find? Would he realize that by the time they collected Juniper at her parents' farm around 11:30 p.m. that her hair was still dripping wet? She remembered sitting in the conference room of the small police department with the weight of her hair sopping the back of her T-shirt and making her shiver with cold. One of the officers wrangled up a dusty blanket from somewhere and tucked it around her trembling shoulders.

It was nearing ten, but Juniper knew that Willa was safe with Cora, so when she pulled into Everett's driveway, she set her phone to silent mode and stuck it in her coat pocket. She wanted it with her just in case—she didn't trust Everett for a second—but she also didn't want it to ring and interrupt them. She had some hard questions to ask Officer Stokes, and she wasn't about to be sidetracked.

"Juniper," Everett said when he opened the front door (sidewalk freshly shoveled, porch light on), "I wasn't expecting a visitor so late." He gestured to the sweatpants and gray ISU sweatshirt he was wearing, but Juniper just gave him a tight-lipped smile.

He swung the door wider and she stepped inside. The last time she had been in his house, she'd entered through the garage into the laundry room and, beyond that, the kitchen. Now she was standing smack-dab in the middle of Everett's living room; only a small tiled square separated the front door from the plush, recently vacuumed carpet that ran through the rest of the house. Directly across from where they stood was the elaborate fish tank and the door that she had peeked through. Juniper couldn't stop herself from glancing toward the office. The door was closed.

"I forgot," Everett said, following her gaze, "you were quite the fan of my fish tank."

Juniper almost told him to cut the crap, that they both knew exactly what she was looking at, but she was hoping to play the ingénue a bit longer.

"I've never seen anything like it," she agreed.

"But I take it that's not why you're here." Everett held up his arms in surrender and gave her a contrite look. "Hey, I'm really sorry about this afternoon. I swear, I wasn't trying to give you the third degree. I was just asking questions. It comes with the job. Guess I'm not very good at it yet."

Bullshit. He knew exactly what he was doing, and his good cop/bad cop performance was pathetically obvious. But she accepted his apology with a shrug. "I overreacted. I don't like talking about—or even thinking about—that summer. Lots of bad memories."

Everett seemed to take stock of her posture, her words, and something inside him shifted. "Do-over?" he asked. "I promise I won't grill you about that night. I think we could help each other."

If he wanted to pretend they were cool, she would play along. "Okay," she said, sliding off her coat and abandoning it on the floor. She followed him into the living room and sank into the corner of the sofa. Everett lingered over her for just a minute, then gestured to the bottle that was sitting on the coffee table. A beer, half gone.

"Can I get you something to drink?"

"I'd love a glass of water." She smiled, calculating the distance between where she was sitting and the office door, and wondering whether she could make it there and back before Everett returned. She couldn't.

When he reappeared a minute later with an ice water, he sat down in the middle of the couch. Their knees weren't touching, but close enough, and it made Juniper feel vaguely threatened. She was exhausted and shaky, and the truth was that Everett made her skin crawl.

"Why are you doing this?" she asked, wiping the condensation from the glass with her thumbs.

Everett's smile was lopsided and insincere. "Doing what?"

"Reopening the Murphy case. Asking questions about that night."

"It's my job," he told her with a self-important smirk.

"Except it's not. You're not a detective, and the DCI unit handles cold cases in Iowa." She gave him a pointed look. "You're a small-town cop in Nowhere, Northwest Iowa."

His smile frosted over, and then he gave up the facade and glared at her. "The murders happened in this town, *my* town. I have access to the files, the evidence, the community."

Juniper nodded once, wishing that she could get her hands on those files and boxes of evidence. "And what have you discovered?"

"That's absolutely none of your business."

"You're accusing my brother."

Everett laughed. "*Everyone* accused your brother. He was found standing over Calvin Murphy's body, quite literally holding the smoking gun."

"No gunshot residue. No motive. He called 911. What killer would do that?" Juniper asked, borrowing from India's playbook.

Everett seemed to consider her words for a moment. Then he leaned forward, bringing himself close enough to touch. She leaned back. "He did it," Everett said slowly. "I know that he did. And I'm going to prove it."

For just a heartbeat Juniper flashed to that night, to the rough-hewn boards biting into the skin of her bare shoulders and the shadow of a man beside her. She felt the blood drain from her face. "You're wrong," she forced herself to say.

"We'll see." Everett grabbed his beer off the coffee table and took a swig. "I find his behavior highly suspicious. He'll trip up."

"He's awake," Juniper said, and tried to hide her surprise when that tidbit of information made Everett's eyes cloud over. The news hadn't reached him yet.

"Good," he said, too late.

But Juniper wasn't sure what to do with his insincerity, so she asked, "Why aren't you looking into the Tates? Franklin? Sterling?"

"Sullivan."

"Him too."

"You're his alibi," Everett reminded her. "And Jonathan's, too. Is there something you'd like to tell me about that night?"

None of them had been where they were supposed to be. It was such an impossible situation. Suddenly Juniper had a splitting headache and she could feel tears forming behind her eyes. Wasn't this where she always got caught up? She couldn't believe that either Sullivan or Jonathan was capable of killing the Murphys in cold blood. And yet, had she felt a sense of familiarity in the barn that night? *Please, God. No. Don't let it be someone I love.*

"Pinning this on my brother won't fix anything," she whispered. "It can't rewrite the past or undo what happened with Carver."

"What do you know about Carver?" Everett said icily.

"Nothing, really."

"Exactly. Nothing. He was a good person, Juniper. Pure and kind, completely innocent. He couldn't hurt a flea, much less murder someone. He didn't know what he was saying, but it ruined everything."

"That's heartbreaking, Everett, truly, it is, but Carver's innocence doesn't prove my brother's guilt."

"He died in a group home. Did you know that? Just a couple of years after it happened. A winter flu turned into pneumonia, and before we even knew what was happening, he was gone."

"I'm so sorry."

"Roxy was never the same."

And you never went back to the only true home you'd ever known, Juniper thought, but she held her tongue and watched as Everett took a long pull of his beer. He never broke eye contact with her.

"You're right, figuring out who killed the Murphys won't rewrite history, but I believe in justice," he said, his voice stiff with emotion. "I believe that when someone has hurt another person, they should be held accountable."

All at once, Juniper knew. "It's you," she

whispered. *That bastard Jonathan Baker,* and his office with all the suspects on the wall like a murder book come to life. The hatred that rolled off him in waves. *Everett* was behind the podcast. He was digging into the past with the singular ambition of destroying her brother.

"What?" He studied her with narrowed eyes.

Juniper's tongue felt thick in her mouth. "You want to know the truth about that night," she improvised. She didn't feel safe in his home anymore and regretted the fact that she had come at all. What would he do if he suspected that she knew the truth about what he was doing?

But Everett didn't seem to notice just how anxious she had become. "So do you. Answer my questions. Help me."

What did he need her for? Everett had already admitted that he had the evidence boxes, access to all the transcripts and case notes, probably even a direct line to the detective who worked the case all those years ago. He held all the cards. Almost.

"You need to talk to Jonathan," Juniper said, stalling. "When he's well enough."

"There's no statute of limitations on murder," Everett scoffed. "He won't talk to me."

"I think you're wrong." Juniper leaned over to put her glass on the coffee table, perching on the edge of the couch. Something had changed in the air, and everything inside her told her to run.

But Everett was only a few feet away. One lunge and he could stop her in her tracks. Do God knows what. Cora didn't know where she was. Neither did India. She hadn't told anyone she was going to Everett's house. And who would suspect a cop? Juniper cursed herself for leaving her phone in the pocket of her coat. It was now crumpled on the floor beside the door.

"I tried," Everett said, and there was a ferocity in his voice that hadn't been there before. He lifted himself up a bit, tilting toward Juniper like he was sure he could convince her if only he said the right words vehemently enough. "He laughed at me."

It struck her all at once that he was painfully lonely. The ripple effect of that night had forever changed his life, too, and she felt a wave of sympathy for the boy who had been so unceremoniously ripped from a home that was safe—maybe even loving—and thrust into a dangerous and scary situation. Juniper's life hadn't been perfect, but she also hadn't been bounced around from foster home to foster home because her stepdad beat her. It had fractured something in him; she could see that clearly now. It broke her heart, but it scared her, too.

Compassion must have shown on her face, because Everett smiled a little. "You get it, don't you? We could finally crack this case."

We? Juniper itched to remind him that there was

no "we," but Everett's tongue darted between his lips and she knew he was a fanatic. A zealot, a die-hard. This—bringing the Murphys' killer to justice—was everything to him. It was beyond right and wrong, it was a matter of retribution to Everett Stokes. Of vengeance. Dread coiled in her gut.

Juniper longed to jump from the couch and fling herself out the door, but she forced herself to stay calm. "How would we do that?" she asked.

"We dredge up the past. Bring it all back. Trigger memories until people have no choice but to confront what happened and whatever role they played in it."

He realized his mistake the moment that Juniper's eyes turned to stone.

"What did you say?" she muttered between clenched teeth. The story was shaping up like the first few frames of an old-fashioned movie reel. Juddering and blurry until, suddenly, a picture so clear and obvious it made her gasp. It wasn't an accident. It wasn't a suicide attempt. "Oh my God. You poisoned Diesel."

Everett's hand whipped out, snake quick, and caught her wrist. "It wasn't like that. I mean, I didn't know that it would happen that way."

Any fear Juniper felt was replaced by a fury so poker hot she could have branded him with it. She ripped her hand from his grip and leapt to her feet so that the coffee table was between them. "You're crazy!"

"It was an accident."

"What on earth were you doing?" Juniper screamed. "How could you possibly think that poisoning Diesel would help anything? And how could you possibly know about Baxter?"

Everett was standing now, too, his beer abandoned and hands out in front of him as if he were offering them up as evidence of his blamelessness. Wrists out: *cuff me.* He chose the last question—the easiest one—to answer. "It's all in the file. All the misdemeanors against the Murphys are included as background information. Jonathan went along with Calvin to lodge the official complaint when Baxter died, so his name came up in the case notes. I just thought if he started thinking about that time . . ."

"Maybe it would jar something loose and he'd *confess* to you?" Juniper's voice dripped with all the loathing she felt, and for a moment Everett withered beneath it. But just as quickly as he seemed to give up, he squared his shoulders.

"I'm an officer doing my job. I didn't know that Jonathan would take Diesel for an early morning walk. And there's no way I could have predicted that stupid animal would run out onto the ice. It's unfortunate that Jonathan was seriously injured, but he's going to be okay. Accidents happen."

Juniper glared at him, speechless, before she

spun on her heel and hurried to the door. If she stayed for another second, she knew that she would launch herself at him, that she'd claw his eyes out with her fingernails, or worse. She paused with her closed fist on the handle and whirled so that her back would not be turned to Everett. She didn't trust him for even a second.

"It was you. It was all you. The phone calls and drive-bys, the harassment that nearly drove my sister-in-law crazy. *You're* crazy. Did you slash my tires, too?"

He took a step toward her and Juniper could see the truth in his feral scowl. She wrenched open the front door. "You'll lose your job over this. Or worse."

"Maybe," Everett said. "But I won't give up."

She whipped around and jogged down the steps. He lunged after her and shouted from the landing: "This isn't over!"

Juniper didn't even break her stride. Within seconds she was behind the steering wheel, car on, no seat belt. She squealed out of Everett's driveway, hoping the neighbors heard, and that they looked out of their blinds and saw him standing there, framed in the glow of his open doorway, shoulders slumped and brow furrowed. Looking guilty as hell.

CHAPTER 24

THAT NIGHT

Light cuts through the night and fractures into a thousand pieces as it slashes through every crack and crevice in the barn. For just a moment I shimmer gold, a dusty glitter illuminating my skin, my tangled hair, the dank dirt floor. Just as quickly as it sparkles, it's gone, but that second of dazzle is enough—it sends a jolt of electricity right through me.

When a door slams, a whimper escapes my lips. There are terrors crouching in the shadows, waiting for me. I thought I had given it enough time, that he was gone and wouldn't come back, but the vehicle in the yard tells a very different story.

My panic is raw and jagged, and though there is much I don't know, I am sure of two things: Cal and Beth are dead, and I'm next.

Hysteria lifts me to my feet, and my skin stings as something—a rusty nail? a chink in the wood?—snags my necklace and rips it clean off. My hand flies to my collarbone, but the necklace is gone, lost in the darkness and completely irrelevant anyway.

Did I cry out? Did the sudden, terrifying choke-hold of the chain make me shriek? I don't know.

Squeezing my eyes shut, I wait for the shout, for the moment when my hiding place is found and the inevitable report of one last gunshot splits the night. But it doesn't come.

Back door. The barn has a back door, and it's my only hope. I'm not safe here, and though I don't know if my feet will carry me or if I'll collapse, I have to try.

One tentative step. My leg trembles but holds. Two. I'm damp and filthy, cobwebs in my hair and dust clinging to the backs of my sweaty thighs. But that doesn't matter now. Nothing does, except getting as far away from the Murphy farm as I can.

The barn door is still open, and outside, the yard is bathed in the dim glow of headlights. He left them on because he's coming for me. I know it. The thought makes my knees tremble, but I take another step. *Go!* I silently scream. *Go.*

But then a real scream rends the night.

"No! No, no, no, no, no . . ."

It's a chilling refrain made all the more terrible because I know that voice.

I don't pause to think, but it wouldn't do me any good if I did because I'm so far past reason. My feet pound in the opposite direction, away from the back door and into the light, toward the only person who can make sense of this horror. Who can fix all that has gone wrong in this monstrous, unimaginable night.

Jonathan.

He's on his knees beside Cal, and in the headlights of his truck I can see his hands bloom crimson when he pulls them away.

"No, no, no, no . . ." he says again, carving a rut with the word. "It wasn't supposed to be this way."

It wasn't supposed to be this way? I open my mouth to call out to him because I'm not sure my legs will carry me any farther, but what escapes my lips is an incoherent howl. At first I think an animal is dying, but when Jonathan's head snaps toward me, I realize the sound is mine. I'm making it, and it's the worst sound I've ever heard.

"June?" He pushes himself up, sliding a little on the gravel or on spilled blood, I don't know. For a moment he hovers there, half bent over his fallen friend as he looks between me and Cal. He's deciding, maybe, who to help. Who to scoop up in his arms and spirit away from this nightmare.

It's too late, I want to tell him. *Save me.* But the words won't come.

When I try to take another step, the earth shifts below me and instinct shatters Jonathan's indecision. He's before me in an instant, fingers digging into my arms as he tries to keep me from falling.

"What are you doing here?" Jonathan growls.

His voice is a strangled cry wrenched from somewhere deep inside. Somewhere secret. He's sobbing, but his eyes are so crystalline, so hard, it scares me.

I'm falling away; I can feel myself going. It doesn't matter that Jonathan is leaving bruises on my skin, I cannot hold myself up anymore, and together we sink to the ground. But Jonathan isn't about to let me just sit there. The second I hit the gravel he wraps his arms around me and heaves me back to my feet, pushing me toward the barn, away from Cal.

"Go!" he screams. "Get out of here!"

There is a streak of blood on his cheek and I can't stand it. I reach for it, brushing it away with my hand, but my ministrations only smear it across his jaw and into the whorls and dips of my own fingerprints. *Guilty,* I think, turning my palm up to see what I've done. Though I know it's illogical, I moan at the thought. Maybe we're all guilty. Maybe we've never, not for a second, been innocent.

"Juniper Grace, look at me." Jonathan lets go long enough to see if I can stay standing on my own. I can, though the world still sways and I cannot focus on him. So he cups my cheeks and forces me to face him. He's backlit in the glare of his headlights, and I can no longer see his eyes. They're holes in his head, black pools. I can hardly look at him, but I make myself comply.

A grimace mars his features, leaving his mouth little more than a sharp slash. "Right here, that's right. Listen to me, June. You have to get out of here."

I shake my head because I know I can't leave him.

"Go. I mean it. I will never forgive you if you don't run. You can do this, June. Through the barn, out the back door. Take the path around Jericho Lake and go home. Take a shower and crawl in bed. Just remember: *you were never here.*"

I nod because he wants me to, but I think we both know that I'm not going anywhere. My legs are trembling so hard we are both lurching, caught in a frantic dance that makes my stomach pitch.

"Go, damnit!" His thumbs dig into the soft flesh beneath my cheekbones, and when I cry out, he only presses harder.

It's just a second, gone in a flash, but the look in his eyes is murderous. *What have you done?* The thought rips through me, shredding everything I believed I knew about my brother and best friend. Then Jonathan blinks and lets go, and in the absence of his touch I can feel the cool, damp breeze. It helps, a little.

"What are you going to do?" I ask, my voice breaking.

"Call 911." His phone is already out of his

pocket, but he stops before punching in the numbers. "Go, June. Please. Take the path by the lake and through the fields. I'll meet you at home later, but you need to listen to me: you were never here."

"Call 911." His phone is already out of his pocket, but he stops before punching in the numbers. "Go, June. Please. Take the path by the lake and through the fields. I'll meet you at home later, but you need to listen to me: you were never here."

"My necklace." It seems like such an inconsequential thing, but my fingers are brushing the place where the chain is supposed to fall. I can feel the narrow welt on my skin. I know it's important somehow.

"What?" Jonathan's brow furrows.

"I lost it. In the barn. It's—"

Understanding dawns. There's evidence that I was here. But he waves his hand, shooing me away. "I'll take care of it. Just go."

"But—"

"Later." He shakes his head. "We'll talk later."

"We were together," I say, backing away slowly. "After the Pattersons', we met at the farm and watched the fireworks from the bed of your truck."

"With Sullivan."

I don't understand, but there's no time to question him, so I say, "Of course. With Sullivan. Then he went home—"

"And you went upstairs to shower," Jonathan supplies.

"But you heard gunshots."

"I did," he says, but he doesn't sound like my brother anymore.

I rush forward and give him a quick, hard hug, wrapping my arms around his neck as if I'll never let go. "Everything is going to be okay," I lie.

Then he pushes me away and bites off one last word: "Go."

I do. God help me, I do exactly as he says. I turn around and run blindly, working from muscle memory and all the years I spent playing on this farm.

Rides on Penny with Cal holding her halter, picking flowers with Beth. "The key to zinnias," she once told me, "is to pinch back the lead when the plant is still young." She took a pair of clippers and lopped off the tallest shoot on a plant that looked nearly ready to bloom. I don't remember what I said, but she laughed and motioned for me to follow her farther down the row. "See?" she said. Here was another small zinnia, but instead of one tall stem, there were half a dozen shorter ones, each centered by the tight fist of a bud all orange and pink like a ripe apricot. "Early adversity leads to an abundant harvest."

Trips to the library together and spending an afternoon in the Murphys' porch rockers while we snapped off the ends of sweet peas. Popping over when we saw the inviting flames of a bonfire or helping Cal pick tomatoes for the roadside stand. The scent of Beth's peaches-and-cream soap. The way Cal whistled for Betsy to follow. His sunbaked brown skin. It's over, all of it. *They're gone.*

I'm weeping by the time I stumble into the parking lot of Jericho Lake, my knees skinned from falling and arms prickling with mosquito bites from the humid night, the proximity of still water. It's the calm before the storm, and just as I reach my car, the first cool raindrop splashes on the back of my hand. It hisses against my feverish skin and I turn my face to the sky, wishing for more. Nothing comes. The clouds are pregnant, overdue, and the atmosphere crackles with the hint of lightning, but for now there is nothing the world can do but wait.

Just as I'm about to wrench open my car door, I see the flashing blue lights of a police cruiser. A second later the sound hits me, the whirring scream of a siren as it races down the road. Before I know it, I'm on the ground, bloody knees now scabbed with gravel as my heart pounds hard enough to crack my ribs.

Jonathan made the call. What does that mean? What will they think when they find him there, stained with Calvin's blood?

But I can't think about that now. When the

cruiser is gone, I slip into my car and start the engine, then pull slowly out of the parking lot. I'm driving without my headlights, on a night filled with shadows and the low rumble of thunder, but our farm isn't far, and I know the way by heart.

I don't even realize that I'm aching for my mother until I pull down our long drive and see that the house is dark. That's not unusual, Law and my mom are often in bed by now, but Law's truck is gone, and there's an air of abandonment over the entire homestead. I'm alone.

Pulling my car as close to the front porch as I can, I cut the engine and sit inside the quiet vehicle for a moment. The night is coming back to me in gasps and starts, still frames that have been taken by an unsteady hand because the edges are blurry and indistinct. Already I wish I could forget. I want to scrub the memories from my mind the same way I'm suddenly itching to scour every square inch of my body. I hold up my hands and there is dirt under my fingernails, but also something darker. Something that looks a lot like blood.

I stumble out of the car, leaving the keys in the ignition even as I understand in some small way that this will look unnatural. My car parked helter-skelter on the grass, my keys dangling, and the driver's seat speckled with grime. I run my hand over the faux leather, trying to sweep some of the mess to the floor, but I only manage to smear it.

Headlights lurching down our driveway make my breath hitch, but there's nowhere to hide, so I stand slowly and watch the vehicle come. If it's a police cruiser, the sirens are not on, but already I know that the slant of light is too high for a sedan. Dad's truck? Jonathan's?

Sullivan.

My body starts to tremble, but even before he's put the truck in park I'm sprinting across the grass toward him.

"Hey," he calls, jumping from the cab. He catches me at the last moment, strong arms enfolding me as he pulls me to his chest. "June, what happened?"

I can't get close enough. I can't burrow deep enough into the hard lines of his body, and I wish for just a second that I could crawl right inside his clothes, press myself against him skin-to-skin. I bury my face against his neck and breathe him in, praying that this has all been a bad dream, a terrible nightmare, and I'm waking up beside him, his fingers laced through mine.

I'm not.

"They're dead," I gasp, the entire awful story folding in on itself until it's nothing but a few essential snippets. "Jonathan called the police. We were together. You have to tell everybody that we were together."

"What are you talking about?" With one hard heave, Sullivan thrusts me away from him so he can look into my eyes. "Who's dead?"

But I don't even have to answer. I can see the moment the truth clicks into place. "Oh my God," Sullivan says, and slams back against the side of the truck, one hand in his hair.

"Who did this?" I ask, thinking for one unreal moment that he knows, that he'll tell me and make sense of this tragedy and ensure that everything will be okay. But Sullivan is already shaking his head. Another thought takes stubborn hold. "Where have you been? I haven't seen you all day. Not since the pancake breakfast. I called and called. I texted . . . What have you been doing?"

It's like he doesn't hear me. Now both hands are in his hair and he's bent over, angling toward the ground as if soon I will be the one who'll have to lift him out of the dirt.

"Get up!" I shout, because I'm scared and in shock and all at once very, very angry. "Get up!"

Sullivan stands and looks at me as if I'm crazy. Maybe I am.

"Where were you?" I want to shake him. I'm thinking, *If you would've been there, everything might have been different.* I know that's not fair, but I'm past logic, and all my rage is suddenly directed at the man I love.

"With my brothers," he says numbly. "All day. I

426

couldn't leave them, not knowing that today . . ."

Was the day. We knew that. It was really *all* we knew, but history had shown us a pattern of small infractions—kid stuff—and we had been lulled into a false sense of security. Or maybe we were so caught up in each other we couldn't see the warning signs. In my wildest dreams I could have never imagined this.

"What did you do, Sullivan?"

"Nothing, June. I swear to you."

I step toward him and lay my hand over his heart. He softens.

"We drank," he admits, and up close I can see his eyes are glassy and bloodshot. "We shot trap. Jonathan was with us for a lot of the day."

"And then what happened?"

"Some of us went to the Pattersons' party."

You? The question is in my eyes; I don't even have to voice it.

Sullivan gives his head an almost imperceptible shake. "When it got dark, I drove with Wyatt to the Murphys' farm. I didn't want to let him out of my sight."

My pulse cartwheels.

"Wyatt shot out the floodlight."

I can't help it, my hand bunches Sullivan's T-shirt as I hold on for dear life.

"Cal must've heard the shot because he came running outside. He went for his truck. I think he was going to grab his gun." Sullivan inhales hard, steadies himself. "So we drove away. I don't know if Cal got a make and model on the truck, or even if he called the police. No one showed up at the farm, anyway. I convinced Wyatt to lay low for the rest of the night because if Cal saw us, he had us dead to rights."

"Did Wyatt go back? Sterling? Dalton?" Each name spills off my tongue, barely a whisper.

"I don't know. I've been driving around, trying to figure out how to tell you, how to make this all right. I was thinking about going to the police station and confessing to what we had done."

"Shooting out a light?" My head feels gritty, my thoughts wrapped in knots. "I don't get it."

"That was just the beginning. The plan was to go back later and set the roadside stand on fire."

I should be stunned. Horrified, even. But in light of everything I've seen, the image of the quaint roadside stand ablaze is almost frivolous. It could be rebuilt. Insurance money would have probably allowed the Murphys to design something even bigger and better. But nothing can fix their bodies broken on the ground.

"They figured they could get away with it if it happened on the Fourth. An errant firework, a drunk drive-by . . ." Sullivan trails off, and I carefully peel my fingers from his shirt. Step back.

"They're dead," I tell him again, unnecessarily. The haunted look in his eyes assures me he knows. "Somebody shot them. I was there."

"Oh, June." Sullivan raises a hand and touches my cheek, running the tip of his finger along my jawline before I turn my head away.

"Did you . . . ?" I ask, hating myself for having to voice something so vile.

"Of course not."

"Do you know who did?"

"No."

His voice is steady when he says it, but there's something closed off in his gaze. I don't know if I believe him. And yet, what choice do I have?

A peal of thunder cracks the night, and a swift wind lifts my hair off the back of my neck to whip it around my shoulders. The temperature drops a couple of degrees as the storm finally reaches the place where we're standing. I'm shaking uncontrollably, and when Sullivan crosses the space between us and gathers me in his arms, I let him.

"We were here," I tell him. "That's our story. We met up at our farm: you, me, and Jonathan. We watched the fireworks from the bed of Jonathan's truck. And then you went home. I went inside to shower. And Jonathan heard the gunshots."

"He's there now?" Sullivan asks, and I can tell that he's crying.

"Yes. And the police will be coming here soon. You have to go."

Sullivan squeezes me hard, crushing me against him, and then he threads one hand into my hair and tips my head back. It's dark, but I can make out his expression in the light coming from the cab of his truck. It's pure anguish. He kisses me, long and so hard I can feel his teeth scrape against my chapped lips. I can taste the salt of our mingled tears.

"Go," he tells me, pushing me away. It's exactly what Jonathan commanded. "Throw your clothes in the washing machine and get in the shower. I'll move your car."

I should thank him, say goodbye maybe, but I don't. I turn and run, skipping every middle step on my way to our porch, and wrenching the screen door open just as the sky erupts. It's an instant downpour, and I whirl around in the relative safety beneath the overhang to make sure Sullivan is okay. But he's already in my car, one arm slung over the seat back as he throws it in reverse and parks it neatly exactly where it's supposed to be.

I watch him for a minute, his long strides as he lopes back to his truck and climbs in. He pauses when he's in the cab and scans the front of the house, looking, I realize, for me. But the house is pitch-black, the rain falling in sheets, and he can't see me standing just beyond the screen door. I lift my hand to my lips and then press the spot where he is, my fingers obscuring him as I say goodbye.

CHAPTER 25

WINTER
TODAY

Juniper pulled over several blocks away from Everett's house and called Cora. Her fingers were numb and unresponsive, and it took her a couple tries to get the number right. But by the time Cora finally picked up, Juniper had managed a few deep breaths and was feeling laser-focused. She trained her eyes on her rearview, watching for headlights or—worse—flashing lights and an accompanying siren, and said without preamble: "It's Everett Stokes."

"Wait. What?" Cora sounded half-asleep. "What are you talking about?"

"He poisoned Diesel. He's been harassing Jonathan for weeks. I think he slashed my tires." She didn't bother mentioning the podcast. It would all come out soon enough.

Cora's voice took on a steel edge. "Are you serious?"

"He's digging into that summer and thought that he could spook Jonathan by replaying the events of the past. He hates my brother. *Hates* him."

"Where are you?"

"Safe," Juniper assured her.

But Cora wasn't appeased. "He's insane. You can't let him get away with this. What if he runs?"

"He won't run. Everett is convinced he's right—and that he's going to catch a killer. He's too self-righteous to be worried."

"Sounds dangerous to me."

"He's a wannabe detective with a vendetta against my brother."

"Exactly my point. But we'll prove him wrong," Cora said.

"I've tried. For fourteen years I've been going in circles, coming up empty."

"The truth is always in the details. What are we missing? Everyone knows the Murphys and the Tates were feuding that summer, but what else was going on?"

Juniper almost dismissed Cora's question out of hand. But it echoed something that India had said, too. Juniper had never kept a diary, and that summer so long ago was entirely overshadowed by the deaths of Cal and Beth. Sure, she had graduated from high school and fallen in love with Sullivan, dreamed of a life far outside of Jericho and gotten pregnant with Willa, but everything else was obscured beneath the shadow of the Murphy murders.

Except.

The memory was sudden and unexpected: a packed suitcase in her mother's trunk.

And then there were more: a craving for jam, an unexpected visit from Cal. An easy poolside laugh followed by the hard look in Law's eyes when he tore his wife away from the Pattersons' Fourth of July party. There were troubled silences and a feeling of disquiet that suffused Juniper's every memory of that summer. Tears in the kitchen. Her mother's bow across her cello like a requiem.

"My mom and Law weren't home that night," Juniper said.

"What?"

"The night that Cal and Beth were killed. When I came home from—" She stopped, shocked by how close she had come to revealing her secret, and quickly adjusted her story. She started again: "When I got back from the Pattersons' party, no one was home."

If Cora noticed that Juniper had lost her footing for a minute, she didn't let on. "So they were watching the fireworks like everyone else in town."

"Law broke his foot," Juniper said, more to herself than Cora. "They were at the hospital in Munroe."

"How'd that happen?"

The thing was, Juniper didn't know.

"What are you saying?" Cora asked.

"I don't know. Nothing. But you're right. There was something else going on that summer."

"Does it have anything to do with Cal and Beth?"

"No," Juniper said, maybe too quickly. "I—I don't think so. There's no way. But I think I missed something really big. I was just a kid . . ."

"And you didn't see your parents as human beings. As real people with their own thoughts and emotions and inner lives."

Cora was teasing, but there was so much truth in her words. Juniper had taken Law and her mom for granted. She had ignored the warning signs, dismissed all the times when her mother was acting strange or inexplicably emotional. Juniper cringed, remembering that she had explained away Reb's behavior that summer by assuming it was precipitated by her daughter's impending departure. How selfish and shortsighted. Her mother was a woman who had once crossed the country alone for love. Who had left her own parents behind, started over, and then begun again when her happily ever after turned out to be a terrible lie. What did Juniper really know about Rebecca Baker? About who she was, and how she loved, and why she did the things she did?

"I have to go," she said.

"How can I help? Should I call the sheriff?"

"Stay put," Juniper told Cora. "Take care of Willa. Keep the door locked. Call the sheriff's department if anything happens—*not* 911. I'll be there soon."

It was with a twinge of guilt that Juniper hung up, but the need to talk to her mother was suddenly overwhelming. It was too late to call, and so she sent a text:

I need to talk to you.

Her mother's reply was almost immediate:

We just got home. Everything okay?

Juniper was stunned. She had left them in Des Moines hours ago. Had it only been that long? It felt like days. Weeks.

Wanted to spend a night in our own bed.
We'll go back tomorrow.

Juniper sat by herself for a few seconds in the dark. Her phone lit up when she moved it, her mother's last text still framed in gray. She thumbed the screen open and typed quickly:

I'm coming over.

Hitting send, she stuffed her phone in her pocket and didn't wait for a reply.

The porch lights were on when Juniper pulled down the long drive of her parents' acreage, illuminating the tall, two-story farmhouse and a patch of deep snow in front of it. Her heart bucked behind her ribs at the familiar sight. When she was a teenager, Law and Reb had always left the porch lights on to welcome her and Jonathan home, even if they had gone to bed hours before. The light poured from the generous front windows like a beacon, the glimmer of a lighthouse signaling shelter. A haven.

But tonight was different. It was close to eleven o'clock, but Reb wasn't sound asleep. Instead she stood framed in the cold flicker of the now rarely used lights. At least one of the bulbs needed to be replaced, and it shuddered out a warning in some incomprehensible Morse code.

"What's wrong?" Reb shouted, holding open the door with one hand and her cardigan closed with the other.

Juniper had barely stepped from her car and was too far away to attempt a response. So she hurried through the shin-deep snow, trying to keep her feet light as she broke through the thin crust of ice. It was no use. The bottoms of her jeans were caked in white and stiff from cold by the time she reached the place where her mother stood waiting.

"Law hasn't had time to shovel the walk," her mom explained, ushering Juniper inside and fussing over her with an old towel that she grabbed from a hook near the door. "You should've gone through the garage. What are you doing here anyway?" she demanded, smacking the snow off Juniper's jeans with one end of the towel. Every slap was more aggressive than the last, and Juniper's frozen calves began to sting with each new blow. She snagged the towel the next time it came near and gently eased it from her mother's hands.

"It's okay," Juniper said. "I'll do it."

"Is Willa okay? Where is she?"

Juniper was surprised by what sounded like raw terror in her mother's tone. Clearly, almost losing her son had been deeply traumatizing—even more so than Juniper had realized. She tossed the towel back on the hook and pulled Reb into her arms. The older woman was slight, more fragile than Juniper remembered, as if long hours in the ICU had somehow diminished her. She was also trembling—though Juniper couldn't tell if it was because she was scared or cold. Maybe both.

"Willa's fine. Everyone is fine," Juniper said, turning her mother toward the kitchen. She kept one arm firmly around Reb until she could ease her onto a bucket seat stool at the counter. "I'm going to make you a cup of tea. When's the last time you ate?"

"What?" she sounded confused. "I don't know. Supper? Did we have supper?"

"That's what I thought." Juniper filled the kettle with tap water and set it on the stove to boil.

Then she pulled open the refrigerator to rummage around for something to feed her mother. There wasn't much. Half a gallon of milk that had just passed its expiration date, a couple of wrinkly apples, and some leftovers that were questionable at best. But there were a few eggs nestled in the divots of a cardboard container. Jackpot.

"What are you doing?" Reb asked, plaintive and sounding not at all like her usual unflappable self.

"Scrambling you some eggs."

"That's ridiculous," Reb huffed, but she didn't say anything more, and in just a couple minutes the nonstick pan was sizzling with butter. The scent filled the kitchen and made Juniper's stomach rumble. She realized that it had been hours since she had eaten, too.

"Where's Law?" Juniper asked, stepping away from the stove to fill a mug with hot water. She set it in front of her mother with the tin of teabags and a sprig of mint she pinched from the plant on the windowsill.

"Chores." Reb waved her hand over her shoulder in the direction of the barn. "I don't know exactly. He said he needed to take care of some things at home, so we left everything at the Rainbow House and hopped in the car. I could have stayed back, you know. I should have."

"Well, I'm glad you're here," Juniper said carefully, grateful that Law wouldn't interrupt them for a while at least. "There's something I want to talk to you about."

"Oh?" Reb paused with the mug an inch from her mouth. "What's that?"

But a whiff of sulfur alerted Juniper to the fact that she had left the eggs too long. She lunged for the spatula to scrape the bottom of the pan. They were fine. A little dry at the edges, but salvageable. She clicked the burner off, turned the fluffy eggs a few more times, then slid them on a plate and put it in front of her mother.

Watching Reb carefully, Juniper said: "I want to talk about the night that Cal and Beth Murphy were killed."

The older woman choked on her tea, eyes watering as she gestured wildly at the flour sack towel hanging over the handle of the stove. Juniper snagged it and tossed it at her mom, watching guiltily as Reb's eyes watered and she struggled to breathe. It was over in seconds, but shock lingered in the kitchen, sharp as the scent of a struck match.

"Not again," Reb whispered. Her eyes were bloodshot and her words savage. "You ambushed us in the hospital and now you want to bring this up *again?* How dare you? Don't you think we've been through enough?"

Juniper felt her resolve fray at the edges. She had once been headstrong and independent, a carefree teenager with the world at her fingertips, but the murders—and everything that happened afterward—had changed all that. When her mother told her to keep still, she did. When she took Willa from her arms, Juniper let her daughter go. And when Reb decided that the best thing for Juniper was to go far, far away from Jericho and leave the past behind, she had done exactly as her mother instructed. "You banished me," Juniper said, finally giving voice to something she had never been strong enough to name. Or even admit to herself.

"What?"

"And you put Willa in my place. You started over."

"Oh, June." Reb shook her head. "Don't you see? I didn't banish you. I saved you. I wasn't going to let you repeat my mistakes."

My mistakes. Juniper recoiled. *Like* I *was a mistake?* she wanted to ask. But she didn't have time for this conversation right now. The clock was ticking, and she expected Law to walk through the back door any second. Nothing made her mother clam up as quickly as a harsh look from Law. "We'll get to that," she said. "Later. Right now I need to know how Law broke his foot."

"Are you kidding me?" Reb threw the towel down on the counter and pushed back as if she was going to leave the room. "I'm not doing this. I am not having this conversation with you. Not now. Not ever."

"Stop!"

Juniper didn't mean to shout. She didn't even know where all that vehemence came from. But Reb stopped. Sat back in her stool and crossed her arms over her chest.

"Please, Mom." Juniper leaned with her forearms on the counter, begging her mother to listen with the desperation in her eyes. "Don't run away from me. We have to talk about this. I was right all along—Jonathan's accident *is* tied to what happened to the Murphys. And this will never be over, we will never be okay until we finish it once and for all."

"What do you want me to say?"

"Let's start with the truth. How did Law break his foot?"

Reb squeezed her eyes shut and yanked her cardigan tighter across her chest. It seemed to Juniper as if she were trying to disappear, to scrunch herself smaller and smaller until: *poof!* It was as if she had never existed at all. It made something shrivel in Juniper's chest. Beautiful, mysterious Rebecca Baker shouldn't feel the need to make herself nothing.

"Mom," Juniper said, softer this time. "Please. I think this might be really important."

For a long moment Reb said nothing, and Juniper was sure that coming home had been futile. But then the older woman's shoulders began to shake, and Juniper realized that her mom was crying. Nothing could have been worse. Juniper could handle shouting or icy silence, fury or disappointment. But seeing her mother cry made Juniper feel like she was six again and Reb was her sun and her moon. Her mommy who still kissed every scrape and tucked her in at night with an almost ethereally sweet rendition of "Somewhere Over the Rainbow" in her lilting soprano. To this day, the first few bars of that tune made Juniper's soul unfurl like the sail of a ship at sea.

"Mom . . ." she whispered.

"I was going to leave him."

"What?"

"That summer. You were off to college and Jonathan was . . ." Reb lifted one shoulder and sniffed. *"Jonathan."*

She knew exactly what her mother meant. Jonathan had been unshakable, unassailable, charmed. Bulletproof. He could have survived anything—and did. But none of that mattered as the truth of Reb's words slowly snapped into place. "You were going to leave Lawrence."

Her mother clapped a hand over her mouth and gave Juniper an anguished look.

Of course. Of course she was going to leave him. She had packed a suitcase, said goodbye in a dozen different ways. She had been composing again, but it wasn't a tribute to her daughter, it was a song of farewell. To her husband of nineteen years. Her family. Her life.

"Why?"

Reb laughed, but it was brief and hollow. "Why do you think? I wasn't in love with him. I'm not sure I ever was. He swooped in and saved me at a point in my life when I desperately needed not to be alone, but gratitude and love are not the same thing. I thought he knew that. We were never supposed to be forever."

Juniper tested those words, put a little weight on them and found out they held. She had always known that Law loved her mother more than Reb loved him back, but no relationship was balanced—someone was always pursuing, the other pushing away. Honestly, Juniper had never seen her parents' marriage as anything other than practical. They were kind and loyal, respectful as coworkers. But was there a spark? Something raw and sacred?

Juniper wanted to say: *What about us?* What about her and Jonathan, the family that they had built? But instead she asked: "Why didn't you go?"

"He found out. I don't really even know how. I covered my steps so carefully . . ." Reb reached for her mug of tea, took a sip out of habit.

"I found your suitcase," Juniper admitted, almost against her will.

"You did?"

"It was an accident. I popped the trunk of your car. You didn't do a very good job of hiding it."

Her mother sighed. "Maybe I wanted to be caught. When I think about it now . . . What was I going to do? Forty-one years old and starting over from scratch. I didn't go to college, never learned a trade. I cooked and cleaned. I gardened and sewed. I was a homemaker. If I would have left my home, what would I have been?" She didn't answer her own question, but it hung in the air between them all the same: *nothing*.

But Juniper didn't believe that. She had forgotten that Rebecca was only forty-one that summer, not much older than Juniper was now. Young and lovely and full of life. She was an artist and composer, a smart, strong woman in her prime. She could have started over, forged a new life far away from the drudgery of a small Iowa farm and a man almost twenty years her senior.

"I wasn't leaving you," her mother said quietly. "I'd never leave you or Jonathan if you needed me. But you were almost adults. I didn't think it would ruin you if your parents divorced. It's not like I was just going to disappear."

"What happened?"

Reb put both hands around the clay mug and held on tight. "We fought. Of course. I was playing the Braga, and he wanted to talk. So we . . . scuffled. The body of the cello was cracked in the process."

Juniper wasn't sure what to say. She knew how much that instrument meant to her mother. But she had to stay focused on the main thing. She wasn't here to talk about her parents' marriage. This was about Cal and Beth. "And Law broke his foot?"

"Not then. I convinced him to go to the Pattersons' party, but it didn't help. He was still so angry."

Juniper could picture the look in Law's eyes as he steered her mother out of the Pattersons' backyard. But the story was starting to collapse beneath the weight of unspoken details, of things that she was struggling to understand. It had been an exhausting day, and it took her eyes a moment to focus after she blinked.

"Mom," she said, hating herself a little for fast-forwarding to the information she sought, "I still don't get it. How did Law break his foot?"

"Why does it matter?" Reb couldn't keep a note of bitterness out of her voice.

"I don't know!" Juniper didn't mean to yell, and instantly tempered her tone. "Look, it just does. Cal and Beth were killed that night, and Jonathan sat in a jail cell without you nearby. I was escorted in a police cruiser to the station for questioning, and because I was just nineteen years old, I didn't even know that I could have refused to go with them. You weren't there when we needed you the most, and to this day I don't know *why*."

Reb looked stricken. But she said, "I was

boiling bone glue to fix the cello. Law was," she swallowed, "trying to get my attention. The pot fell. Broke his second and third metatarsals through his work boot. By the time we got to the hospital it had swelled so much they had to cut through the leather to get it off."

Something inside of Juniper deflated. She didn't realize how afraid she had been until the relief of finally knowing pierced through her doubts.

"He was with you. All night. So there's no way that . . ." She couldn't even voice it. She hadn't even thought it, not really.

But Reb's chin cut to the left just a fraction. "No," she said, refusing to meet Juniper's gaze. She laced her fingers around the nearly empty mug of tea and studied the dregs as if there were a mystery written in the leaves. "He left for a while. Tried to walk it off. That's why his foot swelled up so much."

"What do you mean he tried to walk if off? Where did he go?"

"I don't know. Around. It was a warm night. I cleaned up the mess in here, and when he got back, I drove him to the hospital in Munroe."

Juniper could hardly form the words. "When was that?"

"Quarter to eleven?" Reb guessed. "We didn't get home until nearly two, so . . ."

That night was so suddenly, so viscerally upon

her that Juniper gasped. The cool breeze on her hot skin, gunshots like a car backfiring. Her legs throbbed from the awkward way that she knelt, sweat prickling at the small of her back and the line of her upper lip so that she was afraid for a moment she would sneeze and give away her hiding place. She had believed, if only for a few broken heartbeats, that she knew the killer.

Fast-forward. Rewind. Back and forth, zipping to fragments she needed to relive and then flying past in her search for *something*. Finally, an imagined scene played out in front of the stove beside her. One of her mother's cast-iron pots, a few chips in the indigo-blue enamel. Reb's fingers tight on the handle, wrapped around a folded towel. Law turning her roughly. And then. Liquid bubbling over the edge and down his shirt, his jeans. Pooling between the laces of his boots, funneling past the tongue and seeping into thick socks, singeing his skin.

"What's bone glue?" Juniper asked.

"What?" Reb lifted her tear-streaked face. "I don't understand."

"Bone glue. What is it?"

Reb raised both hands, gave her head a little shake. "I use it to repair cracks in instruments. When my students or . . ." she trailed off. Sliding from the stool, she walked in a daze toward the kitchen sink. She bent and opened the bottom cupboard, and after riffling around, presented

447

Juniper with a small, clear sack of what looked like amber-colored pearls.

It was half-empty, and lighter than Juniper expected it to be. In the split second before she broke the seal and lifted the bag to her face, she contemplated walking away. Hugging her mother. Telling her that she loved her. And going back to the bungalow to pretend that nothing had changed at all. But it was too late for that.

When Juniper inhaled, she breathed in the night that Cal and Beth died. It was muscle and sinew, bones ground to dust. Dirt and stars, a storm rolling in, blood. The scent of death.

CHAPTER 26

WINTER
TODAY

"Why?" The word slipped from Juniper's lips unbidden, the first of many that queued up and jostled for attention amid the growing din inside her head. "Did you know? Did you suspect? I don't understand . . ."

Reb tore the bag from Juniper's hands, spilling the foul pellets all over the linoleum floor. "I shouldn't have shown you," she muttered, dropping to her knees to try and sweep them into a pile. It was no use. They had scattered far and wide, tiny spheres of what Juniper now knew to be a natural adhesive made from animal by-products. Such a distinct smell. Unforgettable.

Juniper crouched in front of her mother and took her by the shoulders. Forced Reb to face her, though the older woman was scowling through her tears and refused to make eye contact. "Why?" she asked again, and when Reb didn't answer: "Mom, I was there." At this, Reb's eyes locked with Juniper's for just a second, but she didn't say anything, so Juniper went on. "I was at the Murphys' farm the night they were killed. Do you understand what I'm telling you? There was a witness. *Me.* And I think Lawrence killed Cal and Beth."

"No," Reb whispered, but there was no conviction in her tone. Suddenly, she tipped sideways, off her knees and onto her hip. Juniper knew she would have kept going, but the cupboard was in the way, and her mother slumped against it, all the fight seeping out of her.

"It's okay," Juniper soothed, changing tactics. Whether her mother knew what happened that night was secondary right now. She had to get to Law, and quickly. So many things were locking into place at once that Juniper could hardly keep up. Had Law seen her crouching in the barn? Had he recognized her? Is that why he spared her life but convinced Reb to exile her only daughter? And did Jonathan know? The hospital marker board flashed in her mind's eye: *Dad.* Had Jonathan been trying to warn her?

"It's going to be okay," Juniper said again, easing her hand from beneath where it was pinched between her mother's arm and the cupboard door. "We're going to be just fine."

Her mother seemed to be in shock, or at least completely numb to the world around her. Sleepless nights, long days in the ICU, and now her entire life imploding before her eyes. What was going through her mind? Juniper had so many questions, but they would have to wait.

She grabbed her phone from her back pocket and unlocked it, then paused with her finger over the nine. Calling the police made the most sense, but what if Everett responded? Juniper couldn't trust him. She also refused to call Cora, and didn't know India or Barry well enough to drag them into this nightmare. Jonathan was in the hospital. She and Ashley were estranged. There was no one in Jericho that Juniper could call. A lightning bolt of longing made her heart sigh *Sullivan,* but she shoved the thought away before it could reduce her to tears.

Juniper was on her own.

The wind had started to howl, and Juniper instantly regretted her decision to forgo her coat and slip out the back door. But the barn wasn't far, and Law was somewhere inside. Juniper ducked her head and ran, her feet sure from a lifetime of walking the path.

The Bakers' barn was larger than the Murphys', and much more modern. Cement floors, large doors for machines, rows of fluorescent lights so that Lawrence could work on engines and honey-do projects after sunset. When Juniper laid her hand on the pedestrian door, it was unlatched and the barn was bathed in darkness. Still, she was freezing, so instead of being careful, she yanked it open and stepped inside.

Juniper should have been grateful to get out of the incessant wind, but the second she crossed the threshold she was aware of only one thing: the scent of gasoline. It was so strong, she pulled her sweater up over her nose and mouth while she waited for her eyes to adjust to the silty dark. Even breathing through the thick fabric, she almost had to back out.

"I wondered if you'd come."

The voice was much closer than Juniper anticipated. She couldn't stop the yelp that escaped her lips. Law's workbench was just beyond the door, and the scrape of his feet on sawdust-covered concrete betrayed his position.

"I guess it's kind of dark, isn't it?" Almost before the question was out of his mouth, Law had flicked on the lights over his workbench. The line of bare bulbs wasn't nearly as bright as the full fluorescents that lit up the barn like daylight, but Juniper had to throw up her hand to shield her eyes anyway.

"What have you done?" Juniper asked. She meant the stench of gasoline, the wide, wet lines of it that she could see crisscrossing the floor like modern art. But Law didn't take it that way.

"You don't waste any time, do you?" He coughed out a harsh laugh. "Not even a hello for your old man?"

Juniper swallowed. "Hi, Dad."

"I'm not your dad."

She had nursed hurt about her biological father for years, but wasn't Lawrence the only father she had ever known? "You were all I had," she said.

Law's face was lined from years of farm work and disappointment, the wrinkles deep as the rows he would disc every spring. It was a hard face, but one she had known since the day she was born, and when it crumpled, she took a step to comfort him. It surprised her as much as it did him.

He stopped her with a raised hand. "Neither of you kids were ever mine."

"That's not true—"

"Calvin Murphy was Jonathan's father."

The final bolt slid home, and suddenly Juniper *knew*. She knew everything as if her whole world had finally snapped into Technicolor focus. Juniper knew that over thirty-four years ago Rebecca Connor had married for convenience. That she had found solace in the arms of a neighbor—someone handsome, someone closer to her age—for a time. Maybe it was just sex. Maybe it was more. Did it matter? Juniper understood that unhappy years had gone by, until Rebecca's daughter was finally leaving home, and the possibility of leaving herself was suddenly a hope she dared to hold in the palm of her hand.

And Juniper knew that over three decades ago, Lawrence Baker had married for love. That he had no idea about his wife's indiscretion, and that his life with her was so much more than he ever dreamed for himself. It was home and family and forever. Juniper could only imagine how devastating it must have been for Law to hear that his wife was leaving. That his son was not his son. That none of it was real.

"Dad," Juniper's whisper was anguished, but Law cut her off before she could say another word.

"Don't call me that."

"But—"

"When she told me she was leaving, when she told me *why,* I didn't know what else to do."

Juniper didn't want to hear any more. She could picture every moment, from the confession and the broken cello to the hot sizzle of bone glue oozing across the kitchen floor like a festering wound. How did he walk to the Murphys' on a broken foot? The pain would have been unimaginable. But nothing compared to the searing agony of his wife's betrayal. Juniper could never forgive him for pulling the trigger, but for just a moment she *understood.*

The perfect murder was a crime of passion. Lawrence did what he believed he had to do. Then he walked home, Reb drove him to the hospital, and the world kept spinning.

"Dad." She insisted on calling him it, perverse as it sounded in the echoing barn. "Let's talk about this, okay? I know we can work this out if—"

Law waved his hand to shush her. "It doesn't matter. I'm taking care of it. It's a blessing, you know? Every day I wondered if you'd remember. If you'd open your eyes one morning and know that it was me." He smiled softly. "*I* knew that it was *you*."

All at once it was there. Every second downloaded as if Law had pushed a button to make it so. Peering through the cracks in the darkness, nineteen-year-old June had known somewhere deep down that it was Law. His height, his breadth. The lumbering sway of his walk. Crouched against the splintering boards she could smell the reek of the still-damp bone glue that must have coated his clothes, but beneath all that it was *him*. It had always been him. In her mind's eye she could see the outline of his leather work gloves curling around the door. That's why his fingerprints weren't on the gun. The gloves must have been so easy to dispose of.

And then: "You went back to make sure I hadn't left anything behind." Juniper was guessing out loud. She wondered how Jonathan had gotten ahold of the necklace—once, when everything had settled down, she'd confessed that she'd lost it that night. But they never spoke about it again. If Law had returned and found it on the dirt floor . . . "You were protecting me. You didn't want the cops to find any evidence of me in the barn and think that I had anything to do with it."

For just a moment the faintest hint of a smile crossed Law's thin lips. There was an entire universe contained in that quick curve: the way he used to throw her high and catch her in his unshakable arms, the summer he taught her to ride a bike, each Baker family meal. All his sure instructions about changing a tire, opening a bank account, fixing a leaky faucet. And every awkward hug and dry, papery kiss on her forehead. He had loved her, in his way.

"I shouldn't have kept it," he said, the smile gone. "Too sentimental. When Jonathan found it in my toolbox a couple weeks ago, well." Law shrugged.

Juniper tried to picture the confrontation and couldn't. What had her brother done when he realized the truth? The only people in the world who knew what happened to her necklace were Juniper and Jonathan. If Law had it, it put him at the Murphy farm that night. It changed everything.

Juniper was quivering, shaking so hard she had dropped her sweater from over her nose and mouth and was fully inhaling the dizzying gas fumes.

"I'm a coward," Lawrence said. "Always have been. I couldn't imagine even a day without her. Still can't."

"Come on. Come back to the house with me—"

"Get out of here, June," Lawrence said, turning away.

"No. I'm not going anywhere. You don't get to tell me what to do." Juniper sounded bold, commanding, but when Law faced her, she felt a ripple of fear. He was holding a slim cigar, a luxury that he indulged in a couple of times a year. He kept a small box on his workbench and hauled them out for special occasions: graduations, anniversaries, the births of his grandchildren. As she watched, Law put the cigar in his mouth and thumbed a flame to life on the small lighter he was holding. After a few quick puffs, the end glowed red.

"You're going to want to leave now, June. I'm not going to say it again. Go."

"No! Don't do this. *Please.*" She was frantic, desperate to make Law see reason. Juniper took a few quick steps toward him, but he exhaled a single smoke ring and then held the cigar out over the gasoline-soaked floor.

"It's better this way," he said. And then, he let go.

The whoosh of fuel as it caught was so instant, and so ferocious, it sucked the oxygen out of the barn. One moment Juniper could see, could breathe, and the next the world was on fire. There was a wall of flame between her and Lawrence, and already the inferno was feeding on sawdust, old boards, moldy hay. Juniper reached for the only father she had ever known, but instead of stepping toward her, he backed away. In a heartbeat, he was gone, devoured by the black smoke that roiled all around them.

Juniper could feel smoldering fingers claw into her nostrils, her mouth, forcing fumes deep inside her lungs. She didn't know how long the barn had been burning, but she could hardly see anymore, and what little air she had left was gone. She had tried to save Law and failed, but if she didn't find the door soon, she wouldn't make it out herself.

The problem was, Juniper didn't know which way was out anymore. Everything looked the same, a black and orange living hell. But through the roar, Juniper thought she could hear something that wasn't the world ending. It was outside the blaze, a sound that was man-made and that heralded help. The sound of sirens.

It didn't make sense. Had her mother called 911? She wouldn't do that, would she? Juniper just didn't know, but in her fevered, smothered state, she believed there were fire engines outside. Water and air and life. When she fell to her knees, she wasn't sure if she was hallucinating or if it was real, but there seemed to be a breath of cool in the place where her fingertips met concrete. Juniper crawled toward it. Scraping her knees along the floor, dragging a body that wanted nothing more than to just lie down and sleep, she kept going one inch at a time. When Juniper felt something solid, she pushed it with one hand. The wind caught the door and flung it wide, ushering in cold night air and drawing the flames toward the place where Juniper crouched. She gulped a ragged breath and fell down the single step as a wave of firemen leapt off the first truck.

She was lying with her cheek in the snow, fire nipping at her heels, when one of them caught her under the shoulder and flipped her over. Scooping her up like a child, he ran, and Juniper buried her face in the stiff folds of his fire gear.

"I loved him," she said. Sullivan. Jonathan. Her unknown father. Even Lawrence Baker.

But when he yelled back, "What?" she was already gone.

It took the volunteer fire department hours to put out the blaze, and nearly as long to comb through the wreckage.

Juniper watched them from the back of the open ambulance where they made her sit with an oxygen mask and a Mylar blanket. The EMTs wanted to transport her to the hospital in Munroe for observation, but after blacking out for a couple of seconds and coming to on a stretcher, Juniper insisted she would be fine and signed a waiver refusing further treatment. She couldn't leave. Not with Lawrence unaccounted for and her mother sedated on the couch inside the farmhouse. An EMT assured her that Reb was not alone, so Juniper sat on the back deck of the ambulance and bore witness to the Bakers' barn burning to the ground.

Law wasn't in it.

Afterward, the emergency workers all gathered in the yard, passing around a thermos of coffee and a sleeve of Styrofoam cups, and Juniper felt gratitude roll off her in waves. It was pure luck that they had come at all. Her mother's 911 call was incoherent at best, but rather than assuming it was a prank, the emergency operator took a chance and sent the full cavalry, including the ambulance and two local squad cars plus a deputy sheriff. No Everett. And when Juniper told the deputy everything she knew, he placed some calls and brought in the state. They arrived just in time to learn that there was no one in the barn—incinerated remains or otherwise— so they organized a search. Over a dozen law enforcement officers, fire department volunteers, and even a couple of EMTs stood shoulder to shoulder in the purple predawn light and walked the field beyond the barn, hunting for fresh footprints in the snow.

Juniper could see the search and rescue mission framed in the ruined skeleton of the smoldering barn, and she knew the exact moment they found him. One emergency worker raised his hand and they all gathered round at the apex of the hill. Juniper could close her eyes and picture the view from that height: the slow rise and fall of fallow fields, and in the distance, the scrub and trees of Jericho Lake giving way to the Murphys' barren acreage.

"We found him. Single GSW to the head." When the call crackled in, the rookie officer who had been assigned to keep an eye on Juniper frantically turned down his radio and gave her a shocked look.

She wasn't surprised. Her stepfather had been a coward to the end.

Still, Juniper was grateful for that one bullet-sized grace. For the knowledge that it had been quick.

Dropping the oxygen mask, she turned her back on the sunrise.

She didn't make it far.

"Ma'am!" A young deputy in a telltale khaki uniform ran after her. "You can't leave. This is a crime scene. We're going to need a statement."

"I'll tell you everything you want to know," Juniper said. Her chest felt empty, void as a deflated balloon. "The man at the top of the hill is Lawrence Baker. He killed Calvin and Beth Murphy almost fifteen years ago."

The deputy's eyes went round. "Wait. How do you—"

"I was there. I witnessed the whole thing."

"But—"

She started walking again, and he tripped over his own feet to fall in step beside her. "I'll

461

explain everything. I'll be in the house. Just . . . ." She didn't know what else to say. She didn't even know what she wanted. To be left alone, if only for a moment before the interviews and the wild claims. The accusations that were so true they stung.

"Okay," he finally said. "Don't go anywhere. We'll need to take you to the station."

But Juniper was already gone.

She let herself into her childhood home. It looked different. Smelled different, even. Maybe it was the bone glue pellets still strewn across the kitchen floor. In another life, Juniper would have gotten down on her hands and knees to clean them up, but she ignored them. She walked past her mother sleeping fitfully on the couch beneath the watchful eye of a social worker and climbed the stairs to her old bedroom.

It was Willa's now. Lavender walls, a tufted cream duvet. There was a corkboard on one wall with dozens of photographs and other paraphernalia thumbtacked to every available square inch. Right in the center was a picture Juniper didn't recognize. Reb must have snapped it without her knowing. It showed nineteen-year-old June sleeping in this very bed, body curled protectively around an infant Willa. The baby was maybe a week or two old. And Juniper didn't look like the scared little girl she had always imagined herself to be at that juncture. Instead, she looked almost happy, lips curled in a soft half smile, even in sleep.

She looked like she had known love. Like she could be the kind of person who would make a good mom.

Juniper was past caring about how it would be perceived or who she would anger. It was time to do the right thing. She took out her phone and looked up the number for Tate Family Farms. She could picture the phone on the desk in the office of the machine shed, and because it was early, she expected the call to go straight to voice mail.

Sullivan picked up.

"Hey," she said softly, recognizing his voice at once. She willed him to stay on the line. To *listen*. "It's Juniper. We need to talk."

EPILOGUE

TWO AND A HALF MONTHS LATER

The forsythia is in full bloom on the path beside Jericho Lake. The golden spires explode like fireworks, each separate blossom a tiny, burning star that makes the air heady with the scent of almonds and earth. In a day or two, if I walk this trail, each little buttercup along these gnarled branches will be spent and fading on the ground. But today they are resplendent.

He's waiting for me at an old picnic table, and just seeing the sunlight drape across his head in blessing convinces me that May could very well be my favorite month. How could it not be? Its blue skies and new shoots, pistachio-colored buds that unfurl into the promise of summer. Everything is filled with hope, made new.

"Hey, you," I say, slipping onto the bench beside him and pulling him into a side hug. Jonathan lets his head rest against mine for a moment, and together we look out at the lake. It's glass this morning, and so opaque that the tufts of clouds above us are reflected on the mirror surface. The world upended.

"Hey, you." His cane is propped against the top of the picnic table, and the presence of it hints at the kind of day my brother is having. We didn't know that after he woke up it would be weeks before he would be able to leave the hospital, or that when he finally did it would be with so many medications, restrictions, and therapies. Now, a cane. It's hard for a man who has always prided himself on his strength and capability, his quick mind and able body, to walk assisted. It's even harder to accept that his heart will never quite be the same.

Still, I thank God every single day that Jonathan *lives*. And that Everett Stokes was convicted of reckless endangerment resulting in serious injury and is serving a two-year sentence at the North-Central Correctional Facility. The gross misdemeanor charges of stalking and harassment were dropped when a court-appointed mental health expert diagnosed him with episodic psychiatric distress. We're told Everett will likely get out earlier due to good behavior, but he'll never work in law enforcement again. It's not enough, but it's what we got. I hope he gets the help he needs.

As for the podcast, it's irrelevant. The whole country knows the story now, the unsolved murder that ended in a blaze one wintery Iowa night. And it's already forgotten. Our story is significant only to us.

"Happy birthday, old man." I pull a Tupperware container out of the tote I've carried from the

465

car. Popping it open, I reveal not the donuts I promised but a thick slice of carrot cake that Willa and I stayed up half the night baking—Jonathan's favorite.

He smiles. "Did you do this? You didn't have to do this."

"It was awful," I admit with a laugh. "You know me—I made Willa shred the carrots and do all the tricky parts. We decided this should be called 'everything-but-the-kitchen-sink cake.' Pineapple, walnuts, raisins . . ."

"Are they golden raisins?"

"Is there any other kind?"

"And cream cheese frosting? Full fat, not that sugar-free crap?"

I nod. "Real butter, too."

"You're a good sister, June."

I hand him a fork. I'm not sure when he started calling me June again, but in the beginning it felt wrong to correct the guy who had just cheated death, so I let it go. Now it's spreading like a virus to everyone else. Even his boys have started to call me Auntie June instead of Aunt Juniper. I don't mind.

"I was going to bring a candle but I forgot. We'll have thirty-three candles at your real party, and you can give yourself a hernia trying to blow them all out, old man."

"No matter how old I get, I'll never catch you, big sister."

I should needle him back, tease him about how he now sports even more gray hair and I've yet to find my first. But Jonathan earned those streaks when he was baptized by ice in the depths of Jericho Lake. Even now, some things are better left unsaid.

Of course, there isn't much we *don't* say these days. *Secrets are lies and bad manners besides—* though that was never a tidbit of wisdom that our family upheld. The night Law burned the barn to ashes and shot himself on the rise overlooking the Murphys' old farm, he took pieces of all of us with him.

For weeks after he died, we said all the things there were to say. About what had happened and how we felt and who was to blame. *Everyone.* It seems we all have to bear our part of the burden of everything that happened in our family, our home, our town.

Yes, Lawrence pulled the trigger, but first Mom broke his heart.

Jonathan went rogue.

I abandoned everything for love.

But the circle is much wider than just us. The Tates were far from innocent, and the rest of Jericho, too. We all turned a blind eye when Cal and Beth were ostracized for being different and beat back detractors who suggested that maybe there were other ways to live and love, to flourish.

"How's Mom?" Jonathan asks around a mouthful of cake.

"Okay." There's no point in lying to him. She moved off the farm and into a small apartment in Munroe. It's not nearly as far as she'd hoped to fly, and yet so far away that she tells me she misses us every day—even though we see each other all the time. This is good for her, we're told. A fresh start. A new beginning away from all the rumors and gossip, the memories that threaten to tear her apart.

I still wonder, sometimes, how much my mother knew—or if she suspected back then who had really pulled the trigger. But guilt and grief and love are sometimes impossible to untangle, and we all have regrets. Our mourning is a layered, complicated thing.

"And when do you leave?" Jonathan is trying to sound nonchalant, but there's a catch in his voice.

"As soon as school gets out."

"You're sure we can't change your mind? Mandy and I—and the boys—would love to have you here."

I shake my head and give him a soft smile. "We won't be gone forever. But Willa wants this. Denver will be a good place for us to start over— to be a real family." I don't tell him that Reb might come with us. We'll see.

"And Sullivan?" Jonathan asks carefully.

"He agrees. Ashley, on the other hand, hasn't exactly been accommodating." But Sullivan has. He cried when I told him, and I knew he was remembering the night she was conceived. Just before the murders when the world was full of promise and we believed we would be together forever. We were so naive. But Sullivan will be a good dad to our girl, I know that. He cried when he met her, too, and for just a moment I could imagine our lives turning out very differently. Still, this is beautiful in its own broken way. We're putting together the pieces like a mosaic. It will just be easier for us all if Willa and I disappear for a while. We have daddy issues, every one of us, but I'm determined to make Willa's relationship with her father work.

"But you and Sullivan . . . ?" Jonathan leaves the question hanging in the air between us. I'm not even sure what he's asking, but I know the intent.

"I'm all grown up," I tell him with more certainty than I feel. "And far more interested in what could be than what might have been."

I heard that Sullivan moved into the suite above the Tate Family Farms offices for a couple of weeks after he learned the truth about Willa. About us. Honestly, I don't know why he married Ashley—if it was love or something different altogether—and I don't know what to wish for now. But I do know that I won't be the reason a family splinters in two, so Willa and I will stay away for as long as it takes for them to figure out what they want. And if Sullivan wants us? I guess we'll have to cross that bridge if we get there.

"I'm going to be just fine," I tell Jonathan. I know this much is true.

My brother nods at this and takes one last bite of cake. "I didn't give you enough credit back then."

"I could say the same thing."

"Nah. I was reeling. Not exactly trustworthy material," Jonathan admits. "When I turned eighteen and Cal told me the truth, it nearly destroyed me. Sure, legally I was an adult, but I wasn't ready for that kind of bombshell."

"I don't understand why you didn't just tell me."

"Cal begged me not to. Beth didn't know the truth about me, and he was trying to figure out the best way to break the news to her. Did you know she couldn't have kids?"

I shake my head.

"It would have wrecked her. As far as I know, she never learned the truth. I think it's better that way." Jonathan sighs.

"But I—"

"You were leaving for college . . . You were so happy, Junebug. Your whole life was before you, and mine was falling apart. I was so hurt and confused, and I didn't want to drag you into any of it. Especially what was happening with the Tates."

"I could have helped."

He nods once. "I should have trusted you."

"You were doing what you thought was right. You're a good son," I tell him, and mean it from the bottom of my heart. A good son to Law *and* to Cal. I always understood Jonathan's desire to protect the Murphys, but knowing who he really is has only drawn everything into sharper focus. "And I'm proud of what you're doing."

"Well, we'll see what happens." Jonathan is careful not to hope too hard, but there is another lawsuit in the works. He's spent years gathering data and working with environmental agencies across the Midwest and beyond. This lawsuit isn't against the Tates but the Department of Natural Resources, the state of Iowa, and several of the larger big ag conglomerates that have contributed to the over 750 impaired waterways throughout Iowa. It's all rather chilling—and exciting that someone is finally doing something about it. My brother.

And this time around, with Sullivan at the helm instead of Franklin, the Tate Family Farms are being used as a case study of how environmentally friendly farm trends can begin to reshape rural environments. I can't help but feel proud that Willa's dad is working to change things. Jonathan and Sullivan are even meeting again for coffee and discussions about preserving biodiversity, reducing greenhouse gases, and conserving soil and water.

"It's amazing. Truly." I squeeze Jonathan's hand where it rests on the picnic table.

"I'm just sorry that—"

"Nope." I stop him before he can go any further. "No more apologies. We did the best we could. We're *still* doing the best we can."

His eyes well, another side effect of his near-death experience, but I wrap my arms around my brother because I know. Sometimes your best is enough, and sometimes it's nowhere near. Sometimes the world is fire and ash, dirt and blood spilled on the ground, and there is nothing you can do to stop it. Sometimes you pour out all of your love, and it returns to you brittle and empty.

But sometimes, we're given another chance. We begin again.

"What are you smiling at?" Jonathan asks when I pull away.

"Nothing," I say, then stand up and gather the container, the fork, the used napkin. I stuff them all into the tote and pull it onto one shoulder.

My brother pushes away from the table and stands slowly, gazing out at the water. I watch him and wonder if he thinks about the ice, the bite of it against his skin and the sudden, savage understanding that life is a fickle, fleeting thing.

A free fall. I hope not. I hope he thinks about the moments when we rise.

"You ready?"

When Jonathan turns, I link my arm with his to walk the forsythia path. He doesn't need his cane. He can lean on me.

ABOUT THE AUTHOR

Nicole Baart is the author of nine previous novels, including *You Were Always Mine*, *Little Broken Things*, and *The Beautiful Daughters*. She lives in Iowa with her husband, five children, two turtles, and a dog. Learn more at NicoleBaart.com.

| Books are produced in the United States using U.S.-based materials | Books are printed using a revolutionary new process called THINKtech™ that lowers energy usage by 70% and increases overall quality | Books are durable and flexible because of Smyth-sewing | Paper is sourced using environmentally responsible foresting methods and the paper is acid-free |

Center Point Large Print
600 Brooks Road / PO Box 1
Thorndike, ME 04986-0001 USA

(207) 568-3717

US & Canada:
1 800 929-9108
www.centerpointlargeprint.com